PRAISE FOR *DECIDUOUS*

"A story of devastating loss, delivered in unapologetic prose, *Deciduous* in unforgettable. The reader remains glued to their seat as they witness the mother's ill-fated attempts to save her children and watch as she struggles to wrap her mind around the gravity of the events. . . .If you love a book that keeps you guessing until the last moment, you'll love *Deciduous* by Michael Devendorf."

—Eliza Stopps, author of the Leslie Kim series and creator of the *ElizaStopps.com* book blog

"*Deciduous* by Michael Devendorf is a compelling thriller pulsing with mystery and suspense. . . . Devendorf delivers this heart-pounding story with a terror and grace found in classic suspense novels. This book begins with loss and grief, so trigger warnings apply, but the author's talent for character, emotions, and mood weaves these painful emotions into a dark tale with some surprising light when all is said and done. Sienna is a well-drawn character. You feel for her from the very beginning, and you wish like @!%!# that she hadn't lost two children, but that's what makes this book and this writer so good. He isn't afraid to go there, do that, and build an emotion-entangled story that hurts you, frightens you, and entertains you.

"Sometimes, to get the best story, you have to plunge into the dark parts you'd rather not think about, and Devendorf does it well—with respect, and measure. I like the unique plot, and the mysterious elements to the story. From the first frantic scene to the final pages, you will be caught up in this drama and will never quite know what could happen next. The unpredictability is appealing. Sienna's husband, Jordan, is also dynamic. The conflict builds to a crescendo, and the secret revealed is a shocker you won't see coming.

"The last quarter of the book is my favorite, and the ending is one of the best I've read in recent years. *Deciduous*, by Michael Devendorf, is a masterful blend of pathos and suspense verging on horror. Not to be missed."

—ReaderViews (Tammy Ruggles for ReaderViews.com book blog)

"A gripping psychological suspense, Devendorf keeps you on the edge of your seat as secrets of Sienna's past unfold. *Deciduous* will have you desperately turning pages in the search for Sienna's truth—a captivating and powerful read."

—Ashley Wutke, book blogger and creator of the *Turning Pages* book blog

". . . *Deciduous* constantly looks at relationships under strain. The book excels at showing the tension between in-laws and family members, especially at two people seeing the same thing and reacting in entirely different ways. Strain can strengthen relationships, too, like the growing friendship when neighbor Yvonne steps up to help Sienna in her grief.

"It's clearly Sienna's story, but even Yvonne is a realistically complex person. She has a strong belief in yoga and meditation, but can't quite quit smoking when she's lonely and stressed. This is just another minor character detail showing realistically how strain and sadness affect us. After her divorce, she barely thinks about her ex-husband, but misses her former stepchildren constantly, facing a different kind of loss even as she helps Sienna. . . . *Deciduous* tells a story about grief, but it's also a story about what we keep secret in ourselves and what we don't question in others. Without revealing too much, the narrative takes unexpected twists, both in the unfolding discoveries and in how Sienna copes with her loss, to tell a surprising story about mother love and a mother's strength."

—Meg Stivison, book blogger and creator of
TheFictionAddiction.com book blog

"Written in a smooth, captivating way, the emotions of the characters are clearly drawn and completely relatable without being too overwhelming (tough to do with this topic). The settings are described beautifully and often very poetically, lending at times an almost surreal feel to the story. There seemed to be paranormal elements under the surface, and while I won't provide spoilers about that, the plot twists and the mystical elements keep the reader wondering and engaged until the final page.

"Overall, it was a fascinating book with likable characters, beautiful imagery, riveting action, and enthralling emotion that will draw you in, put you through the wringer, and leave you feeling very satisfied. A great read!"

—Kenner Alexander, author of *Exposed* and *Blindsided*,
and International Thrillerwriters' Association website editor

"Like any novel, *Deciduous* lives and dies by the acting of its principal characters. Sienna and Jordan are active and emotional, agents of change for good or ill. They, more than their circumstances, drive the story forward, and their flaws provide the story's depth. Jordan, the ambitious career man, works to keep the media at bay and protect his wife from the investigators' suspicions. Sienna, the compassionate mother, tries to make sense of the details of her children's deaths, even as she begins blaming herself for losing them. . . . If you enjoy family dramas with intense emotion and a complex mystery, give *Deciduous* a try. It's sure to take you off the beaten path. It just might take you a bit farther into the wilderness than you had expected."

—William R. Hunt, author of the Last Colony series

"A mature, measured piece of writing about a woman who teeters on the brink of unreliability throughout, in the most intriguing manner possible.

". . . truly impressive offering to the genre."

—Mark Weinstein, author and *New York Times*-Bestselling acquisitions editor

Deciduous

by Michael Devendorf

ISBN 978-1-64663-339-5

Published by

 köehlerbooks™

3705 Shore Drive
Virginia Beach, VA 23455
800-435-4811
www.koehlerbooks.com

DECIDUOUS

MICHAEL DEVENDORF

VIRGINIA BEACH
CAPE CHARLES

CHAPTER ONE

SIENNA COULDN'T BRING HERSELF TO say it out loud, but it was true. Kai was dead. She froze in the cathedral doorway fifty feet from her son's closed casket. A gasp stuck in her throat at the sight of the child-sized silver box that concealed his body and shined as though electrified or radioactive, even with the lights dimmed for the funeral. Through tunnel vision, the room stretched away. Tilting her head to the vaulted ceiling, she broke the optical illusion and willed herself to take a deep breath.

The stone arches overhead glowed in a kaleidoscope of ruby light filtering through the stained-glass windows. She closed her eyes, letting red seep across her retinas, then opened them and lowered her gaze, avoiding the coffin. Shadowy candlelight dulled the pastel floral wreaths and sprays that blended into a hovering grey cloud that matched her spirit.

Drained from all the crying and not having eaten a meal in days, Sienna lingered in a fog. Heavy double doors closed behind her, extinguishing the morning sun, spurring her to move.

In unison, hundreds of mourners turned their tear-streaked faces to her. As if in a dream, she walked the center aisle toward the altar as weepy eyes of friends, family, and strangers followed her somber progression.

With her arms crossed and hands cupping her elbows, she took a seat in the first pew. A jolting pain of grief stabbed her gut, reminding her she was awake and in agony, lost inside the thirty-seven-year-old body that resembled her former self.

She smoothed the skirt of her black dress—her funeral dress—the one she also wore to Kira's services ten months earlier. Leaning into the shoulder-rest of the unforgiving wooden bench, she struggled to admit or comprehend that first her daughter, and now Kai, was gone too.

She wondered how many hours had passed since she last held him. Talked to him. Trying to tune out the whimpering that assailed her, Sienna focused on her last conversation with Kai, the final words he spoke to her, desperate to burn them into her memory.

⚜⚜⚜

She recalled typing away at her computer like any other day. The words spread on the screen like black mold overtaking a wall as she added her thoughts to the page with haste and enthusiasm until her momentum waned. The task stumped her. At her desk, hands hovering over the keyboard, she pondered the forest conservation project she consulted on part-time. Trying to avoid coming across as an extremist ready to chain herself to a tree for the cause, she revised and softened her description of their goals in the grant proposal.

After a few minutes of struggling to find the right words and revising her next sentence in her mind, the screen saver came on and turned the monitor into an inky black mirror. Sunlight spilled through the window into the small bedroom she used for her home office and illuminated her face on the computer screen. Struggling with the phrasing kept her from noticing her own reflection staring back. Her slim face, long sandy-blond hair, and bright, grey-blue eyes highlighted by the dark silhouette of a pullout sofa and bookshelves in the background, all flashed into focus when Kai shouted to her from downstairs.

"What? Come up here!" Sienna said.

Multiple sets of footsteps stomped on the hardwood stairs as he came bounding up to the office along with his friend Shane.

Kai barged in, taking extra breaths after having run upstairs to the end of the long hallway. "We want to paint the treehouse. Can we get some paint from the garage?"

The request to play outside surprised but delighted her. "Really? You two want to do something other than play video games in a dark room all day?" Sienna grinned.

Kai nudged his friend in the side. "Shane's sick of losing."

"Not every video game has to be as serious as a life-or-death duel, Kai. Go outside and play, but you're not painting the treehouse. I don't want you up there unless I can watch you, and I've got to finish working. I don't want you to get paint everywhere. And you could fall."

She pictured them swinging limb to limb as they painted high off the ground in the massive maple tree with thick, widespread branches like arms outstretched to receive a giant gift box.

"I told Shane you would say that. You're always worried. Why do we still have the treehouse if you won't ever let me go in it? Please!" Before she could answer, he tried to defuse her argument. "We won't fall. We just want to paint the inside."

"Paint the inside?"

"Dad said we should paint over all the carvings and drawings on the walls. It's kid's stuff."

Sienna couldn't help smiling at him. "Because you're no longer a kid?"

"I'm almost thirteen."

Shane smirked and pushed Kai's shoulder. "Yeah, he just looks ten."

"Most of that paint is old and has probably dried out," Sienna said, shaking her head.

"There are like fifty cans of paint in the garage. I'll find some that's still good. I don't care what color it is. It's embarrassing. I want to paint it."

At least for the moment, Kai was no different from any other kid enjoying the summer. Playful and happy, not mourning his big sister. Sienna didn't want to spoil the normalcy of the day.

"Promise me you'll be careful up there and won't make a mess. You'll go slowly and just dip a brush into the can without dripping it everywhere?"

"We'll be careful. And we won't make a mess," Kai said as he and Shane dashed out of the room before she could change her mind.

"And don't get it on your clothes! Better yet, put on old clothes!" she said as they vanished.

Sienna turned back to her computer and swirled the mouse around until the screen saver cleared, and the swarm of tiny letters like black sugar ants popped into view. A few seconds later, the back door slammed as the boys ran to the garage, searching for loot. After trying unsuccessfully for several minutes to regain her train of thought, she grabbed her water bottle, drained it of the last ounce of lukewarm liquid, and took a break to get another.

As she arrived in the kitchen, Sienna struggled to suppress the urge to call the boys back into the house. Jordan kept telling her to quit being a helicopter mom, to stop always assuming the worst or she would stifle their son's development, but she couldn't resist checking on them.

She walked through the mudroom to the back door and stepped down off the covered porch to get a vantage of the treehouse on the other side of the yard. The boys were sprinting from the garage across the deep lawn to the giant maple. Kai had a gallon can of paint, and Shane had a plastic grocery bag of painting supplies.

Anxiety flared, and she crossed her arms, about to shout to them that she changed her mind and didn't want them making a mess, but she hesitated when they laughed and teased each other and began their ascent. She waited as they climbed, and with them safely inside, she returned to the kitchen, leaving them to have their fun in the summer afternoon. Taking a fresh bottle of water from the fridge, she opened it and swallowed a long gulp then headed back to work.

As evening settled over their suburban neighborhood, Sienna finished her writing for the day and descended to the kitchen to start dinner. After plugging in her cellphone at the counter to charge, she assembled chicken breasts, tomatoes, and other ingredients for one of only four entrées in their regular dinner rotation. Putting everything aside, she walked outside and down off the porch. Facing the treehouse, she shouted across the yard that it was time to come in.

The setting sun beamed rays of light, creating a halo around the dark structure suspended in the tree, but she didn't see the kids.

She stepped inside the house and over to the hallway and called up to Kai's bedroom. When he didn't answer, she listened for video game explosions of grenades, or the squealing of sportscar tires, hesitated, then climbed the stairs to his open door. He wasn't there.

Sienna hurried out the front door and around to the open garage, but there was no sign of Kai there either. Her neck flushed in bright red blotches. They spread onto her chest and up to her cheeks as though she had run a marathon, but she simply stood in the garage without clear, undeniable confirmation of her son's whereabouts.

She told herself to stop panicking. That he was close by, but she couldn't suppress a fierce need to protect Kai. Again came the familiar urge to double over and vomit from the knot in her stomach whenever he wasn't within her line of sight or earshot.

Shaking her head, she tried to convince herself she was foolish for worrying. That she was overprotective like Jordan would so often tell her, but her instinct overrode her intellect.

She ran down the side yard to the gate, calling out Kai's name. Sally, their sixty-pound yellow Lab mix, greeted her with two paws planted on her waist. Sienna ruffled Sally's neck, and the dog responded by springing on her hind legs begging for more attention.

"Where's Kai, girl?"

With no sign of Kai, Sienna hurried the two hundred feet across their expansive lawn to the base of the tree, Sally trotting behind. "Kai! Are you up there? Shane?"

She looked around the yard and back to the house. The roof and eaves caught the setting sun's rays like a face turned up on a craned neck, but the rest of the house was in shadow.

Stepping back from the base of the tree several feet, she tried to get a vantage into the treehouse. "What are you guys doing up there?" Sienna asked, glimpsing the sole of a tennis shoe in the recesses. "Answer me, Kai!" she said.

Grabbing hold of the bottom rung when he didn't respond, Sienna climbed the wooden slats nailed into the tree trunk. "Kai?" she said again as she hoisted herself up the first few feet.

As she got halfway up to the structure, she looked down for the first time. Sally barked at her from ten feet below. The unabated barking propelled her even faster up the rungs.

"Kai?" she said, trying not to lose her balance as she neared the dark opening without another glance to the ground. She grabbed the two maple sapling trunks that served as grip bars fastened to each side of the doorway and hefted herself up into the small, dim space.

Kai was on his back, framed by a scattering of dried leaves from the prior autumn. A single leaf drizzled in blue paint clung to his cheek.

Sienna vaulted off the wooden slats into the treehouse screaming her son's name. "KAI!"

She dodged a can of spray paint at Kai's feet and kneeled next to him. The grocery bag Shane had carried was near Kai's head. She scooted it out of the way. Leaves stuck to it, covered in paint that had leaked onto the floor. Kai was motionless. Sienna slid closer to him, shoved her arm under his neck, and lifted him to her face.

Dried leaves fell away from him and floated back to the floor where his body left an outline as if he had tried making a leaf angel by sweeping them away with outstretched arms and legs.

"KAI!"

She brushed the leaf off his face, put her ear to his nose, and held the air in her lungs, listening for his breathing. Kai was unresponsive.

"HELP! SOMEBODY! PLEASE HELP!"

Her screams echoed inside the treehouse.

Holding his chin, she shook his face side to side. "Breathe, Kai!"

A fine mist of blue paint speckled his nose and his mouth. He remained limp in her arms as she laid him on his back and kneeled over him. Again, she turned her ear to his nose and mouth. Her rapid heartbeat pulsed and throbbed in her ears, obliterating all sound.

She didn't know what to do and glanced back out the doorway, desperate for a face to appear. "Somebody!"

But no one came. Pinching Kai's nose with one hand, she held his jaw with the other and breathed into his mouth, emptying her lungs. Without waiting, she turned her face and took another deep breath then breathed into his mouth again. And again.

On top of his chest, she placed one palm over the other and

pushed. She had no idea how hard to press down. Over and over, she compressed his chest and pleaded to anyone who could hear her. "Help us! Please! Help us!"

As she alternated between respiration and compression, her concept of time vanished as though she had entered a time warp. The world accelerated to the speed of light, but Kai remained still as she leaned over him, trying to breathe for him. Everything around them, the treehouse, the leaves and tree branches, the paint can, the sliver of sky through the doorway and the window, all stretched into ribbons of color spinning around them as the earth turned.

Her own breathing became labored. Each deliberate inhalation and forced exhalation resonated in the treehouse like an astronaut breathing into the helmet of a spacesuit. She became lightheaded and paused long enough to place her hands on the sides of his head and look into his face. He steadied her. He grounded her, and she caught her bearings. The spinning stopped, but her vision was blurry. It took a moment for the definition of the treehouse to regain a structure she could see.

Time was immeasurable. It might have been ten seconds or ten hours. CPR wasn't working. Kai didn't move. Again, she slid an arm under his neck and the other under his thighs. As though lifting an infant from his crib, Sienna hefted Kai's limp, eighty-five-pound body from the floor of the treehouse. Spinning on her knees into the doorway with him dangling in her outstretched arms, Sienna screamed into the void of summer evening air. "HELP ME!"

Adrenaline pumped in her system. Kai hung weightless in her arms. She leaned out the doorway scanning the world for anyone who could help, but they were all alone. There was no movement anywhere. No airplanes overhead. No noises in the distance. Eons might have passed, and all human life on earth might be long extinct.

She leaned out farther. Kai's legs and feet bumped against

the doorframe. The roof of Yvonne's house next door peeked over the tops of the trees that ran along the fence line separating their properties.

"Help!" It was the only word she could vocalize.

Turning her head, she shouted into the canopy of leaves that obscured her other neighbor's house an acre away. Her voice was as hopeless as a message tucked in a bottle and tossed into the sea. She screamed, but no one came. As if in a nightmare, no one could hear her. Sienna knew what was happening in that nightmare—Kai was dying. The rest of the world continued on without noticing.

She peered to the ground twenty feet below, and her vision narrowed. The earth pulled away as though she floated higher and higher in a hot air balloon. She had to get him down from the tree. Had to get him to the hospital.

"Hold on, baby. I can do this," she said. Without making a conscious choice, without further consideration or fear, Sienna righted Kai in her arms, brought his chest against hers, and with his head hanging over her shoulder, clung to her son's body. Using one arm to squeeze him into her chest and the other to hold the wooden grip bar in a vise, Sienna turned and edged over the lip of the treehouse opening. She backed down with her right leg onto the first step and again cried out as she brought her left foot down to meet the right one.

"Somebody! Somebody, help us!"

"Sienna? What's wrong?" It was Yvonne's voice in the distance.

CHAPTER TWO

CLUTCHING HER SON TO HER body, Sienna slowly lowered her foot down another rung. In her peripheral vision, the hot pink of Yvonne's bathrobe caught her eye as her neighbor stepped around her pool house on the other side of the wall between their properties. From that perspective, Yvonne was as tiny as a child's Barbie doll. "Call 9-1-1, Yvonne! Call 9-1-1! Kai isn't breathing! Hurry!"

"Oh my god! Be careful, Sienna!"

As Yvonne disappeared back around the pool house, Sienna moved with surreal strength. She steadily lowered herself and Kai, jostling him down from one rung to the next, never fearing she could slip and plummet to the ground.

"Please breathe, baby," she whispered. With eyes fixated on Kai's chestnut brown hair as strands of it whisked into her face, Sienna's fingers dug into the wooden slats, and her thighs strained. Kai's limbs bounced against her back with each step on the rungs.

Seven feet from the ground, her tennis shoe slipped off the

edge of the wooden rung, and her precarious maneuver downward became a freefall. As though the earth stopped rotating, she launched into the air, but then the world resumed its spin, and she and Kai crashed. As she fell, she kept her arms laced tight around him.

Sienna landed on her back in the grass, and Kai landed on top of her. He knocked the wind out of her, and she fought to breathe, never releasing Kai from her embrace.

The giant maple loomed above. She lay in the grass for ten full seconds with her mouth stretched wide in a panicked but useless locked gasp for breath. Sally ran up and barked as Sienna's reflex engaged. She caught her first chest full of air as a lone maple leaf dropped from a limb overhead and landed on Kai's face.

She squeezed Kai with both arms as she turned with him onto her side. "I've got you," she said, taking another deep breath. "You're going to be okay."

"They're sending an ambulance!" Yvonne called over the wall. "I have them on the line. I'm coming back there!"

"Tell them to hurry." The words left her mouth as air without a sound. Gasping more breaths, she twisted up onto her knees and slid Kai off to the side. She placed him prone in the grass, his arms and legs limp and askew. His mouth was ajar, his jaw slack, hanging off to the side out of alignment. "Kai? Breathe. Please, baby. Breathe!" she said, hoping he would open his eyes.

Laying her head on his chest, she listened for a heartbeat and tried to feel his chest rising, but she detected neither. She pulled his arms tight against his body, straightened his legs, then tilted his head back. Taking a deep breath, she again breathed into Kai's mouth, repeated, then compressed his chest.

"Please, Kai! Breathe!" Over and over, she repeated the breathing and compressions. And over and over begged her son to breathe.

"Sienna!" Yvonne said.

Sally's barking intensified as Yvonne raced up, but Sienna never took her eyes off Kai.

Yvonne slid to a stop in the grass and kneeled with her hands on her knees, inches from Kai. She had toenails painted the same bright red as her fingernails and still only wore the hot pink silk bathrobe that clashed with the fiery red of her wet hair that had soaked the back of the garment. Winded from running, Yvonne gasped for air then shrieked into the phone.

"What do I do?" One of her feet bled from a wound caused by a stone or twig as she raced from her backyard to Sienna's backyard without shoes.

"Don't hang up until they get there," said the operator over the speakerphone.

"No, I won't. Please hurry," Yvonne said.

"Do you know CPR?" asked the operator.

"No, I don't know what to do!"

"If he's not breathing, I will talk you through it.

"Call his name. Is he responsive?"

"Where is the ambulance!" Sienna asked as she continued chest compressions on her son.

"KAI? CAN YOU HEAR ME?" Yvonne shouted as if it would make a difference.

"Can you tell if he's breathing?" asked the operator.

"No, he's not breathing. His mother is giving him CPR."

The operator rattled off proper CPR instructions as though Sienna could stop to take notes.

"Where is the ambulance?" Yvonne asked as Sienna paused the compressions and gave a rescue breath.

"They're on the way. The station is very close to you. Continue with CPR. Thirty chest compressions, then two deep breaths, then back to compressions."

"Wait! I can hear the ambulance coming," Yvonne said as sirens blared down the street.

"Put Sally inside and bring them back here!" Sienna commanded.

Yvonne jumped up and shepherded Sally inside, pulling her by the collar, but Sienna didn't stop. She continued methodically compressing Kai's chest with focus and determination as though she was turning a combination lock on a vault with her son trapped inside. If she could manipulate the dial and crack the code, a door would swing open, and her son could catch his breath.

⁂

"Stand clear, ma'am!" said the first EMT to approach Sienna, still performing CPR.

Sienna waited to move until the EMT physically took over the space she occupied. She continued kneeling next to her son.

Yvonne bent and placed an arm over Sienna's shoulder and tried to pull her to her feet, but Sienna was an immovable tree stump rooted to the ground.

"Please help him!" Sienna said. "He's my baby. Please help."

The EMTs worked on Kai in tandem.

"What happened to this boy?" asked the lead EMT.

"I'm not sure. I found him up in the treehouse. He wasn't breathing!"

Dried, crumpled bits of leaves were stuck to Kai's clothes.

A fire truck pulled up out front with sirens blaring, and the EMT used the radio attached to his shoulder to call for a stretcher.

"Please help him!" Sienna said, begging them with Yvonne pulling on her to stand. Sienna wouldn't budge.

"Still no heartbeat," said an EMT who cut open Kai's shirt as the other prepared a defibrillator, positioned the paddles, and jolted Kai's lifeless body.

"He's not dead!" Sienna said as she stared into Kai's face. "Open your eyes, Kai! Breathe!"

The lead EMT radioed again. "Medical Command, advise the ER we have a possible cardiac arrest and asphyxiation. Could be huffing related. Patient is a male child, approximately eleven to thirteen years old. He's not responding to life support." Moments later, two additional fire department personnel hurried through the side gate carrying a stretcher.

"Please help him!" Sienna said, her voice cracking.

"Ma'am, is this your son?" asked the lead EMT as the others placed Kai on the stretcher.

"Yes, I'm his mother. He's twelve."

"He's unresponsive."

"You have to keep trying. Please! Please try!" she said, staring into the man's eyes.

"Come with us in the ambulance, ma'am," he said, helping her to her feet as others lifted Kai off the ground strapped to the stretcher. "We will continue to do everything we can until we get to the ER."

"Yvonne, my phone is in the kitchen. I have to call Jordan," Sienna said as she hurried along with the team of EMTs down the side yard.

Yvonne nodded, pulled the silk robe taut around her waist, and raced inside to retrieve Sienna's phone. She charged out the front door, phone in hand, as they loaded Kai into the ambulance.

"Here! Sienna!" she said, passing the phone off to Sienna climbing inside with her son. "Do you want me to call him for you?"

"I'll call him now."

"What can I do?" Yvonne asked, staring into Sienna's stunned face.

"Pray," Sienna replied as the ambulance doors closed and the sirens reactivated; she didn't hear them. Trapped in a vacuum where time was irrelevant and sound was impenetrable, she squeezed Kai's hand and dialed Jordan's phone. Kai's hand was soft and limp; she brought it to her lips. The call went straight to voicemail. She left an urgent plea for him to call her back and then redialed without hesitating, but she got voicemail again. "Jordan! Call me right away. We're taking Kai to the emergency room!"

Shaking, she hung up and ran a hand over her scalp and cradled her head while holding Kai's hand. She felt a leaf in her hair. It was one of the deep purple-blue leaves off the maple they'd transplanted to their backyard from their lake house. Letting it fall to the floor of the ambulance, she pressed her hands together in prayer with Kai's hand clasped in between.

Sienna begged God to save her son as the EMTs radioed medical control and outlined the advanced life support they had tried. She kept squeezing his hand as they followed their protocol like robots, continuing to administer life support until they arrived at the emergency room.

ᴥᴥᴥ

Running alongside the stretcher, she didn't release Kai's hand as they wheeled him into the ER. A nurse forced Sienna aside with one hand and with the other yanked a curtain on a track to encircle a medical team who would try to revive him. Staff scurried around Kai performing the same evaluation as the EMTs looking for any sign of life, but they found none. His exposed torso and face were the color of the sterile white hospital walls. The ventilator didn't help him, and neither did more defibrillation. The ER doctor stopped and stepped over to Sienna, standing at the end of the gurney.

"What is your son's name?"

"Kai. His name is Kai. You have to keep trying."

"I am so very sorry," said the doctor, who paused, clasped her palms together and held them against her chest. She then took a deep breath. "I'm sorry, but Kai is deceased."

The doctor's words hit Sienna with the force of an explosion and deafening blast that rang in her ears. Sienna gripped the sleeve of the doctor's white coat. "Please don't say that. Please!" she said as all oxygen left her lungs in a whimper and her knees buckled.

"I'm sorry. We couldn't resuscitate him. He's gone," the doctor said, reaching out and grabbing Sienna's elbows to steady her.

"NOOO! No, he's not! NOOO!" She released the doctor from her grasp, leaned down to Kai, slid an arm under his neck, and hugged him with both arms. "Not my baby boy. Please, no!" she said, sobbing. Kai's chin rested on her shoulder as though quietly napping while she released a choking cry.

The hospital staff stood silent, seeming to will themselves immobile as Sienna, lying across her son, realized her absolute worst fear was real.

"I'm sorry, the EMTs did everything possible," the doctor said. "Robin, one of our counselors, is on the way to help right now. Is there anyone we can call? Kai's father?"

"You can't say that!" Sienna said. "No! Please! You can't say that!" Her choking cry caught in her throat, and she fought to breathe.

The counselor arrived as Sienna cradled Kai, but Sienna didn't acknowledge her. Stepping closer, the counselor said in a gentle, calming voice, "My name is Robin. This is Dr. Marta Singh. What is your name?"

It took time for the question to register in Sienna's mind. There was only room for thoughts of Kai. "Sienna," she said at last. She laid Kai back down and placed her hands on the sides of his face. Tears rolled down both cheeks.

"What happened to you, baby? What were you doing?" Sienna raised his shoulders again, hugged him, and wept, tears falling onto his bare shoulders, her own shoulders quivering as she sobbed.

Dr. Singh and Robin stood by as Sienna cried. After several minutes, Robin asked, "Can we call Kai's father?"

"Jordan. My husband." She inhaled a long, deep breath, her lower lip trembling. "I called him, but he didn't answer. Will you call him again?" Sienna asked between gasps and sobs as she took her phone from her back pocket and dropped it on the gurney. As quick as a blink, she wrapped her arms back around Kai, lifting him to her.

"We will. We'll call him again right now."

CHAPTER THREE

JORDAN'S PHONE VIBRATED. SIENNA WAS calling. Pressing the decline button, he continued his pitch to his potential new boss.

"Mr. Whitburn, I can assure you, and my record shows, I am just as comfortable with commercial real estate as with residential." He swallowed the rest of the Maker's Mark and swirled around the golf ball of ice resting on the bottom of his tumbler.

With a quick nod toward his glass, he signaled the bulldogish waiter. Jordan smoothed the lapel of his expensive jacket and noted he could be mistaken for Mr. Whitburn's son. They both had sleek, side-parted hair and wore stylish, fitted suits along with crisp, white shirts.

As the two huddled in a curved, red leather booth in the Montrose Hotel Club Room, Jordan hoped the historic hotel bar in downtown Madison impressed the businessman. With its intricate walnut paneling, glass lamps suspended high overhead, and a wall of liquor bottles backlit on shelves of golden honey onyx, it was the perfect upscale sanctuary for big deals. He assumed he was about to close one.

Already three drinks in, Jordan continued his pitch. "I have sold more commercial real estate than any other residential agent in the firm. Two years running!"

His phone rang again, interrupting his flow, but he rejected the call, again, continuing. "I started in residential like most agents do, but I'm ready for this. I think of it as a promotion. Joining your team is the next step in my career. I'm thirty-eight years old. I've got lots of energy to work very hard. I've got fifteen years of experience. I've already worked with the premier agency in Wisconsin. I'm ready."

The waiter arrived with Jordan's fourth bourbon. He picked up the glass as he spoke. "I bring with me all of my past commercial clients," he said when his phone rang again. Jordan noticed Mr. Whitburn use the interruption to glance at his watch, so he turned off his phone and placed it on the seat instead of the table. "Including RBMS Group, which I helped source property for Aspire Plaza."

Mr. Whitburn drained his cocktail and set his glass on the table. "That's three calls in three minutes. Your clients are getting antsy," he said as he stood and buttoned his suit coat. The waiter dashed over, but before he could offer another drink, Mr. Whitburn added, "Jordan's got this one, right, Jordan?"

Caught off guard by the abrupt dismissal, Jordan stood too, not wanting the meeting to end. "Yes, of course. So, what do you think about me joining your team?"

The waiter cleared the empty glass and slinked away.

"Jordan. I like that you're eager, but one big deal doesn't make you an expert on the commercial side."

"Aspire Plaza was a huge deal, and I made it happen," Jordan said.

"Yes. It's what got you this meeting. You sure there wasn't a conflict of interest at home? Your wife? The environmentalist. Surely, she wasn't so happy about your influence on a project like that."

Jordan knew he meant Sienna—spokeswoman for every celebrity environmental pet project that needed a pretty face and commanding demeanor to help them sway legislators and corporate executives to yield to their objectives.

"My name is not officially attached to any of the environmental workarounds I coordinated. Anyway, she's a stay-at-home mom now. She's there to support me in my career. She does some consulting stuff from the house, but she gave up the other job when—" His voice trailed off. "She's there to take care of our son and support my career. I did what I had to do to facilitate the deal, and that meant clearing some hurdles the conservationists set up."

"I like your resourcefulness, Jordan. Now return those phone calls and close a deal tonight." He extended a hand, which Jordan shook in his firm, well-practiced, hyper-masculine manner. "We'll talk again."

Jordan watched the self-made man leave after an unabashed effort to impress him and get a job offer. But Sienna's incessant calls had cut the meeting short, and Jordan was irritated.

Sitting back into the stiff leather seat, he raised his fingers in the air and snapped to signal he needed another drink. After the waiter acknowledged him, he picked up his phone and turned it back on. There were five messages—three were from Sienna, two from clients. He wanted to put off talking with Sienna as long as he could and could never escape the constant neediness of his clients. He drained the glass and mumbled to himself as the waiter set another glass of bourbon before him. "I deserve this change."

"Sorry, sir?" the waiter asked.

"Huh? What? No, nothing else," Jordan said, and the waiter moved on to the next table as Jordan took a sip of the bourbon.

He wanted the offer. Confident he'd convince the man to

make him one sooner rather than later, he swirled the brown liquid in the glass, loosened his tie and unbuttoned his collar, then slurped more of the expensive bourbon.

He reminded himself he could not let anything sidetrack him. He had to stay focused. Working directly for the developer, being the sole source of real estate acquisitions, would catapult his career. His timing was right, he reassured himself as he downed the last of his drink, allowing the glass of alcohol to serve as a sounding board that reinforced all his thoughts.

He sucked an ice cube into his mouth and then raised the glass and rattled the remaining ice to signal for another.

As his cocktail arrived, Jordan sat unwittingly shaking his head side to side. His train of thought had shifted back to Sienna and her voicemails. And how in the last year, she had morphed into another person. Different from the woman he married. He used to get a rush just thinking about her. That rush fizzled into a pang. Draining his cocktail, thoughts of how Sienna had changed surged in his mind. Gritting his teeth, the muscles in his jaw bulged. Slurping the last remnants of his bourbon from the glass, more ice water than liquor, he patted the table three times with an open palm to signal he was ready for another. Delaying going home, Jordan asked himself for the one-thousandth time if things could have been different or if they would always end up this way. It left him wishing he had never proposed.

↓↓↓

Jordan remembered his mother pushing them to get married while they vacationed in Hawaii for his parents' anniversary. "Mom was the first one to guess Sienna might be pregnant," he said to his rocks glass. He regretted asking Sienna to join them on the trip. They hadn't even been dating a year. She had been so excited to see the rainforests. Back then, he felt like her hero but now realized she was probably more excited about the rainforests than being with him.

He replayed their second morning at the Kiralani Kai Resort. Sienna awoke and rose from bed to use the bathroom but launched into a sprint and gripped her stomach, saying she was about to throw up. She shut the door, but he heard her slink down to the toilet, slam the lid back, and wretch.

"You okay in there?" Jordan asked through the door.

"I'm fine. Just a little nauseous."

"Too many Mai Tais last night? You need me to hold your hair for you?" he said, smiling.

A moment later, Sienna returned to the bedroom. Jordan had opened the drapes of their fifteenth-floor suite, revealing a brilliant blue sky that melded into the sparkling ocean, creating a view of intertwined elements as if staring down from the stratosphere. Sitting up in bed, his light brown hair hung over his forehead, and a cowlick at his left temple created a wavy curl. The morning sun traveled into the room and illuminated his sapphire blue eyes that matched the view out of the wall of windows.

"I was beginning to think you were secretly trying to poison me," Sienna said with a grin. She joined him in the enveloping white sheets and comforter and snuggled into his muscular arms.

"When I saw *Sixth Sense*, I did file it away in my memory that you can poison someone slowly with Pine-Sol," he said and squeezed her in his arms and kissed her temple. "You know, just in case I need it."

"Just in case," she said, smiling. "Maybe something at dinner didn't agree with me. I'm okay, though."

At breakfast, Jordan asked his parents if either of them got sick from the seafood dinner they shared the night before. When they said no, he told them about Sienna dashing for the bathroom, ready to vomit first thing in the morning.

"You're pregnant!" asked Jordan's mother.

"What? No. I'm not pregnant, Frieda," Sienna said but then hesitated as the idea dawned and showed on her face.

Jordan turned to face her. "You're not? Are you?"

"Stop. I'm not pregnant," Sienna said.

"You've gone as pale as a ghost. Is it possible?" Frieda said, clasping her hands in prayer for it to be true.

A drugstore pregnancy test the two used in the privacy of their hotel room later that day proved Sienna wasn't pregnant. But his mother had spent the day assuring them they were meant to be together. She said the idea they could be pregnant while celebrating an anniversary was divine intervention. *Providence* was her word, he remembered, and that notion lodged in his brain. He thought Sienna was beautiful and wildly intelligent, and she made him feel invincible. Staring at his glass of bourbon, he only saw Sienna as she was then, and he smiled to himself before taking a long swallow of his drink.

The idea of providence, divine intervention, was the reason he asked Sienna to marry him that night, on his parents' anniversary with an August super-moon holding court in the night sky of stars reflecting off the bay. He wanted divine intervention in his life. Standing barefoot on the beach as the sand spread between their toes and the ocean splashed over their ankles, he proposed to her. But Sienna didn't accept right away. She said they were too young, and she wasn't ready. So, he chased after her until she agreed a year later.

✦✦✦

Jordan squeezed his phone as he savored the last icy drop of bourbon, raised the glass in the air to signal for another to sip while listening to his clients' calls before calling Sienna back. He played one as the waiter placed Jordan's check on the table, instead of the drink he wanted, and stepped away. Putting the phone to his shoulder, Jordan whistled after the waiter as though calling a dog. "Hey! I was ordering, not asking for my check. Another Maker's. A double," he said and resumed the voicemail.

When he finished listening to his client's message explaining he was taking his house off the market rather than continue his efforts with Jordan to sell it, Jordan slammed his fist down onto the table with a thud. The rattling of glassware caused two nearby customers to turn at the commotion.

Jordan would not let the twenty-thousand-dollar commission go without fighting for it. He couldn't afford to lose it. Before calling the man back, he first played the message from the other client who said she wanted to discuss raising the asking price for her house by another one hundred thousand dollars after they had spent a few days reviewing comps and agreeing on the list price.

"There's no way in hell. It will never sell at that price!" Jordan spouted and ended the voicemail. While fuming about being on the verge of losing two commissions, he returned the call of his first client.

When his client answered his call, Jordan launched into schmooze mode to convince him not to pull the listing. The waiter arrived with Jordan's seventh drink, the double he wanted, and his check. Jordan flung a hand at the waiter, who had turned away, and then swallowed a mouthful of the bourbon between syllables.

By the time he unsuccessfully finished trying to sway his client, another fifteen minutes had passed, ten minutes since he finished his drink, but the waiter had not returned while Jordan was on the call. As he argued into the phone and slapped the table for emphasis of his points, he ignored the glances from the customers he distracted with his raised voice.

Jordan's call ended, and he tossed his phone onto the seat. "Another Maker's!" he called to the waiter serving cocktails to two women in the next booth.

"I'll be with you in a minute, sir," the waiter said.

Jordan got up from the booth and stepped to the bar with his empty glass and soggy cocktail napkin. "Maker's Mark and ice," he said to the bartender.

"Sir, I think you've had enough," the bartender replied.

"What the hell are you talking about? I'm fine. I'm here working."

"You're cut off. You've been rude and loud."

"That's bullshit! Get me the fucking manager! Now!" he said, his raised voice causing other patrons to pause in the middle of their conversations.

"I am the manager. You're cut off, and I'm putting you in a cab. There's one right out in front of the hotel," the bartender said, leaning forward toward Jordan with both of his palms down on the edge of the bar, elbows locked. "Now, please pay your bill."

"I'm not getting in a cab! This is fucking ridiculous!"

"A credit card, please," asked the bartender, staring Jordan down.

"Were you bitches complaining about me?" Jordan said, barking at the two women as he turned to face them. He lost his balance and stumbled into a heavyset customer seated on a barstool next to him but steadied himself by grabbing onto the bar top.

"Hey! Watch it!" the customer said.

"What do you mean, watch it? You're hard to miss, big guy," Jordan slurred and tossed the balled-up cocktail napkin into the man's face.

The bartender reached over and grabbed the house phone. "That's it. I'm calling security."

"Asshole," the heavyset man mumbled.

"Mind your own damn business!" Jordan slurred as he spun back toward the man and accidentally bumped his arm, causing the man's beer mug to hit his mouth. The man screeched as blood trickled from his lip.

"Security, we need you now!" the bartender said into the phone.

"You son of a bitch!" the heavyset man said, holding his hand against his lip. "You just assaulted me!"

The bulldogish waiter loomed next to Jordan as if daring him to take a swing.

"What? No. Wait," Jordan said. "No, I didn't do that."

"Call the police," the customer said.

"I was trying to pay my bill," Jordan said and then noticed the security guard dressed in her Madison Police Department uniform, including her holstered firearm, round the corner from the hotel lobby into the bar. Her long black hair pulled into a ponytail swung side to side as she made quick, deliberate steps toward him.

"This one's drunk and just assaulted this customer," the bartender said.

The officer looked from Jordan to the customers, some standing and ready to intervene, all facing Jordan and the heavyset customer holding his mouth, blood spilling between his fingers.

"Sir, I'm a police officer. Step back toward me," she said.

"Wait, I'm trying to pay and leave," Jordan slurred but didn't budge from his spot inches away from the injured customer.

"Now! Step away from the bar. Right now!"

Jordan kept his eyes on the officer, but all the patrons stared at him, eyes fixated, some whispering to each other, disgust on every face. He reached into his coat for his wallet to pay the bill and leave.

"Freeze!" ordered the officer as she drew her gun and aimed it at Jordan.

Jordan realized his mistake and stepped away from the bar toward the officer.

"On the ground! Now!"

The officer holstered her gun and then handcuffed Jordan with his hands behind his back.

"This is a mistake. It was an accident," Jordan said.

"I want to press assault charges," the heavyset man said as he reached for napkins from the stack.

The officer radioed dispatch then escorted Jordan to her patrol car parked outside the hotel and put him in the backseat. She read him his rights as Jordan continued to argue that it was all a misunderstanding.

She drove Jordan down to the police station, where they booked him on assault, public intoxication, and disorderly conduct charges. He begged to be let go.

"The courthouse is already closed," she told him. "You're going to spend the night in jail."

CHAPTER FOUR

"JORDAN'S STILL NOT ANSWERING HIS phone," Robin said to Sienna in the hospital grief room. The two women sat on the edge of a plush blue sofa positioned on coordinating industrial carpet in the austere space. Matching curtains too large for the window like king-sized bedsheets on a twin sleeper shut out the night. The furniture did little to differentiate it from a patient's room. It had the same fluorescent lighting, the same tan plastic water pitcher and reusable cups, a tiny bathroom with a shower, and ports in the wall for connecting oxygen tubes.

Sienna's elbows rested on her knees, and she leaned forward, staring ahead without really noticing the painting of towering maple trees on the wall above the TV. Robin's words summoned Sienna back to the moment.

"I wish you would let me call someone else. You shouldn't be alone right now."

"I should have washed his face," Sienna said, looking up at Robin. An aura of calm emanated from the counselor's petite frame. Sienna recognized empathy in her dark brown eyes as she pulled another tissue from the box and wiped her nose. "Picked the dead leaves out of his hair."

"The medical examiner will want Kai's body left exactly as it was," Robin replied. "Whenever there is an accidental death, they have to investigate. It's a matter of routine." She folded her hands in her lap. "This room is completely private. No one's going to bother you here, and it's yours as long as you need it. I'll stay with you as long as you'll let me, but is there another family member I should call?"

At the mention of the investigation to come, Sienna braced for the police asking her how such an accident could happen when she was nearby. When she was at home with her son. And just like when Kira died, she didn't have an answer.

"Sienna, is there someone I should call?" Robin repeated.

"Jordan needs to know first. I can't talk to anyone anyway," she said, afraid that as soon as she talked to someone, it would make it all real, and she wanted to pretend it wasn't real for as long as she could. "I should have wiped the paint off. Can I go see him again?"

"Don't worry. Kai will be all cleaned up. They will take very good care of him. Let me try Jordan again," Robin said before Sienna had the chance to protest. This time she dialed his number into her phone instead of Sienna's, but again she got voicemail.

Sienna picked up her phone from the sofa cushion. The display indicated it was after nine. She had been at the hospital for over three hours, unwilling to leave Kai's side, even after Dr. Singh pulled a white sheet up over the boy's face. In time, they persuaded her to go to the grief room to wait for Jordan and so they could move Kai's body.

"He was in a meeting earlier this evening. It would be over by now. Let me try the house phone again. He might already be home."

"The police would have brought him here or at least notified us if he arrived at the house."

"Are the police at my house?" She fully expected the police to scour the house just like they did after Kira's death. Digging. Digging. Convinced if they looked hard enough, they would find her guilty of hurting her daughter. She took a shallow breath imaging them showing up at the hospital any minute, wanting to put handcuffs on her.

"Yes, they are likely still there investigating, which they do anytime there is a child death. They will want to visit with you when the time is right."

"I know. I know how this works," Sienna said as someone knocked on the door.

"Come in," Robin said.

Dr. Singh stepped into the room and clasped her hands together. "I'm so sorry for your loss. I wish we could have done more to save him."

"I can't believe he's gone," Sienna said as her crying reignited. She choked as she sobbed and wiped her red, puffy eyes with the backs of her hands.

Dr. Singh sat on the sofa and put her arm around Sienna. The three women sat together without uttering a word while Sienna fought to recover from the pulverizing blow that left her dazed and teetering.

She pushed her hair behind her ears and looked up at Dr. Singh. "What happened to my son?"

"The medical examiner will make that determination, but I see evidence of SSDS—Sudden Sniffing Death Syndrome. It's caused by inhaling paint chemicals resulting in sudden heart failure. It can occur even the very first time someone does it. Toluene in spray paint is a highly toxic chemical."

"They were going to paint the treehouse. I didn't think they would do something like this. Is Shane okay?"

"Who is Shane?" asked Dr. Singh.

"Kai's friend. They were going to paint the treehouse together."

"I'm not sure about that, but I did come in here because I have some information about your husband," Dr. Singh said as Sienna plucked more tissues. "The police have dispatched an officer to the hospital. Officer Lisa Rodriguez. They have your husband in custody."

Sienna spun to face the doctor. "What?"

"He's okay, but he has been arrested. Are you able to speak to the officer?"

"Yes! Please! What's going on?"

"Officer Rodriguez, you may come in," said Dr. Singh loudly enough for the officer to hear through the door.

Stepping into the room and closing the door behind her with a gentle hand, Officer Rodriguez removed her hat, revealing her sleek black hair pulled into a ponytail. She stood with her arms bent at the elbow behind her back, head up, and shoulders back as though standing at attention in an honor guard.

"Ma'am, I'm Officer Rodriguez of Madison PD, and on behalf of the entire department, I want to express our sincerest condolences for your loss."

Sienna stood from the sofa. Dr. Singh and Robin stood along with her. "Thank you, officer. What has happened to my husband?"

"I was the arresting officer, ma'am. When I heard he was the victim's father and the owner of the home where officers are investigating a child's death, I asked to be the one to come over here."

Sienna didn't flinch.

"There was an altercation in the bar at the Montrose Hotel. Everyone's fine. Calmer heads eventually prevailed, and the parties involved have decided not to press charges against your husband. He's being held now only because he's heavily intoxicated, and the district attorney must agree not to pursue it."

"Does he know what's happened?" asked Sienna as she crossed her arms.

Officer Rodriguez remained at attention as she spoke. "Negative, ma'am. We decided not to tell him while he's inebriated and in a holding cell. Instead, he was told you would be informed about the arrest. He couldn't tell you himself because we don't typically allow intoxicated detainees to use the phone until they have sobered up. In any case, he didn't have his cellphone on his person at the time of the arrest, and maybe because of the alcohol, he doesn't seem to know or can't remember your phone number. We fully expect he'll be released first thing in the morning."

"What am I supposed to do?" Sienna asked. She sat and stared at her hands in her lap then up into the room again, missing Kai and worrying about how she was supposed to handle it all on her own. It was then the painting registered for the first time. Her heartbeat fluttered, and her head cocked to the left as she gazed at it. The center featured a glorious Crimson King maple tree with vibrant purple leaves tinged with blue at the edges. She could tell the blue was the artist's attempt at a light effect. A dense forest of smaller maples with the same colorful leaves surrounded it.

"That looks like our forest," she said.

The women turned to the painting as Sienna spoke.

"We have a house on the lake. Kai loves hiking through the forest. There's a meadow deep inside it with a group of maples in the center like that. There's a large old maple surrounded by smaller ones. The leaves are a deep purple fringed with midnight blue from iron ore deposits, I think. You can see the hint of blue when the sun shines through the leaves. Kai said the small trees were like the Queen's Guard in London with their colors flying there to protect her in the center," she added, staring into the artwork, wanting to escape to that sanctuary and find peace among the trees. Leaning forward, she put her face in her hands, resting on her lap, confused and foggy.

"I don't know what to do," she said into her hands.

"You don't have to do anything tonight," Robin said, caressing her back. "Arrangements can be made tomorrow when Jordan is available."

"Can you tell me what happened, Mrs. Clarke? Are you up to that?" Officer Rodriguez asked. "It would be very helpful to our investigation. Help figure out exactly what happened to Kai."

"Yes," she said, looking up again with tears spilling down her cheeks, wanting to talk about her son, but braced for the inevitable questions that could all be distilled down to, "How could you let this happen? Again!" She sniffled and righted herself.

"I found Kai in his treehouse," she began and noticed the officer open her notepad and take notes. "I came down to cook dinner, and since it was getting late, I called out for him and then went looking for him. He and his friend Shane were supposed to be painting the inside of the treehouse. Is Shane okay?"

"Yes, he's fine. Not long after officers arrived, Shane and his mother showed up. She noticed the paint on his hands. He told her they tried huffing paint, so she took him back to your house. Shane told the officers he got scared and biked home and that he never meant for anything to happen to Kai."

"He could have come to get me. Why didn't he come inside?" Sienna asked.

"We'll be speaking to him again. Understandably, he was quite upset and fuzzy about the details," said Officer Rodriguez. "Where did they get the paint?"

"From the garage."

"So, you did give the kids permission and knew what they were doing, like Shane said?"

"I told them they could paint the inside of the treehouse."

"Do you know if Kai or Shane ever huffed paint before?" asked the officer.

"No, never. Kai has never done anything like this before. It's why I still can't believe this is real," Sienna said, her throat aching from the repressed sobs.

"You found Kai in the treehouse?"

"Yes. I climbed up there and found him unconscious. I screamed for help and tried CPR. I don't know how long I tried. I kept screaming for help, but no one came."

"Your neighbor heard you?"

"Yvonne heard me yelling. She called 9-1-1."

"How did you manage to get him down out of the treehouse?" asked Officer Rodriguez.

"I don't know. I just picked him up and started climbing down."

"Your neighbor says you fell."

"Yes, I was almost down, and my foot slipped. As soon as we got down, I tried CPR again until the ambulance arrived."

"Were you or Kai injured in the fall?"

"No, it was just a few feet. I had the wind knocked out of me when Kai landed on me. He was unconscious," Sienna said through sobs. After a few moments, she stifled her emotion and wiped her eyes with the crumpled tissue so she could continue.

"And then what happened?" Officer Rodriguez softly asked.

"I kept trying CPR," she said, taking a deep breath. "My neighbor was there with me. She had 9-1-1 on the phone, then the ambulance arrived, and they brought us here."

"You didn't bring anything else down with you or remove anything?"

"No. I didn't touch anything else."

"And you were the only one in the treehouse?"

"Yes."

"You didn't go back up after you came down with Kai, do I have that right?"

"Yes, that's right. I don't know if I will ever go back in that treehouse."

Officer Rodriguez flipped closed the cover of her notepad.

"Ma'am, I want to tell you again how very sorry I am. I know this has been difficult, but I appreciate you helping us trying to put together what happened. We have what we need for now, but we will need to talk with you again. And with your husband. You can expect Jordan to be released in the morning by eight or earlier."

Officer Rodriguez made a barely perceptible motion to hug Sienna but stopped herself and instead nodded in a long, solemn bow. She then turned to Dr. Singh. "Thank you, doctor," she said and then stepped from the room.

It wasn't until the door closed that it occurred to Sienna that Officer Rodriguez hadn't asked about Kira's death. She hadn't pressed her about the similarities. Hadn't forced her to relive those moments, too. Moments she feared would cause her an irreversible breakdown if she allowed them to surface right then. She kept them buried and wondered if maybe the police had not yet made the connection that she was the same mother who lost another child ten months earlier.

She couldn't face the scrutiny again. The questioning of her fitness as a mother. And the accusations. The evil accusations. She'd barely survived all the speculation that Kira's death was her fault and not an accident. If it wasn't for Kai and her need to endure it for him, the police investigation would have killed her. Sometimes she doubted Jordan believed her. She wouldn't survive if they said the same about Kai.

Dr. Singh rose from the sofa. "I'm afraid I must get back to my patients. I'm going to prescribe a mild tranquilizer. Something to help you sleep tonight. You can fill it here at the hospital on the way out. You'll have it if you need it. I'm so sorry. I wish there were something we could have done." She again opened her arms to Sienna.

Sienna stood and accepted another hug. "Thank you, doctor."

"Get home and get some rest," she said and excused herself.

Robin stood with her cellphone in hand. "You should probably let me call someone for you now since Jordan won't be coming tonight."

"I don't think I should tell family until Jordan knows. I think he deserves that, regardless of . . . His parents are retired and live in Hawaii. My mom is in Texas with my stepdad, where I'm from. My dad's gone. My sister and her family are there. Jordan's brother is in Minneapolis, but he's got problems and is estranged from the family. No one's coming tonight."

"Can I call one of your friends? Or someone from your church?"

"We don't go to church. No, will you drive me home? I just want to go home."

"Yes, of course I will, but I don't think you should be at home alone tonight without Jordan. Please let me call a friend."

"I just want to be at home. There is nothing anyone can say or do. There isn't anyone in the world who can make things better. Including Jordan."

CHAPTER FIVE

"WAKE UP!" A CELLMATE SAID as he kicked Jordan's feet down off the stainless-steel bench bolted to the wall. It doubled as a bed and wrapped around the perimeter of the ten-by-ten drunk tank at the Madison Police Department Jordan shared with two other men.

Jordan's legs fell off the bench along with his feet, forcing him to sit halfway up. "What the hell, man?"

He rubbed his eyes from the glare of bright fluorescent lights illuminating the small windowless space resembling a military-style sleep deprivation interrogation chamber. Still a little drunk and groggy, Jordan's head spun as he took in his surroundings. A metal door with a small glass cutout large enough for two eyes to peek inside was the room's single orienting characteristic, but he had no idea what time it was.

Jordan ignored the sleeping cellmate lying on his side and wearing a camouflage jacket. Instead, he focused his eyes on the talking cellmate. He was baldheaded, a hairless scalp, but had a long and greasy, unkempt beard that hung off his face. It was unnatural since it didn't connect to any hair on his head like a soiled, fake beard one might wear to dress as a hobo on Halloween.

"You were talking in your sleep. Maaan," slurred hobo beard, parroting Jordan. He sat up and leaned against the pale green, cinderblock wall. "No one wants to hear you rambling about your fucking wife. You're not the only one trying to sleep."

Jordan's head throbbed both from the excessive bourbon and the steel pillow. Shaky, he stood and removed his suit coat, wobbling off balance from the alcohol, then balled it up and lay back down on the bench a few feet further away from the cellmates. After a moment, he realized his shirt collar was open, and his tie was missing. He had a vague memory of his jail booking and the officers taking the tie off. Flopping over onto his side, he suspected they must have taken it to prevent him from committing suicide with it. Some inane protocol measure. With his eyes closed to block out the view of the two other prisoners, both unshaven and unwashed as though they had been sitting in the cell in the same rumpled clothes for days, Jordan smirked at the idea of suicide in jail.

"Why are you wearing a suit?" hobo beard slurred.

The other cellmate in camouflage snored facing the wall, his back to the room, oblivious.

Jordan opened his eyes and raised his arm to shield them from the fluorescent glare. "What?" He noticed a dingy smudge down the entire sleeve of his white dress shirt. Grime transferred from the steel bench. He ran his hand down the shirt to wipe it off, but the charcoal-grey tinge remained.

"What were you doing that you got arrested wearing a suit?"

Jordan closed his eyes again. "I drank too much."

"You're still drunk. Ha! So am I. You get a DUI?"

Jordan remained still trying to sleep and didn't open his eyes.

"I wasn't driving. I was at a bar minding my own business. You ought to try it."

"You got arrested at a bar for minding your own business?"

Jordan moved his tongue around inside his mouth, tasting the dryness of dehydration from excessive drinking. "Right."

"So, the bartender just had it out for you? Is that it? You weren't doing nothing, he just wanted you arrested 'cause you minded your own business?"

"He wanted me arrested 'cause a fat drunk said I assaulted him."

"Did you?"

Jordan sat up and leaned back into the cinder block wall and leered at the man. "I was having a meeting with a client. That's it."

"You look guilty. Like you assaulted him. What did he do? Grab your wife's ass?"

Jordan shifted on the bench. "Why were you arrested?"

"'Cause I assaulted a man who grabbed my wife's ass," hobo beard said with a grin.

Jordan stared at the man, unamused, then eased down onto his back and rested his head on the suit coat pillow. He slid his feet up the metal bench, his legs bending at the knees. He raised a foot, crossed it over, and rested it on his knee, flexing it back and forth, stretching it at the ankle. He exhaled a deep breath and tried to go to sleep.

"Those are nice shoes," the cellmate said. "Shiny. I bet I could see my reflection in those shoes. How does a man keep his shoes that shiny?"

"By buying new ones every three months." Jordan sat back up, letting his feet fall to the floor, and reclined against the concrete wall, which he found as unforgiving as the metal bench.

"Every three months? A rich man. Wow. Are those real leather shoes? Genuine? Can I touch 'em?"

Jordan ignored the goading. He just had to get through the

night. He slid down the bench to the corner of the tiny room and nestled into the *V* where the walls met, braced himself in place with both feet planted on the floor for support, and stuffed the balled suit coat behind his head. The pressure of his head leaning into the wall held the garment in place.

"What do you do, rich guy?" hobo beard asked.

Jordan closed his eyes and adjusted his head on the coat. "I'm a realtor. One of the top realtors in Madison. And I'm about to take a step up too," he said, boasting, the alcohol fueling his ego. "I have multiple job offers at my feet, and I'm about to get another. One that will make me a very rich man. I handled the largest commercial land development real estate transaction in the state a few months ago. I made it happen. That's why I was at the bar. Meeting with the owner of the biggest commercial real estate firm in the state."

"Is that who grabbed your wife's ass?" he asked, provoking Jordan.

Jordan opened his eyes and turned his head to the side so he could see the man. "What?"

"You said you're here 'cause you hit a man who grabbed your wife's ass. You probably screwed up your job offer," he slurred. "There goes your chance at getting rich. Not many people get the job after they assault the boss."

Jordan turned his head back toward the ceiling and closed his eyes as he readjusted the coat pillow. "I didn't assault anyone. And my wife wasn't there. She was at home babying my teenage son."

A moment later, he continued. "She quit her real job making real money to sit at home with him. She spent a decade in school and racked up a hundred grand in student loan debt getting her PhD in biology and conservation environmentalism. Now she *consults* from home wearing sweatpants all day with her hair in a ponytail." Jordan crossed his arms over his chest and tilted his head further back into the coat. "Now she doesn't earn enough to pay the interest on her loan debt, much less pay for anything else."

Jordan rambled on with his eyes closed to shield them from the harsh fluorescent bulbs that hummed a high-pitched tone as loudly as the camouflaged man snored.

"She's lucky I'm good at what I do. I don't need her income to make the mortgage. I'm out there turning over every stone, looking for every opportunity, working deals. I'm working a huge deal right now. I can't afford to sit at home and work only when I want to. The burden is all on me. The mortgage, the home equity loan, our cars, her student loan debt. All at once, everything became my responsibility when she quit to consult part-time from home.

"I liked that she used to travel," he continued, his train of thought unbroken despite the alcohol still flowing through his blood that his liver and kidneys hadn't yet had enough time to purge. "She had work trips at least once or twice a month. She would head off to give some presentation or an interview about her research and be gone for a couple days at a time. I had my own space. A break. Now she's home every night. Not once did she ask me if I thought it was a good idea," he scoffed as hobo beard began to snore, joining the man in camouflage.

Jordan opened his eyes. The man's head was hanging down, his double chin providing a cushion on his chest. With his lower jaw pushed to the side by the weight of his head, he appeared to be sneering. As the man slept, his sleep apnea kicked in. He exhaled a rough, deep breath but didn't inhale for what seemed an eternity, then he gasped and choked, gulping for air. The cycle continued. Jordan figured he wouldn't get much sleep.

He stood and stepped five feet over to the seatless steel toilet that matched the adjoining sink and bench riveted to the walls. After relieving himself of the pressure on his bladder from all the liquor, he stepped to the small window in the door.

He peered into the hallway that was as bright as the cell itself, but no one was in sight. A similar door was down and across the hall, but he couldn't tell if it was another cell or an entrance to the police department.

After waiting a minute to see if anyone would appear, he banged on the door, not caring if he woke the other drunks. "Hey! Officer! I need to call my wife."

A few seconds later, the outside door cracked open, and a young night desk officer who didn't appear old enough to be out past ten on a school night stuck his head through the opening. "Just lay down and sleep it off. Your wife knows where you are. You'll be out of here in the morning. Go to sleep, buddy. You'll want to be rested when you see her."

CHAPTER SIX

SIENNA SAT QUIETLY IN THE car as Robin drove them out of downtown Madison and north to the historic preservation district of Montfort Heights. With her arms limp at her sides and hands cupped together in her lap like a nest waiting for a bird to land, the headlights of passing vehicles flashed in her eyes. She imagined them as a long, unending stream of human spirits emanating their light into the night and wondered if Kira and Kai traveled as angels in tandem like headlights. Their souls two inseparable bright orbs together on a journey to some unknown destination. Her eyes filled with tears refracting the glow and blurring it out of focus. Visualizing headlights as the blinding, golden auras of her departed children, she let the light sear her eyes. Light as bright as lightning.

The thought of lightning reminded her of the first time she stepped foot in the meadow in the forest behind their lake house, searching for Jordan's childhood treehouse. "He wanted to hug me, and I wouldn't let him," she said, her voice soft. They were the first words Sienna had spoken since they got into the car fifteen minutes earlier.

"What's that?" Robin asked.

"I wouldn't let him. I couldn't let him. I hope he knows I was trying to keep him safe." Her voice trailed off, and Robin didn't push her.

But the memory of that day in the meadow surged and replayed in her mind. "It was too dangerous. I hope he knows I wanted more than anything to hug him. If we hadn't gone out to that meadow, we never would have built the treehouse." Sienna leaned into the doorframe without uttering another word as grief and guilt melded in her heart.

"Sienna, every grieving mother wants to punish herself over the smallest of incidents and decisions wishing she handled them differently. You're probably destined to replay a thousand different scenarios, wishing you had the chance to make up to Kai for some imagined wrongdoing or neglect. When those thoughts creep in, you can look for solace in remembering how much you loved your special little boy and that you only ever wanted the best for him."

Sienna didn't respond and was grateful for the silence that followed as she ran through a hundred regrets. Leaning back into the headrest, she revisited in her mind, regretting the day they decided to build the treehouse. If they hadn't gone on that hike, hadn't sought out Jordan's childhood treehouse in the backwoods of the forest around their lake house, her kids would be alive.

She regretted every decision that day in the meadow and wished she had done more to make Kai feel safe. Kira was strong. Independent. But Kai had been too terrified to move.

As someone who spent countless hours conducting research in forests around the country, she was sure she had checked the weather before agreeing to set out for the outskirts of their sixty-acre property. That would have been a matter of routine. She reminded herself that the morning started sunny and warm.

The endless canopy of green leaves shielded them from the late spring sun as they weaved their way through the maze of tree trunks and sidestepped saplings, underbrush, and ferns. With each footstep, their shoes disappeared into six inches of crunchy leaves over a moist layer of decaying twigs, branches, and soggy leaves that blanketed the forest floor like fertile compost.

She remembered thinking halfway through the walk that they picked an ideal day to hike farther than usual and have a picnic. But by the time they reached the boundaries of their property an hour later ready to set up lunch, the sky had clouded over, a breeze picked up, and a fine mist began to fall. It moistened the bug spray on her skin she made them all apply liberally from head to toe, behind their ears and over socks before they left the house. She could taste the poison at the corners of her mouth as it trickled from the accumulating drizzle.

Jordan had led the hike through the dense forest with Kira, Kai, and Sally in tow. Now Sienna wished she had insisted right then that they turn back before the weather worsened. If she had, they would never have built the treehouse. Instead, she and the kids followed like a family of partridges as Jordan ducked under a moss-covered and rotting fallen tree propped up at a forty-five-degree angle by a smaller neighbor.

"It can't be too much farther," he said.

Sienna was last in the line and kept reminding them all to stay at least ten feet apart, so the tree limbs and saplings they trudged through didn't spring back and slap the person behind or poke someone in the eye.

"It amazes me that your parents would let you come out this far without them," she said, ducking under the same fallen tree as Jordan.

"Things were different in the eighties and nineties. It was nothing for us to hike all through these woods or take the kayaks out on the lake by ourselves. There was no Lyme disease and no cable news to convince us that a child abductor lived on every corner."

"This is too far out for you two to hike on your own," Sienna said. "Are either of you getting tired?"

"We've hiked much longer than this before," Kai said.

"Yeah, but not in sections this dense without trails."

"Drink some water, Mom. You need to stay hydrated," Kira said, mocking the tone Sienna used when issuing the frequent reminder.

"I'm just asking. You weren't that much younger when you would get tired ten minutes in."

As Jordan led them into a small meadow and open sky where the woods yielded to knee-high grasses, Sienna noticed the grey clouds building on each other. "The clouds are getting denser, Jordan. We need to start heading back. I think the picnic will have to wait."

Jordan had the compass app open on his phone and held it out in front of him. "We've come this far. Now I have to see it. I haven't been out here in years. I'm pretty sure this is it. This is the right direction. Cell service doesn't work here, but the compass still does."

Sienna remembered the meadow was seventy yards across and equally as wide. In the center of the meadow was a large maple surrounded by a dozen smaller, all with the same unusual and distinctive deep purplish-blue foliage.

"Ahh! Look at those leaves. Gorgeous. They might be Crimson Kings. I don't know. That's more blue than purple. Maybe it's the light of the grey sky."

"It's a mini forest within the forest!" Kira said.

"I remember them being blackish-purple. Maybe this is the wrong spot."

"Crimson King maples have blackish-purple leaves. These are deep purple with midnight blue. Absolutely gorgeous."

"No, look. This is it! You can see it from here. Up in that big tree in the middle. That's what's left of our treehouse from when I was a kid," Jordan said, pointing to a few small sapling poles strapped together to make a rudimentary treehouse floor wedged in among the branches.

"Your uncle Lance and I built it when we were not much older than you guys. I think it was here for two or three years before my parents even knew about it. This was our hideout. When you get to our property line a hundred feet to the east, it's staked with survey posts, and beyond that is state forest land for a hundred miles. My dad may not have been smart about most things, but he got it right when he bought this land."

Kira launched into a sprint toward the tree, raising her knees high to hurdle the grasses, and Kai and Sally ran after her.

Jordan took Sienna's hand and led her after the kids. "We would spend all day out here in the summer. We got to where we could make it from the house to here in thirty minutes. The trees became our signposts. We didn't need trails."

Kira reached the base of the tree first and stared up at the shell of a treehouse that was more debris than a structure. "There's nothing left of it!" she said.

"Lance destroyed it. He was mad at me. He came out here without me and pretty much dismantled it. We cut and trimmed small trees, saplings, and branches to build the thing. We spent most of a summer on it."

"Why would he do that?" Sienna asked as they waded through the grass to reach the base of the large tree.

"I don't know. Something petty, I'm sure. You know how he is."

Kai jumped, trying to reach the lowest branch, but it was several feet out of reach. "How did you get up there?"

"There used to be a rope from that branch."

Sienna remembered noticing among the handful of smaller trees several tree stumps jutting one and two feet from the ground. It was the moment she regretted most. She allowed the discovery to distract her from focusing on the brewing storm. "What happened to these trees?" she asked Jordan.

"We cut them down. Come on. Come look at the treehouse," Jordan said, placing his hand on Sienna's back to guide her. "I want you to see this."

Sienna stepped back to the stumps, more interested in them than the treehouse. "No, these were recently cut. See the sap on them? That's a natural process for newly sawed saplings, not old dead stumps from decades ago."

"That's what Lance and I used for some of the treehouse lumber. See those poles up there? Those were these trees," he said, taking her hand and pulling her away. "We cut those trees because they were just slender, straight poles without a lot of branches. Perfect size for the floor. Come here. I want to show you."

Sienna released Jordan's hand and stepped back to the stumps. "You chop a tree down, the stump doesn't keep growing," she said and slipped her backpack off and swung it around by one of the straps and set it against the nearest stump. Unzipping the front pocket, she retrieved a small pocketknife. After opening the longest blade, she squatted in front of another nearby stump and dug the knife down into it and pried away the bark. "There is still a green layer behind the bark. That's chlorophyll!"

Jordan stepped back among the stumps and put his hands on his hips. "Come on, we came to see the treehouse. Forget about the tree stumps, will you?"

She jumped over to a different stump a few feet away and again dug the knife behind the bark and again found green chlorophyll. "These stumps are still alive!"

"Yeah, so. We didn't cut any roots," Jordan said.

She ran over to another stump. "You cut the tree, and the stump dies. Often with deciduous trees, if the roots are strong enough and there is enough stored food, the stump will sprout new shoots, and the new leaf growth can fuel a new tree, but if not, if there is no new tree, the stump dies. This one's alive too," she said after digging behind its bark.

She stood and closed the pocketknife as the mist turned to fat drops of sprinkling rain. "This center maple must be a hub tree, a 'mother tree' some people call them, keeping these stumps alive. Pumping chlorophyll to them through the intertwined root system. They were her saplings," she said.

"What are you talking about, Sienna?" Jordan asked. "You're not working! You're with your family. We came to see the treehouse, remember?"

They all stared at her as she ran through the idea aloud, talking to herself more than her family. "This is a hub tree. Maybe a concentration of iron in the soil gives them this deep purple color with a blue tinge. Iron will do that. Or soil acidity. I can see why you would build a treehouse here in this meadow. It's almost magical," she added as a bolt of lightning spanning the sky flashed overhead. They all instinctively ducked their heads, keeping their eyes fixed on the clouds.

Dark clouds churned like squid ink released in seawater. Within two seconds, thunder crashed like a car slamming into a wall. The ground shook. One second later, another streak of lighting flared and seared their eyes as if a mirror reflected the sun directly into them. An explosion of thunder rocked the forest, leaving them with ringing ears.

"Duck your heads and drop your backpacks right now!" Sienna shouted.

Stunned by the concussive crash of thunder and successive eruptions, the others hesitated.

Sienna spun to Kira and unsnapped her backpack, which jolted Jordan into action, and he did the same for Kai. They tossed the packs into the meadow away from the trees. Jordan removed his as another splintered bolt of lightning like blue veins down a pale forearm streaked for miles across the sky, followed by the rapid cannon blast of pounding thunder.

Kai ran up to Sienna and threw his arms around her waist and looked up at her, panicked, his eyes peeled wide.

"Stay away from the open meadow!" Sienna said. "Keep your heads down! Kira, crouch at the base of this tree and cover your head with your arms! Kai, stay down and get to that tree over there and do the same! Make yourself into a tiny ball. Go! Now! Jordan, take Sally and get to that tree. Stay down. Crouch. Make yourself small."

Too terrified to move, Kai wouldn't release his grip on her.

Another cascading explosion of blinding flashes and bone-rattling thunder splintered across the dark sky directly above them. Wind tore through the canopy, ripping leaves from their branches as the storm rolled overhead.

Sienna took Kai's hands and pried them off her waist. "We all have to stay at least fifteen feet away from each other! We have to minimize our conductivity!"

A bolt of lightning tore open the sky, followed instantly by crashing waves of thunder that wracked their bodies and the ground with the intensity of an earthquake.

Kai cried and threw his arms back around Sienna's waist. She hunched over and walked him to a nearby tree and again pulled at his hands. "Kai, I need you to do what I say. Squat down here and cover your head with your hands."

Kai didn't seem to comprehend. He didn't budge. He simply stared into Sienna's eyes.

The lighting flared again, sending bursts of white light flashing across the grey sky and bullwhipping their eardrums.

"Kai, right now! Crouch! Now!" Sienna said. Her raised voice broke through Kai's stupor, and he did as she told him.

His tears mixed with the raindrops as he huddled at the base of the tree, staring at his mom as she left him.

Sienna remained hunched over and hurried to another tree, careful to avoid the largest in the center of the island of trees. She felt marooned.

The lighting strikes competed for attention and dominance of the sky. One bolt after another, each broader than the last. Explosive roars and unrelenting jagged volts of electricity arching across the sky.

Squatting on her knees, thighs flat against her calves, Sienna turned her head to find her children. Both were crying with terrified grimaces. She couldn't hear their pleas over the storm as torrential rain poured through the umbrella of branches and leaves, drenching them in a freezing cold bath.

Kai's eyes were twice as wide as normal, and Kira had hers closed in a tight squint. "No one move!" Sienna said. "Stay put and let the storm pass!"

A ribbon of lighting brighter than the sun struck the metal thermos attached to Jordan's backpack in the meadow. The crack of thunder caused their ears to ring and the pressure in them to pop. A moment later, another bolt flashed and connected with a large tree at the edge of the forest beyond the meadow. It seemed to take hold of the tree and shake it, not wanting to release it from its electrified grasp as though if it held on long enough, the tree might animate. Kira and Kai shrieked as the bolt retreated to the sky, leaving the tree licked with a fiery gash down its trunk. Sheared open by the strike, a quarter of the tree split away and crashed to the ground.

"Stay down! Don't move!" Sienna said as her children screamed, and flames crackled in the heart of the tree. Smoke wafted as the pouring rain worked to extinguish the fire.

It took three seconds before thunder reached them after the next few lighting bursts. Then five seconds. The storm was moving away. Within minutes, as all four kneeled in a position of worship at the base of separate trees, hands and arms shielding their heads, the lighting and thunder slipped to the backdrop. Even before the flickering fire in the torched tree was out, the deluge slowed to sprinkling rain. But Sienna never took her eyes off Kira and Kai. They were only fifteen feet away, but it was as though she watched them through a video monitor, helpless to comfort them.

Kai sat up once the rain diminished, but Sienna ordered him to stay down. He slumped, resuming his cowering crouch at the base of the maple.

"I think it has passed us. The worst of it," Jordan said as the sprinkling rain sizzled on the smoldering tree.

"Give it another minute!" Sienna said. "Everyone, stay down another minute." Once she was sure they were safe, sure the freak lightning storm had ended, she jumped up and ran to her kids, who dashed to her, colliding in a group embrace. Sienna spread her arms wide to capture every inch of her family she could. Jordan was seconds behind and leaned in to hug them all.

"It's okay. It's over. I'm sorry," Sienna said, cooing, trying to reassure her kids. They were both still crying and shaking under her embrace. She craned her head toward Jordan.

"We should have headed back. I know better."

Jordan kissed Sienna on her temple and then again on her cheek as he released his grasp. "I should have listened to you when you told us to go back."

"We're all okay. It's over. Thank you, God!" But the children weren't soothed. "Come on now. We're okay." She kissed them both on their heads and squeezed them to her chest. "I'm sorry, but we had to be apart. If we stayed together, we would have been a bigger target to attract lightning. I know you were scared. I'm sorry, but we're okay."

Jordan turned toward the smoldering tree trunk, the flames extinguished. "That's more than I can say for this tree." As he stepped over to the section of the tree that cleaved away and fell partially into the meadow, the sun broke through the clouds and filtered to them through the leaves.

Sienna stood and rubbed Kira and Kai on their backs with her open hands. "Take some deep breaths and shake it off. We're all okay. I love you guys," she said as she kissed them both again on their heads. "Kai, I think Sally needs a hug, too."

He bent and put his arms around the shaking yellow Lab, trying to calm her.

"My backpack is toast," Jordan said. "Imagine if I had been wearing it."

"It was the metal. The metal attracted the lightning," Sienna said.

"It was kind of cool," Kai said, sniffling and trying his best to sound convincing.

"Shut up, Kai. That was as cool as jumping out of a plane without a parachute," Kira said, wiping away tears with the backs of her hands, her eyes and cheeks red and inflamed.

Jordan inspected the section of the tree split open by the lighting. "I've never in my life witnessed anything like that."

"I have. That's what makes me so mad at myself. I know how dangerous it can be. I guess I was just too awestruck by the masterful craftsmanship of your treehouse to think clearly." Sienna smiled, trying to add levity to defuse everyone's sense of fright as she wiped the rain from her face and pushed her wet hair back. "What did you name it? Graceland II? Monticello, Jr?"

"I'm thinking about putting a picture of it on my business card to show clients the beautiful architecture of the kind of real estate I represent. Hey, let's build a treehouse at home!" Jordan said, clearly hoping to dispel the looming anxiousness.

Sitting in the passenger seat of Robin's car, the thought grated Sienna's brain. *Why did we build the treehouse? Is that what fate had planned all along?*

"Yes! A big one!" Kai said, raising his hands in a cheer.

"You're going to build a treehouse, Kai?" Kira scoffed.

Jordan squatted and rubbed Sally's neck. "Sally wants a treehouse, right girl?" The dog's legs were still trembling as raindrops fell from her coat. "We can take a couple of the poles from my old treehouse to put in the new one. They can commemorate this adventure."

"Adventure?" Kira asked. "We nearly died!"

"And a treehouse can enhance the property. Make a huge house homier. Family friendly. Like it's lived in."

"Always marketing," Sienna said.

"Come on, Kai, let's pull a pole or two to take back," Jordan said, putting his hand on Kai's back and guiding him toward the largest maple in the center of the grouping.

Sienna and Kira stepped into the sunlit meadow, already humid as the wet grass heated. The sun's rays shined onto the wet leaves of the distinct maples that glistened with iridescence.

"The leaves look like fruit, like leaf-shaped plums," Sienna said. "See how the sun filters through them? Maybe they aren't Crimson Kings. A similar species of maple. Maple leaf viburnum is blue in fall."

Jordan was up in the tree, wrestling two thin poles from the group laced together to form a floor as Kai stared up at him, waiting for them to drop.

Kira pulled a large leaf off its branch, held it to the sky, and looked at the sun through it. "It is blue with the sunlight coming through it. Like feathers." She spun the deep blueish purple leaf in her fingers.

Sienna pulled a couple of leaves and turned them in the sunlight. "Look for a big shoot or a nice sapling of these Crimson Kings, or whatever they are. We can pull it up and take it home. You and I can plant it around our silver maple. It will be our tree, and they can build the treehouse."

Jordan loosened and tossed the old saplings to the ground.

"Watch out. Stand back."

Kai raced to retrieve them. He was already gleeful, and Sienna hoped the trauma had faded. Grabbing one in each hand, he turned them vertical like four-foot walking sticks. He and Jordan dragged them back through the forest to their lake house, talking the entire way about the treehouse they would build. Jordan promised it would be a real treehouse. They would hire people to help them build the biggest treehouse they could. They ended up using the sapling poles as grip bars fastened to each side of the treehouse doorway.

⚘⚘⚘

Sienna sat back upright in Robin's vehicle and crossed her arms over her body. "We never should have built that treehouse," she said again, trying to shake off the fear she was too callous toward Kai when he needed her or that she overreacted. She regretted prying his arms off her and forcing him to cower all alone when he was so frightened.

"You can't let regret tear you up. *Coulda* and *shoulda* and *woulda* are not your friends," Robin said.

"It's not regret. It's blame. The blame is on me. You can blame me for my kids dying."

CHAPTER SEVEN

"OF COURSE YOU'RE NOT TO blame," Robin said as the navigation system guided them into Sienna's neighborhood. "No one is to blame. It's natural to feel that way, but trust me, it's not true. Looks like we're almost there."

For a second, Sienna questioned if she was doing the right thing. She wasn't sure she wanted to enter an empty house. To feel abandoned with her thoughts.

She sat upright as they pulled onto her street. Countless times she had passed the other two-story Victorian homes with attic dormers giving them the appearance of a third floor. But as if the car's windows were an out-of-focus camera lens, every detail about her neighborhood blurred together. The idea of going inside the house suddenly overwhelmed her. Her chest collapsed as a panic attack washed over her. Grabbing the grip over the door handle, she squeezed it as the rows of cupolas along both sides of the street jutted into infinity. All the expansive wraparound porches with thick columns seemed to extend as far as her eyes could see.

Her breathing quickened and became shallow. The houses' colorful facades of clapboard siding and ornate, carved moldings painted white all blended into a rainbow. Then her breathing became labored as her chest tightened into a balled fist.

Robin turned toward Sienna and slowed the car. "Are you okay?"

Sienna nodded and feigned assurances, but her vision dimmed. She grabbed the center console with her other hand. The strategically placed landscape lights that illuminated every house and sprawling lawn and stand of trees that separated the two-acre lots all began to twinkle in her eyes. Her pulse raced, and veins danced in her neck. The spotlights trained on lush shrubs and trees in each yard became a moody, mysterious backdrop stage set for *A Midsummer Night's Dream*.

With her head swimming, she rolled the window down and felt a cool evening gust hit her face. Breathing in the fresh air, time slowly shrank back to normal as she stared into the night sky.

"That's good. Take deep breaths. It's okay. Everything's okay," Robin said. Her words trailed off as she pulled into Sienna's circular, cobblestone driveway that branched off toward the detached garage along the side of the house. Yellow tape that read *Police Line – Do Not Cross* stretched across the drive and down the side yard, blocking the path to the garage.

"What's all this?" The sight of yellow police tape took her right back to the moment of Kira's death. It was a moment of déjà vu that would claim her sanity if she allowed it to couple with the present.

"It's an ongoing investigation," Robin said. "They'll want to preserve the area for a day or so in case the medical examiner wants to come out or the investigators have questions. I'm sorry you had to see that. Let's get you inside."

Sienna didn't look back at the tape. "I'll be okay. I was just . . . I just started to panic for a second, but I'm fine. I'll be fine. Thank you for your support tonight, and thank you for the ride."

She opened the car door wanting nothing more than to get into bed—any bed—cover her face, and cry, but then she paused before unfastening her seatbelt. She inhaled deeply and looked up at the house but didn't move.

"You shouldn't go in there alone," Robin said when Sienna hesitated. "May I come in for a while? Make sure this panic attack has passed. Maybe make you some tea or something to eat?"

"Maybe some tea." But still, she didn't move.

Robin extended her hand and squeezed Sienna's forearm then turned off the engine and unbuckled her seatbelt, prompting Sienna to do the same.

They walked toward the porch without urgency, Robin's arm draped over Sienna's shoulder. Sienna looked up at the second level of the white, two-story house, and her eyes locked on the contrasting black windows of the corner room that reflected the moon back into the night sky. She realized Kai's bedroom was now as empty as Kira's. It was a massive house, now without any children to fill it, and she knew instantly it no longer felt like her home.

They found the front door locked, and as Sienna was about to tell Robin they could go around to the side door, Yvonne called out from the edge of the driveway. Yvonne was dressed as though just returning from the gym.

"Sienna! I have your keys, sweetheart!" she said, hurrying up to the covered patio with Sally on a leash. "I told the police I would watch for you, so we locked up the house."

"Thank you, Yvonne," Sienna said, kneeling to ruffle Sally's neck. She then stood into Yvonne's waiting arms.

"I'm so terribly sorry, Sienna. God knows you tried to save him," she said as they embraced under the glow of the porch light for the span of a half dozen deep breaths.

Sienna thought she was all cried out but discovered she had an untapped reservoir, which slipped over her eyelids and flowed down her cheeks. "He's gone," she said as she released Yvonne and wiped away the tears with the back of her hand.

"Let's get you inside," Yvonne said, wiping her own tear-streaked face. "Otherwise, you're going to have other neighbors eager to offer condolences, which I'm sure you don't want to endure." She unlocked the door, and Sally charged in ahead of them.

"Is Jordan still at the hospital?" she asked as they entered.

"Jordan is away right now," Sienna said, taking a few steps toward the staircase, crossing her arms. Rubbing her elbows, she turned back and said, "He won't be home until tomorrow."

"Oh, sweetheart, were you alone all this time? Why didn't you call me?"

"I've been in a daze. Or maybe it's shock."

"I didn't know if I would be intruding at the hospital, so I stayed here with Sally and my cellphone, and then the police arrived." She unclipped Sally's leash and hung it on the coat closet door lever. "They never mentioned you were alone. They just asked what happened. They only left an hour ago."

Fanning her face with both hands to cool her puffy eyes and dry her tears, her red nails flashed under the light of the chandelier. "I didn't know what else to do, so I told them I'd stay and watch for you since you gave me a key to the house for emergencies. Sweetheart, I wished you had called me."

"Thank you for calling 9-1-1," Sienna said and squeezed Yvonne's hand.

"I'm Robin Johnson, a grief counselor and family therapist at University Hospital," Robin said from the doorway, extending a hand to Yvonne, which she shook with a polite, but somber, smile.

"Robin has been with me all night," Sienna said, feeling drained after the walk from the car to the house. Making the short distance for the first time since the death of her son, she felt as though she had survived a river crossing treading water up to her neck that threatened to drown her.

"Thank God you had someone there with you," Yvonne said.

Robin stepped further into the house. "I'll make some tea. Which way to the kitchen?"

Yvonne pointed past the living room and through the dining room visible from the foyer. "Toward the back of the house. Down this hall. You want me to do that?"

Robin shook her head and made her way to the kitchen without a word.

Yvonne guided Sienna into the living room with a hand on her elbow and the small of her back. Sienna collapsed onto their tufted-leather sofa that faced the veiny marble fireplace and the baby grand piano next to it.

Yvonne joined her on the sofa. "Do you need me to stay tonight?"

"No, I just want to crawl into bed, but thank you. Thank you for everything this evening."

"I was here waiting, thinking Jordan might show up. When the police arrived, I just knew it was bad. I told them how you fought to save him, Sienna. I told them I was useless and panicked on the phone with 9-1-1, but Kai wasn't breathing, and you somehow managed to give him mouth-to-mouth even though you could barely breathe after your fall. A mother's love is that remarkable."

"Thank you, Yvonne," Sienna said. "My heart breaks again every time I think about it. How many times can it break before it kills me?"

"Oh, sweetheart. Please know I'm here if you need me for anything. Anything at all."

They sat for a moment, and then Yvonne said, "It was a miracle that you got him out of that treehouse. After the ambulance got here, several of the other neighbors came out. I don't know if you saw them. Everyone was asking me what happened before I could even get home to change from my bathrobe. I had just turned off the shower when I heard you screaming, and I ran out back. Everyone was so worried. I told them how you managed to get Kai out of the tree all on your own. Just miraculous. One of those stories you hear about. A mother's strength. You did everything you could have done."

Sienna leaned into the deep sofa, brought her feet up, and hugged her knees. Kai died when she was just inside the house. Kira, too. Just feet away. No one could convince her she did everything she could. She was the only one home with them. If she'd been a better mother, her kids would be alive. This pain was her punishment. Her heart told her she deserved it, but she shunned the thought. Instinct told her she wasn't in the mental state to grapple with the facts.

Her eyes focused on the piano, and she pictured Kira playing it beautifully as she so often did. Pictured Kai practicing his lessons on it. Then she closed her eyes.

"Kai died before his thirteenth birthday. Kira died before her fourteenth," she said and then covered her face with her hands, knowing that if she opened her eyes and saw the empty house, she would start crying again. "They're gone," she said, her voice muffled. "Both of them. They're gone. I've been so afraid I was going to lose Kai, too. I knew not to let him paint the treehouse. I knew better."

"Don't do that to yourself, Sienna. This is no one's fault. There is no way you could have known what was going to happen. You couldn't have known. But I do know this," she said, clasping her hands together and bringing her index fingers to her lips. "I had just finished my steam yoga and meditation when I heard you yelling. Maybe because my mind was clear and wide open to receiving energy, I don't know . . . I think I sensed Kai's soul departing this world."

Sienna looked at Yvonne. She could see concern and sincerity in her wide, green eyes. "What do you mean?"

Yvonne ran her hands through her barrel-curled red hair to push it back from her face. "I could feel him, Sienna. His entity, hovering above us up in the treehouse as you gave him CPR in the grass."

Sienna sat up and let her feet fall to the floor, crossing her arms over her chest in a self-protective motion.

"I know that sounds insane or like new-agey nonsense. I know. After you left, I meditated again in the backyard. I was trying to recapture the feeling of his spirit when the police showed up, and I knew then for sure that he was gone, and so was my sense of him. It was just something I felt at that very moment we lost him, and then, what I think, is his soul soared up to heaven."

Sienna bit her lower lip and then slowly took a deep breath through her red and swollen nostrils, making a vibrato sound as though her lungs were sputtering.

"I'm sorry. I don't know why I'm telling you this right now. It was peaceful is what I'm trying to say. I felt a sense of peace. That's what I felt. Almost as if I was remembering something I already knew. It was like a flash of emotion you get remembering a happy memory. I don't know how else to explain it."

"It's chamomile. This should help you relax and try to sleep," Robin said, returning to the living room with three mugs of tea, each with a teabag string dangling over the edge. She handed them each one and then took a seat in a wide armchair.

"Sally's chowing down in the kitchen. Are you sure you don't want me to fix you something to eat?"

"Thank you, Robin. I think I'm going to take this up to my room. I need to get into bed."

"I have some reports to work on. My laptop is in my car. Why don't you let me work down here for a while until you fall asleep?" Robin asked.

"I will be fine. You don't have to do that," Sienna said as she stood.

"I can work quietly for an hour and then slip out of here once you've drifted off. Is that okay? I don't have anyone waiting for me at home." When Sienna didn't answer, Robin hopped up and headed toward the door. "Okay. I'm going to run and grab my laptop."

"Do you have anyone coming tonight? Family?" Yvonne asked.

"No, I really just need to be alone, and Jordan doesn't know what's happened yet. I'll see him first thing in the morning, and then we can let the family know. He deserves that."

Yvonne set the mug down on the coffee table and stood to leave. "He doesn't know?"

"I can't reach him tonight. I just have to get through until morning."

"You know I don't have anyone waiting on me, either. Please call me if you want me to come over when Robin leaves. I'm happy to stay over."

"Thank you, Yvonne. I appreciate it."

Yvonne bent and hugged Sienna a final time as Robin stepped back into the house. "Try and get some rest, sweetheart. I know it's hard, but try and clear your mind and sleep. Do not hesitate to call me. Okay?"

"Thank you," Sienna replied, and Yvonne issued a weak smile and left.

Sienna stood holding her mug and rubbing her upper arm with her free hand. "I'm going up to bed now. Thank you for the tea."

Robin removed the medication bag from her purse. "Here's your prescription from Dr. Singh."

"Will it keep me from dreaming? I don't want to take anything that will keep me from dreaming. I want to get into bed and dream about my Kai all night. I want to remember him while I'm sleeping."

"Dr. Singh prescribed Valium. It's a mild tranquilizer to calm your nerves. It should help you doze off, but that's it." Robin opened the bottle and gave Sienna one of the orange pills. "I'll put these in the kitchen," she said, shaking the prescription bottle, rattling the remaining pills inside.

"I'll put them in my medicine cabinet. We keep all pills out of the kids'—" She stopped speaking as a pang stabbed in her stomach. She swallowed the pill with a sip of her tea and stood, pushing the bottle into her jeans pocket.

"Thank you for being here. I don't feel like I have to relive it all over again with you. You were with me. I don't have the strength to relive it again for any family or friends. Not tonight. Just lock me in and drop the key through the mail slot in the door." She started for the stairs, carrying her mug. "I'll be fine once I fall asleep."

❧❧❧

As she rounded the corner and stepped into the hallway, she looked up the stairs to see Sally standing at the top of the staircase looking into Kai's room.

Placing her foot on the first step, Sienna's legs felt phantom and too weak to support her. With all her impulses and instincts held hostage by mourning, she struggled with ordinary motor functions. She mounted a few more steps and used the railing like a hiker's climbing rod, but each step made her feel she was moving in the wrong direction. The staircase seemed to extend and add five new steps for each one she climbed. As though walking backward, Sally and the doorway to Kai's room seemed to get farther away. Her head spiraled from vertigo, the floor seesawing beneath her, and she dropped her mug, sending it to crack into big ceramic shards on the wooden step, spilling tea at her feet.

"Sienna?" Robin said, running into the hallway.

Sienna stood frozen three steps up from the first floor, the mug cracked at her feet.

Robin ran up to her and placed an arm around her waist. "Let me help you upstairs. I'll clean that up. Let's just get you into bed."

"I'm sorry. I'm a little lightheaded. I want to sleep in Kai's room," Sienna said as they ascended the staircase.

"I think you'll have an easier time clearing your mind like Yvonne suggested if you try sleeping in your own bed."

"No. I have to be near him. Sally and I are sleeping in his room tonight."

Sienna stepped onto the second-floor landing, and she reached into Kai's bedroom, flicking on the light switch for the ceiling fan. The dark room burst into view. Kai's twin bed with blue sheets occupied the space under the dormer; the slant of the roof angling over it was within reach from the pillow. Sally followed her inside, but Robin stood in the doorway rather than trespass on sacred ground.

Sienna turned on the desk lamp, which shined on Kai's video game collection stacked next to it, and wished he had just played video games like he always did.

Robin turned off the overhead light switch. "I'll let you sleep." Then she headed back downstairs.

A crumpled sheet of paper on Kai's desk caught her attention. She read the printed-out webpage describing how kids get high huffing paint fumes, markers, duster, and other inhalants. It seemed more like a how-to overview rather than a warning, even though that's what it was supposed to be. Someone had folded and refolded it a dozen times, and she suspected kids must have passed it around. Crumpling it up in her hands, she squeezed it in a fist and threw it into the trash.

Sienna lay on Kai's bed and pulled the sheets in a ball up to her face. She breathed in his scent, which from the day he was born she had known as vanilla ice cream. It was unmistakable. "He's gone, girl," she said, and her eyes watered. With Sally on the floor at the foot of the bed, Sienna tapped a fresh basin of tears that breached their banks.

Sienna reached into her pocket and removed the prescription bottle. As she sobbed, she opened it and poured all nine into the palm of her hand, wanting the ache in her heart to stop. Closing her fingers making a tight fist, digging her nails into her palm, she massaged the pills together nestled inside. Sienna sobbed, knowing Robin could hear her and knowing she would leave her alone to grieve. Then she opened her hand and poured the pills back into the bottle.

For thirty minutes, she wept until her breathing became rhythmic gasps like a toddler crying herself to sleep with red cheeks and hair damp with sweat. The Valium and fatigue and grief quilted together to swaddle her and rock her to sleep, and she started dreaming.

CHAPTER EIGHT

OFFICER RODRIGUEZ FINISHED HER REPORT about Jordan's arrest and decided to check in on him before focusing on formalizing the statement she accepted from Sienna. She stepped into the bright corridor and over to the drunk tank. Through the little window, she spied Jordan asleep on the metal bench, his body tucked into a fetal position. It occurred to her he might have many sleepless nights ahead.

Several hours had passed since the arrest, but she doubted he'd be sober yet. He was barely coherent in the patrol car on the drive to the station. It wasn't until later when she learned his son died huffing paint, and that his daughter died months earlier, that she understood his drunken condition. Like many people in pain, she figured those grieving must have found fleeting solace in the alcohol. Still, she hated Jordan was in there, ignorant to the hell that waited for him. If it was up to her, she'd unlock the doors and get him home. Drunk or not, it wasn't right to keep him in the dark.

"Poor sap," came a man's voice over her shoulder. Detective

Harris entered the corridor and stepped over to Officer Rodriguez. The fluorescent lights were unmerciful on his heavy eyebags. "But it's best this man's in here rather than get this kind of news when he's drunk. I've asked the night officer to arrange a ride home for him first thing in the morning. Do you have your writeup on your interview with the mother for me?"

"That's the next thing I'll do," Officer Rodriguez said. "I'll have it to you shortly."

"Good. I want to study it before I interview her tomorrow. Had I been informed the mother of this boy also had a daughter die at that house ten months ago, I would have taken her initial statement myself. What's your impression of her?"

"She's heartbroken."

"Did she mention her daughter's death?"

"She only talked about her son, and I was unaware of the girl's accident."

"Accident? I don't know if we're dealing with accidents. Maybe we are, but how many kids die in accidents while Mom is standing by? I'm on this case to find out for sure. I want you with me when I go to see her tomorrow. I want you looking for any deviation from what she said yesterday. Any change in her demeanor or attitude, no matter how insignificant," he said, stepping back to the corridor door. "Get me your writeup within an hour."

"Yes, sir," Officer Rodriguez said, watching the detective leave. She turned back to Jordan, mumbling in his sleep. She hoped he was having pleasant dreams because he was going to wake to a nightmare.

CHAPTER NINE

AT FIRST, SIENNA DREAMED ABOUT the painting hanging on the hospital wall. She was back in the grief room, standing up close to the painting, staring into it, mesmerized by the hundreds of five-lobed maple leaves she was so familiar with. The vibrant purple leaves with blue edges were like those in the meadow at their lake house. Lost in the brushstrokes, she watched as the leaves began to flutter as though a gentle breeze stirred them. The breeze caressed her cheeks, and it blew through her hair, giving her a chill and making her shiver.

Staring into the leaves, she reached out to touch the papery softness of them between her fingertips. Smiling, she plucked several of the deepest midnight leaves for Kira, who loved the color.

The wind picked up, and a ferocious gust blew through the trees in the painting and whipped around the room. Sienna's hair swirled along with leaves ripped from their branches. She raised her arms to protect her face and ducked her head. A wild torrent of wind burst from the painting, churning into the room, knocking her off balance, and sending sofa pillows onto the floor.

The painting fell off the wall and crashed to the carpet. The wind stopped as if someone closed a window during a storm. The room was still again, and silent as leaves floated to the floor.

Sienna looked down at the painting. All the leaves had turned black. She leaned closer and saw they were no longer maple leaves. Picking up the artwork, she brought it closer to her face. Each leaf had morphed into a broad palm with five long and sleek, wispy digits, all pointed at the end. The digits started fluttering on the painting. Tree limbs, covered in leaves like skeletal hands, quivered as if beckoning her.

Sienna dropped the painting. Long limbs covered in leafy hands jutted out of it and swatted, grabbing at her legs. She screamed and shuffled back, nearly falling over, then ran for the door.

She yanked open the grief room door. The hallway was dark with only a faint light filtering in like immense shards of amber glass through rectangular windows in the exit doors at the other end. Clinging to the tiled hospital walls were vines and mosses and roots. A dank, dark forest smelling of rot and mold had overtaken the hallway. As she ran down the hall, the tile floor beneath her feet became rotting logs, soft and decayed. Her feet squished into them with each step until she made it to the main door.

Sienna burst outside and into the meadow near their lake house, no longer at the hospital. A heavy haze of smoke drifted overhead, blotting out the sun and leaving the world gauzy and grey. Her throat constricted, and she coughed acrid air as heat washed over her back. She spun around. Fire engulfed the forest behind her. The trees were giant torches with flames from the ground to the sky, creating a wall of fire. The meadow was her only escape.

Sienna ran into the open grasses, but the smoke got thicker and unfurled from the forest and engulfed her like a gossamer blanket. Ahead, in the center of the meadow, there was a single enormous tree. A Crimson King maple with masses of deep-bruise-blue leaves that ruffled on a fiery hot wind like bat wings. The tree was hundreds of feet tall and had branches spanning a hundred feet across. Larger than any maple she had ever seen.

The smoke hovered and burned her watering eyes as she looked up into the deep recesses of the branches and saw a structure. The treehouse from the backyard. She raced closer, screaming Kai's name as she neared. The doorway was dark.

When she reached the base of the tree, she yelled up to him again. There were no ladder rungs. The branches were out of reach. Stepping back, she called his name again.

Kai sat up from the floor of the treehouse and stared at her from the doorway but didn't make a sound. She shook her head in panic and disbelief as leathery, blue maple leaves crawled over Kai's body. The fives lobes of the leaves like the fingers and thumbs of hands chopped off at the wrist. The leaves walked on the lobes from every corner of the treehouse and clung to Kai's skin, grabbed at his hair, and covered his face. The thin maple branches growing in the window and through the panels stretched and laced together over the doorway, locking Kai inside.

"Kai!" she said, but he didn't make a sound. "Jump to me, Kai! I'll catch you! Kai!" Sienna said again as Robin shook her awake.

"Sienna! It's okay! Sienna!" Robin said, nudging Sienna's arm.

🍂🍂🍂

Sienna sat up on Kai's bed, her face glistening with sweat and cadaver pale in the feeble light from the desk lamp. It took her a moment to realize she had been dreaming. Shaking as she brought her knees up to her chest, she wrapped her arms around them. Her terror converted into despair the instant she remembered Kai was gone.

"It was awful. I dreamed about him in the treehouse. I couldn't get to him." Her voice trailed off as she began crying and bent her head to her knees.

Robin sat on the bed next to her. "You were having a nightmare. I knew this would be a tough night. That's why I didn't want to leave you alone."

Sienna wiped fresh tears from her cheeks. "What time is it?" Her whispered words were strangled by grief and panic, her heart still racing.

"Almost midnight."

"The Valium gave me a terrible headache," she said, rubbing her throbbing forehead.

"Do you have some Tylenol?"

"Yes, I'll get it. I'm sorry. I didn't mean for you to have to stay this late," Sienna said, twisting her body and letting her feet fall to the floor, trying to shake off the sense of terror and despair. "I'll be fine now. I'm going to take Sally out and then go to sleep in my room." She stood and nearly lost her balance, her arms bouncing up to steady her. "I'm still a little lightheaded."

"I'll take Sally out. You sit back down for a second and get your bearings, then go get into bed. Come on, Sally," she added without giving Sienna the chance to protest as she led the dog from the room.

Sienna sat back on the bed and scanned around Kai's room. A basket of clean clothes she told him to fold and put away earlier that morning still rested on the floor by his chest of drawers. She realized there was no need to bother with that anymore. Closing her eyes, she again saw Kai in her dream, but his haircut was wrong. It was the longer, wavy hair she had him wear most of his early childhood until he got older and insisted on cutting it short and parting it on the side like his dad. It was his young boyhood haircut in her dream. Not like her Kai anymore at all. She felt a surge of panic, a momentary shortness of breath and needle pricks on her scalp, worried she would forget how her kids looked and start to remember them different than they really were.

They both had chestnut brown hair like their dad, but they'd gotten her grey-blue eyes. Her heart sank as if it had deflated and lost all blood pressure when it occurred to her that she might forget the minute details that distinguished her kids, those maybe only perceptible to a mother, that were as unique as their fingerprints.

Closing her eyes again, Sienna thought of Kira. She imagined her vivid, shining memories of her daughter as a cavern full of precious jewels and coins spilling from hidden treasure chests. The memory of brushing Kira's fine, silky hair into a ponytail after breakfast as they got ready to work in the yard that fateful fall day flashed in her mind. Sienna wondered how much Kira would have changed. It had been almost a year. Trying to imagine what a nearly fifteen-year-old Kira would look like, she could only see her sweet little girl, the talkative, inquisitive girl who loved animals and loved the piano and who was always singing.

She couldn't see Kira in her mind as a teenager. It struck her in that moment that not only might she forget details about them, but she also would never know what her children looked like as they moved through their teenage and then adult years. Sally's loud barking in the backyard arrested her downward spiral.

Tucking her hair back behind each ear, she stood and left Kai's room and shut the door. Walking down the hall, she paused at Kira's door, opened it up, and whispered into the darkness, "I miss you, baby girl," then with a gentle hand pulled the door closed again until she heard the soft click of the latch.

☙

Entering her own bedroom at the end of the hall without turning on the light, she could see out her window the giant silver maple in the distance near the back of their lot. Flanking it were smaller maples, including the little purplish-blue maple they transplanted from their lake house the year before. Like a tossed snowball arcing in mid-air, the white moon illuminated the yard. It was a sea of murky blue, the trees black and veiny. She stared at the treehouse, a black box nestled into the branches, its doorway concealed by night, and then twisted the blinds closed shutting out the view. She stepped to the side window to close the blinds. Light from Yvonne's bedroom window next door shined bright through the tree canopy that obscured her house during the day.

"I think Sally was looking for Kai," Robin said from the hallway. "She was barking up at the treehouse. Poor thing. She can smell him and must be wondering where he is."

Sienna joined her in the hallway to find Sally staring at Kai's closed door. "Come on in here, girl. Come sleep with me tonight. She usually sleeps on the couch downstairs," she said, patting her leg, her signal for Sally to come.

"I'm here. Why don't you let me stay on Sally's couch tonight? I wouldn't be able to sleep if I left."

Sienna leaned into the doorframe. "I never meant to be an imposition or for you to feel obligated to stay overnight. You've been so kind. In the hospital, I could see the compassion in your eyes. We have a guest room at the other end of the house, and of course, you're welcome to it, but really, I'll be fine. You don't have to stay. It was my choice not to call anyone. I don't want to be your burden."

"I have an idea what you're feeling, Sienna. I lost my son, Reginald, in Iraq four years ago. An IED. He was nineteen."

"Oh, Robin," Sienna said, sucking in her breath and placing her hand on Robin's upper arm. On contact, the alchemy of shared pain welded a bond of empathy between them, like transforming lead into gold.

"I know from experience that you're going to need your family and friends. I couldn't leave you here alone. Our church helped me survive. I've been a psychologist for fifteen years, but losing Reginald is why I now work as a grief counselor and PTSD therapist. Maybe the Lord needed me in this job and knew I would need Reginald as my guardian angel looking over me in order to do it. I'm here tonight because I'm supposed to be."

"Do you have other children?"

"No, Reginald was my only child."

"How often do you dream about him?"

"He visits me in my dreams all the time. It's how I know he's okay."

"In my dream, Kai wasn't okay."

"That was your mind processing the trauma. It will take time, but you will eventually have powerful dreams that seem so real you'll wake up feeling like you just spent time with Kai."

"I think about my daughter every day, but I haven't had a dream about her in a while. I lost her ten months ago. Kira," she said, looking from the floor up into Robin's eyes. "She was Kai's big sister. She died in an accident here at home just like Kai."

Robin covered her mouth with her hand, silencing a gasp. Despite her training, she had no words.

"It's a rare thing for a mother to lose two children in less than a year," Sienna continued before Robin could utter a sound. "It happens in war. Or from famine. Disease. Only the cruelest of circumstances. It doesn't happen when their mom is home taking care of them," she said, wiping fresh tears from under her eyes with the tips of her fingers. "I'll never see my children grow up. The world will never know how special they were. All that's left are my memories. The only thing keeping me from losing my mind is that my memories of my kids are kept there."

"Cherish those memories as you cherished them in life, Sienna. Visit those memories often. You'll have difficult days ahead, but your memories can help ease the pain." Robin guided Sienna into the bedroom. "Go ahead and lie down."

"My memories of my children could never be replaced, and there will never be any new memories created. If I lost my memories, it would be like my children never existed at all. They would vanish and be forgotten," Sienna said as she eased down onto the side of the bed.

Robin sat next to her. "That's not going to happen. You won't forget, no more than you could forget how to breathe."

Sienna crossed her ankles and straightened her back.

"Yvonne once tried to help me connect with my memories of Kira by meditating. She has a little yoga studio out back and also has one in town where she holds classes. A few months ago, she caught me outside, and I invited her in for coffee, and she noticed the piano. She asked if Kai played. I told her he played some but that we got the piano for Kira. It was nice talking about Kira with someone new. I got to boast about her again and tell her how proud I was of my daughter. I told her Kira was a natural at the piano. She could hear a song and, in no time, teach herself how to play the chords and melody. I told her Kira even started creating her own melodies and that there was one in particular she would play on the piano and hum all the time. That's when I realized I couldn't remember the melody. I didn't know it. I couldn't recall how it went. There was no written music of it, either. I started crying, thinking her melody was lost forever. Yvonne said that maybe I could remember it if I meditated. Cleared my mind."

Sienna took a seat at the foot of the bed and gripped the edge of the mattress, bracing for Robin to ask if she had recordings of Kira performing. If she captured the music on a cellphone video as she practiced or maybe from a recital. Sienna would then have to admit she'd been too busy working and traveling to catch every performance or attend a routine practice. She had old clips, sure, but none of Kira playing her own melodies.

Sienna stared into emptiness as she spoke, her mouth going dry from the Valium. "Yvonne took me to her backyard studio and tried to teach me to clear my mind and focus on my breathing and the ringing of a bowl to find my 'inner peace' as she called it. It didn't work. The melody didn't come back to me. I can't remember my daughter's melody. I think that memory is gone."

She hugged herself and rubbed her own upper arms.

Robin placed a hand on Sienna's arm, and Sienna felt her plunge into the abyss slow. "It's not gone. It's in your memory somewhere. Yvonne is right."

"I don't know Yvonne very well, even though she's been our neighbor for close to two years. Kira died months after she moved in. I was too busy traveling for work to get to know her in the beginning. And then, after Kira, I didn't do much socializing with anyone. I've pretty much lost contact with most of my friends. I quit my job that required me to travel so I could be at home with Kai."

Embarrassed, or maybe just hurt, Sienna did not mention that all her work friends and acquaintances disappeared pretty fast. Followed soon after that by their couple friends, too. Even her one or two good friends had stopped checking in. It was obvious people didn't know what to say. No one knew what to say to a person who lost a child. Add the police and media attention. It was all too much.

Sienna also left out that she and Jordan didn't even know what to say to each other, rarely if ever discussing their daughter's death.

"Jordan gave Yvonne our house key back when I used to travel. I forgot she had it," Sienna said. "Before she left earlier tonight, she said she *felt* Kai's presence after he died and was meditating, trying to recapture a sense of his spirit, when the police arrived. Do you believe in anything like that?"

Robin folded her arms and sat next to Sienna. "I believe in concentrating to connect with that part of your mind, in your subconscious, that is reserved just for your memories of that loved one. It's a grief therapy tool medical professionals and therapists call guided relaxation or hypnosis. Yvonne might call it meditation. It can help when the time is right for it."

"She made it seem like something more than meditation. Like a physical presence or something. Not a memory."

"I know Yvonne meant well. She wants to help ease your pain, but no, I don't think he was physically there."

"She said he was floating above us. Not a memory. Even Sally was barking at the treehouse. Maybe I should go out there and see if I can feel him there?"

"No, I shouldn't have said that. I regretted it as soon as I did. Sally smelled the paint. She smelled him, I'm sure. I'm sorry. I'm so sorry, Sienna, but memories are all we have. Eventually, your memories of Kai and Kira will stop hurting, and you'll learn to bask in them, even old memories you don't know you have. It just takes time."

"Memories aren't enough," Sienna said through tears.

"I tell my patients to think of climbing a high dive and walking to the end of the diving board. When completely relaxed, it feels like diving into a pool, leaving you awash in the love you felt and shared together and swimming in memories of them. Knowing you can always return to that pool and revisit those memories can help with grief and healing."

Robin stood. "It's hard, but you need to try and sleep. Let the tranquilizer do its job. There is a lot to attend to tomorrow morning, and if you don't sleep, it will be that much more difficult for you." She bent down and petted Sally's neck as she dozed on the floor.

Sienna exhaled deeply and again wiped her eyes with a bent index finger, nodding her agreement as Robin stepped into the hallway, pulling the door closed.

"I've lost Kira and Kai. I couldn't keep them safe," Sienna said to herself as the light from the hall dimmed with the closing of the door. Sitting motionless on the edge of her bed staring at the floor, she wondered if Yvonne really sensed Kai floating above them after he died.

CHAPTER TEN

YVONNE GOT READY FOR BED while sipping wine at her bathroom vanity. She applied her nighttime moisturizer and brushed her hair. And she changed into her favorite green nightgown that was really a billowy silk kimono, but because it was so comfortable, she had been using it to sleep in for months.

It was close to eleven, and she knew she should get to bed for her early morning class but kept thinking about Kai and poor Sienna and couldn't shake the peculiar feeling at the moment of Kai's death. Too wound up to sleep, she carried her wine and cigarettes out to the pool, hoping the warm summer night air and the intoxicating combination of nicotine and alcohol would calm her spirit.

But even as she emptied half the bottle, her mind continued racing, wondering what precisely she'd encountered. She couldn't ignore the prickly barb in the back of her mind that there was something transcendent, honest, and human about what she felt when Kai died. Maybe the cosmos opened up to receive him. And perhaps she sensed it. She felt silly each time the notion crept back in. But the wine only lubricated the thought. She couldn't deny she felt something, even if she had only imagined it. She wanted to get out of her own head. To stop dwelling on it. The phrase "hysterical pregnancy" popped into her mind, and she suspected that's what was happening. She was manifesting the feeling, and that made her feel foolish, not just silly.

Her phone chimed. It was her friend Robby texting. "You up?"

Reclining on a lounge chair, Yvonne called him rather than text him back. "I'm up. I can't sleep. I'm trying to calm my nerves the best way I know how. Cigarettes and wine by the pool," she said as she inhaled from her Virginia Slim. Anxious, she twirled the gunmetal chain-link shoulder strap of the pink crossbody resting in her lap she used to conceal the packaging of her embarrassing habit.

"Don't wreck your skin. Botox and fillers can only do so much."

"I'm quitting soon, Mr. Muscle & Fitness. I promise. But not tonight. You know this is just while I deal with my divorce," Yvonne said as she pulled in another deep puff. "I'm glad you called. I was thinking about calling you when the bar closed."

"You're the only other night owl I know," he said, interrupting her. "I had to tell you about this customer. You should have come into the bar tonight. You should have seen it. This guy got sloppy drunk. Absolutely trashed. Started acting like an asshole. Cussing and yelling. Then he hit another customer in the mouth. Everyone started screaming. We had to call the police, and they had to pull a gun on him to arrest him. It was crazy. He was a hottie, though. Handsome and volatile. A great combination. A bad boy. I should have tackled him and held him in a bearhug—pun intended," he said with a chuckle and continued on. "He looked like he was in his late thirties. I'm probably six or seven years older than him. Oh, but I could make him so happy. Help him deal with all that anger. Probably wasn't gay, though. But he did have a gay haircut. You know the type."

Yvonne didn't reply.

"What's wrong? I can tell something's up. Is it your ex-husband again? What did he do this time?"

"No, that's not it. It's my neighbor. Poor thing. Her son died this evening."

"What? Oh, god."

"It's the same neighbor I told you about whose daughter died in their backyard last year. The one I tried to help meditate. Ugh, this is just so awful." She inhaled the last remnant of pleasure from her cigarette and snuffed it out on a white china saucer. It left a black smudge as she swirled it around the porcelain surface.

"Jesus. What happened?"

"He huffed paint, and it killed him. I heard his mom screaming for help in their backyard. I called 9-1-1. An ambulance came, but they couldn't save him. He was just a child," she said as she opened the mini-purse and plucked another cigarette from the cellophane pack. She lit it and exhaled into the night air.

"The police came over while I was still there. Five of them scouring over the yard, taking photos. They asked me all kinds of questions. Even about the girl's death. And they grilled me about their mother, Sienna. I told them I watched her try and save her son's life. I watched her give him CPR until the ambulance arrived, never once giving up.

"Ugh, I can't talk about it. I can only imagine how she's feeling. Hell couldn't be any worse. She's utterly devastated. This is just awful. I'm still a nervous wreck."

"Do you need me to come over?"

"No, just talk to me for a few minutes. Help me take my mind off it." She lifted her wine glass from the woven rattan patio table, taking another generous swallow of cabernet. "So, is the customer banned or invited back for a drink with you?"

"I'm sorry you had to go through something like that."

Yvonne brought the cigarette back to her lips for a quick puff then snuffed it out on the plate. "I'm serious. You can look up his mugshot online and track him down," she said, trying to change the subject.

"Maybe I will. Oooh," he said with a May West effect. "What about you? Have you seen that guy again? What's his name?"

"Bill. And no, I haven't seen him again. I guess it was just a one-night thing. We had fun."

"Fun? What kind of fun? I thought it was dinner. You didn't tell me this part."

"Stop."

"Sometimes having a little fun is enough. You deserve it."

"He hasn't called. It's been well over a month. I couldn't help talking about my divorce. Ugh, I was being stupid."

"Don't say that. He's the stupid one. You're gorgeous. Funny. You own your own business. You were in a Calvin Klein CK One commercial in the nineties," he added, chuckling into the phone.

She felt the wine kicking in and stretched her legs out, crossing them at the ankle. Yes, talking about something else, anything else, helped.

"You know my ex-husband totally exaggerated my brief modeling success to stroke his own ego. It was the one thing his friends seemed to remember about me. I don't think Bill has an ego. Just the opposite. He seemed nervous."

Talking about men reminded her that Jordan was away, and Sienna had to deal with the loss of their son all alone. Her sadness returned and swallowed her up faster than she swallowed the last of her wine. "I'm sorry, I'm rambling. I've had too much wine. I'm being ridiculous. Of all the heartache and suffering in the world. All that Sienna has to face. Why didn't you tell me how shallow I was being?"

"Right, because I called you to gossip about a hot alcoholic who got arrested. I can't call out anyone for being shallow. You're going through a hard time. Add to that seeing a kid put into an ambulance. If I had your money, I'd probably be sitting by the pool drinking wine at midnight, too."

"You're probably tired. I'm sure you didn't intend to be on the phone this long. I'll let you go."

"I'll call you tomorrow."

"Okay. Bye, sweetheart."

⚜⚜⚜

The instant she hung up the phone, thoughts of Kai and Sienna flooded back. The silence, the moonlight, the vastness of the night sky, the sprawling yard, her home in the background, all closed in on her as though the solar system was shrinking. There wasn't enough room for her thoughts and the planets. She realized she couldn't escape the gnawing sense she'd witnessed something. Maybe something remarkable. The idea she might have sensed a child transitioning from this world into the next scared her, but it was clear that wine and cigarettes and distractions would not wipe away the troubling suspicion.

She thought this would be another time her husband would tell her she was too emotional. His go-to dig. "You're too emotional." Whenever they argued, he would throw her emotions at her as an insult. But she admitted to herself he wasn't wrong. It wasn't a new criticism. She'd always been oversensitive. A crier who couldn't even watch a Dodo viral video of animals, even though they always end in a happy moment, because she'd have to suffer through twenty seconds of tragedy first. It was too much for her. Meditating gave her a way to harness what she felt. She considered meditating again to try and connect with the same emotion, the same energy she'd sensed earlier, but a welcome drowsiness caressed her. The wine flushed her cheeks and made her tongue feel thick.

Leaving her purse and wine, she stood from the lounge chair and headed inside for bed, planning to get up extra early to meditate before dawn. At five, which would be roughly twelve hours after Kai's death. If he died at five, she wondered if maybe five could be some sort of cosmic window she could peer through to find him. Twelve was definitely a significant number. She remembered from her numerology studies that it signified completion and was the end of the numerology spectrum. And there were twelve astrological signs. The Twelve Olympians. Also, the twelve days of Christmas. The human body had twelve cranial nerves, which she recalled from studying the science of meditation. Yes, five in the morning—twelve hours later—would be a good time to try, she told herself as she climbed the stairs to bed, unsure if she'd actually be able to fall asleep.

CHAPTER ELEVEN

AS ROBIN'S FOOTSTEPS ECHOED DOWN the hall, Sienna lay back into the stack of pillows on her bed, still wearing her jeans, slip-on loafers, and the fitted blouse she'd put on that morning. She didn't have the energy to undress. Closing her eyes, she tried pretending sleep was possible, but despite complete exhaustion, she was still awake more than an hour later. With her eyes closed, she saw Kai's lifeless body the way she found him in the treehouse. When they were open, pooled tears caused the blinking green light from the smoke detector to refract and intensify. It was an incessant tapping on her forehead, reminding her Kai was gone.

"Are you my guardian angel in heaven? Did you find Kira?" she said into the darkness. Eyes open or closed, she couldn't stop thinking about Yvonne saying she sensed the moment Kai died and his ascension. She leaned over and picked up her cellphone from the nightstand to call Yvonne and ask her what she meant, but it was close to two. Instead, she got out of bed, looked out her window between the blinds that bent with an aluminum ping as she separated them. Yvonne's bedroom light was off.

Sienna stepped to the large window overlooking the backyard. She twisted open the blinds, and the moonlight splashed into her room and illuminated her face like a beam from a lighthouse. The wooden shingles of the treehouse roof glistened like river rocks in the distance, but the night shielded the doorway that beckoned her with the inescapable gravity of a black hole.

She picked up her cellphone again and turned on the flashlight app. It cast a bright white spotlight on the wall illuminating her dresser, and it reflected at her in the mirror. Sally lifted her head with a quizzical tilt and then settled back down.

"Be a good girl," Sienna said and turned off the light then moved to the doorway and quietly turned the knob.

The hallway was as still and dark as a black and white photograph. A row of closed bedroom doors, first Kira's, then Kai's led to the open guest room door at the other end of the hall. The guest bedroom light was off. She stepped into the hallway, closing her bedroom door, and slipped down the stairs, through the kitchen, and out the backdoor.

On the porch, she opened the phone's flashlight app and used it to guide her path across the deep lawn to the maples a couple hundred feet away. When she reached the base of the silver maple, she turned off the light and slipped the phone into her back pocket then closed her eyes and inhaled a deep, long breath.

The crisp night air filled her nostrils and lungs. A breeze caught the leaves and rustled them like fingers through long hair. Police had staked a box around the tree trunk and laced police tape around it. The tape fluttered in the breeze like a kite's tail. Crickets chirped, and a squirrel or mouse scurried away from her into the stand of trees along the property line. But she didn't sense Kai. She couldn't feel him.

Sienna looked up to the treehouse and the darkened doorway.

Hope summoned her to try and connect with her son inside. Pulling a section of the tape down from the stake that held it in place, she reached out and hopped onto the rungs. At the top, she peered into the treehouse. She pulled her phone from her pocket and switched on the flashlight. It was close to three, roughly ten hours since she'd found her son in the treehouse. Slowly she lifted the light to the doorway and shined it inside, hoping to sense what Yvonne had felt.

A gust of wind swirled around her and into the treehouse, making a hushed howl as if she held a conch shell to her ear. The breeze died back, and her hair settled against her shoulders. Directing the light around, she gasped, and adrenaline surged in her veins at what she thought was a limp body resting against the back wall. Her eyes adjusted to the faint light, and she realized it was a shallow mound of leaves blown into the shape of a small child. She watched and waited, expecting movement, expecting someone mummified in leaves to sit up, but her fear subsided, and the leaves resolved into nothing more than dried, crinkled debris from the prior year.

Moving the flashing light around the floor, she searched for the outline of Kai's body, his leaf angel she noticed before, but it was gone. Instead, the leaves had scattered around the dried blue paint spilled and splattered on the floor. Movement of someone passing the treehouse window startled her, but it was only the gusting wind that caught slim, wiry branches with sparse leaves that had sprouted in through the back window and protruded through gaps in the walls. They had twisted and angled as they grew to reach for sunlight they never found. These leaves were a pale green but had a purple hue, like unripened plums.

Grabbing hold of the sapling grip bars fastened to each side of the doorway, she climbed inside and kneeled, unable to stand without having to hunch over to avoid the low roof. Shining the light down onto the floor and panning it around, she found a partial footprint in the dried paint. She reached down and ran her hand over it. It was the same paint that killed her son. She could still smell it and the propellent from the aerosol can. His body, the spray can, and the plastic bag, the rags, and gallon can had been removed.

The instant she climbed inside, she got the answer she feared. "Kai? Can you hear me?" she said. She sat perfectly still and listened. "Can you hear me in heaven?" But she knew there would be no response.

Sienna scooted over and sat in the doorway and leaned against the frame. It struck her that she shouldn't be there. *Robin's right,* she thought. *I shouldn't be alone.* She shined the light out the doorway toward the ground. No one would have allowed her to be out there. To be in that particular spot on the planet. *Not alone.* But she wanted to be alone so no one would stop her from going out to the tree, stand at the foot of it, and beg to know why her kids were gone. Beg to know what they would have become. Beg to remember every detail of them for as long as she lived and never forget a single aspect of their lives or personalities or features or their uniqueness.

Convinced she was doomed to lose other details about her children, Sienna set the cellphone onto the floor. The light shined up and illuminated walls and the roof like a campfire. She pressed her palms together and rested her lips on her fingertips and cried for her children as images of them flashed in her mind. Their births. As babies breastfeeding. Images of them taking their first steps and talking for the first time. First days of school. Hiking at the lake as a family. Teaching Kira to brush her teeth. Teaching Kai to tie his shoes. Kai talking just that morning about his thirteenth birthday.

She kept her eyes closed as tears streamed, and she leaned her head back into the wall and wondered if maybe she wasn't supposed to be a mom at all. Did she not possess the natural, maternal instincts that other mothers relied on to keep their children safe? How else could she have lost both? She'd failed them. They were gone because of her.

She opened her eyes, and the bright white cellphone flashlight shined into them. Quickly closing them again to preserve the images of her kids, she noticed the light changed from white to blood-red. In that moment, it occurred to her she might have other memories of her kids she needed to perceive differently. Memories that required a different process to retrieve. Maybe her memories needed to be free to come to her passively, just like the light through her eyelids she could see even with her eyes closed. That's what Yvonne had tried to teach her. She remembered Yvonne telling her to keep her eyes closed. Keep her eyes closed and focus on her breathing.

Hoping she might recall Kira's melody, maybe find some long-forgotten memory of Kai she could cherish like new, Sienna took a deep breath. She smelled the tree, the leaves, the woody, earthy fragrance of the bark mixed with the paint. As she focused on the light through her closed eyes, letting it clear her mind of all other thoughts, she begged for a moment with her children.

Sienna leaned her head back further against the wall, and with her eyes closed, she began controlling her breathing just as Yvonne taught her. She slowed each breath in and each breath out. Long, deep breaths in through her nose, exhaling slowly. She repeated the deliberate, measured respiration for ten or twenty minutes, she didn't know. Unsure of what else to do, she willed a sense of calm to find her and rescue her from grief, so she could visit her children. An overwhelming need to relive every memory, every nuance of their unique beings encoded into her brain, every long-forgotten ordinary moment that might feel like a new experience if found and revisited, gave her the strength to focus and breathe and discover her children in the recesses.

When her limp arms at her sides began to tingle, she imagined the sensation spreading. Rapidly it traveled across her legs and then over her entire body to the tip of her nose. Then all her senses seemed to mute; even the cellphone light that shined red through the skin of her eyelids dimmed as her eyes instead focused inward on her mind.

Robin's words came back to her. Robin said she told her patients to think of a diving board, so that's what Sienna did. Free to visualize without distraction, she imagined a mile-long metal ladder before her leading to a diving board she couldn't see but knew was there, waiting for her. A distant light shined down behind her and illuminated the rungs. Still, a pitch blackness shielded everything around it as though the metal ladder was set into the moon pointed out into space with the sun at her back one hundred million miles away.

She visualized, placing her hands on the rungs, stepping onto the ladder, and climbing toward the top to reach the diving board Robin told her would help her dive into a pool of memories of her children, leaving her awash in their grace and love. With slow, deliberate movements, Sienna climbed the ladder, counting each step in her mind along the way, eager to dive.

With the cellphone light in her peripheral vision, and while controlling her respiration, maintaining a steady, peaceful rhythm like reading a lullaby to her child, Sienna climbed the mile-long ladder and soon lost the knowledge she was only visualizing the action. She could feel the metal rungs in her hands, ridged for traction. One hundred steps, and she kept climbing. Then two hundred steps, but her thighs never tired as she frequently glanced up, searching for the diving board, counting each step along the way.

The ladder continued into the endless darkness of space that surrounded her. Six hundred steps. Six hundred and one. Then the climb got easier, as though she was becoming weightless, her legs and torso floating up off the rungs only held in place on the ladder by her hands, gravity free. One thousand steps.

One thousand and one. The singsong of her breathing and the flashlight of the cellphone kept her from floating off into the vacuum of the cosmos. She neared the top. The diving board was within sight.

Sienna held onto the curved chrome rails of the ladder and brought her feet down to the diving board. Gravity returned the instant she stepped onto it. The long, slender, white board bounced as it accepted her weight. The blackness of space was all around her and above, but below was the shimmer of a pool as vast as an ocean. The water rippled and shined a bright blue and white as though the ocean had swallowed the sun. Sienna tiptoed to the edge of the board, ready to dive into her pool of memories and remember every detail about her kids and see exactly what they were supposed to become. The people they were and the people they were meant to be.

She stretched her arms out at her sides then pointed them up over her head, bounced twice on the diving board, and without hesitation or fear, jumped off headfirst, arms aimed at the water, freefalling through the dark void.

CHAPTER TWELVE

INSTANTLY, SIENNA SPLASHED INTO A neural bank where she stored her memory treasure. Neurons fired and flashed before her eyes and struck her as bright as fireworks. As their bright, colorful light burned out, the world around her resolved into a sunny Hawaiian sky shining above the terrace where she sat overlooking the beach—sixteen years earlier. It was the first time she was pregnant.

She was on a trip to Hawaii with Jordan's parents. She remembered the four of them sitting at an outdoor table covered in a white tablecloth that fluttered in the gentle breeze off the water. She blamed her morning sickness on too much alcohol or bad seafood, but Jordan's mother knew better. She figured it out over breakfast at the resort where they celebrated their parents' anniversary.

"You're pregnant?" his mother asked, glee displayed on her face.

Sienna's stomach rose into her throat when she said it aloud.

It wasn't from the white plates loaded with omelets garnished with strawberries or the centerpiece constructed of plumeria and pineapple. It wasn't Jordan's father's meat lover's breakfast that consisted of a ham steak, sausage links, bacon strips, and a Danish on the side, which all repulsed her. It was the notion she might be pregnant and someone else knew. She had suspected it soon after arriving but tried desperately to convince herself it wasn't true and pondered what it would mean for her future. She was in the middle of her doctoral program. Several organizations had already offered her research grants, and she was eager to launch her career crusading for the world's forests. She'd moved from Texas to Wisconsin to study and was alone.

She wanted children someday, but not then. She remembered feeling selfish for wanting to delay having children. For wanting to contribute to the world in a different way. She decided she couldn't have children before she had the chance to work with renowned scientists and ecologists. Not before she had the opportunity to write and make a difference.

"We have to take a pregnancy test," Jordan said after breakfast, and they broke away from his parents.

They found a drugstore within walking distance of the hotel and strolled to it hand in hand. Sand from the beach dusted the concrete sidewalk path.

"If you're pregnant, I want to get married. Right away," Jordan said with the Hawaiian sun warming their skin, the sound of the surf a backdrop to their anxious conversation. "We're going to do it eventually anyway, right?"

"Oh! We are?" Sienna said, placing her free hand on his bicep, taking comfort in her genuine feelings for him. She felt his muscle flex. A subconscious action.

"You feel it. I know you do. We're right for each other."

"Jordan. I'm not pregnant. I don't know why I let you talk me into taking a test. Your mom is projecting what she wants to see. I would know if I was."

"Humor me, please. Wouldn't that be the most perfect sign from the universe if we find out you're pregnant on the same day as my parents' twenty-fifth wedding anniversary? You have to admit that would mean we're supposed to be together forever."

When they got back to the hotel room, Sienna closed the bathroom door, and Jordan waited on the bed while she took the test.

Sienna hadn't recalled the moment in many years. It was a memory she chose to conceal, even from herself. It was her biggest regret that she lied to Jordan and didn't have the baby. Instead, she chose to keep her pregnancy secret. She simply ran the pregnancy test under the faucet and then stepped back into the hotel room to wait the tortuous five minutes alongside Jordan. The inevitable negative, not pregnant symbol appeared in the tiny test strip window.

"I told you, Jordan. I'm not pregnant," she said after kissing him on the cheek and then resting her head on his shoulder.

Jordan embraced her, and they both reclined onto the bed.

Neither of them said a word for several minutes. Their terrace doors were still open from the morning. The sheer drapes billowed into the room, briefly leaving the floor before settling back down only to aviate again moments later.

When Jordan turned onto his side to speak, his face was inches from hers. His words tickled her ear. "I thought for sure you were. You look different. More alive. Maybe the test is wrong."

"It's not wrong. But we need to be more careful, or we could end up getting pregnant before we're ready."

"Would that be such a terrible thing? Imagine how special our children would be. You're smart. I'm smart. You're beautiful. So am I," he said, smiling at her, teasing a smile from her in response.

Sienna's memory jump skipped to the moment she took a pregnancy test in private after they got home days later, and the strip showed positive. It was the very next day she made an appointment with a clinic for an abortion.

⚘⚘⚘

As she continued her controlled breathing, no longer having to will herself into a relaxed state, and as she sat reclined in the treehouse, her memory jumped again to the moment she stepped into the medical center.

"Before we proceed, I want to make sure you've thought about your options," the doctor said, his nurse standing silently behind him. "My aim is not to influence your decision but simply confirm you are aware that you have three distinct choices."

Sienna shivered in a white hospital gown as she sat on the edge of a gurney. At the same time, she could feel her cheeks and ears flare rosy, and she started to sweat. Her feet dangled over the edge, and she wished she had socks on. She felt uncomfortable and vulnerable and wished they had the conversation before she removed her clothes.

"This hasn't been an easy decision. I've never been pregnant before and never anticipated my first pregnancy would end like this, but I know I'm not ready. I'm not ready to have a child."

"Very good. As I said, there are three distinct options. Option one is becoming a parent. Option two is adoption. Option three is abortion."

"Is that the preferred order?"

The doctor cleared his throat twice. "No, I don't mean to suggest there is an order."

Sitting in the treehouse, Sienna subconsciously felt a chill as a cold breeze fluttered around her, lifting her hair, but her mind remained focused on the memory. She recalled leaning back and the doctor positioning her feet into the stirrups.

Her memory morphed into a nightmare as the doctor performing the procedure vanished, and the clinic transformed into the treehouse. Now, she was still in her gown lying on the gurney, feet in stirrups. Before she could move, the grip bars fastened to the treehouse doorway sprouted tree shoots like vines from each sawed end that whipped around the stirrups holding her feet. The tree shoots sprouted little, bright, electric blue maple leaves. Before her eyes, the leaves instantly grew larger as the shoots laced around her feet and then twisted around her legs and spread and entangled her lower body.

She pulled and tore at the shoots with her free hands, but new shoots immediately replaced each shoot she ripped. The shoots crisscrossed her body and held her down like ropes made of vines. Tied up, she couldn't move. The shoots grew longer, spread, and wrapped around her entire body and head. They encased her as more searing blue leaves sprouted. The leaves grew wide and covered her in a blanket, obscuring her body. She could see nothing but bright blue maple leaves. The shoots spilled and draped to the floor, enveloping her and the gurney as leaves filled the treehouse.

Then the leaves started dying. Sienna stared wide-eyed as the leaves turned brown and crisp. They dropped away from her body and from the gurney and piled into a mound as if raked up in fall. She lay on top of them like an altar of leaves. Then her memory changed. Her thoughts switched to Kira.

CHAPTER THIRTEEN

RECLINING IN THE TREEHOUSE AND focusing on her breathing, Sienna's mind flickered away from the memory of her abortion and turned to Kira.

It was ten months earlier, and she, Kira, and Kai, along with his friend Shane, were raking up leaves in the backyard so they could bag them. Unseasonably warm for October, they removed their coats as they piled leaves into a wide four-foot-high mound in the Saturday midday sun.

"You're a moody one lately," she said to Kira. "You used to love playing in the leaves in fall."

"This is stupid," Kira said as Kai and Shane jumped into the pile, sending confetti of red, yellow, orange, and brown leaves up into the air. "This is going to take forever if they keep jumping in them." She held a leaf up to the sky and twirled it in her fingers, letting the sun's light filter through and illuminate its segments of ruby and spinel fall color.

Sienna mounded them back up to cushion another jump.

"Oh, come on! One jump."

Kai and Shane helped reshape the pile, and when they had an enticing heap, Sienna flung the rake aside and grabbed Kira's hand. "Come on! One, two, three!" She sprinted, pulling Kira with her, and they both leaped and disappeared into the leaves. Moments later, their heads reappeared, both giggling.

Sienna pulled leaves from Kira's long hair as they laughed. "See. You remember how fun it is? Don't be in a bad mood."

Kai dashed to the tree, his twelve-year-old legs pumping and arms swinging as Sally chased behind, and then he sprang onto the rungs and climbed. "I'm going to jump from the treehouse into the leaves!"

"Yeah, jump!" Shane said, watching Kai climb.

"No, you're not, buddy," Sienna admonished as she and Kira climbed from the pile.

Kira trailed after him. "Fun! Let's do it!"

"No, ma'am," Sienna replied.

"Come on. It's a huge pile!" Kira said as she hurried up the rungs behind Kai.

Kai reached the top rung and climbed into the treehouse. "Jump with us, Mom!"

Kira squealed as she climbed inside. "Yeah, Mom! Let's jump."

"Kira, you'll break your leg if you jump from there," Sienna said, looking up to her kids twenty feet off the ground hanging out the treehouse doorway. "Climb halfway down, please, and you can jump from the ladder."

"I'm first!" Kai said, nudging Kira out of the way and maneuvering himself into a good jumping position. He stared down at the enormous mound of leaves. "Whoa! It is too high to jump from up here."

"I told you," Sienna said. "Climb down halfway."

Kira squeezed past Kai. "It's not too high. It's a giant beanbag!"

"Kira, I said no. Climb halfway down."

Kira hurried down several steps. When she was ten feet from the ground, she leaped from the tree and plunged into the leaves like a cannonball dive into a pool, disappearing deep inside the pile.

"Hey! I was first!" Kai said as he scurried halfway down the ladder, and before Kira's head resurfaced, he jumped. With an acrobat's skill, he spun himself around to fall into the leaves and onto Kira's legs, narrowly missing landing on her head.

"Ahhh!" Kira shouted as Kai's tennis shoes dug into her shins.

"Kai! Watch it!" Sienna said.

The mound rustled from within, the leaves crunching and crinkling as Sally barked, waiting for him to reappear. Kai pawed at the leaves and grabbed onto Kira's arms to pull himself back into the sunshine. Kai hit Kira in the shoulder with the side of his fist.

"It was my idea. I was supposed to get to jump first!"

"Don't hit me!" Kira said and scowled, climbing from the leaf pile now half as tall and twice as wide as before they jumped.

"Kai, don't hit your sister," Sienna said.

"Then tell her to quit being so stupid!"

"Hey, enough! You could have hurt her jumping on her like that."

"Good. I wish I landed on her head."

"I said that's enough."

"Yeah! That's enough!" Kira chimed in.

Kai shoved Kira from the side with both hands. "Shut up!"

"You shut up!" Kira said, shoving him back.

"That's it, Kai. To your room!" Sienna said, pointing back toward the house with an outstretched arm. "Shane, it's time you went home."

Kai kicked at the leaves and stormed back to the house without another word.

"Pick up your coat! And no video games!"

Kai swiped up his coat from the ground without stopping and continued inside, Sally trailing after him.

"Kai can play tomorrow, Shane," Sienna said as Shane walked toward his bike in the front yard glancing at them over his shoulder.

"Kira, you can't push your brother, either!"

"I didn't do anything! He started it!"

"I want you to rake these leaves and start bagging them up. I'm going to make lunch, and we'll help bag them after we eat."

"Why don't you make Kai do it?"

"Because he was having fun doing it. He's being punished in his room," Sienna said, turning away from Kira, grabbing her own coat from the lawn, and striding back inside.

Still controlling her breathing, the cellphone light glowing. Jordan called to tell her his client wanted to see several other houses, so he would be out most of the day. She told him Kira had finally gotten out of her mood, and they were actually having fun jumping into the leaf pile—until they started bickering.

⁂

After the call, Sienna circled through the house, collected all the dirty clothes she could find, sorted them, and started a load of laundry before returning to the kitchen. She rinsed and loaded the breakfast dishes into the dishwasher and turned on its rapid wash cycle. She remembered scrubbing eggs stuck on a skillet and washing and drying it by hand and then microwaving frozen burritos for lunch while she checked her email. It was like reliving that day, every detail crisp and vivid. Even that she and Kai had beef and bean burritos and Kira's was bean and cheese.

Sienna's eyes swept side to side under her closed lids as if she was in REM sleep rather than propped up against the treehouse doorway focused on recalling her children. As clear as if it was happening then and there, she stood at the microwave removing the cooked burritos, emptying the wrappers onto plates, and setting them on the bar across from the sink.

From the base of the stairs, Sienna shouted up to Kai's room. "Kai! Come down for lunch!" She then walked through the mudroom, out the backdoor, and stepped down off the covered patio into the yard, her hand resting on the white handrail. "Kira! It's time to eat!" But she didn't see her. Kira's hot pink coat lay on the ground like a tiny piece of chewed bubble gum in the distance.

She stepped back inside and walked to the base of the stairs and, just like she had a thousand times before, called both Kira and Kai down for lunch. Kai's video games blasting and exploding from a make-believe warzone echoed above. A few minutes later, he shuffled down the stairs and toward the kitchen.

"Go tell Kira to come down here, please."

Kai spun around on his heels and headed back upstairs to Kira's room next to his. He opened the door without knocking, but she wasn't there.

"She's not in her room," he called as he descended the stairs.

"Then she's still outside. Take Sally out and go get her."

"Come on, girlie," Kai said, and as he stepped through the kitchen, the yellow Lab slid off the sofa and trotted out with him.

Sienna took the soda from the refrigerator, poured both kids a glass and set them next to their plates, then stepped outside and down into the yard. Kai was standing at the base of the tree calling out for Kira.

"Is she in the garage?" Sienna asked across the yard.

Kai shrugged and jogged around to the side of the house, and she turned back toward the kitchen. But as she twisted, she noticed Sally stayed by the tree, staring down into the leaf pile. She didn't follow Kai to the side of the house.

Sienna stored her memory of that terrifying moment in its own jewel box of tarnished and oxidized silver she never polished and rarely opened. Tears began to spill from her closed eyes and drip from her chin onto her chest, but she remained still against the treehouse doorway and focused. She lifted the box and removed the corroded lid, and the memory treasure spilled over her.

Before her eyes, the midday sun glistened in the sky like a ripe, summer citrus fruit with rays descending to burn the image into her retinas and into her brain. Sienna stepped further into the yard then hesitated, hoping for movement in the leaves as Sally stared down at them. Her breathing became labored and heavy though she had walked only ten feet. Then her breathing became rapid, anticipating what she would find. She launched into a full sprint over to the leaves almost two hundred feet away. As she rushed up, Sally stood looking into the pile without turning her head away.

Sienna shoveled away the leaves using both arms, brushing them back as though she was swimming in water. She stepped into them and kept pushing them away, feeling deeper into the pile until her hand felt a leg. Then another. Frantic and in leaves up to her neck, Sienna swiped them away.

"Kira!" she said as she shuffled further into the leaves, shoveling them away from her daughter until she reached her arms and shoulders. She leaned into the leaves, grabbed hold of Kira, and heaved her up using her own body weight and gravity to roll out of the mounded leaves and into the grass.

As she rolled with Kira in her arms, blood spilled from her daughter's headwound. But then Sienna's memory changed. The instant they toppled out of the mound of leaves onto the ground, every leaf, thousands, all bounced up into the air. Like water splashing up into droplets on a beaten drum, the leaves sprang up off the ground from the impact of their weight.

But the leaves didn't fall back to the ground. They separated and formed into groups like flocks of starlings and returned to their original trees. Each leaf fluttered and swayed on a course through the air back to its original branch, and its stem reattached to its original place. The leaves recaptured their bright green color. The browns and oranges and reds receded, and vibrant spring green seeped into each leaf as though reversing months of time. All but one tree rejuvenated.

The blue leaves of the maple they relocated from the lake

house continued swirling in the air, the sun radiating through each leaf, turning them into shiny, bright blue votive candles. Thousands of them. Gradually the leaves drifted into place on their branches. As they settled, an image began to emerge on the tree. The leaves fell into order like strokes of an artist's brush. With each reunited leaf, new definition formed. A jawline, then cheekbones, a nose, then a mouth. The last of the leaves landed in order revealing the eyes and face of Kira in the canopy of the tree.

A portrait of her daughter made from fiery blue leaves glistened and gleamed from within the tree, the sun's rays shining through the leaves with a crystal blue light. But slowly, the light faded, dimmed to a faint glow, and then extinguished. The tree and leaves wilted and turned a dark midnight blue devoid of life. A dead thing rooted to the ground. At the same time, blue flames ignited from the tip of each grip bar attached to the doorway. Neon blue flames flickered like taper candles framing the entrance to a mausoleum.

Sienna squeezed her daughter tight only to realize she was again clutching Kai to her chest—no longer Kira. All the leaves were in place. It was warm and sunny. It was the day before. Kai's hair was in her face after falling with him from the treehouse and landing on her back. His bodyweight again knocked the wind out of her. Choking for breath, her lifeless child in her arms, the treehouse loomed above. A single electric blue leaf swayed in the air. Slowly it drifted closer and landed on Kai's face and sparked small saplings to sprout from every crevice in the treehouse, every sawed edge, every joint, and from every sanded knot. Like a cancerous tumor, the saplings absorbed the treehouse, their tiny stalks capped by bushy mounds of sapphire blue maple leaves that opened and fluttered and beckoned.

With her reflexive breathing still caught in her throat, Sienna tried to inhale as stringy, webbed roots shot from the ends of the grip rails by the doorway. They stretched in long, leathery, fibrous ribbons down to the ground and latched onto Kai's head. The roots burrowed into his nose and mouth. Clinging to his face, the roots lifted Kai by his head and begin pulling him from Sienna.

Sienna coughed, gasping for air, then caught her breath. Twisting her arms and body side to side, wrestling with the roots, she refused to release Kai. He was limp in her arms. She squeezed him, begging him to live but knowing he was dead.

Sienna released a guttural, primal scream. There were no words. Only the utter devastation of losing her child. The sound of her own voice wrenched her back to the present. No longer mining her memories for treasure, a bright white light shined into her eyes. She held up a hand to shield her vision. She was again in the treehouse, hovering above her own body, sitting in the doorway. She could see herself. Her own body on the treehouse floor reclined against the wall by the door, surrounded by dried leaves like a dead body dumped in the woods. Her hands lay limp at her sides with her legs extended out across the floor. With her eyelids shut, her eyes twitched side to side. The cellphone flashlight was still on, and it beamed straight into her eyes as she looked down upon herself.

She watched herself wince, her face grimace in pain, then felt a stabbing pain in her abdomen. Staring down at her own inanimate body, she saw blood pool from beneath her and spread across the treehouse floor and flow over the dead leaves. As it seeped, the dried, withered leaves absorbed the blood, soaking it up like blood-sucking leeches. Their brown color changed to a deep purplish-blue, then to bright shiny blue as they plumped back to life, regaining their former leathery texture and shine. One after another, they sprang to life until she lay in a bed of fresh leaves the bright color of blue gems. But her blood continued to flow and spread across the floor toward the dried puddle of blue paint. The moment the two substances connected, blue sparks sprayed into the air, igniting a blue flame that raced across the trickling blood like gasoline set on fire. The flames torched the floor and lapped beneath her causing searing pain to seize her abdomen.

Sienna screamed again and opened her eyes. No longer in her self-hypnotized state, she was awake and alert and found herself standing in the treehouse doorway. She held onto the two grip bars behind her as she teetered on the verge of falling.

CHAPTER FOURTEEN

YVONNE WOKE WHEN IT WAS still dark out with no hint of daylight breaching the edges of the window shades. She glanced at her phone. It was four fifty-nine. One minute before her alarm was set to go off. She had hardly slept. Not even the Xanax she took a few hours earlier could calm her mind. For most of the night, she'd pictured Kai's lifeless body in the grass as Sienna tried CPR.

She sat up in bed, thinking about the last time she had seen him alive. It was the week before when he was riding his bike. His tanned, gangly limbs. Hands gripping the handlebars as he sang aloud in his little boy voice some song she didn't recognize. Just a normal kid enjoying the last of summer before school started, oblivious to the world. He seemed so little. Younger than twelve or thirteen.

It occurred to her the last time she talked with him, maybe the only time they exchanged anything more than a hello. He had rang the doorbell. It was before his sister passed away. A year ago, maybe. He was with a girl about his age. She was selling Girl Scout cookies door-to-door, and he apparently had tagged along with his friend. The girl was quiet. Kai was outgoing and took the lead with an exuberant sales pitch. Of course, Yvonne bought lots of cookies, she recalled with a smile. She couldn't resist the confident little guy. But now he was gone forever. Her heart sank into her stomach and then rose as a lump in her throat, buoyed by grief.

Before despair could sink its teeth, Yvonne swung her legs from the bed and slipped her feet into loafers. Grabbing her phone and the lukewarm bottle of water from her nightstand, she headed to the guest house she used as a yoga studio to meditate, hoping to be granted even a glimpse of that same sensation she felt at the time of Kai's death.

Outside, the moonglow reflected off the dark, placid swimming pool creating symmetrical panels of diptych art with the night sky. She opened the studio's double French doors, pulled a yoga mat from the stack, and dropped it in the doorway on the hardwood floors. She sat and crossed her legs then closed her eyes.

With her back to the room and its wall of mirrors, she fought the temptation to allow thoughts of Kai to enter her mind until she felt centered and ready to process them.

Yvonne focused on her breathing to purge her mind of thought. It was a degree of calm she could only achieve by breathing slowly and deliberately enough to lull every cell in her body with it. As they did, she became lighter, and gravity lost its effect. When she felt she could float off the ground, she knew she had reached her full meditative state of absolute serenity.

Then her anxiety kicked in again, and she returned to the ground. Yvonne again tried to focus on clearing her mind like she had studied and practiced with obsessive earnest since her divorce. But her yoga techniques failed her. It was hard not to think about the boy and about Sienna and what it would be like to start life over after losing children. She struggled to find a purpose after her husband left, and she didn't even love him anymore. Yoga had become her purpose, she reminded herself, again focusing on her breathing. Of feeling weightless.

After another few restless minutes, she figured looking up at the tree and the treehouse might assuage her spirit, helping her to find a cadence to her respiration. Seeing them might disrupt the anxiety that plagued her.

She rose from the mat picturing the tree canopy as amorphous, unable to tell where it ended, and the smaller maple trees that surrounded it began. Their leaves merged into voluminous green fabric billowing in the air. The evening sun sparkled on the individual leaves, turning them into shiny green and gold paillette sequins on a gown.

Stepping out of the studio onto the pool decking, the moonglow refracted off the swimming pool and bathed her in rippling light waves that crossed over her body and face and bounced off the mirrors on the wall behind her. An ethereal sensation enveloped her. The night was bright under a moon that seemed to have magnified in the lens of the earth's atmosphere.

Wanting to see the tree and treehouse, to welcome the tree's energy to guide her, she walked around to the side of the pool house closer to Sienna's property. The large silver maple was on stage under the moon's midnight blue spotlight. A surge of static electricity coursed through the air and washed over her. It prickled against the back of her neck and caused the fine red hairs on her arms to rise. Raising an arm out, she looked at her forearms as the invisible current manipulated the tiny, wispy strands. It was the signal Yvonne needed. She couldn't see the static electricity but could feel it on her skin. It was the same way she knew she really had sensed Kai's spirit.

She continued walking around the pool house until the treehouse came into view. A bright, artificial white light shined from inside the treehouse, causing her to stop in her tracks. Then she saw Sienna leaning out of the doorway, her hands on the grip bars. Yvonne sucked in a breath, and her pulse quickened. "Sienna!" Without waiting for an answer, she raced toward Sienna's backyard to the base of the tree.

"Sienna! Watch out!"

CHAPTER FIFTEEN

SIENNA JOLTED AWAKE PERCHED AT the edge of the treehouse, perilously close to falling out. She ducked back inside and fell onto her back, knocking the phone out of the way. Its light spun like a strobe. Her mind reeled as a searing pain seized her abdomen. She clutched herself around her waist, leaned forward, and doubled over.

A faint morning glow broke at the horizon but wasn't bright enough to shine into the treehouse. Her mind as hazy as the light, it took another moment for Yvonne's voice to filter through.

"Sienna! What's going on?"

Sienna gripped at her lower stomach and pulled in a deep breath, filling her lungs. Her abdomen seized again, and she shrieked in pain.

"Sienna, you're scaring me! What is it?"

Sienna lay back and turned on her side, drawing her knees up in the same spot she found Kai. She took shallow breaths, trying to dispel the pain. She tried to sit up, but her abdomen cramped again, and she cried out.

"Sienna? I'm coming up there!" Yvonne said.

Sienna exhaled a deep breath and tried to sit up again. Shooting pain gripped her, but she scooted to the doorway as Yvonne climbed.

"It's the baby. I think I'm losing the baby. I have to get out of this treehouse. I have to save my baby."

"You're pregnant!" Yvonne froze in place, her kimono billowing, before scurrying up the remaining rungs and shuffling into the treehouse.

"Help me down," Sienna said between gritted teeth as Yvonne scooted over to her. An orange light radiated into the treehouse framing Yvonne in black silhouette reminiscent of a Halloween-themed diorama. "Help me out of here. I won't let anything hurt my baby."

Yvonne slid next to Sienna lying on her side in a pool of her own blood. "You're bleeding! Oh my god! I'm calling an ambulance!" She pulled her cellphone from her kimono and dialed 9-1-1 for the second time in two days.

Sienna sat up and winced again and fell back down. She then tried to drag herself to the doorway. "Help me down from here."

"No, wait for the paramedics, Sienna! We could fall."

"9-1-1. What is your emergency?"

"We need an ambulance at 11515 Prescott Ave. Hurry, please. My neighbor is bleeding. I think she's having a miscarriage. There's so much blood. She's in pain. We're in the backyard. In the treehouse."

"Sorry, ma'am, I didn't understand that. Where are you?"

"There's a treehouse in the backyard at the far end of the property. She can't climb down due to the pain."

"Is she alert?"

"Yes, she's awake and alert, but she's bent over in pain. I can't get her down from here."

"I've got paramedics en route. I'll stay on the line with you until they arrive."

"My children died here. I can't stay. I have to save my baby. Help me down."

Yvonne moved Sienna's hair from her face and spoke softly. "Just stay calm, Sienna. I'm going to stay with you until the ambulance arrives."

"My baby is in danger."

"No one's going to hurt your baby. Just focus on my voice. Listen to my voice, Sienna. You're okay. I'm with you. Listen to my voice. The ambulance is on the way. Focus on my voice and only my voice. Is Jordan in the house?"

Sienna closed her eyes in a squint as shooting pain spread across her abdomen. "No, he's not home yet. Robin's in the house."

"I'm not going to leave you here alone. Do you have Robin's phone number?"

Sienna grimaced. It took a minute before her spasm subsided and she could respond. "No, I don't know it."

"I'm still on the line. Is she alert?" asked the operator.

"Yes, she's in pain, but she's alert."

"I'm going to call your house phone," Yvonne said. "Maybe she'll answer."

Yvonne scrolled until she found the entry and dialed. The phone rang six times and then went to voicemail. She redialed. Again, after six rings, it went to voicemail. She tried a third time, and then a fourth before Robin answered the phone.

"Clarke residence," Robin said.

"Robin! This is Yvonne from next door. I'm in the backyard with Sienna. I found here up in the treehouse. She's bleeding and is in terrible pain. I'm on the phone with 9-1-1. They're sending an ambulance. When they get here, you need to bring them out back."

"My God! Okay! I'll wait for them."

"I'm up here with her. I'm not leaving her," she added and hung up the call.

"There's too much blood," Sienna said. "God, please help me."

"I hear the ambulance, Sienna. You're going to be okay."

"All my children die. I can't stop it. How do I stop it?"

Yvonne took Sienna's hand and squeezed it. "You're going to be okay. They're coming. I can hear them," she said to Sienna and the operator on the call.

"Do you want me to stay on the line?" the operator asked.

"No, I think they're here. Thank you! Thank you so much," Yvonne said.

Within minutes, Robin brought two paramedics into the backyard. They climbed up to the treehouse with a bodyboard. "We have to strap you to this stretcher, and we're going to lower you to the ground. Is that okay?" asked one of the paramedics.

Sienna sat up halfway and rested on her bent arm. "I can climb down. If you help me, I can do it."

"Ma'am, I'd rather not risk further injury. It's safer if you let us lower you. You'll be okay."

Sienna nodded and lay back down as they positioned the slim red board next to her frame.

"How far along is your pregnancy?" asked the paramedic.

"Less than two months," Sienna said through tears.

With four straps laced over her body, the paramedics angled her out of the doorway and slowly released the rope. Cool morning air blew across Sienna's face as she dangled twenty feet off the ground. As though they were lowering her into a deep well created by the towering trees that enclosed the yard, the darkness of the ground crept closer with every jerk of the rope.

She closed her eyes as the pressure of the straps dug into her thighs and torso. They reminded her of the saplings wrapping around her body when she was in stirrups during her dream, or meditative state, or her nightmare, she didn't know which. All she knew was that it left her shaking.

As she touched the earth, the pressure from the straps eased. After the paramedics hurried down the tree and began the trek with Sienna through the backyard to the waiting ambulance, she locked eyes with Robin.

"Jordan doesn't know about Kai. He doesn't know. He's coming home this morning."

Robin ran alongside. "Do you want me to wait for him?"

"I don't know what else to do," she said, her face the same grey pallor and glistening with sweat just as it had been after her nightmare hours before.

"I'll show him my hospital credentials and explain it to him. I can drive him to the hospital to be with you."

Sienna nodded as they rounded the side yard.

When they reached the ambulance, Yvonne slipped Sienna's cellphone into her jeans pocket. "I'm going to run home and change, and then I'll head to the hospital. I'll be right behind you. You're going to be all right."

As the paramedics slammed the door, Yvonne turned to Robin. "She's not able to cope," she said.

The sirens activated, and the ambulance rocked like a boat on a choppy sea when they pulled out of the driveway and raced toward the hospital. Even as the vehicle transported her, Sienna worried that her baby was in danger.

The trees that lined her northern suburb, visible through the two windows in the back of the ambulance, created a corridor of green leaves hanging over the roadway that caught the morning sunrise. But the beauty didn't reassure Sienna. She clutched her abdomen and prayed the baby was all right as the paramedic reactivated the blood pressure cuff on her arm and again checked her vitals. Lying on the stretcher, breathing from the oxygen mask, the pain in her abdomen diminished, and as it did, her hope the baby was alive heightened by an equal measure.

The paramedic repositioned the blanket draped over her. "You're cold due to low blood pressure," he said and then adjusted a dial to increase the blanket's warming level. "Your oxygen levels are normalizing. We're almost there."

Freezing cold but sweating at the same time, Sienna's teeth chattered together, causing the oxygen mask over her face to vibrate. Her rapid pulse kept time with her clicking jaw as her heart pumped faster than it should. She closed her eyes, and it struck her that she wanted, needed, her child. Until that morning, until faced with losing the baby, she wasn't sure what she thought about having another child. She didn't want them to be one of those couples that had a baby trying to save a failing marriage. But in that moment, her love for her unborn child sparked. She needed the baby no matter what happened with Jordan.

CHAPTER SIXTEEN

SIENNA'S PAIN HAD DIMINISHED BY the time they arrived at the emergency room. She was alert as they wheeled her down a center aisle that separated two rows of semi-private exam rooms with short walls that didn't reach the ceiling. Wide curtains closed off each space for privacy. Hospital staff shuffled in and out of them, dragging the curtains into the path.

They situated Sienna in a treatment area, and nurses pulled the curtain enclosing her. Moments later, Dr. Singh stepped in and evaluated her while a nurse changed the IV fluids the paramedics had started in the ambulance.

But Sienna focused on her baby, ignoring the nurses as they removed her clothes, connected various parts of her body to beeping equipment, and positioned an enormous circular light on a suspension arm above her. A nurse grabbed a new oxygen mask and tube from stacks of plastic-wrapped supplies and boxes of gloves in wire shelving attached to the wall. She placed it over Sienna's nose and mouth while another readied the ultrasound machine.

Once they had Sienna draped in a gown, Dr. Singh prepared the internal ultrasound. Soon the finessed device produced an image on the monitor the doctor studied. "There is a heartbeat," she said after an agonizing two minutes, and the tiny group of cells that in time would develop into a heart flickered on the screen.

Sienna issued a choking cry of relief. She pulled the mask down below her chin and wiped at her nose.

Dr. Singh finished her preliminary testing while Sienna cried. "Sienna, you're in stable condition. Your blood pressure is a little low, but steady, as is your heartbeat. The fluids are helping. You've lost some blood, but the fetus is still viable. I'm going to request that a specialist come to see you, okay? He's not on the premises but is on-call, so I'm going to ask him to come in, okay?"

Sienna nodded and lay back into a small foam neck rest that served as a pillow.

"A nurse will be back to check on you shortly, okay?" said Dr. Singh.

Sienna again nodded her consent, and the doctor ducked behind the curtain. She silently thanked God for her baby while also wondering what happened to it. What happened to her. She remembered every detail of her meditation in the treehouse. The maples morphed into a brilliant blue, like sapphire, and mutilated every memory she tried to embrace.

She looked down at the cords and cables and tubes connected to her body and coiled on the floor. They reminded her of the roots reaching for Kai and of the saplings with blue leaves wrapping around her legs and body. Staring past the coiled equipment, she recalled how the saplings attacked her in her meditative state. How they infected the treehouse. These unnatural things that preyed on her children during her meditation and tried to destroy her unborn baby.

Sienna's breathing became heavy, her chest rising and falling rapidly. Blotchy redness erupted on her chest and neck. With wide eyes, she stared without seeing as she relived the images of the grotesque blue maples attacking her family. Then the curtain slid back several feet on its rod, and Sienna snapped back to the present.

An elderly admissions clerk with a puff of white hair came in holding an open laptop computer she placed on a rolling table.

"Good morning," she said with a smile. "Dr. Singh says you're doing well, so I'm going to get you in the system." She whispered using a soft tone one would use at the library as though they weren't supposed to be talking. "Are you feeling better?"

Sienna nodded and crossed her arms across her chest, cupping her elbows.

"Let's start with your name."

Sienna hesitated but welcomed the routine, clinical interaction and allowed it to bring her back to the moment. "Sienna. Last name is Clarke, with an 'E.'"

The admissions clerk tapped her keyboard using only her right index finger. She looked from the screen down to the keys and back to the screen again for each letter she typed. Blue veins bulged on the back of her hand as she worked.

While the clerk asked her questions and slowly made her entries, Sienna noticed a large placard hanging above her exam room indicating she was in number four. The room at the end of the row. The same room Kai had been in. Lowering her gaze, she again found the cables and tubes from equipment coiled and overlapping each other on the floor. This time she could see they formed squiggly letters. She could make them out clearly. *K I R A*. Her throat tightened. "Do you see that?" she managed to say to the clerk. "Do you see the letters on the floor?"

"What's that, dear?"

Sienna pointed. "See the cables jumbled together there? Look to the right. Do you see that thick one how it makes the letter *K*?

And that thin oxygen tube you see it swirls to make the letter *A*?"

The clerk craned her neck to see over the bed then stepped around it. "I'm sorry, I just see a bunch of cords."

"That black one is curved into an R."

Trying to get a better look, the clerk pushed the cart holding the monitor back a foot, and all the cables slid into new positions. "I don't see any letters."

"No! Wait! No, now they're gone." The cords shifted and stretched, and the letters she saw before vanished into the coiled pile.

"These are just cords. You sure you're feeling all right?"

Sienna blinked twice. "Yes, I'm fine. I'm just tired. I didn't sleep last night."

After a tortuous ten minutes, the clerk had all of Sienna's identifying information, including her next of kin. "Can we call Jordan for you?" she asked.

"He is without his phone, but a friend is probably here in the waiting room. Her name is Yvonne Mills."

"Okay, Sienna, I'll check. If she's here, should I send her back?"

"Yes, that would be fine. Thank you."

A few minutes later, a different woman wearing scrubs pulled the curtain back. "Yvonne is here to see you."

"Sweetheart, I've been on pins and needles out there worrying myself sick. Is everything okay? Are you still in a lot of pain?"

Sienna lifted her head off the pillow. "If I lie still, it's not bad. They gave me some Tylenol."

"That's a good sign."

"This is the same room they put Kai in," Sienna said. "This is the same spot I got to hold my baby boy for the last time."

Yvonne stepped to the hospital bed and squeezed Sienna's hand. "Oh, sweetheart," she said.

Sienna teared up again. She lay back against the pillow and rolled her eyes up in her head as far as she could to keep new tears from escaping as she imagined Kai's body tucked away in some dark, scary place. Yvonne bit her lower lip.

"I haven't been able to reach Jordan yet. I've called him a couple of times over the last hour that I've been in the waiting room. I Googled his name and found several real estate listings. They all had the same cellphone number for him. I got his voicemail. I told him I'm here at the hospital with you and that Robin is a representative from the hospital waiting at your house. I can't imagine how that's going to go. It's all just so awful."

Yvonne glanced at her phone, but there were no missed calls from Jordan.

Sienna wiped at her eyes. "Jordan is in jail. He got arrested yesterday for public intoxication. I haven't spoken to him, but the police told me he would be out first thing this morning. He has no idea what's going on," she said as she reached for her phone resting next to her on the gurney and turned it over to see the screen. No one had called or texted.

"You should have said something," Yvonne said, lifting Sienna's hand off the bed in hers and squeezing it again. "I feel terrible that I left you alone."

"I think I needed to be alone. Alone to grieve. I never imagined I would end up back here. I'm scared."

"Is the baby okay?"

"Yes, they did an ultrasound."

"Oh, thank God!"

"A specialist is supposed to be coming to see me. There was so much blood."

"Maybe you were injured in the fall from the treehouse. I'm sure it will be fine. It has to be fine." Yvonne issued a weak smile, her eyes brightening.

Sienna hesitated. She felt foolish mentioning what she experienced in the treehouse. "Have you ever had nightmares while meditating?"

"Sure. Meditation helps you process and clear tons of emotions and psychic energy. Sometimes those forces are pretty toxic and can feel just like a nightmare."

"I meditated in the treehouse early this morning, and I saw blue maples attack Kira and Kai. They had bright blue leaves. Glowing blue. They tried to hurt the baby, too."

"Oh, sweetheart. You're exhausted. Your heart is hurting. Going up into that treehouse to meditate wasn't a good idea."

"I meditated like you showed me, and it helped me see more clearly. It opened my eyes." It felt like pulling a curtain back from a window to see what she didn't want to see before. "I could see that something horrible, something . . . something horrible happened to my kids." After a moment, she added, "They weren't accidents."

"It was horrible. What happened to Kira was horrible. What happened to Kai was horrible. Meditation unlocks your subconscious so you can process energy and confront and cope with your feelings. Afterward, it can leave you reeling. No different from a night terror."

Sienna couldn't shake off an eerie feeling of dread. "Everything I see reminds me of the trees in the meadow attacking me and my kids. It was a vision, not a memory. A vision, Yvonne."

She gripped the metal railing along the side of the gurney and used it to pull herself farther up on the exam table. Her eyes grew wide as she spoke.

"I tried to focus on memories of my kids, but every memory was corrupted by thoughts of these trees from our lake house. We have acres of forest, and in the very back, there is a meadow where Jordan built his childhood treehouse in a grouping of maples. They are a deep purple, and some have a blue hue around the edges. I saw the leaves morph into something sinister. They turned bright electric blue and attacked my children. They invaded my thoughts to show me what happened to my kids. They weren't accidents. This baby isn't safe."

Yvonne whispered, taking Sienna's hand in hers, "You're going through something no one should ever have to face. I suppose it's easier to imagine they weren't accidents. I can't possibly understand the pain you're in. But don't interpret what you see in meditation literally. No matter how real the aftereffects feel. You're exhausted. Physically and mentally, I imagine. I can help you try again if you want. Help you breathe and focus, but for now, you need to rest." She released Sienna's hand and smoothed the blanket covering her.

Sienna thought of the mother tree in the meadow. There standing watch, guardian, over the other smaller maples and the stumps from the saplings Jordan and his brother, Lance, chopped down. The mother tree of the maple sapling they stole from her protection in that isolated place and relocated to their backyard. Her breathing became heavy, and her eyes grew wide, thinking maybe it was the mother tree fighting back. Protecting her saplings. The mother tree saw them as a threat. Her family was a threat. To the mother tree, they were no different from a swarm of caterpillars there to eat the maple leaves or beetles determined to strip them of bark. The mother tree's natural defenses, toxins she would pump into her leaves, electrical signals she would send pulsing through the roots and limbs, the pheromones, they all could have affected her kids. Could have hurt them.

Yvonne's worried glance forced Sienna to push the idea aside rather than make herself sound more insane than she already had. She restrained herself.

"I saw what my subconscious already knew. They weren't accidents."

"You're hurting. I don't think we're supposed to be able to ever understand how or why something like this could happen. This is just your subconscious searching for some way to reason, some way to make sense of losing two children."

Sienna cried and dropped her head back to the pillow. The

tears flowed as freely as they ever had, with no hint they could ever stop flowing.

"If it's not the trees, then it's me. A mother is supposed to protect her children. I failed mine. Kira and Kai are dead because of me."

"That's not true, and you know it. No one is to blame. You need some rest. You need to allow yourself some time to grieve. You need to be with Jordan."

Yvonne reached to the back wall and pulled several tissues from the box resting in a metal bracket and handed them to Sienna. A nurse stepped back into the room through the curtain.

"I'm going to recheck all your vitals," she said as she stepped to the monitor to review the readings. The automatic cuff on Sienna's arm had activated and then deflated every few minutes, even without any staff there to observe it. "You're doing okay. Your blood pressure is looking good. Has the acetaminophen kicked in? How's the pain?"

"It's better. Thank you." Sienna again wiped her puffy eyes and then tapped on her phone resting against her leg, disappointed that the illuminated screen didn't show a missed call or a text.

"The OBGYN should be in shortly. I'll check back on you in a few minutes," the nurse said and then excused herself with a smile.

Sienna bunched up the tissues and twisted them in her hands. "What did you mean last night when you said you felt Kai's presence above us?"

CHAPTER SEVENTEEN

YVONNE LOOKED AT SIENNA'S HANDS wrestling with the tissues, then back up into her eyes. "Sweetheart, is that why you were in the treehouse? I didn't mean to upset you. Really, it was just the opposite. Listen, right now, you need to put all your energy into making sure this baby is okay."

"Yvonne. Please," Sienna said.

But Yvonne hesitated and looked to the seam in the curtain, seeming to beckon a nurse or the specialist to rescue her from the topic.

"Please."

Yvonne took a deep breath. "When I was six years old, my cat died. A big white Persian cat named Charlie. I loved him so much. Such a pretty guy. My mom and I buried him in the backyard and had a little funeral for him. At that age, I didn't understand what death meant, of course."

She leaned into the edge of the bed. "After the funeral, I stayed outside by myself, crying and talking to him. Then I heard him meowing. His meow. I knew it. But it seemed to come from behind my eyes, not from the outside world. Like I was remembering it without trying or thinking of it. I closed my eyes, and the sun hit my eyelids. I saw him. He was in the arms of a young woman who caressed his neck and cradled him. I didn't recognize her. But she whispered to me and said she would take care of Charlie for me until one day when I would see him again.

"I ran inside and told my mom about it. I wasn't scared. The woman didn't frighten me. She made me feel happy. At first, my mom didn't believe me. I described the woman. Her long brown hair parted in the middle. All her freckles. I could see the look on Mom's face. She ran and grabbed a photo album and showed me a picture of the woman. I said that was her, the woman holding Charlie. My mom said it was my dad's sister. She died when she was twenty. Years before I was even born. I know you probably think I'm crazy."

Sienna's hands were shaking; she desperately wanted to believe Yvonne.

"Throughout my life, I've experienced little things like that. I don't know what they mean. I don't know if they are real. But they feel real. It was the same after Kai died. I felt his spirit. I felt the essence of him. A sweet and innocent young soul. When you were giving him CPR there in the grass, something compelled me to look away from him and up into the treehouse. I couldn't see him but sensed his spirit there as if he was staring from the other side of a two-way mirror. It wasn't my senses that told me he was there. Intuition, I think, a different primal instinct, told me a part of him—a spiritual part of him—was in the treehouse."

Yvonne ran both hands through her hair, pushing it back from her face, and then dropped them down into the back pockets of her jeans, elbows bent at forty-five-degree angles.

"Have you seen that viral video of a raccoon with cotton candy that he drops into his water bowl, and the pink candy instantly vanishes? After that, he can't see it or smell it or taste it or feel it. None of his senses work to detect it, but he knows it's there. You and I know it's there. Logic tells us it's there. It's just there in another form. It was the same with Kai. Kai was there in another form."

"I don't understand."

Yvonne moved to the foot of the bed and paced as she toyed with the canary diamond ring that replaced the engagement ring and wedding band that used to reside there. "It was because of the meditation. It cleared my mind. I was meditating the moment Kai died. It's like packets of sugar poured into warm coffee that you can't see but still taste. Or the fragrance in the air from a burning candle that you can smell, but you never see. Things can change form, and then you detect them differently. I don't know how just like I don't know how I'm able to wiggle my toes without thinking or trying. I couldn't see Kai, but I could hear his emotions in my head like whispers. Emotions that weren't my own. I think his soul connected with mine for a brief second. Before I had time to think, the feeling was gone."

"What feeling?"

"Peace. Safety. Comfort. Tranquility." Yvonne stepped to the side of the bed and again took Sienna's hand in hers. "Maybe it's silly. Maybe I'm completely nutty like my ex-husband says, but I believe that all things in the universe are intertwined. The known universe, and the universe we can't possibly understand. Kai became part of the unseen universe when he died. I was there at that moment in a meditative state, and for a few seconds, I could hear the universe carrying his voice. I heard him."

Sienna stared at Yvonne, and the room around her dissolved into a blur of white. She focused on the sound of Yvonne's voice no longer aware of the din traveling over the low exam room walls and through the thin curtains.

Yvonne swallowed the lump forming in her throat. "I heard

Kai say, 'Mom, it's time to sleep for now, but we'll be together again when I wake up. I'm going to dream while I sleep. When we remember them, dreams become new memories. We create new memories when we dream. When I wake up, I will tell you about all the memories that I dream.'"

Yvonne placed both hands on her own chest just below her neck, trying to steady herself with deep breaths as she continued.

"It felt like he received a squeezing hug from you, and as you embraced him, I felt your soul joining with his. I could feel them fuse. It was like atoms colliding in the sun. A warmth radiated through him. That warmth radiated out into the universe, carrying Kai with it. Along with that part of you forever bonded to him. He drifted off, and I lost my sense of him above us in the treehouse."

Sienna looked straight into Yvonne's eyes, but she didn't see her there, only the image of her son's face in her mind as tears streamed down her cheeks.

"We create new memories when we dream," Sienna repeated and leaning back into the pillow on the gurney. "That's what he said? 'Dreams become new memories if we remember them'?"

Yvonne smiled, causing tears to spill from the corners of her crinkled eyes.

"Last night I told Robin I was afraid of losing my mind because my memories of my kids are stored there, and that's all I have left of them since there will never be any new memories created."

"I guess it's true if you think about it. Each time you dream of your kids, you'll have a new memory of them. I might sound foolish or trite, but maybe we've evolved to dream about loved ones as a way to be close and connected to them until we're together again someday. Your dreams can be a window through which you can see Kai."

Sienna looked down at the sheet covering her body. "I went into the treehouse hoping to connect with Kai, too. Like you did. Instead, it was like a nightmare. I felt attacked. I didn't sense Kai there. What I sensed was terrible. Maybe I'm losing my mind. It's my punishment for what I've done and what I didn't do. I might spend the rest of my life being punished. I'm glad Jordan had one more night without knowing the pain of losing both his kids."

CHAPTER EIGHTEEN

JORDAN STOOD AT THE JAILHOUSE booking counter while the night officer opened the envelope containing his belongings. His back was stiff from the bare metal rack he had slept on, and his head pounded. He wished he could have another couple of hours' sleep in a real bed to ease his hangover, knowing things were about to get worse once he was facing Sienna.

He watched the fresh-faced young officer he recognized from the middle of the night tick his personal items off the inventory as he fought the urge to puke. His Phillipe Patek watch he bought for himself after a particularly lucrative commission. His Luis Vuitton wallet that matched his iPhone cover. He picked up the watch from the counter, wound it, and set the time to seven thirty-five based on the wall clock behind the officer then slipped it on his wrist.

He needed breakfast. Something greasy to absorb the alcohol. Before heading home, he thought he might swing by McDonald's and allow himself a rare fast-food meal after picking up his car at the hotel. He couldn't face her on an empty stomach.

"Can I get some water?"

"There's a fountain in the waiting area behind you," the officer said. He kept glancing up at Jordan and then back down to the form in front of him but didn't say another word as he processed Jordan for release.

Jordan picked up his silk tie and stuffed it into his suitcoat pocket. "My cellphone's not here."

"Then you didn't have it on you when you were brought in."

"I'm not going to call my wife or anyone else to pick me up from jail. I need an Uber. I don't know how to get one without my phone."

"I've got Officer Susienka standing by to take you home." He gestured to an older officer standing near the exit doors.

"Take me home?"

Officer Susienka stepped forward, holding his hat in his hands, with a somber expression. "I'm happy to take you home, son. You shouldn't have to try and drive at a time like this. We're all very sorry about the loss of your son. The arresting officer and our chief reached out to the court as early as possible this morning to get you released so you could be with your wife."

Jordan's mind reeled then sputtered. He didn't know how to respond. He stared at the man without uttering a word, and the man stared back. Jordan turned his head to the young officer behind the desk, who seemed frozen in place, eyes down on the inventory sheet.

"Is he ready to go, Johnny?" Officer Susienka asked as he placed a hand on Jordan's back.

Jordan was rooted in place. "What's going on?" he said.

"He hasn't been informed, Susienka."

The officer blanched. His white-blond eyebrows and eyelashes disappeared into his pale skin as the color drained away from his face and lips. His mouth opened as the horror of his gaff struck him. "I . . . uh . . . I thought Officer Rodriguez informed him." He whipped his head back and forth from Jordan to the young officer. "No one said he didn't know."

Jordan stared at the man absentmindedly twisting his car key in his fingers.

"Mr. Clarke," the young officer said. "There was an accident yesterday. Your son passed away."

Jordan hung his head down. He stared at his feet and didn't move an inch, as though he was a cutout poster of himself starring in a movie.

The young officer tried to recover from Officer Susienka's catastrophic mistake. "Why don't you take a seat, Jordan?"

Jordan sat in one of the red waiting room chairs that resembled school desk chairs with its chrome legs and disks the size of quarters for feet. He put his head in his hands.

"Are you telling me Kai is dead?"

"Your son. He— We don't know all the details. 9-1-1 was called to your home. Some kids were apparently huffing paint."

The two officers averted their eyes.

"What happened to my son?" Jordan whispered.

Before either officer could respond, Officer Rodriguez entered the waiting room. "Officer Susienka, get this man home, will you? Mr. Clarke, the bar and the patron don't want to press charges, and the DA has dropped it. Right now, I think it's a good idea for you to head home."

Officer Susienka took a seat across from Jordan. "I screwed up, Rodriguez. He knows."

"What happened to my son?" Jordan repeated.

Officer Rodriguez laced her fingers together behind her back. "I'm sorry, Mr. Clarke. I never meant for you to find out this way. This all happened after you were in custody, so we decided it was best to wait until morning when you could be with family."

"What happened to my son!" he barked.

Officer Rodriguez hesitated for a second, trying to find the most appropriate words.

"The medical examiner will say for sure, but it seems he died from huffing spray paint in the treehouse at your home. Your wife did everything she could to save him, but it was similar to an overdose. There wasn't anything she could do. A witness says your wife carried him down from the treehouse by herself. I was out there last night helping with the investigation and saw how high it is. I'm amazed she was able to carry him down by herself. She tried CPR. Unfortunately, it was all too late."

Jordan's mind reeled as he placed his head in his hands. After a minute, the silence broken only by the rustling of uniforms as other officers came and went in the background, Jordan jumped up and faced Officer Rodriguez.

"My son is dead, but I've been sitting in a jail cell you locked me in."

"I'm sorry, Mr. Clarke. You were heavily intoxicated, so for your safety and public safety, you were held overnight. I personally visited your wife at the hospital and explained the situation to her. I told her I would work to get you released early this morning, so she's probably expecting you."

Jordan stared into Officer Rodriguez's eyes. "You visited her? You visited my wife in the hospital? You left me in jail, but you visited my wife?"

"Sir, all of us are terribly sorry about what happened. Under the circumstances, me being the arresting officer, I thought it best that I explain to her you were all right. The last several hours must have been terrible for her. I wanted to do what I could."

"Terrible for her!" Jordan shouted. "I've been in a fucking holding cell when I should have been with her! And with my son! You kept me from them!"

"Take it easy, Mr. Clarke," said Officer Susienka as he stood up next to Jordan. "We didn't have any choice here."

Jordan turned back to Officer Rodriguez. "Maybe if you hadn't locked me up, I could have been there to save him!"

"Jordan. Listen," Officer Susienka said as he extended his arms, palms facing Jordan. A gesture that meant, "I know this is highly emotional, but let's keep our cool."

"It's okay, Officer Susienka," Officer Rodriguez said. "This man has just lost his son. I think he's entitled to feel whatever he does. Just know that I'm sorry, Mr. Clarke."

"Stop saying you're sorry! *Sorry* doesn't help! I might have been able to save him if I wasn't sitting in jail! My wife certainly wouldn't be dealing with this on her own."

Officer Susienka crossed his arms. "Mr. Clarke. I know you want to blame someone. It's natural. I see it all the time." He again put his hand on Jordan's back. "Your boy made a tragic mistake."

"I'd like to come by later today and take a statement, Mr. Clarke," Officer Rodriguez said. "If you think you're up to it. For our report to the medical examiner's office. This evening, maybe? I have Sienna's statement already from my visit at the hospital."

Jordan stepped away from Officer Susienka. "Really! My statement! Somebody get me a goddamned Uber!" Adrenaline coursed through him and was the antidote to his hangover. He took a few breaths as all the officers, including two others in the background, not part of the conversation, stood and stared at him. "What could I possibly have to say? You made sure I wasn't there to help and then hid his death from me all night."

Officer Rodriguez looked away from Jordan's stare. "I truly am terribly sorry for your loss, Mr. Clarke. We all are."

"There's usually a taxi out front first thing in the morning," said the young officer behind the desk. "If you prefer to take that, I just need you to sign here accepting your property, and we're done."

Without a word, Jordan picked up the pen attached to a tiny chain and signed his name.

The desk officer tore off the pink carbon copy from the back of the form and handed it to Jordan.

꙳꙳꙳

The morning sun shone in through the double glass doors and framed Jordan in a spotlight. His hair still parted and neat. The light caught his eyes from the side and brightened them, so they radiated blue light. "Where is my son's body?"

"At University Hospital with the medical examiner," Officer Rodriguez said. "They'll release him to the funeral home once you and Sienna have made arrangements and he has finished his report. A day or two."

Jordan slipped his car keys into his pocket and stepped out the glass doors into the sunshine that basked the entire facade of the century-old, historic precinct building. Parked at the curb was a taxicab with its center light on indicating it was available for hire. After approaching and tapping on the rear window with his knuckles, he ducked into the backseat and gave the driver his address.

The driver pulled away from the curb as Jordan stared ahead without focusing his eyes. The driver turned up the news radio, and the meter ticked away as he headed to the pricey, outer suburbs of town.

"The tragic death of a child has again devastated the same Madison Heights neighborhood where a second child has died in less than one year," announced the news reporter. *"Witnesses say a family grieving from the death of their daughter is now also dealing with the death of their son just ten months later."*

The driver changed the station to a traffic report.

"Wait! Turn that back!"

CHAPTER NINETEEN

YVONNE SQUEEZED SIENNA'S FOREARM. "IT might feel like you're losing your mind. How else should something like this feel? Sweetheart, if I thought it would help, I'd tell you to embrace a little temporary insanity. But I don't think it does. Your baby needs you."

Sienna lowered her head to the pillow and looked up at the ceiling. Tears flowed down the side of her temples and traveled along her ears and trickled down to her neck. "Maybe I'm not supposed to be a mom. A mom is supposed to protect her children."

"Stop that. You're a wonderful mother. You put your career on hold to ensure Kai would be okay after losing his sister. Stop thinking like that." Yvonne ran her hand over Sienna's shoulder.

"Showering Kai with all my love helped me cope with losing Kira. I wanted nothing more than to hold him every second and never release him from my arms. I don't know if a baby is enough to help me cope with losing them both."

"You don't have to cope on your own. You have your husband,

and if it's meant to be, you have this baby."

"Jordan doesn't know I'm pregnant, either. I conceived on our wedding anniversary two months ago. We went out to dinner and drank wine and laughed. We had a wonderful night. Something I think we've both felt guilty doing since losing Kira."

Sienna closed her eyes, remembering that night. How he reminded her of why she loved him. And of him showing her he still loved her, too. That night she thought maybe there was hope. Maybe a chance for their marriage. He was so much like the old Jordan. He was talkative and excited about this new career opportunity. She slept that night in his arms. But the next day, he turned right back into the career-obsessed person she didn't really know anymore.

Yvonne took Sienna's hand and squeezed. Losing one child changed them. Losing two children might destroy them. And their marriage. But a baby wasn't the answer, and she regretted not telling him about the pregnancy since taking the test a week earlier. She waited, hoped, for a happy moment to share it with him, but there hadn't been one. And now it felt like something she was hiding.

⚘⚘⚘

Dr. Singh pulled the curtain back and stepped into the exam room and smiled at Sienna and Yvonne. "Oh, good, you have company. Hi. I'm Dr. Marta Singh," she said to Yvonne but didn't extend a hand.

"Nice to meet you, Dr. Singh."

"And this is Dr. Fuller," she said, motioning to a young doctor who stood behind her with the curtain draped against the back of his head and shoulders, just inside the room. "He's an OBGYN. I've discussed with him what was found on the ultrasound."

"Hi, Sienna," Dr. Fuller said, crossing his arms and stepping closer to the bed. "How's your pain? Any better?"

"Somewhat. I don't know if it's alleviated or if exhaustion has taken over, and I've gone numb. Is the baby okay?"

"Yvonne, will you give us a minute?"

"She can stay. What is it?"

"Let's run another ultrasound. Is that okay?" he asked.

"Yes, of course."

Dr. Fuller donned latex gloves as Dr. Singh readied the internal ultrasound.

"Do you know if Jordan is on his way already this morning?" Dr. Singh asked.

Sienna picked up her cellphone resting against her thigh, but there weren't any missed calls. "We haven't been able to reach him yet. Robin stayed at my house last night. She knew I was alone and couldn't find a way to convince herself it was okay to leave. She agreed to wait at the house for him."

Dr. Singh stood back as Dr. Fuller initiated the ultrasound. "We're happy to discuss this with him too when he gets here," she said.

"Sienna, you have a very reasonable chance, and I have a reasonable expectation that you can carry your baby to term. Dr. Singh says you're between eight and ten weeks along. But there is a complication. May I speak freely in the presence of your guest?"

Yvonne stepped toward the curtain. "Sienna, I'll go see if I can reach Jordan again. Or get a number for Robin from the front desk."

Sienna wasn't sure she could take another blow. If there was to be one, she wanted support. "No, it's okay. Stay. What's wrong?" Sienna looked back and forth between the two physicians.

"Right now, everything's okay," Dr. Singh said. "Your baby is fine."

"You have fibroids," Dr. Fuller said. "Common, right? The problem is that you have many of them of different sizes. This is the fetus." He paused and held the wand in place while they all watched the tiny, rapid flicker of a cluster of heart cells like a twinkling star on the black and white screen. Using the wand to take measurements, the doctor added, "You're nine weeks along."

He resumed his examination of the rest of her uterus. "See here?" he asked, pointing to the monitor. "These are fibroids. Some are small. Some of these others are much larger. Women with fibroids deliver perfectly healthy, normal babies all the time. But as the uterus expands, fibroids can tear or rupture. It can be extremely painful and cause significant bleeding. That's what you experienced. The fall likely caused a fibroid or fibroids to rupture and bleed. It wasn't a miscarriage, but uncontrolled bleeding of a ruptured fibroid could threaten the fetus, and as you've experienced, it's quite painful."

"But the baby's okay?" Sienna said as she scooted herself further upright in the bed.

"The fetus is intact and thriving and perfectly viable, but you'll have to be mindful that physical exertion can cause a rupture. Especially in the first trimester. Have you not experienced pain or discomfort before this morning? Even before your pregnancy?"

"No, I haven't." She bit her lip, thinking she had been so focused on Kai over the last year, she probably ignored her own body. But she also knew she wouldn't have allowed herself to acknowledge any pain if it meant distracting her from Kai.

"I've had fibroids. And cysts on my ovaries," Yvonne volunteered. "I had pain, and my doctor removed them. Can't you remove these?"

"Surgery to remove fibroids while pregnant is not advisable. That would trigger bleeding in the uterus, and that would endanger the fetus," he said as he returned the wand to its cradle. "The bleeding has stopped. Your pain has diminished. I'd like you to stay here under Dr. Singh's observation for another couple of hours, but I don't see any reason to admit you. You should be at home resting. You'll want to make an appointment with your OBGYN as soon as possible."

He stood back from the bed and removed the gloves. "Dr. Singh will let me know if your condition changes, but otherwise, I suggest you rest here a while longer and then head home later this morning. And Sienna, I'm very sorry about the loss of your son."

She nodded and smiled. The doctor smiled back and then stepped to the other side of the curtain.

"Okay, Sienna, I'll be back in an hour," Dr. Singh said. "A nurse will be back in before that to check on you. Okay?" Sienna nodded.

"Are you comfortable? Are you cold?" Yvonne asked once the room was cleared.

"I'm fine." But really, she felt like she was in a fog. There was too much to comprehend. She looked at her phone again then dropped it back onto the gurney when she saw no one had called.

Yvonne picked up a plastic bag containing Sienna's personal effects resting on a small chair then sat down with the bag in her lap.

"Jordan hasn't called yet. He lost his cellphone," Sienna said, "but I thought he might call from jail this morning. It's almost eight. I don't know if this is too early for the police station to release someone or not."

"Well, let's call them and find out. Do you know where he is?"

"Yes, I talked with an officer. She arrested him downtown. He's at the downtown precinct."

Yvonne opened her browser and soon found the phone number for the police department and dialed the call on speakerphone.

"I'm here with Sienna Clarke calling to find out if her husband, Jordan Clarke, has been released this morning."

"Yes, he was released about fifteen or twenty minutes ago. You're with Mrs. Clarke?"

"Yes, she's here at my side."

"May I speak with her?"

Yvonne pressed the phone to her chest. "Do you want to speak to them?"

"This is Sienna Clarke."

"Mrs. Clarke, my name is Officer Susienka. Jordan left in a cab headed home to you about twenty minutes ago. I'm sorry, but I misunderstood and inadvertently told him about your son's passing. Please forgive me. Please forgive me for interfering. You should know he was understandably quite upset that he wasn't able to be with you last night."

"Is he in any trouble?"

"No. No, there are no charges. Again, I'm so very sorry for your loss."

"Thank you, officer," she said and hung up and handed the phone back to Yvonne.

"I didn't think to get Robin's cell number so we could find out if he's home yet. I was so rushed, but I'm sure someone here has it. If not, I'll try the house phone again."

"I need to start calling some people."

"Do it when you're ready. In the meantime, I'm going to get Robin's number from the front desk and tell her you're all right and that you'll be released soon and that Jordan is on the way. Let me just call the studio and tell my assistant he's teaching the class this morning."

"No, you don't have to do that. I can call my best friend Monica and let her know what's happened."

"Call her, but I'm staying until they release you." Yvonne was already dialing and stepped away through the curtain as her assistant answered the studio phone.

Sienna opened her texts and scrolled to find the last time she and Monica communicated. It was over the July Fourth holiday weekend. Monica had typed *Happy Fourth!* and included a fireworks emoji. And, *Let's get together when I get back in town.* Sienna responded with, *Yes, let's do! Be Safe!*

She hadn't known Monica left town for the weekend and had no idea where she was for the holiday. Before losing Kira, before their friendship changed, Monica would have spent hours talking with Sienna about planning the trip. Monica hadn't texted in the weeks since.

Sienna changed her mind and called her mother instead. She waited a few minutes, knowing once she uttered the words, there was no turning back. She would no longer be known to the world as Kai's mom. Bracing herself, she pressed the call button.

Her mother answered the call after a few rings. "Well, hey, Sienna! How are you, hun?" she chirped in her Texas drawl.

"Mom, it's awful. I have to tell you something just awful." Tears were already streaming down her cheeks.

"Sienna, what is it?"

"Mom, Kai passed away." They were the only words she got out before a choking cry seized her again. Her ribs were sore from sobbing.

"WHAT! Sienna! What! Oh my Lord! Sienna!"

After a moment, Sienna caught her breath and fought to stifle her sobbing, which left a lump the size of a golf ball in the back of her throat. "He huffed paint, and it killed him."

"Oh, no. Oh Lord, no. Sienna, that can't be. When did this happen?"

"Yesterday evening. I couldn't bring myself to call."

"I know he was having trouble after Kira, but you said you thought he was doing okay."

"It was an accident. He had been playing with a friend in our backyard. I said they could paint the treehouse, and they took some paint from the garage. I found him alone and unconscious a couple of hours later." Her voice cracked. "He's gone."

"Oh, dear Lord. Okay. My Lord. I'll get up there just as soon as I can. Oh, that sweet boy. Sienna, I'll work it out. I'll get up there as soon as I can."

"Will you tell Janelle? Go ahead and tell the rest of the family, too? I can't do this. I can't talk about it."

"Oh, hun. Are you going to be all right?"

"I don't know."

"Sienna, I'll pray for you, hun. The Lord will protect you and watch over you. I know he will."

"Mom, I'll call you tonight. Okay?"

"Hun, I love you so very much."

"I love you too, Mom."

As Sienna pulled the phone from her ear, it buzzed for an incoming call. The incoming call was from Kai's phone.

CHAPTER TWENTY

THE TAXI DRIVER PULLED UP to the house and let the engine idle with his foot on the brake as Jordan fished two twenty-dollar bills out of his wallet. Sunlight seared the tops of all the trees that lined both sides of the property. Like lit matches, each treetop glowed orange, but the world below was in shadow, still gripped by the memory of night even as dawn seeped over the world.

"Keep the change," Jordan said, stepping out of the car. He walked up to inspect an unfamiliar SUV in the driveway as the cab pulled away. It was empty except for a yellow umbrella tucked into the pocket attached to the back of the driver seat. He ignored the police tape stretched across the garage and dashed toward the house.

Before he reached the porch, the door opened, and Robin stepped outside.

"Hi. Are you Jordan?"

"Yes. Where's Sienna?"

"Jordan, my name is Robin Hardin." She extended her hospital badge for him to inspect. "I work with University Hospital. I'm a grief counselor. Sienna thought I should wait here for you."

Jordan walked past Robin and into the foyer. "Where's Sienna? Sienna!" he shouted.

"Sienna is at the hospital. She was taken by ambulance a couple of hours ago, but she's okay now. Your neighbor Yvonne is with her. I just got off the phone with her. They are going to release her shortly."

"What happened?"

"Jordan. I need you to listen to me. Okay? Sienna is fine. She'll be home soon. I'm here because of your son," she said, holding her hands up so he would pause a moment and hear her words.

"Kai is dead. Is that why you're here?"

She laced her fingers together, her empty palms on display. "Yes, I offered to stay here and wait for you. I understand the police department has already informed you."

"Yes. I guess I'm still in shock. This can't be happening. Even when I heard about it on the radio, it didn't seem real. I saw the police tape around the garage, but it still hasn't sunk in. I'm reliving the death of my daughter."

"Sienna told me about Kira. I'm so sorry. The police were out here last night investigating Kai's accident. I think the police tape triggered something in Sienna when she saw it. She didn't want to come inside the house."

"This is surreal. I need my wife to tell me exactly what happened."

"Shock coupled with disbelief is a normal response to hearing something like this. Why don't we sit down?" she said, motioning into the living room. He took a seat on the sofa, and she sat in the same chair she used for tea the night before.

Robin started calm and measured, explaining the sequence of events.

"I offered to stay here until she fell asleep last night. She didn't want me to call anyone. She ended up having a nightmare, so I said I would stay over. About five-thirty this morning, Yvonne found her leaning forward about to fall out of the treehouse."

"The treehouse!"

"I think she was desperately trying to feel a connection to him. I don't know how long she was out there."

"Why did an ambulance take her to the hospital?"

"I think you need to speak with her. I can drive you to the hospital if you want."

Jordan recognized Sienna's old iPhone on the coffee table. Kai had inherited it and put it inside a chunky plastic, silver, and black phone case that made it resemble a toy that could transform into a robot. "I need to call her." He leaned forward, grabbed the phone, and scrolled through the recent call list until he found the first entry of *Mom* and then pressed the call button.

Sienna answered the phone and hesitated three or four seconds afraid to speak.

"Hello."

"Sienna, it's me. I'm at the house with the hospital rep."

"Jordan. Oh god, Jordan. Kai's gone," she cried.

He cleared his throat. "Are you injured?"

Sienna sniffled, reached for tissues, and wiped her eyes. "I never should have let him go up into that treehouse. The maples . . . "

"Are you hurt? Why are you at the hospital?"

"I wish you never built it. I'm a terrible mother. I knew not to let him go up there. Not after Kira. But I let him go anyway. He would still be alive if I listened to myself and didn't let him go up there. Every time I close my eyes, I see the maples with bright blue leaves smothering him."

"What were you doing in the treehouse?" He heard her stifling her crying into the phone.

"Jordan, there is a lot I need to tell you, but I don't want to tell you over the phone."

"I am coming to the hospital. You can tell me when I get there. I'll be there in fifteen minutes."

"I'm sorry, Jordan," was all she could manage.

"You don't have anything to be sorry for. I'll be there soon." He hung up the phone and slipped it inside his jacket pocket. He then turned to Robin.

"She won't say why she's there. Did she have a nervous breakdown during the night?"

"Yvonne found her up there. She thought she was about to fall. Understandably, she's having a tough time coping and blames herself. Apparently, she told Yvonne she's been having nightmares of maples with blue leaves hurting her children. She's struggling to make sense of what happened, and her thoughts are conspiring against her."

"She just said the same thing to me."

"She needs time. Grief can play tricks on the mind, just like any other emotion. It makes people say and do things they wouldn't ordinarily. Think of the things people do for love. The things they do for hate or rage. Jealously. What jealously makes people see and believe. Her emotions are raw right now, and that's normal and expected. She's dealing with it the best way she can. I offered to work with her in grief counseling when the time is right. Shock is your coping mechanism. That's how you're able to function and take care of your wife right now."

"Is that why she is at the hospital?"

"It's not because of her emotional state. It's physical. Like I said, she's okay, but I do think you need to get to the hospital to see her right away."

"Why are you both being evasive? What's going on with my wife? What? Did she try and kill herself? Tell me!"

Robin looked into his eyes. "Jordan, it's not my place. You need to go see her and hear it from her. Would you like me to drive you?"

"No. I'll take her car. I'll be fine. Thank you for staying with her. I take it that's not part of the job description."

Robin stood and picked up her laptop bag from the sofa and slung it over her shoulder. "It's exactly the job description." She then extended a hand to Jordan. "It's the reason I took this job."

Jordan looked into Robin's brown eyes, which were bleary from crying. He took her petite hand in his. "Thank you . . . Robin, you said?"

She nodded.

"I'm glad she wasn't here alone, Robin. I'm going to let the dog out, then I'm headed to the ER to be with her. I'm emotionally numb right now, but I'm going to be strong for her. Should I be concerned about these things she's saying?"

"At this point, no. Like I said, she's vulnerable and grappling with overwhelming pain. If you're able to talk with her and reason with her, then I wouldn't worry. It's the duress she's under that's fomenting these irrational thoughts. In time, the duress will ease. Until then, she's bound to see purpose, search for it, where it doesn't lie."

Jordan nodded and smiled weakly. "Let me walk you out."

"I don't have to tell you there is no specific way you're supposed to think or feel after something like this. There are phases of grief. Shock is one of them. Whatever your response is today, it's the right response. It's normal. Whatever your response is tomorrow, it's the right response. It's normal. When you're ready, I'm happy to talk with you, and with Sienna."

He reached and opened the door for her. As they stepped onto the porch, the side door of a local news van parked at the curb slid open, and a young reporter leaped out along with a cameraman. The camera light was already on. Jordan and Robin looked on as he walked across the grass to the front porch. "Uhh. Mr. Clarke?" he shouted with a raised, waving hand. "Excuse me! Are you Mr. Clarke?"

Before Jordan could react, the reporter rushed up onto

the porch and thrust a microphone in his face. Jordan stood without uttering a word. He recognized the TV reporter; he aired a weekly, sensationalized newscast focused on consumer fraud and corruption.

"Mr. Clarke, we are terribly sorry for your loss. This is a tragic situation. Our thoughts and prayers are with you and your family."

"Thank you, but I just learned my son has passed away. This is not a good time for us. I'm still trying to wrap my head around this."

"Your neighbors told us about your wife carrying your incapacitated thirteen-year-old son down a treehouse ladder. It's remarkable. And a testament to a mother's strength when her child is in danger. The community is heartbroken that she couldn't save him."

"My wife and I are heartbroken. If you'll please excuse me." Jordan turned to Robin, who handed him her card as she made her way down off the porch.

"Might we have two seconds with your wife? Hear from her about what happened?"

Jordan ripped the microphone away from the reporter and threw it to the ground. "I just learned my son is dead! Please show some respect . . . some humanity."

Robin stepped in front of the reporter. "There has been a tragedy, and this family is grieving. Please. I am a grief counselor with University Hospital." Robin motioned for Jordan to go back inside.

"I'm sorry, Mr. Clarke. I really am," the reporter said as he picked up his microphone. "This isn't live. It's not meant to be an ambush. I apologize if it seemed that way or if I've been insensitive."

Jordan turned away from the camera and started for the front door, shaking his head in disgust as he walked.

"Robin, thank you again for being here this morning. Thank you for your help during this incredibly difficult time." He waved over his shoulder and shut the door.

Robin hurried to her SUV and tossed her bag into the passenger seat, leaving the news crew on the porch. She stood in the open car doorjamb as the reporter and his cameraman whispered to each other.

The reporter leaned in and spoke through the front door. "Mr. Clarke, about two thousand children a year die as a result of an accident at home, including falls and poisonings. This is the second accidental child death at this residence in ten months. What are the police investigating? They have indicated this is an active scene."

Jordan leaned against the closed door with his back. Sally stood only feet away and stared at him blankly. At thirteen and almost deaf, he didn't imagine she heard the reporter's crass question. For a split second, he thought it would be nice to live in such oblivion.

After waiting a few seconds for Jordan to reappear, the reporter added, "Statistically speaking—"

"Every accidental death is investigated," Robin interrupted from the doorjamb of her car. "This was not a suspicious death, sir. I find it highly inappropriate for you to be here. Cruel, in fact."

The reporter continued waiting for the door to open, but when Jordan didn't reply, he pressed further. "Are the police certain these deaths were accidental, Mr. Clarke?"

Jordan spun around to rip the door open but then thought better of it as his hand gripped the knob. He stepped back a few feet, figuring it was better to wait for the crew to leave.

After another thirty seconds, the reporter continued. "Mr. Clarke, who was home supervising these children?"

Jordan blinked several times, fuming from the reporter's implications. He didn't know whether to ignore the comments or order the intruders off his property. He wondered how either action would look on TV.

"Was their mother the only one home at the time of these accidents?"

Sally stepped up to Jordan and sniffed at his leg. Jordan hardly noticed as he stood frozen in the foyer.

"Are there any other children in the household?" the reporter asked.

Jordan ripped the door open and glowered into the reporter's face.

"Please leave now, or I'll call the police," he said through clenched teeth. "My wife loved our children with all her heart. She would do anything for them. For you to suggest, even hint otherwise, is nothing short of evil. It's absolutely evil. And I assure you, you'll deserve exactly what I do to you if you say something like that again. Now get off my property. I'm not joking. I suggest you leave now."

The reporter backed away, and the cameraman followed his lead back to the van. Jordan watched as they hopped inside.

"I'm sorry, Jordan," Robin said. "Try and tune them out." She then climbed into her vehicle and started the engine.

Jordan stood in his doorway to make sure they were leaving. It wasn't until they pulled away and headed down the street, and Robin backed down the driveway, that he closed the door.

He walked toward the back door, patting his leg. "Come on, Sally, let's go outside. Hurry, girl. Hurry. I need to get to your mom."

His cellphone chimed. Reaching into his coat pocket, he pulled the phone to read a text message from Sienna.

"The doctor just came by and said my vitals are stable. I asked to leave, and she said I can go. Yvonne is going to drive me. No need to come up here. I'll be home soon."

He quickly typed his reply. "What's going on?"

"I'll tell you when I get home. I don't want to be here."

"You sure you're okay?"

"Yes. See you soon. I love you."

"I luv you!"

Jordan stepped off the back porch and stared up at the ancient silver maple on the other side of the yard. From that distance, the treehouse appeared no bigger than a bird's nest in a diorama of a manicured park. He raised his hand and extended his thumb, blocking out the tree from his view. It vanished like a magician's trick, but his jumbled mix of emotions remained. He tucked his thumb back into a fist, and the tree reappeared, along with the treehouse that to him now looked more like a coffin.

CHAPTER TWENTY-ONE

YVONNE PULLED HER SMALL MERCEDES roadster to the curb and waited. A hospital orderly wheeled Sienna outside wearing a long one-size-fits-most hospital gown that engulfed her frame as if she had a sheet cinched at her waist.

"I'm sorry I didn't think to bring you some clothes. I feel like I haven't been much help," Yvonne said, opening the car door from the inside and pushing it outward.

Sienna eased into the passenger seat then ran her hands through her hair and sighed. "You have. And I appreciate it. The gown is fine. I just want to get home." She held the plastic bag containing her clothes and clutched it to her chest like a child's security blanket. As they pulled away from the curb, her phone buzzed.

"It's my friend Monica calling. Do you mind if I take it?"

"Of course not. Anything you need, sweetheart."

Sienna wasn't prepared to say it aloud again. She breathed deeply several times as though she was about to plunge beneath the surface of water and hold her breath.

"Monica?"

"Sienna! I just saw it on Instagram and Facebook! Is it true?"

"Is what true?"

"Your sister. Janelle. About an hour ago, she posted a picture of herself with you, Kira, and Kai and said that her nephew passed away yesterday from an overdose. She tagged you in it. She tagged the National Institute of Drug Abuse. She has several hashtags like *huffing* and *high on paint, RIP*, and *Rest in Peace*. It already has over a hundred comments and shares. Is it true?"

"Yes," she said as her voice cracked. "Yesterday."

"Oh my god! What happened? Are you okay!"

"He tried huffing with a friend and accidentally—" Sienna's voice caught in her throat as she uttered the words aloud. Instantly, the weight of her words acknowledging his death dropped in the air and crushed her chest, squeezed her stomach, and pinned her back into the seat.

"What can I do?"

All Sienna could do was sob into the phone.

"Let me get someone to cover my meeting, and I'll be right there. Are you at home?"

Sienna struggled to stifle her crying and finally said, "I'm on my way home now. Jordan was away yesterday. He's there waiting for me now."

"Sienna, why didn't you call me?"

"I just needed to be alone. I wasn't ready to say it. To believe it. Now I have to start telling people if it's on social media. I don't know if Jordan has told his family. I don't know if I can get the words out."

"I'll make those calls for you if you want me to. If you're not up to calling people, then don't. No one knows what you're feeling. I can go straight to your house. I can be there in an hour."

"No, I need some time with Jordan. I'll call you later today."

"Okay. If there is anything you need, anything, you promise you'll call me?"

"Yes, I will. I'll call you later."

Sienna dropped the phone in her lap and covered her face with both hands. "Oh god, my heart is breaking. My sister, Janelle, posted about Kai on Instagram and Facebook."

Yvonne continued maneuvering the roadster toward their neighborhood. "It's too soon. You can have her take it down."

Sienna picked the phone back up and opened Facebook. Immediately she noticed her alert counter read eight hundred fifty-three. She ignored them and swiped to her own page. The posting from her sister was at the top and began playing. A collage of pictures rotated on her screen; one faded out as another slowly appeared. Pictures of Kai. Some she recognized from her own Facebook and Instagram. Her sister copied them into her posting. One of Kai knee-deep in the lake, another of him waving from a school bus, which Sienna remembered capturing on his first day of middle school. The pictures rotated again to one of Kira and Kai together, playing in the snow. The collage changed to a group photo of Sienna and her sister along with Kira and Kai at a picnic table from their last visit to Texas three or four years earlier.

Sienna's phone screen was doused with tears.

As more alerts continued to tick up the counter on the bottom of her screen, Sienna read her sister's posting aloud. "*I'm devasted. I can't believe both of these precious little babies are gone. I don't know how my family is supposed to ever recover from this. Last night my nephew Kai Clarke died from huffing paint. It was an accident he never did anything like that before. I was thinking about visiting him for his thirteenth birthday next month now I'll never see him alive again. I'm still dealing with the loss of my niece Kira Clarke who died just last year she was Kai's sister she died in a tragic accident at home too less than a year ago. Now these two angels a brother and sister that were the happiest most loving kindest kids I've ever known are together in heaven. Please send us your prayers. I love you my sweet sister @SiennaClarke. I know you did everything you could to try and save Kira and Kai. They were lucky to have you as their mother."* Sienna paused as the words sank in.

"She has all kinds of hashtags. She's not trying to inform the family. She's trying to get the whole world to see this post."

"There is no guidebook for posting about death on social media. I wouldn't know the right way to do it, either. I'm sure she's just speaking from the heart, but she really should have talked with you first. She'll take it down if you ask her to."

"She tagged me and has over a thousand shares," Sienna said as she clicked on the link to open the latest string of comments. Her heart deflated as she read what perfect strangers had to say.

Two dead! Come on. Their mom is a serial killer, the last comment read. *Too coincidental. Somebody killed those kids!* another stranger posted. Sienna scrolled up over a hundred comments. *Doesn't happen. Two kids don't accidentally die at home back to back like that.* Some of the hundreds of post included links, one to Kira's obituary from the funeral home's website. It, too, had its own thread of dozens of people talking about her daughter's death. Sienna put her hand over her mouth to stifle a scream.

"What's wrong, Sienna?"

"There are people posting that I am a murderer, that I should go to jail."

"You need to make your account private. Tell your sister to do the same. People are cruel. Don't pay any attention to that stuff." Sienna scrolled and read another stranger's comment. *♪♪ABC. So simple as 123. ABC, 123, Baby You Killed Your Kids, Girl♪♪.'*

"Some of these people think I killed my kids. This person says, 'Better cancel Sienna Clarke's passport quick before she flees to Mexico.' Yvonne, what's happening?"

"People are idiots. That's all. They love to jump on something, glom onto it, and rant about it. Say the most disgusting and vile things. They don't care who they hurt. Don't read any of that."

Sienna wiped tears from her eyes but kept scrolling. "They have no idea what happened!"

"Put your account on private. Do you know how to do that? Go to settings. Ask your sister to make her account private or delete the post."

Sienna closed out of Facebook and scrolled through her contacts to find Janelle then pressed dial. She blinked away fresh tears as the phone rang.

"Sienna? Oh god. How are you?" Janelle said. Every word echoed through the interior of the tiny two-seater.

"Janelle, have you seen what people are saying online? It's awful. I need you to take down that post."

"I still can't believe what's happened. I've been crying all morning. How are you holding up?"

"Janelle, will you take down that post, please?"

"What? Mom said you wanted us to tell the family. I was on the phone all morning, but it's so hard saying it over and over again, so I posted it online. Didn't you say to tell everyone?"

"Yes, but I didn't think that meant putting it on Facebook. I'm not sure Jordan has had the chance to tell all of his family. I don't want them hearing about it this way. I'm going to put my account on private. Will you do the same, please?"

"Sienna, there's nothing wrong with the post. We need to use Kai's death to bring attention to the danger of huffing. Don't let his death be in vain."

"What are you talking about? Random people are accusing me of killing my kids, Janelle!"

"I know you're in pain right now. I know I shouldn't say it, but Sienna, that's just like you to focus on a few negative comments that don't mean anything from people who don't mean anything.

Did you bother to read the hundreds of comments from people offering condolences? People from all over are sending us love and prayers. Praying for us right now. Some are even sharing their own overdose experiences. My post is already helping people. Can't you see that?"

"Please, Janelle. For me. For now. Will you please take it down or at least make it private for our family?"

"It's already out there, Sienna. If I take it down, it won't matter. People have already added to it. It's a thread that's trending. Kai's death and Kira's death only months ago has touched a nerve with a lot of other people who are hurting, too. There was a comment from a mother who lost her son to huffing who asked if we could start a support group. Did you read that one? I think that's a wonderful idea. A way to honor Kai's memory."

Yvonne chimed in. "Janelle, my name is Yvonne. I'm Sienna's friend and neighbor. I don't think you're hearing your sister. She's telling you that your post is causing her terrible pain, and she just wants you to respect that. Maybe you should have talked with her first."

"Who the fuck are you?" Janelle snapped. "I don't have to ask anyone to post on my account. Kai was my nephew. I loved him, and I loved Kira. I don't see anything wrong with me sharing with my friends and family that I'm grieving. That we're all grieving."

"Janelle, this is more than friends and family. Please don't tag me in anything else without asking me. Can you do that for me?"

"I really thought all the loving support from around the world would be helpful. That you could find some comfort from all the kind words. Hundreds and hundreds of touching comments. I don't know why I didn't expect you to be selfish since that's the only way you know how to be. I should have known that you would turn an outpouring of love from friends and family and even complete strangers into a negative. That you'd only see the negative.

"Go ahead and make your account private. What do I care?

But there are other members of our family, like our mother, Kai's grandma. Did you forget about her? They're devastated and are taking comfort in the compassion and sympathy from others. It's helping me and Mom. I'm keeping the post up, and I hope it keeps going viral. I hope the whole world sees the tragedy of huffing and can learn something from Kai's death. I am going to try and start a support group in his name. Don't worry. I won't tag you."

"Janelle, I appreciate what you were trying to do, but—"

"Listen, Sienna, I love you. I know you're devasted. I want to be there for you. I really do, but I can't help you if you're going to be irrational and try and control every little thing. Kai was your son. I get that. But you're my sister. He was my blood, too, and I loved him with all my heart, just like he was my own son. You know that, right?"

"I can't explain how it feels for a random stranger to accuse you of killing your child."

"Oh, Sienna, you want me to go in and delete all that shit? I can just ignore it, but if you can't. If you get stuck on what some internet troll says, then I'll just delete those comments. Is that good enough for you?"

"I miss my boy. I miss my little girl. That's all. I miss them. Those comments are a stab in my heart. Not to mention how Jordan's going to feel about it. I have no idea how Jordan is coping."

"Well, I know this. Jordan will have to live his whole life regretting not being there to protect those kids."

"What? What's that supposed to mean?"

"I'm just saying that maybe if Jordan had been there, these accidents might not have happened. Maybe Jordan could have prevented them."

"How dare you say something like that to me?"

"Mom says you knew he had the paint. I bet Jordan would not have let a kid play with inhalants. He told me he wouldn't have let Kira jump from the treehouse, either."

"I didn't let Kira jump! You know that. And I didn't know Kai had spray paint. I didn't know!"

Yvonne extended her arm and reached toward Sienna's phone. "Hang up the phone, Sienna. Hang it up."

"I'm not saying you knew. That's between you and God. But maybe you should have known. Have you thought about that? Has Jordan asked you that?"

CHAPTER TWENTY-TWO

JORDAN WAITED AT THE WINDOW to see if the news crew would double back. When they hadn't shown up after a couple of minutes, he headed out to the garage, shutting Sally inside.

A cool mid-morning breeze tussled with the police tape that cordoned off the area. With each gust of wind, the plastic made the snapping sound of a kite in flight. Rather than duck under the tape, Jordan ripped it down and balled it up as he continued inside the garage to retrieve the chainsaw. Tossing the tape aside, he checked that it had gas and hefted it up along with a pair of safety glasses.

With the morning sun at his back, he walked to the rear of the property. The sun's rays reflected off his shiny leather shoes like black onyx nestled in dewy grass that glistened and sparkled as though a pavé of tiny emeralds adorned each blade and reflected the sunshine. When he reached the base of the maple, he glanced up at the treehouse. He never thought of it as sinister, but in that moment, it looked unnatural to him. Grotesque. His childhood treehouse blended with his kids' seemed like a great idea at the time, but now he felt foolish for not having removed it and wondered if people might think it was odd that they left it in place after Kira's death. *Was it a mistake?* he wondered.

He put on his safety glasses and yanked the chainsaw's starter, and the saw roared to life. The saw's engine bored into his ears as he tilted the blade on a forty-five-degree angle. After chewing into the trunk for thirty seconds, wood chips and dust covered his hair and forearms. He made a similar cut, leaving a Pacman shaped bite a foot deep into the side of the tree trunk six feet wide. Within another minute of cutting, the tree that dominated their back property even before some long-forgotten family built the house eighty years earlier, the tree that reigned with outstretched arms like a pontiff presiding over a congregation in the square, began to creak.

Jordan let the saw idle and stepped back several feet and shut off the saw and scurried back several more feet. The trunk protested with a cry as it slowly snapped, spraying shards in Jordan's direction. He stepped back a few more feet. The wood creaked and splintered faster like rapid gunfire that ricocheted around the yard and reverberated off the other trees back to Jordan as though they were responding with their collective screams. Their horror of the tree falling before them.

With a crescendo of exploding fireworks, the trunk ruptured, and the tree crashed. Several limbs snapped and flew into the air, and others bounced off the ground with the splintered log in a futile last gasp to get back up and stay upright. Then the tree settled to the ground with the finality of an executed prisoner on a firing line.

Jordan stepped back to the tree and climbed around the fallen branches to inspect the remnants of the treehouse. Demolished in the crash, little of it remained intact. He restarted the chainsaw and cut into the few recognizable remnants. It took less than five minutes to eradicate the tree that had existed for nearly a century, and the treehouse that called it home.

He dropped the chainsaw to the ground, walked back to the middle of the yard, and turned back toward the tree. The massive black trunk and limbs covered in green leaves lay like a shipwreck across the lawn. The vastness of the sky once obscured by limbs seemed endless, like looking through a telescope. He wondered how many critters and birds died when the tree hit the ground. Squirrels and chipmunks for sure. Plenty of birds called the tree home, too. He pulled the cellphone from his pants pocket, opened the browser, found a tree and landscape service, and dialed.

"I need a fallen tree removed and the stump and roots ground up. It has to be done right away. It's huge. Eighty to one hundred years old. Easily a hundred feet tall. I'll pay triple your rate if your crew gets here within thirty minutes and starts pulverizing the stump and carts the whole thing away."

"Is the tree blocking the road or something?"

"Does it matter if I say no?" he asked as he ran his hands through his hair, breaking up the remaining pomade held–style, knocking out the sawdust.

"No, I was just wondering about the urgency. Where are you located?"

He wiped off his arms and clothes too. "Montfort Heights. Can you have a crew here in thirty minutes, or do I need to call another service?"

"For three times our rate, I'll have my husband and son out there to cut the tree up personally. What's the address?"

⚓⚓⚓

Jordan wound up the yellow police tape into a ball and walked back to the kitchen. He pulled a chair out far from the breakfast table, scraping the legs along the hardwood floor. Something he would have reprimanded the kids for doing. The room was warm from a yellow glow of sunlight coming in through the window. He sat and arched his back into the wooden slats until some of his vertebrae cracked and popped. He then relaxed his back and crossed his foot over his knee to slip off his shoe. At the same time, a car pulled up in the street in front of the house.

Jordan hopped up, jogged to the front room, and eased the curtains back two inches, suspecting the news crew might have returned, but it was Yvonne's black Mercedes. He hurriedly reached the passenger door before Sienna had the chance to open it. The sun beamed off the window, turning it into a mirror and obscuring Sienna's face. His own reflection and disheveled hair were all he could see. Without realizing it, he ran a hand across his side part to smooth the strands back to his liking. At that exact time, he grabbed the door handle and pulled but found it locked. Sienna opened the door, and he rushed to lean inside with his hand on top of the retractable roof for support of his weight.

"I'm sorry. I'm so sorry I wasn't here for you."

Sienna became tearful when their eyes met. He lowered his head and eyes from her gaze, convinced she was both devastated by the loss of her son and angry at him for drinking and getting arrested.

When she tried to speak, her voice cracked, stolen from her by the pain of speaking the truth aloud, forcing him to raise his face back up to hers.

"We've lost Kai," she mouthed, barely audible. She sucked in a breath and tried again. "He's gone," she said with more force.

Jordan leaned into the car and hugged her over the seatbelt. "I know. I know. Robin told me what happened. I'm sorry. I love you, Sienna," he whispered into her ear.

"It's my fault."

"No, it's not. Don't say that."

He felt her crumble in his embrace as she buried her head in his neck.

Jordan held onto her as she cried, but aware of Yvonne, he remained stoic, refusing to show any emotion. He pulled his head back to see Sienna's face, but she was staring over his shoulder at the house. "Let's get you inside. Can you walk?"

Sienna sniffled and tossed her head back, trying to recover as Yvonne took the plastic bag from her lap. "This isn't our home anymore, is it? This place will never feel the same without the kids."

Still embracing her, Jordan reached and unfastened the seatbelt. "Come on."

Without waiting for a response, Jordan stood. Holding both of Sienna's hands, he helped steady her as she eased up out of the seat.

Yvonne stepped around the car. "Don't forget this."

"Thank you, Yvonne. I might still be up in that treehouse if it wasn't for you," she said, accepting the bag.

"Do you need help with anything? I can make you something to eat."

"No, I've got to get into bed. I haven't slept. I don't know if I can, but I'm going to try. I'm operating on some sort of autopilot, and I'm about to crash land," Sienna said as Jordan helped her down the walkway toward the door.

"I can come to check on you later."

"You don't have to do that."

"I'll stop by in a few hours on my way into the studio. Jordan, you let me know if either of you need anything. And you get some rest, too," Yvonne said, walking back to the driver side of her car.

Jordan smiled at her and nodded, concealing his irritation. Yvonne telling him to get some rest meant she knew he spent the night in jail.

"Thanks for being there for her this morning. And yesterday. After the accident. We'll definitely call you if we need anything," he said.

A female couple walking their collie lingered in the street, chatting in hushed voices and glaring. Jordan could feel their eyes on them as he helped his wife to the door.

CHAPTER TWENTY-THREE

YVONNE'S CAR PULLED AWAY, THE engine revving as she headed home, and Sienna sensed a distance open between herself and Jordan. The farther away Yvonne got, the wider the gap grew, as though the car was towing away the prized cargo of relaxed familiarity they'd accumulated over years of marriage. They were now different people, childless, and transformed by grief. Their relationship had transformed, too.

Sienna thought of a bride in an arranged marriage meeting her groom for the first time, before ever having kids, long before gaining comfort with the absence of conversation. They were strangers. She didn't know what to say or do all alone with this man and didn't know if a blind union between the betrothed would work.

She let him guide her to the house, stepping inside just far enough so he could close the door and shut out the world. The instant quiet and isolation turned the foyer into an ancient tomb sealed with artifacts of her past life. Her marriage. Her children. There wasn't enough oxygen. Her chest constricted and threatened to squeeze the life out of her. Heat rose in her cheeks.

Sally's tags rattling on her collar broke the silence as she lumbered forward to greet them with a fraction of her usual enthusiasm. Sienna took a deep breath, extended her hands, and scratched behind Sally's ears.

"I think she's grieving, too," she managed to say. "She knows he's gone. Dogs can tell." It was small talk, but she preferred it to silence or telling him all the other thoughts clogging her mind.

"Come sit down and tell me what's going on. Why were you at the hospital?" Jordan asked, leading her into the living room.

She followed him to the sofa without another word and sat next to him on the oversized chesterfield. She looked into his eyes, and he still held her hand, waiting for her to speak. He squeezed her hand, prompting her when she stalled. Holding his gaze, wanting to read his response, she said, "I'm pregnant." As the words left her mouth, her stomach flipped like she was riding in an elevator coming to a halt.

Jordan pulled his head and neck back on his shoulders, stunned. "Pregnant?"

It was out of character for the pokerfaced salesman to show surprise. No one ever caught him off guard.

"Yes, pregnant. I'm nine weeks along," she said, looking straight at him awaiting his reply, but there wasn't one. "Well? Say something."

"Did you know you were pregnant?"

"I've known for sure a few days now."

She looked away from him for the first time since taking a seat. Embarrassed that their relationship had devolved back to a phase not much different from the first time she hid her pregnancy from him a decade and a half earlier.

"You should have told me."

"I wanted to tell you. I was waiting for the right time. I didn't know how you'd react."

"It's okay. I get it. Things have been strained between us. I'm sorry." He pushed her hair back behind her ear and caressed her ear between his index finger and thumb. "But why were you at the hospital? Is the baby okay?"

"Yes, but I have several fibroid tumors that put the baby at risk. The doctor said pregnancy hormones caused them to grow very rapidly, and one of them ruptured. He thinks it happened when I fell from the treehouse carrying Kai. Hours later, there was blood, and I was in so much pain. That's why I went to the ER. I don't remember everything he said. I was scared. He gave me some discharge instructions. Yvonne put them in the bag. He says I have to be careful to avoid another fibroid rupture, but that there's a good chance I can carry the baby to term. I didn't want to tell you over the phone. I wanted to see your face and see your reaction. I wanted to see if you were disappointed."

"No, of course I'm not disappointed," he said and leaned back into the sofa. He put his hands behind his head, arms bent at the elbows, laced his fingers together, cradling his head, and looked up at the ceiling.

"Is there a state of mind beyond shock? What do you call it when you get in your car and drive to work but have no recollection of how you got there, and you simply look up and find yourself in your parking spot? That's how I feel right now. Out-of-body experience. That's what it's called. I'm here, but my mind is somewhere else trying to escape reality.

"It's going to take me a minute to wrap my head around a new baby. The idea clashes with trying to figure out how to accept that we've lost Kira and now Kai. I'm not sure there's room in my head for a baby."

"I was terrified I lost it. There was so much pain. This baby will be Kira and Kai's little brother or sister. I'm not going to let anything happen to it."

"I can't believe Kira and Kai are both gone. This just doesn't seem real. This can't be happening again. Robin from the hospital and the cops said you found him in the treehouse, huffing paint."

"He was unconscious. I tried to save him."

"I'm sorry I wasn't home with you last night. The whole thing at the bar was stupid. I drank too much. You shouldn't have had to deal with another . . . with the accident all alone. I wish now you hadn't talked me out of cutting down that tree."

Sienna's mind switched back to her meditation in the treehouse. The mother tree attacking her kids in her vision that left her with an unshakable fear, like a warning bell, a tornado siren going off in the middle of the night, that their deaths weren't as they seemed.

"What if it wasn't an accident?" she asked, tears welling.

Jordan continued holding Sienna's hand and paused, her words a spell that suspended his animation. Sally jumped up onto the sofa, breaking his stupor. He repositioned himself and brought his calf up to rest on the edge of the cushion.

"What do you mean? You think Shane hurt him?"

"No, I don't mean Shane. I was in the treehouse last night. Yvonne said she sensed Kai there after he died, so I went up there thinking maybe if I meditated, somehow, I could be closer to him. I don't know. But that's not what happened."

"Don't listen to her foolishness. It's pretty pathetic that she would put that kind of nonsense in your head at a time like this."

"Nobody put anything in my head, Jordan," Sienna admonished, shaking her head, her agitation building. "Please. I'm trying to explain to you what happened. My subconscious took over and showed me what I needed to see. What I already knew. When I meditated, I saw the maples from the meadow. The mother tree that's there. All of the leaves turned crystal blue, and they attacked Kira and Kai. And they tried to hurt the baby. I don't think the kids died accidentally. I think something happened to them. It took meditation for me to see what's in my subconscious. What I allowed myself to ignore and deny."

Again, the mother tree flashed into her mind. Sienna sat up straight on the sofa, crossed her arms over her chest, and gripped her sides, recalling how mother trees protect and nurture the saplings around them until they grow into established trees with deep roots of their own. She pictured the mother tree in the meadow, still feeding water and nutrients through her root system to those sapling stumps unable to photosynthesize. The ones Jordan and Lance cut down to build a treehouse. And then her family returned and took another sapling out of the meadow. She knew she would kill for her own children. Do anything to protect them. Anything. That might be what the mother tree tried to do. Fight back from the infestation she perceived her family as by using her natural defenses. Defenses mother nature gave her. Kira died not long after they transplanted her sapling. Maybe that wasn't a coincidence, but she knew how ridiculous it sounded. Her logical mind told her not to say it aloud. Not to fuel his worry about her frame of mind.

"They weren't accidents."

"Sienna! You're not making any sense. You think it was something deliberate?"

She looked from him down to her hands, not knowing how to explain what she didn't understand herself. Maybe it was a mother's intuition. Perhaps it was simply that she knew her kids better than anyone and knew they wouldn't make the mistakes everyone else accepted so quickly.

"I don't know," she said, looking back at him. "I don't know." She held his stare. "Yes. I do. I—"

Jordan interrupted. "Is that easier than believing Kai would do something so reckless? That Kira would be reckless?"

"Kira didn't jump. I never believed she jumped. She said it was too high. She didn't fall. I don't think she even went up there."

Jordan put both of his hands to Sienna's cheeks and cupped her face with a gentle touch. "But she did. The police confirmed it in the end. I think all this is from guilt. You can't accept that another child has died from an accident while in your care. That's what your subconscious mind is trying to get you to deal with. This was another accident."

Sienna leaned back into the sofa cushion and again crossed her arms over her chest and gripped her sides. "In my heart, I don't believe that."

"Did something else happen you're afraid to tell me? Is there something else?"

"Jordan, the vision I had of the mother tree when I meditated seemed so real. I woke up from it with absolute certainty that something happened to my kids! I feel it! Inside." She patted her chest.

"Just stop now! Enough of this. You haven't slept. Robin said it's common for people to grasp at explanations. Kira jumped or fell and hit her head on roots bulging through the soil and suffocated in the leaves. Kai died huffing paint."

Reaching out, he took her in his arms again and pulled her close. He squeezed with tender strength then rocked her side to side, a motion no more perceptible to her than the rotation of the earth.

"Do you want to talk to Robin?"

"I'm trying to talk to you."

He released his embrace and gripped her shoulders. "I'm not going to listen to this! You're not making any sense. You've had trees and forests on your brain for too many years. At times you've been obsessed with them. You write about them all day. *Trees!* It's always trees. This isn't about trees!"

Sienna exhaled and allowed herself to consider that maybe Jordan was right. He put everything into real estate terms. He saw through the lens of an agent. She wondered if maybe that's what she was doing now. At a breaking point, she was putting the death of their children through the lens of an environmentalist, a biologist. Maybe she was having a nervous breakdown and applying science to something that science couldn't explain.

"If it wasn't the trees, then I'm the only one to blame."

"They died in accidents." Jordan let his words linger. "I think the mother tree is you. You're talking about yourself. I have to ask you something, Sienna. Is there something you're not telling me? Did something happen when you were up there with Kai? When you were home with Kira? Or is this just guilt overwhelming you?"

Sienna couldn't bring herself to say no. She would never be absolved of responsibility. She may not have hurt them deliberately, but she didn't protect them, either. Grief was to be her penance.

Before she could answer, Jordan stood and looked down at Sienna.

"You have to stop talking like this. I don't want to discuss it anymore. You can't blame yourself. You can't blame anyone. You're exhausted and losing your grip on reality. It's sleep deprivation. That's what this is. You've been awake since yesterday morning, and your mind is foggy. You have to get some sleep. No more of this. Come on now, let me help you up," he said, taking her hands.

They both turned their heads to the front window as a diesel truck rumbled down the street, towing a metal trailer. It bounced and clanged and vibrated the front windows before coming to a halt at their house.

Sienna made it onto her feet alongside Jordan and pulled the hospital gown taut around her frame. "What's that?"

"They're here to haul away that tree. I cut it down. I took a chainsaw to it. It's on its side. I should have done that after we lost Kira."

"YOU DID WHAT?"

She had fought him from cutting the tree down after Kira died. She never wanted the ancient maple harmed.

"It's destroyed, and these guys are going to haul it away."

"Jordan, the treehouse is where Yvonne said she sensed Kai. I wanted to meditate there again . . . How could you?"

He again put his arms around her, but she kept her arms wrapped around herself. "He's gone. Kira's gone."

Sienna looked up at Jordan, tears rolling off her chin. Just then, the doorbell rang.

"Let me go talk to these guys really quickly, and I'll meet you upstairs," Jordan said. "Why don't you head up to bed? Give me two minutes with them."

He released her and walked back one deliberate step at a time without taking his eyes off her as though she was a toddler standing on her own for the first time, and he might have to catch her fall at any moment. "I'll tell them to rip out the maple from the meadow since you seem fixated on it," he said as he stepped outside to greet the crew.

She sat back on the sofa, listening to Jordan issue matter-of-fact instructions to the men when, by contrast, all she wanted to do was bury her face and cry until God felt sorry enough to return her children.

CHAPTER TWENTY-FOUR

JORDAN RETURNED MINUTES LATER, JUST as the diesel truck engine restarted.

"They're going to saw it into sections and chip it into a dumpster they towed here and grind up the stump and roots, too. It's four guys. I told them to start with the treehouse debris. They said it won't take them too long, but it's going to be loud. I didn't think about that, but I want you to lie down and try and sleep anyway."

He glanced out front as the truck pulled onto the side yard, towing the dumpster across their lawn and gouging tracks like a plow tilling for seed on a farm. "We'll have to re-sod. Come on. Let's get you up to bed," he said, walking over to her and extending a hand.

Sienna's phone chimed in the plastic bag, and they both glanced at it.

"I need to get my phone from the hotel. It must have been left there. My car, too. I can't leave it at the hotel another night. I guess I'll have to Uber over there later," he said while she rooted around in the bag for her ringing phone.

"Use Find My iPhone to see if it's there. Though I'm not sure you should be going back. At least not right away." She pulled the phone from the bag and showed him the display. "It's your mother calling. She must have tried to reach you on your cell. You take it. I don't want to talk to anyone right now."

Jordan let the call go to voicemail. "I'll call her in a minute after we get you to bed." He tossed the phone onto the sofa and dropped his hands to his sides.

Sienna stared at Jordan, who was in silhouette from sunlight coming in through the sheer drapes behind him. The abrupt ending of the phone ringing left a void in the room until seconds later when a demonic orchestra of roaring buzz saws accompanied by the concerto of a milling woodchipper reached them from the backyard as though a demon was conducting hellish music. The sound of the tree's destruction joined with the pulsing of blood in her inner ears as her heart pounded from competing emotions.

"She saw my Facebook. Janelle posted about the kids using hashtags, and it went viral. It's been shared over a thousand times by people who don't even know us. Some people don't believe the kids died accidentally. They're reposting it with links to news about Kira. Links to child murders."

Jordan leaned back into the sofa and inhaled a deep breath. "People are assholes. They would never dare say something like that to our faces. Not a chance in hell. Online, they can hide behind a ten-year-old photo of themselves before they gained weight and chime in with their two worthless cents without knowing a single detail or fact. Delete Facebook. Get rid of it. And Instagram. The internet is filled with heartless bullies looking for someone to troll."

"Monica called me when she saw it on Facebook, too. Janelle tagged me in the post. She's already communicating with people all over the country about it."

"She shouldn't have posted anything without talking to us. She had no right."

"Did you tell her you blame me for Kira's death?"

"What? No, I never said that! Did she say that?"

"She said the two of you talked about it and that you said you wouldn't have let her jump from the treehouse and that you implied I allowed it."

"I barely said two words to her at Kira's funeral. Don't listen to her. What did Monica say?"

"She offered to come over. Maybe I'll call her later today. I'm glad she reached out."

"You need to rest. I'm sure she'll understand that. You said you're supposed to be on bed rest for the baby?"

"He said rest until I can get in to see my OBGYN. It's on the discharge paperwork," Sienna said, motioning to the plastic bag from the hospital.

Jordan leaned to the other end of the sofa and stretched to grab the bag. He slid it across the cushions onto his lap and peered inside. A tri-folded document printed on white paper like a letter waiting for an envelope and a stamp rested on top. He plucked it out and read the doctor's instructions aloud.

"Rupture of fibroids. Ultrasound reveals multiple fibroids of varying sizes. Patient advised of miscarriage risk. Recommend immediate consultation with primary OBGYN. Patient in overall good health. Four pregnancies, including this one. Two live births. One abortion. No history of prior miscarriage."

Sienna's body tensed. An electrical current surged through her seizing her limbs and spine. She managed to turn her head toward Jordan as he looked up from the printout. He said nothing. It was clear from the confusion plain on his face; he was trying to comprehend what the doctor's words meant.

He turned and faced her. "Abortion?"

Sienna couldn't answer.

"Sienna? What about an abortion?"

Her forehead throbbed, but she closed her eyes and took a breath. The memory of lying on the gurney for the abortion surged to the forefront of her mind.

"I made a mistake, Jordan," she said without looking at him. "When I was in the treehouse, I expected to meditate and relive memories of our kids. That's all I wanted. I focused only on remembering our kids. The first memory that came back to me was of a pregnancy you don't know about. From before we got married."

"What are you talking about?"

"Do you remember when we went to Hawaii for your parents' anniversary, and Frieda thought I was pregnant? I was sick, and she thought it was morning sickness. I said it was something I ate."

"You were pregnant?" he interrupted.

Her cheeks and eyes were red and puffy from crying. She could feel heat radiating. She looked at her hands and realized she was picking at her nails and cuticles, so she stopped and looked at Jordan for her reply.

"I was pregnant, yes."

"We took a test."

"I didn't really take it then. I wasn't ready to be a mom. We had only known each other for nine or ten months. I was a single woman in my early twenties who had never even had a real job outside of work programs for school. I didn't have any family here. I was all alone. I didn't know if I was going to stay in Wisconsin after I finished my graduate degree."

"I asked you to marry me."

"We weren't married. I didn't know then if we would ever get married."

"You aborted our baby without even talking to me? That was our decision to make. Together! You deprived me of being a father to my child. You took that away from me. I didn't know you were capable of something like that. Of being that deceptive. How can I ever know what else you've hidden from me? Lied about. Were you never going to tell me?"

"I realized this morning that I had to tell you. The memory of that conversation in Hawaii. The memory of taking the test. It all came back to me. I relived it. When I was meditating, I concentrated on our children, and the first thing I remembered was being in the clinic, situated in the stirrups for the procedure. But then the memory changed. I was in the treehouse, and the blue maples began to sprout everywhere and hold me down and strangle me."

"I don't want to hear about the trees!" he shouted. "This has nothing to do with the trees!" He stood and walked to the window then walked back to the sofa and back to the window again.

"You're fucking losing it, Sienna. Are you going crazy? Seriously? I'm asking. Do you think you're having a nervous breakdown?" He continued pacing the room, but Sienna didn't say a word. "What did you do?"

"I didn't protect my children."

"Protect them? Are you saying you're responsible?"

"I am responsible. They're both gone. The police can investigate. They can do an autopsy. They can say these were accidents, but they weren't."

"I'm asking you. Did you hurt our kids, Sienna?"

The words stung. Just then, Kai's phone rang. They both glanced at it. By the fourth ring, Sienna wanted to answer it rather than use the last of her energy defending her sanity. Voicemail picked up the call, leaving the room in silence. Gone was the din of saws and the woodchipper.

"I'm sorry. I didn't mean that," Jordan said. "You know that's not what I meant."

The phone rang again, but Sienna didn't take her eyes off the front window. The trees and lawn and the house across the street were fuzzy through the sheer curtain.

"You should get that," she said.

"It's the number for the lawn crew, I think," Jordan said.

Without acknowledging him, she picked up her phone from the cushion next to her and stood.

"Sienna, I don't mean deliberately. You know what I'm asking."

As though she wasn't only childless, but also a widow, she left the room without looking at him.

CHAPTER TWENTY-FIVE

YVONNE GOT HOME AND TRIED to nap before heading into the studio. No sooner than she slipped out of her jeans and climbed into bed, the roar of chainsaws and heavy equipment obliterated her chances of sleeping. Jumping up, she raked her jeans back on, grabbed her crossbody mini purse from the dresser, and headed outside to investigate the sound.

Stepping off her back porch, she lingered at the edge of the pool, waiting for a break in the mechanical cacophony, and lit a cigarette. She puffed multiple times, but it was clear the work would continue unabated, so she walked around the pool house to get closer to the wall and listen for voices coming from Sienna's backyard. The new abundance of open sky behind her pool house stopped her in her tracks. Gone was the ancient, towering maple with branches that stretched for hundreds of feet in all directions at the edge of the marshy land preserve that bordered the neighborhood. Blue sky and puffy clouds illuminated by the midday sun were her new vista.

"They cut it down," she said to herself. Her lips pulled tight into thin strips, and she clenched her jaw and shook her head when the tragic death of the child popped back into her head. She didn't blame them one bit.

Men's voices carried over the wall during the intervals between cutting and repositioning of saws. "Turn it off!" one man said over the din. Yvonne stepped up against the wall to try and hear what they were saying. "Hey! Johnny! Turn off the woodchipper! I'm getting a call from your mom! Guys! Guys! Cut the saws for a minute!" She dabbed out the cigarette butt on a decorative cast stone planter and pressed it into the soil.

One by one, the gas engines of the equipment shut off, leaving a pronounced void, like a mute button pressed on a TV during the climactic scene of an action movie. The trilling of a cellphone replaced the roaring until the man answered the call.

"What is it, Meg?"

"John, I've been calling and calling!" a woman said in a high-pitched, excited voice. The call was on speakerphone.

Yvonne looked up as though seeing the top of the wall might improve her hearing. She listened as the woman told him about Kai's death in the treehouse that she watched on the news and told him to stop what he was doing until confirming it was okay with the police.

Yvonne stood straining to hear the muffled conversation.

"Nobody touch anything else," the man said as a ringing phone came through his cell speaker.

"Hello?"

"Mr. Clarke, this is John Rusk out back behind your house. I've got a couple questions for you. You mind coming 'round for a minute?"

"Uh, John, I'm talking with my wife right now. Just chop it up, chip it up, blast it up, whatever you need to do."

"It'll just take a second, sir."

"All right. Give me a minute, and I'll walk back."

"Thank you, Mr. Clarke."

Yvonne pulled her cellphone from her pocket to check the time. It was almost noon. Despite the sun shining directly overhead, the high wall that separated their properties cast shade over her like an awning. A few minutes later, she heard the voices resume in the distance. She held her breath, straining to hear.

"What is it, John?" Jordan asked.

"My wife called and said there was an accident here yesterday."

"Yes, that's right. My boy."

"I'm terribly sorry to hear that. We all are. Have the police finished everything they need to do here?"

"What do you mean?" Jordan asked.

"Well, my wife saw this tree on the news with police tape around it. Now, there's no tape here now, so I assume the police took it down, is that right?"

"I don't know. I don't remember any tape. I came out here this morning, and the instant I saw the tree, I just knew I needed to cut it down. It doesn't belong here. It would be a constant reminder of what happened. So, I cut it down. Honestly, I don't even really remember doing that. I was acting on adrenaline and allowed myself to release some of my anger and emotions on the tree through the saw. That's a natural thing to do, wouldn't you say?"

"Well, sir, do you have permission from the police to remove the tree?"

"Permission? I don't need permission to cut down a fucking tree in my own yard!"

"Sir, I agree with you, except they may not want it removed just yet. I think me and my crew ought to put this job on hold until the police say it's okay."

"No, John! It's not fucking okay. I don't want my wife to have to see it. As you can understand, she's in a terrible state right now. You can't imagine the pain we're both in. This tree, where my son died yesterday, it's no different from hanging on to a crashed car that a child died in after a car accident. We wouldn't be expected to keep it in our driveway. No one can expect us to keep this tree. It has to go. It has to go now. Now!"

"I'd like to help, Mr. Clarke, but like I said, I really need the police to give us the okay. I'd hate to mistakenly disrupt the job they have to do."

"Do you have kids, John?"

"Yes, this is my oldest boy, Johnny. I've got two other sons."

"I'm sure you love them as much as my wife and I love our kids. My son died playing in a treehouse that was up in this tree! My daughter died in a fall from it! We'll never recover from losing them, but we can't even begin to try and put our lives back together while this tree is here. It's like having gallows on our property. It's tormenting. Get it the hell out of here!"

"You have my deepest sympathies, Mr. Clarke, but I'm afraid we're going to have to pack it up for today. I'll leave the receptacle here. As soon as you get the go-ahead from the police, we'll be back out here ASAP to finish the job. You have my word. And there will be no charge, sir. I couldn't ask you to pay. My wife wouldn't let you pay, either. Mr. Clarke, you've got our office number. You just let us know when—"

"My wife is fixated on this tree. Losing our son might have broken her. She's saying all kinds of irrational things about it. And the treehouse. It has to go. And this smaller one here. This purplish one. At least cut that one down before you go."

"Mr. Clarke—"

"Give me the fucking saw, then," Jordan said. Within seconds, the engine of a chainsaw buzzed to life. He revved it and then it tore into the wood. Three seconds later, the motor stopped, and the sound of the small tree falling to the ground replaced it, leaves and branches ruffling like a delicate train of a gown.

"I'm going to say a prayer for your family, Mr. Clarke. For you and your wife. And your boy and your daughter, too. God bless you, sir. We'll plan on coming back in a few days."

Yvonne blinked, dumping plump tears from her lids. They landed in the grass like fresh dew. Her heart ached for Jordan. The emotion he was trying to hide was evident in his voice. He expressed it as anger. As hostility. Wiping her eyes, she wanted to yell out something, anything that would comfort him or provide any solace, but she held her tongue. There wasn't anything she could say to ease the pain of losing his children.

As the men tossed heavy equipment into the back of the truck, Yvonne walked back toward her house at a slow, indecisive pace as she scrolled on her phone, searching for the last group text between herself and her step kids. It took a second to find it way down the list. It had been months since they communicated. She read the last series of texts. They were from her birthday. "Wish you were both here celebrating with me," she typed to them. They both responded with *Happy Birthday!* and emojis of cake and party hats. She had initiated the text. They had forgotten it was her birthday. She missed them terribly, but it struck her that it must be only a fraction of the pain and sense of loss Sienna and Jordan felt. Her step kids were alive and well, just not interested in talking to her. She wondered what she had done wrong or had failed to do that kept them from wanting to spend time with her now that she was just Yvonne and not their stepmom. Maybe they didn't love her like she loved them. The idea stabbed, and for a moment, she wondered if it hurt more to lose a child to death or lose a child to unrequited love.

Walking along the edge of the pool, the rippling grey-blue water reflecting the sun like a thousand floating, bobbing candle flames, Yvonne opened the camera roll of photos on her phone and scrolled through the folder of family pictures. She had one after another of them laughing and enjoying time with each other from when they were eight and ten years old, to others from just a year ago after her stepson's college graduation. Pictures of them at the park, at the zoo, at amusement rides. Pictures of them at the mall, at the movies, shopping, and one from the time her then sixteen-year-old stepdaughter came home from the salon with her blond hair dyed black.

Every picture she flipped through was of the three of them without their father. He was always too busy to spend any time with his kids. While he worked at the law firm during their visits every other weekend for more than a decade, he left it to her to plan fun and exciting things for them to do. She helped raise his two kids, not him. He didn't want to spend time with them. Her irritation with him flared, remembering how he rejected having another child for years. How he always used the law firm as a reason it wasn't a good time for them to have a baby. He was too busy working. So, she got to be a stepmom, but now at almost forty-six, she wasn't even that anymore and had spent the last year and a half alone.

Yvonne opened her crossbody and tweezed another cigarette from the packet. It was nearly empty, though she was sure she unwrapped a new pack early that morning. She puffed and swiped back to the last group text message with the step kids and typed a new message. *Thinking of you both today. And often. I miss you guys. How about a pool party at my house before summer is over? Bring your friends. I'd love to meet them.*

After a few seconds, a small grey bubble with three blinking dots appeared. They were already responding! Then the grey bubble vanished with no comment from either of the step kids. Afraid a pool party might be too much, too pushy, she typed out a new message. *Or we could always get together for dinner. I would love to treat you both to one of my favorite restaurants.* Again, her eyes locked on her screen like it was a heart monitor displaying the lifeline of their relationship. She held her phone and waited, and waited, but didn't get a response.

She ran a hand through her hair, smoothed it down the back of her neck, and headed back into the house. When she reached the covered porch, the doorbell was ringing.

Not one to use the peephole, Yvonne opened her front door and instantly recognized the face. Starbucks flashed in her mind. She recognized her barista. Then she noticed the cameraman walking up the grass from a few feet behind, aiming the lens in her direction.

"Hi, I'm Mark Cranson from Channel 6 Eyewitness News. Are you Yvonne Mills?" The man in her doorway extended a microphone to capture her response.

"Yes," she said, blinking repeatedly, looking back and forth from the reporter and the man holding the camera.

"Mrs. Mills, you're not on TV or anything. This isn't live." At the same time, a white light attached to the camera turned on. "I understand you were the first to go back and help Mrs. Clarke yesterday after she found her son. Is that right?"

"Yes, I told a different reporter yesterday, and the police, I heard her yelling for help, and by the time I got out back behind my pool house to see what was going on, she was climbing down from the treehouse with her son in her arms."

She looked past the news crew to her elderly neighbor with a sour expression marching toward them across the lawn.

"Ask her if that boy was alive before his mother dropped him?" the elderly woman said. "Go ahead and ask her," Mrs. Erlish urged. "Is that what killed him? A fall from that treehouse? It's the same thing that happened to his sister."

Mrs. Erlish reached the patio and stood with her hand resting on the white railing of the steps that led to the doorway, but she didn't climb any of them.

"Didn't you tell her to wait for the ambulance so she wouldn't fall with that boy or drop him!"

"We didn't know how long they would take. Her instinct was

to get him down. And thank God she did. The 9-1-1 dispatcher walked us through CPR."

"How did she manage it?" asked the reporter.

"It didn't seem like he weighed any more than a bag of groceries."

The old woman flung her arm in the air in protest. "Impossible! She would have had to have her arm around the back of his neck to get him down from there. She might have cut off his oxygen."

The reporter brought the microphone back to his mouth. "Mrs. Mills, you can see that there is much concern in the community about—"

Yvonne cut him off. "I know what people are saying online. Is that why you're here, Mitch? You're a real piece of work."

"It's Mark. I'm an investigative reporter. It's my job to ask tough questions. Even questions that seem provocative. Sometimes that's the only way to get to the truth."

"I witnessed Sienna desperately begging him to breathe. She wouldn't give up CPR. Even when it was obvious he was gone, she kept at it. The paramedics had to pull her away from him."

"That's because she dropped him," said Mrs. Erlish. "She knew her goose was cooked. She might have gotten away with it the first time, but she's not going to get away with it twice without putting on a show."

"It's not just online, Mrs. Mills. Some of the other neighbors we've talked to say that Mrs. Clarke has acted strangely since the death of her daughter. They say she's become reclusive. Your neighbors say they've tried talking to her, and she ignores them outright. Some of them think she's hiding something."

"Ugh! I'm not going to stand here and let you malign a grieving mother. A woman who has been grieving for the last year, and who maybe hasn't wanted to chit chat with her neighbors and listen to them say how sorry they are over and over when sorry doesn't bring her daughter back."

"I understand that a second 9-1-1 call was made by you early this morning. An ambulance was dispatched to the Clarke residence."

"Had half the neighborhood standing in the street terrified we were going to have another body come out of that house," Mrs. Erlish said.

"Well, that clearly wasn't the case," Yvonne replied as she stepped back into her entryway, starting to close the door on the circus act performing on her patio.

"You have firsthand information, Mrs. Mills. I'm sure you'd rather have facts out there, not just opinions and conjecture. I ask questions, and I go where the facts take me. Your neighbors say Mrs. Clarke was lowered from the treehouse on a stretcher. What happened to her?"

"It was some ritual," Mrs. Erlish blurted. "She was up there performing some sort of ritual. Why else would she be up there at night, in the dark? The place where her kids died!"

"Oh, that's ridiculous," Yvonne scoffed. "It's the stupidest thing I've ever heard you say, Mrs. Erlish, and that's saying something. You've said a lot of stupid things since I've lived here."

Mrs. Erlish clasped her chest. "Ahh!"

"Why did paramedics have to help her down? She was able to climb down before holding her son," the reporter said.

"I don't have children. But I can imagine that if I did and my child was in danger, I would find the strength to climb skyscrapers, not just trees. That's what Sienna did. She found strength in herself that she didn't know she had. I spent the last several hours with her. She's heartbroken. That's not even the right word. She's destroyed. Make sure and get this on tape, Mitch," she said, moving the reporter out of the way with her arm as she stepped around him and looked directly into the camera. "Sienna Clarke didn't hurt her kids. Neither intentionally nor accidentally. Anyone who suggests otherwise is a heartless piece of shit who could benefit from a dose of reality in their own life. Maybe then they'd have a little more compassion. And maybe if the news didn't try and sensationalize every tragedy hoping to get ratings out of someone's pain, maybe society wouldn't be so quick to assume the worst. We always assume the worst. This time, everybody has it wrong. We'll never know why, but shockingly, tragic things do happen in this world. Not everything is fodder. Leave that family alone. Let them grieve. Now get off my property."

She turned from the camera and stepped back into her house, shutting the door. Her hands were shaking. She wanted to punch someone. Instead, she opened her crossbody purse and plucked a cigarette like she was picking a single grape from a vine. She lit it inside the house for the first time ever, took a long pull, and exhaled into the room, then turned and peered through the peephole. The news crew headed back to their van, Mrs. Erlish in tow. She stepped to her front window as the vehicle started up and drove down to the street to Sienna's house. It made a U-turn and parked on the opposite side of the road, rolled down a window, and took photos of a landscape service truck pulling from Sienna and Jordan's lawn.

CHAPTER TWENTY-SIX

SIENNA SWIPED OPEN HER CELLPHONE, seeing a voicemail from her mother-in-law. She didn't have the energy to call her back, but she played the message.

"Sienna, is it true?" Jordan's mother asked as though yelling into a bullhorn rather than talking into a cellphone four thousand miles away in Hawaii. Her shrieking voice filled the stairwell.

"It's all over Facebook. What is going on in that house? Call me back. Please! And try to get Jordan to call his brother. He can be there much faster than I can. I'm useless from here. Lance can help with whatever you two need. I know he will if Jordan would just reach out to him. He's got his drinking back under control. He can be some support. Those two shouldn't be fighting at a time like this. Please call me. I'm going to try Jordan again."

Sienna reached the master bathroom to shower away the stench of the hospital and the cold shivers that enveloped her when Jordan asked if she hurt their kids. It was a typical tactic of his. Throw out a jab, then rephrase it and say it wasn't what he meant. But it was always what he meant. He would just try and massage it, so his spite wasn't so obvious.

He hadn't always been like that, but she couldn't remember when it started. Then she second-guessed herself and thought maybe he had always done that. She told herself that if she ever talked with Robin or any other counselor, she would ask if that was passive-aggressive behavior, or cunning behavior, or both. He almost had her thinking she was delusional.

Sienna closed the outer bathroom door, something neither she nor Jordan ever did, hoping to shut out time itself. She didn't have to turn on the bathroom lights. Sunlight illuminated the large en suite covered from floor to ceiling in grey and white marble. The skylight doubled the sun's rays flooding from the windows over the tub to brighten the room. Reflected light glistened on the shiny chrome throughout the space. The towel racks. The faucets. The handle for the shower doors. It was a place that once gave her respite and comfort but now felt like solitary confinement, leaving her tortured by her own thoughts.

Stepping to the wall of mirrors above the vanities, she looked up at herself. They were her grey-blue eyes that looked back, but they were also Kira's eyes and Kai's eyes. Both her children had her eye color and shape. They had Jordan's hair. It struck her that she could always look in the mirror and see a reminder of her children.

But her eyes were also bloodshot and her lids puffy. The sight of herself, so haggard from crying, was yet another reminder of her reason for crying. She clutched her gown into a fist over her chest and could feel her heart breaking in two. Closing her eyes, she remembered the sight of herself on the treehouse floor as she hovered above, looking down as blood pooled from beneath her.

She opened her eyes, wiped them dry with her free hand, and plugged in her phone. Then she removed the hospital gown, balled it up, placed it in the trash, and slipped into her white terrycloth robe. Before tying it, she stepped back from the mirror to scrutinize the full length of herself. With the sunlight from overhead bouncing off her head and face making her hair and eyelashes shine golden, she turned sideways and inspected her abdomen in the mirror, but there was no hint of pregnancy. The light from above changed. She looked up as deep purple maple leaves fringed with blue edges fluttered and settled on the skylight like putrid contusions in the sky. A dozen leaves, then a dozen more as though a disease was spreading, they covered most of the glass. She froze, a gasp caught in her throat, the bathrobe hanging free around her.

※※※

Jordan knocked on the bathroom door and spoke to her without opening it.

"The crew left. They'll come back when the police say it's okay. The maple from the lake has been felled, too. I cut it down myself. Barely made a whisper as it hit the ground."

Wind swept the leaves away from the skylight, but Sienna kept her eyes on the glass, waiting for them to return.

"Sienna? Did you hear me?"

"Yes. I'm going to take a shower and then lie down."

"I thought you'd want to know."

Sienna didn't know how long he lingered, but she didn't say another word as she stepped into the shower. She draped her robe over the hook along the back wall of the enclosure, picturing the ancient tree that had lived longer than her grandparents, that survived as the world changed around it, but couldn't survive her family. She wasn't surprised he cut it down without asking. It was months before he finally stopped demanding they cut it down after Kira died. He never could understand why she didn't want the tree punished.

He was right, she realized. Had they cut it down, Kai wouldn't have been up in the treehouse. She wondered if Jordan was thinking the same thing and waiting for the chance to say, *I told you so.* But he didn't have to say it. She knew and would never forget.

She turned on the shower faucet, hoping the spray would serve as white noise, like the noise emitted from devices designed to help people shut out all thought so they could sleep.

As the water warmed and droplets splattered onto the shower floor and walls, her mind flashed with images from her meditation in the treehouse. Sienna turned off all the other spigots, but left the shower running, then picked up her phone. She opened the app controller for the speakers in the ceiling to select the piano music that used to be her standby. Since Kira died, music seemed like a pathetic attempt at salving a wound, so she didn't bother. But she had to try and shut off her mind or risk falling apart and knew she couldn't take a Valium this time.

She scrolled through her music library for the album she wanted. After turning up the volume a hair below maximum, she pressed play on "Nuvole bianche." The first solemn chord erupted through the room, blasting away thought. Focusing on the sound of the piano pedals that could be heard in the opening between notes, she allowed the music to swaddle her like a newborn baby after a feeding with no thought beyond that exact moment. It was that very moment where beautiful music charmed her into a state of automation. She climbed into the shower.

꙰꙰꙰

As the piano notes progressed and the melody ascended, Sienna found her mind drifting to the holidays five years earlier around the time she discovered that piece of music. She had taken two weeks off from work to be at home with the kids during their holiday break from school. It was a few days after Christmas. "Nuvole bianche" had played in the house a few dozen times over a week leading to Christmas Day and again several times in the days since. Jordan was working, so he wasn't there to object or play one of his eighties Christmas compilations. Kira seemed to like the music as much as she did, and Kai, at age seven, was already addicted to the PlayStation he received as a gift that year.

Like every year, she had a handful of gifts to return to the mall. Clothes that were the wrong size mostly. And always the passive-aggressive present she received from her mother-in-law, who never failed to include the receipt as though there was an expectation she would have to return it. Whether it was an enormous dress made for a woman who weighed one hundred pounds more than her, or undergarments in maternity sizes, or shoes five sizes too big, or the extra-large, puffy neon green tracksuit she received that year that would make her resemble a tennis ball. A trip to the mall for returns was part of the holiday tradition.

As they were leaving the mall after making their returns and exchanges, the three of them, happy with their replacement gifts, climbed onto the escalator and descended. At the base of the moving staircase, a young man in a tuxedo sat at a black baby grand piano. The first note was unmistakable. Then came the soft piano pedal before he struck the next chord.

Kira looked up at Sienna with a beaming smile. "It's 'Nuvole bianche!'"

Sienna nodded, the width of her smile matching her daughter's.

They rode to the bottom level as the young man extracted the melody from the piano and sent it high into the mall's rafters. They approached to listen to the performance but stayed back at a polite distance. Other mall shoppers dashed around and didn't seem to take notice. It wasn't "Jingle Bells" or "Silent Night," and they didn't recognize or appreciate any connection of the music to Christmas.

Kira set her shopping bag down, its flat bottom kept it upright, and she stepped up close to the pianist. In awe, she stood watching his arm and back movements and his fingers connecting with the keys. She stared at his feet pushing the pedals and his legs moving his body on the piano seat. Fixated, she absorbed his every action.

When he finished, he turned his head and smiled at Kira as she applauded while bouncing on her tippy toes and springing off the ground with delight. Sienna and Kai also clapped, but none of the other shoppers bothered as they hurried by on their mission to reach the next store, so the young man jumped straight into another song. "Joy to the World."

"Can I try?" Kira interrupted.

"What's that, sweetie?" he asked, able to play the simple song and still carry on a conversation.

"I've never played a real piano. Please, can I try it?"

"After that standing ovation you gave me, sure, you can try it." He slid down the piano seat to make room for her.

With wide, bright eyes as though she was opening an overlooked Christmas gift, Kira sat at the piano and caressed the shiny keys with both of her hands. Gentle, slow strokes as though the piano was made of glass and might break into pieces if she exerted an ounce of pressure. "It's so pretty! I got a keyboard for Christmas. It connects to the computer so I can learn how to play it. My dad set it up for me."

"She has only stopped playing on it to eat and sleep," Sienna said.

Kira found the middle C and pressed it with only enough force to produce a faint tone then with more confidence pressed three keys building the C-minor chord. She glanced up at the young man and smiled then turned to Sienna to show her the same proud grin. Then she tried other keys, producing A minor, then multiple keys and black keys to summon C-sharp minor. Within a minute, she tried chords with one hand and then chords with both hands.

The pianist clapped for Kira, clearly impressed with her grasp of the keyboard. "Who taught you all that?"

"I taught myself. It's easy." Kira smiled. "You were playing 'Nuvole bianche.' That's my mom's favorite song," she added as she simultaneously pressed the keys.

Sienna watched Kira, tentative at first, as she tested keys while humming the music to "Nuvole bianche" in her high-pitched nine-year-old child's voice. The man held his breath, anxiously waiting for Kira to correctly identify the successive keys nodding each time she got it right and moved on to the next chord.

"You're a natural. Can you play these for me?" he asked, reaching and pressing keys on the higher end of the register, demonstrating what he wanted her to do. He then lowered his fingers to the keyboard like doves landing in a nest and again played "Nuvole bianche."

Without guidance or prompting, her timing perfect, Kira struck the higher-pitched chords adding an ethereal, angelic quality to the evocative melody the two played together.

Astonished at her daughter's talent, Sienna hugged Kai around his chest as he stood in front of her.

By then, a small crowd of shoppers noticed Kira accompanying the young pianist. They formed a semicircle around them as she added delicate chords to the classic piece. The young man and Kira mesmerized the crowd with their duet. The tinkling high notes she added changed the tenor of the music into holiday music, a Christmas song they had never heard before.

꽃꽃꽃

Sienna repositioned herself under the shower spray, allowing the water to splash her face and combine with her tears. She didn't know how long she'd been in the shower. The bottoms of her feet tingled from a diminished blood flow after standing in the exact same spot for too long. Hot water steamed up the room and clouded the mirror. Thoughts of her children floated in the air with the vapor mist, as other songs from "Una mattina" reverberated through the bathroom and vibrated the glass shower doors.

She recalled telling Jordan about the events at the mall that day and them agreeing to get her into piano lessons and the need to have a real piano for her to play and practice on. Sienna smiled, remembering that by then, Kira had surpassed in skill and technique anything her first instructor, Nicholas, the young pianist from the mall, could impart. Kira dazzled him with her ability to improvise. When Kira began creating her own melodies, he conceded she needed a higher level of training than he could provide.

A pang of guilt broke her train of thought, and her smile vanished. It was her first smile since finding Kai in the treehouse.

"I miss you, baby girl," she said and smiled again, refusing to let guilt steal the memory of her daughter's gifts.

Shower spray flowed over her head, and she tilted it back, allowing the water to massage her scalp. For the one-thousandth time, she wished there was sheet music of Kira's compositions. She often encouraged Kira to create sheet music, but her response was always the same; the music was in her head and she didn't need to write it down. And it did seem she had an endless capacity to retain different songs. Still, she wished she had insisted. Had she only known.

For the first three years, Kira used an electronic piano keyboard connected to their laptop. It was another three years before they bought the large Victorian house and had room for a baby grand piano like the one from the mall. Kira might have inadvertently recorded onto the hard drive some melodies she created during some of her online lessons and endless practice sessions. Maybe even the particular tune that had become Kira's signature. The one she couldn't remember how to recreate no matter how hard she concentrated.

Turning off the shower and lifting a plush bath sheet from the hook, she remembered they gave Kira that old laptop. She swept the towel over her hair then padded her face and arms and legs dry. When Jordan got his Mac a few years ago, Kira inherited the old one as a hand-me-down to keep in her room. Wrapping herself in the wide towel, she stepped from the shower and turned off the music. She had to check Kira's laptop for any trace of the music she composed.

Sienna slipped into her robe and headed down the hall to Kira's room. As she crossed the staircase landing, she heard Jordan whispering downstairs. She figured he was on the phone but had no idea who he was talking to—and she didn't care. Nothing mattered to her except checking the laptop for Kira's music.

At the closed door, she hesitated. Nearly every night since Kira's death, Sienna opened the door and blew a kiss into space and said, "I miss you, baby girl. I love you," but she found it impossible to penetrate the barrier that repelled her each time she tried to enter. As though ether filled the room, she couldn't step inside without getting dizzy and struggling to breathe. She knew it was her anxiety but accepted she wasn't ready to experience intimacy with her daughter's things if she couldn't also be close to her daughter. It was a tradeoff she didn't want to accept.

She opened the door and waited. The distinct smell of her daughter's hair and her clothes wafted over her, but rather than succumb to despair, she allowed it to intoxicate her and revive her and embolden her. Sienna inhaled deeply, stepped inside, and closed the door behind her, shutting Jordan out.

CHAPTER TWENTY-SEVEN

"SHE'S OUT OF THE SHOWER," Jordan said to his mother-in-law when the music blaring in the bathroom abruptly stopped. "Hang on a second. I'm going to go to the study." Jordan stood from the sofa and picked up from the coffee table the slim maple tree branch heavy with the midnight leaves he brought inside after cutting the tree. He thought they looked like a bruise, but Kira loved them, and he wanted them as a keepsake. A memento. Jordan slipped down the hall to the wood-paneled study with windows closed off by wooden shutters that blended into the walls. He softly closed the door as the latch clicked into place.

"I'm worried, Doris. You should listen to the things she's saying. She honestly thinks they weren't an accident. She was the only one home! When I press her to stop and think, she turns inward and says it's her fault. I don't think she has any idea what she's saying. I'm getting scared. She might have done something to them."

"We both know that's not true. She's overwhelmed with guilt like any grieving mother would be."

"You didn't hear her! I don't know what to think."

"Don't press her right now. Let her have whatever it is that's getting her through this, even if it doesn't make sense."

"Are you kidding? I'm supposed to let her talk herself into insanity? You have to get up here and help me with this."

"I know. I think I can get up there day after next. Two more days at most. Has Sienna told you that her stepdad can't be left alone for more than a few hours?"

"Yes, she said he's not getting around very well. But I need help here."

"I'm trying to find someone to come stay with him. My pastor is asking some of the parishioners. I might have to get someone from one of those in-home care websites, but I don't want to do that. He doesn't want that, either. Some stranger helping him to the bathroom."

"She was very bad off after Kira, and I had to handle that without your help. But even then, she didn't say these kinds of things."

"Sienna told me not to come for Kira's services. I wanted to be there, but she knew I didn't have anyone to take care of Abe. He's much worse since then."

"This time, she's much worse! If it's just a guilty conscience, then it's at a breaking point. I'm worried it's more than just that. She just told me she had an abortion before we were married. Did you know that?"

"This isn't the time to get into that, Jordan."

"Did you know?"

"Jordan, please focus on what's important right now."

"Did you know!"

"Yes, I knew. I agreed with her decision."

"You agreed she should lie to me about it all these years?"

"What do you want, Jordan? An apology from your wife for something that happened before she was your wife? That was such a long time ago. It has nothing to do with your marriage today."

"It has everything to do with it. She killed our first child without telling me. Maybe what people are saying is true. Maybe it is too much of a coincidence for our other two children to die in accidents."

"Stop with that! You don't really believe that. I know you don't. You're hurting, too, but don't turn on her right now."

"What do you expect? With everything she's been saying, I don't know what to think. She needs a mental-health professional or facility or something. I might have to admit her for observation."

Jordan ended the call, shoved Kai's phone into the pocket of his suit pants, and turned his attention back to the maple leaves. In the hazy light of the study that even lamps couldn't adequately brighten during the day, he twirled the branch in his fingers, and the leaves fluttered like feathers of a blackbird. He set them on the desk and turned to the bookshelves lined with hundreds of reproductions of classic novels intended to infuse the study with an air of refinement like a home staged for sale. Each book had the same burgundy binding, and since no one ever bothered to put them in alphabetical order, finding a particular title was no different from solving a riddle.

Jordan scanned the rows, taking slow steps down the bookshelf and back again until he found it. Pulling *Charlotte's Web* from the shelf, he carried it to the desk and opened it to the first page. *"Where's Papa going with that axe?"* He read the first sentence aloud and pursed his lips. It was Kira's favorite story when she was younger. The one she always asked him to read to her whenever he offered.

Plucking off the branch a couple of the largest, pristine leaves with the deepest blue hue, he set them inside the book between the opening pages and then closed it up with a clap. He patted the cover solemnly, lamenting, and then tucked it under his arm.

He pulled Kai's cellphone from his pocket, swiped it open,

and found *Dad* under the recent calls list. As he moved to the window and angled the wooden shutters for a view of the street, he pressed *dial*, hoping someone found his phone.

The news van was on the other side of the street. "Bastards," he muttered as the phone rang. And rang. No one answered. Jordan pictured the phone sitting in a lost and found bin under the bar then shook his head. The cell and Louis Vuitton case were worth fifteen hundred dollars. Its finder might want to become its keeper.

He dialed again, but it went to voicemail, and the greeting he loved, but that he knew some people despised, played.

"You've reached Jordan Clarke. I'm sorry, I must be at another closing of a real estate deal because that's the only thing that keeps me from answering when my clients call. Leave me a message, and I'll get right back to you."

He pressed the pound key to gain access to his voicemail messages, but before he could enter his password, a police car pulled up at the curb along with an unmarked vehicle. He hung up and returned the phone to his pocket while watching them get out into the sunshine.

Jordan recognized Officer Rodriguez as she stepped from her squad car, but not the man from the other vehicle who wore an ill-fitting suit of a greenish-grey color he hadn't seen since the nineties. Even from a distance, he could tell it was cheap, as was the abstract necktie from the same era as the suit. Officer Rodriguez joined the man at the unmarked car. She referred to notes she had on a pad as she explained something to him.

The driver door of the news van opened, and the cameraman from earlier that morning stepped out, lugging his camera. The reporter sprinted around the vehicle as the police turned to face the news crew.

"Excuse me, officer! Excuse me! Mark Cranson, Channel Six News. What can you tell us about your investigation?"

The man in the suit stepped away from his car and headed

toward the house. "We have no comment at this time," he said without stopping or looking at the reporter. Officer Rodriguez followed behind and matched his gait as they rushed to the door.

"Officer, are you investigating foul play?"

Neither officer responded as they reached the walkway leading to the covered porch and steps.

Jordan hurried from the study, the book still under his arm. He reached the front door before the police had the chance to ring the bell.

"May we come inside and talk with you and Mrs. Clarke? I don't think they'll let up until we're off this porch," Officer Rodriguez said, pointing with her thumb over her shoulder at the reporter and his cameraman still in the street at the curb.

"Sienna is sleeping. I don't want to wake her," he said softly. He closed the door, wondering how the scene would play out on the news. How he would look and how business would probably suffer. "You said you wanted to take a statement, but I didn't think you meant before I had the chance to sleep. I was just able to get Sienna calmed down. This really isn't the best time for this."

"It's important we conduct these interviews, Mr. Clarke. While memories are fresh. This is Detective Harris. He's overseeing this investigation."

The men shook hands.

"You may not be aware, but my wife was at the hospital part of the night. She's in a vulnerable state right now. I'm not about to wake her up."

"Why don't we sit down?" Detective Harris said. "We can revisit her statement later. We need to talk to you about Kai."

"Let's go into the living room," Jordan said, waving across to the foyer, leading the way. He shook Sally awake from the sofa. "Come on, girl, get down."

The big dog barked at the sight of the officers, and Jordan shushed her. "It's okay, Sally. Get down," he said, pointing to the floor. "She's thirteen. Doesn't hear well."

The group watched Sally stagger into the kitchen, still groggy from her nap.

"Mr. Clarke, we are aware that your wife was in the emergency room last night," said Detective Harris. "I take it she's okay since she wasn't admitted."

"No, detective, she's not okay. Our son is dead."

"Yes. I'm sorry, Mr. Clarke. I'm here because we are trying to understand how this happened," Detective Harris said.

Jordan tossed the burgundy bound edition of *Charlotte's Web* onto the coffee table. "Understand how this happened! I don't know how a twelve-year-old dies huffing paint, but I do know this isn't the best time for you to force my wife to relive the details of it. Can't you give us a few days? My god. Where's your sense of decency? That goddamned reporter out there doesn't have any! Why don't you two go out there and tell him to get the hell out of here? I don't want Sienna to see him!"

CHAPTER TWENTY-EIGHT

SIENNA HAD RECOGNIZED SALLY'S ALERT bark. She paused at the laptop and listened for a moment but heard nothing more, so she returned to trying to guess Kira's password. It had taken all her willpower to enter the bedroom in search of Kira's music, but she didn't have her password and had tried various possible codes—her daughter's favorite composer, favorite composition, her favorite pop artist, favorite movie and actor and actress, her favorite food. She tried her favorite color, favorite animal. She ran down the list of logical options. She sweated, fearing the very thing she was searching for was right in front of her, but out of reach like an overlooked last will and testament locked in a bank vault. She tried Kira's favorite book, tried her birthdate, and her middle name. Then she heard Jordan shouting.

Closing the laptop lid with a snap, she stepped out into the hall. Multiple voices carried up to her as she crept to the upper landing and listened. She pulled the robe tighter around her chest and neck. The collar was wet from her hair.

"Detective Harris and I are not here to upset you, Mr. Clarke," Officer Rodriguez said.

Sienna recognized the voice and descended a few steps to see the officer who interviewed her in the hospital along with another man she didn't recognize. Next she heard her husband scolding them.

"You two show up here expecting to find us having lunch like it's any other damn day! You have no idea what kind of pain we're in. My wife was barely clinging to her sanity after we lost Kira. Now we've lost Kai, and I'm terrified of what's happening to her."

Sienna's heart fluttered.

"Kai's autopsy is complete, Mr. Clarke, and we need to discuss it with you and ask you and your wife some questions."

"Autopsy?"

"When the cause of death is uncertain, the law requires an autopsy. As in this case here," Detective Harris added.

Jordan turned to Officer Rodriguez. "*Huffing.* You said it was huffing."

Officer Rodriguez turned her open hands to Jordan as she explained.

"Kai's friend Shane confirmed the boys were attempting to huff paint. Shane is traumatized and having a hard time giving us any answers. I also spoke with the ER doctor, who proposed SSDS based on the presence of paint on Kai's mouth and nostrils. That assessment was also supported based on the inhalants found at the scene and the manner they were bagged for huffing, but the autopsy is required to determine the actual cause and manner of your son's death."

"SSDS? What is SSDS?"

"Sudden Sniffing Death Syndrome," Detective Harris said. "Huffing-induced cardiac arrest is typically associated with SSDS, but it's a term that also encompasses other huffing-related causes of death. Seizure, asphyxiation, hypoxia. Suffocation in certain circumstances, including this one."

"Kai suffocated?"

He nodded, acquiescing, and pulled his lips tight against his teeth, taking a moment before speaking. "I'm afraid so, Mr. Clarke."

"How? On the paint? The paint choked him?"

The detective raised his hands in protest. "Listen, Mr. Clarke—"

"No, you listen! What happened to my son?"

The detective issued a nervous cough and cleared his throat. "There was no evidence that paint blocked Kai's airway or lungs. Initial speculation is that he lost consciousness with his head in the grocery bag or face down on the bag. That would explain what the medical examiner found."

Rooted in place on the stairs, Sienna couldn't see the detective's expression, but his words punched her in the stomach. Hearing him describe Kai's death was no different from hearing a madman calmly describe how he had tortured him. She wanted to attack him for the things he said, lunge at him and wail on him, but she resisted the instinct knowing no matter how much it hurt, she needed him to finish. Needed him to say what happened to Kai. She walked down the stairs until they could see her face and paused.

"What did the medical examiner find?"

The police turned toward her voice, and Jordan jumped up from the sofa and stepped into the foyer.

Sienna descended and reached Jordan on the lower landing. He placed a hand on her arm, but she didn't take her eyes off the detective and stepped past Jordan.

"Mrs. Clarke, I'm Detective Harris," he said, standing, prompting Officer Rodriguez to do the same. "Please forgive the intrusion. That's what we're here to discuss. It's important that we document precisely what happened yesterday. Exactly what you observed. Every action you took."

Sienna stood in silence, stiff and unyielding.

"What did the medical examiner find?" Jordan repeated.

"I want to be delicate. I apologize, but we are seeking clarity about how you found Kai, Mrs. Clarke. Paint markings and cloth fibers on his face match paint markings on the bag and fibers from rags we collected from the scene. The medical examiner didn't find any evidence of prolonged inhalant abuse. It's possible he never tried huffing before. The toxicology results will take more time. Weeks. They will provide a greater understanding of factors, including the paint chemicals that may have contributed to Kai's death, but the physical examination of his body is conclusive that he suffocated. It's now the manner of his death we're investigating. It appears it was mechanical suffocation from the grocery bag. What he found is more consistent with a homicide. It's rare, but losing consciousness with the bag over his face would look much the same. It's similar to a baby in a crib who suffocates on bedclothes."

When Sienna heard the reference, it conjured memories of Kai as a baby in his crib as she wrapped him in a blanket, smiling and giggling. Within a breath, the memory switched to the day before, thirteen-year-old Kai in the treehouse with leaves piled around his body and lifeless face. Until she looked up, she was unaware that everyone's eyes were fixed on her.

"Did the leaves suffocate him? The leaves from the treehouse. They were all around him."

"We noted the presence of leaves inside the treehouse. But little clumps of dried, dead leaves wouldn't be dense enough to obstruct his airway," Detective Harris said.

Sienna looked up from the floor into the detective's face. "The bag wasn't on his face when I found him. You sure it wasn't the leaves?"

"No, even if that amount of leaves were wet, they wouldn't cause him to suffocate, and the leaves in the treehouse are dry. But it's daylight. I plan to take another look out there. Our photos were taken in the evening."

Jordan shifted on the sofa closer to Sienna. "The treehouse is gone."

"It's gone?" asked Detective Harris.

"Yes, I cut down the tree early this morning. I had a crew out here that began chipping it up and pulverizing the roots, but they stopped halfway through the job when they found out about Kai."

"Mr. Clarke, there was police tape around the tree. And the garage. This is an active investigation," Officer Rodriguez said. "I was out here and personally helped secure the scene."

"It's not a scene, this is my home! Five hours ago, you told me he died huffing paint," Jordan said. "You told me that! You told me he died up there. I got home and saw that treehouse, and I wanted to smash it to bits. I wanted the treehouse and the tree that held it to vanish. I didn't want the tree to live if my boy couldn't live. I got my chainsaw and—"

"And you destroyed evidence," Officer Rodriguez huffed.

"Evidence? Kai's not up there waiting for you to figure out if it was a bag or leaves. You said you all were already out here last night and did whatever you do. Collected everything. Would you hang onto a crib that your baby suffocated in? Would you hang onto the bedsheets that suffocated him in his crib?" Jordan asked, but neither responded. "No, you wouldn't. I didn't have any choice."

"What's left of the treehouse?" Detective Harris asked.

"Nothing, I imagine. A four-man crew was out there working. You can go see for yourself," Jordan said, pointing the way through to the kitchen.

The detective nodded for Officer Rodriguez to inspect the remains of the tree and treehouse. She stood, but the detective continued his questioning. "Can we start with you telling us again exactly what happened yesterday?"

Officer Rodriguez paused in the kitchen doorway. "Mrs. Clarke, would you feel more comfortable if you changed?"

It wasn't until then Sienna remembered she was only wearing a robe. "Yes, give me a minute to change," she said, standing and tying the robe tighter.

As she reached the upper landing and headed to her bedroom, she heard Jordan speaking to the detective, but her hearing seemed diminished and her head foggy. She could hear Jordan ask if Kai suffocated on paint fumes and not the bag or leaves, but the detective explained that Kai's suffocation was from physical obstruction of his breathing, not chemical interference with his breathing.

Sienna felt her body and mind numb as though she had taken another Valium. As she pulled on a pair of jeans and a loose T-shirt, she realized why. It was an instinctive response of self-preservation after hearing that Kai suffocated and that the police wanted to question her.

She braced for it as she slipped her feet into a pair of shoes. But what did surprise her was that she wasn't crying.

She wondered if feeling numb was one of those phases of grieving. After Kira's death, she only experienced varying degrees of sadness, but numbness was a respite from her tension, anxiety, fear, and despair that left her red and blotchy with hives. Yes, she was still standing in a room on fire, with flames licking at her skin from all angles, but the numbness was her insulated, reflective fire suit that kept her alive.

As she left her room and walked to the stairs, she could hear Jordan's aggressive sparring. She grabbed the banister, thinking if the death of his child couldn't break his exterior, then nothing would.

"I've never seen her touch our children. Are you saying this is possibly a homicide?" Jordan said.

"While suffocation is typically associated with homicide, it isn't always. Huffing-related suffocation is, unfortunately, becoming more common. Did you notice anything out of sorts

with her recently? A worsening of her depression? Anger? Acting
out in some way?"

"She's been grieving our daughter. We all have."

"Did you see anything unusual yesterday?"

"I got arrested yesterday! I spent the night in jail! I was
oblivious to the fact that my family had completely fallen apart!
I had the privilege of hearing about my boy's death from a perfect
stranger who blurted it out like the bad timing of a joke. That's
how all of this feels. Like a really shitty, bad joke." He stopped
and craned his head up to the ceiling and inhaled deeply. "Oh
God, my boy," he said.

Jordan closed his eyes, the silence underscoring his words.
Before anyone said anything, he swiftly stood from the sofa and
turned his back to the officer and detective. He bent over at the
waist as though he might collapse. Bracing his upper body with
his arms extended and his hands on his knees, he inhaled several
deep breaths. Filtered light from the window bathed his face, but
he kept his eyes closed tight.

The detective didn't give him the chance to fall into despair.
"Did you give a statement to the media?"

"No, I shut the door in his face," Jordan said, righting himself,
wiping his eyes and retaking his seat on the sofa.

As Sienna reached the bottom of the stairs, Officer Rodriguez
re-entered the living room. She stared at Jordan as she spoke.

"The tree has been cut down." She then faced the detective.
"It's on its side back there. The treehouse isn't there anymore. It
must have crashed apart in the fall."

"Well, if it's all right with you, I'm going to get the tree service
back out here immediately so they can finish the job."

The detective held up a hand. "Let's hold off for now."

Sienna joined the group, and everyone's attention turned to
her. "What about the media?"

Jordan made room for her on the sofa. "One of those cheesy

investigative reporters was out there this morning. He's back out front now."

"Mrs. Clarke, I'd like to review your statement and ask a few questions," Detective Harris said. "I want you to concentrate and recall every detail, no matter how painful. Can you do that?"

CHAPTER TWENTY-NINE

"SIENNA," SHE SAID, NODDING. "CALL me Sienna."

"Sienna, what were the boys doing with the paint?" Detective Harris asked.

"Kai asked for permission to paint the treehouse. He said he wanted to cover up old drawings. But I knew he wanted to change it so it no longer had the same connection to Kira's death. I thought it was a healthy step for him. A progression since he never talked about the treehouse or went back into it that I know of. I didn't want him up there, but I also didn't want to hinder any sort of healing or therapy that might come from it."

"Tell us exactly what you saw and what you did when you got up into the treehouse."

Sienna inhaled then spoke slowly.

"My son lying on his back on the floor, covered in dead leaves. Like he'd been rolling in them. He was pale. I realized he wasn't breathing, and I screamed for help. I kept checking him and shaking him so he would breathe, and I was screaming out the doorway at the same time. I tried CPR. I don't know if I did it right. It seemed like forever. Like I had been screaming for help forever. Like minutes flew by each time I blinked. I don't know how long I was at it. I just detached and didn't see or hear anything. My mind went dormant, so I could keep doing chest compressions and breathing for him without falling apart, but the CPR wasn't working, so I picked him up and carried him down from the treehouse to call 9-1-1."

"Explain what you mean by your mind went dormant."

"Like I wasn't there. I didn't feel or see anything. I wasn't aware of anything. I didn't think about anything. I just . . . I just acted. On impulse. On instinct."

"Which one? Impulse or instinct?"

"My instinct was to save him. That's what I tried to do."

"How long were you in the treehouse?"

"I don't know. I would guess a couple of minutes."

"Your neighbor placed the 9-1-1 call at five eighteen p.m. You told Officer Rodriguez the boys went up there around three-thirty or four, right?"

"Somewhere around that time, yes."

"I want you to think. This is crucial. Close your eyes and tell us what you saw in the treehouse when you first got up there."

Sienna closed her eyes but then opened them right away. "Just Kai. I only saw Kai and the leaves clinging to him. No one had been up there since the prior fall. Leaves blew in and piled up. It's been neglected. Spindly young branches grew in the window and through the gaps in the wallboards."

"Did you see the plastic grocery bag?" the detective asked.

"Yes, it was on the floor next to Kai."

"It wasn't over his head or on his face?"

Sienna closed her eyes again and saw the bag on the floor a few feet from Kai's hands.

"No."

"Could the wind have blown it off his face?" Officer Rodriguez asked. "Wind gusting high up there might have caught the bag and whipped it off his head."

"Possibly. I want to re-examine the paint splatter. Paint was on the floor but nothing on the walls. Was he face up?" Detective Harris asked.

"He was on his side."

"What else was on the floor next to Kai?"

"A can of spray paint, and a gallon of paint, and a couple of paintbrushes. Jordan's old T-shirt that we cut up into rags."

"Was there anything else already there when you got inside?"

"No, I can't remember anything else."

"Shoeprints in the paint?"

"I must have stepped in the paint. It spilled from the bag. I remember that."

"We'll want to try and match up pictures of those prints with your shoes. Where are they?"

"They're in that hospital bag. You can take them."

Jordan pulled the loafers from the bag one at a time and handed them to Officer Rodriguez. She examined the bottom of each and showed them all the blue paint on one heel then set them on the plastic bag as the detective continued.

Sienna nodded to Officer Rodriguez. "That blue is the same blue as Kai's bedroom. He picked it out." She nervously picked at all the cuticles of her hands. "Do you think if we didn't paint his room, if we didn't have any paint, he wouldn't have gone up there, and he would still be alive?"

An awkward silence fell until the detective spoke. "I imagine it's been a very difficult ten months since the death of your daughter."

"You imagine right," Jordan interjected. "Difficult doesn't begin to describe it."

"Did he have leaves in his mouth like Kira?" Sienna asked without looking at anyone.

"No, there were no leaves in his throat," Detective Harris said.

Sienna didn't see the midday sun shining into the room or the people staring at her. The unpolished jewel box where she kept her memories of Kira was open.

"I found Kira in the leaves. She suffocated, they said. They said she hit her head, knocking her unconscious, leaving her brain dead when she fell into the leaves. I don't think she fell. That's what they said. That she fell. Facedown, they said. But she was breathing. They found bits of leaves in her mouth and throat. She suffocated, they said. She tried to breathe. I don't think she fell. She didn't jump."

"The medical examiner would have called out something like that in his report, Sienna. If he choked on leaves, he would have recorded it."

"Are you sure? Did they check? I want them to check."

"Yes, I'm sure. I was present. As part of the investigation."

Sienna caressed her upper arms as she spoke to the detective. "I wanted to see Kai in the hospital again after they took him away. I wanted to clean the paint off his face. Remove the leaves from his hair. They wouldn't let me. They said the medical examiner would investigate and needed him to stay just as he was."

She looked to the ground, remembering how she felt after they had taken him away to the morgue. She remembered the urge to hug and kiss him one more time. No one said a word until she asked Detective Harris, "Were they careful with him?"

"Yes, the medical examiner was very careful with Kai. He was very respectful of your son. When they had to turn him to take photos, there was another person to help. They treated him like he was their own child."

"They took photos of him?" she asked.

"Well, yes, photos of some bruises on his face and some abrasions. The paint on his face. Photos of the paint on his skin in the shape of leaves that transferred from leaves in the spilled paint. The leaves that stuck to him from the spilled paint. They document all those details."

Sienna closed her eyes and pictured the leaves skittering around the treehouse like decomposed severed hands as Kai lay unconscious. They settled on his nose and mouth, over his eyes, and quickly obscured his face. A large leaf wider than a hand dropped onto Kai's face, covering his nose and mouth so he couldn't breathe. Then the blue leaf morphed into a hand holding the plastic bag over the boy's face.

Jordan cocked his head to the side as their dog might. "His face was bruised?"

"Indistinct, but likely fingertip bruises. It's reasonable for Kai to have some bruising following a traumatic episode," the detective said.

Sienna pictured a hand clasped over Kai's face.

"Earlier Sienna said she had a feeling Shane might have hurt him. Accidentally."

"The bruising is likely from Shane trying to help him. He says he can't remember," Detective Harris said. "Or they were self-inflicted. He might have fallen with enough force to cause slight bruising but not injure his hands. He might have even panicked and clutched at his own face instinctively, trying to breathe."

Jordan became tearful. "I should have been home," he said, the words catching in his throat as he lowered his head.

Jordan's movement and his choking words wrenched Sienna back to the moment. She allowed the numbness to steady her again as she watched him fight the idea of their son's final moments. He blocked his face as though he could hide. If no one saw him, if he didn't see them, then they weren't there. He could pretend their words were imaginary, like a ghost's screaming and howling he hadn't really heard and his rational mind could ignore.

She placed her hand on his free arm, but he recoiled and brought it up to join the other arm, shielding his face.

"My boy," Jordan said as he rocked forward and back, his face buried in his hands, only fragmented whimpers escaping.

"I'm sorry to ask you to go through this," Detective Harris said.

"Are the bruises from me? From the CPR?" Sienna asked, placing an arm around Jordan's shoulders. She clung to him as his back jerked every couple of seconds as if convulsing with tears.

Jordan sat up with red and watering eyes, his cheeks puffy. He swallowed hard and wiped his eyes on the rolled sleeve of his shirt.

"No, Sienna," Officer Rodriguez said. "You didn't cause the bruises."

"Well, I pinched his nose and held his face. I might have." Sienna stared at her with a solemn resignation, unafraid to look away or shy away from the details. She sat in front of Rodriguez braced for whatever she had to say. Unconsciously, she pressed her hand over her abdomen to stifle the dull pain that threatened to flare.

"There were slight abrasions on the sides of his nose and his mouth," Officer Rodriguez said and then turned to Sienna as she continued. "The medical examiner attributed them to post-mortem CPR attempts. There was no sign of bruising at the abrasion sites. He was already gone when you tried CPR."

It was confirmation of what Sienna already knew, bringing both hands to her lap, palms up toward the sky. She silently acknowledged that Kai was dead when she entered the treehouse. She had attempted to bring him back from the dead, hoping that God wouldn't take another child from her, hoping that a mother's love could bring forth life not just once at birth, but a second time when death came too soon. Hope had compelled her to try.

Jordan cleared his throat and adjusted his collar, making sure it was straight. He then smoothed his hair back into place. Sienna frowned through her heavy, closed eyelids. She knew it was Jordan's best effort to cope by injecting a degree of normalcy.

The detective turned to Sienna. "Do you know if Shane or Kai were roughhousing, or tussling, or in an argument?"

"No, I didn't hear anything like that. I don't know what happened outside."

"As Officer Rodriguez said, he's traumatized," Detective Harris said. "He can't remember where the bag was when he fled. He hasn't been much help. His parents are heartbroken and have given us permission to speak with him again. We haven't been able to get the full story from him."

"There's something wrong with that kid," Jordan said.

"What do you mean?" Detective Harris asked.

"He's got a foul mouth. Never when an adult is around. He puts on an act in front of us," Jordan said, nodding to Sienna. "But I've overheard him use profanity many times. Shocking language for a kid. We've considered not letting them play together but worried this wasn't a good time to complicate Kai's life."

"Did Kai or Shane know you had concerns about their friendship?" Detective Harris asked.

"Not really, no. Should I be worried that he might have—"

"I don't think Shane hurt him," Sienna interrupted. She didn't want them tormenting Shane. "He has older cousins he tries to impress with his language and the attitude he pulls sometimes. Tries to act older and tougher than he is."

Jordan placed a gentle hand over Sienna's hands resting on her churning abdomen. "You okay?"

She nodded, and Jordan pulled his hand back. "He should have gone inside. Gotten Sienna. She could have called 9-1-1 right away."

Detective Harris nodded slowly several times with a weak, sympathetic smile.

"Sienna, during the 9-1-1 call last night, the dispatcher on the line heard you say that all your children die and that you couldn't stop it. Do you remember that?"

"It's true, isn't it? My children are dead. I love them more than

I knew was possible. I'd trade my own life for theirs. I'd volunteer to spend an eternity in hell if only my children could live ordinary lives. I'd trade my soul, my health, my sanity, everything I have to give. But it didn't matter. My love for them didn't keep them alive."

The pain flared again, but it was a mild nuisance compared to the pain she'd felt in the treehouse early that morning.

"I think I need to lie down," she said to Jordan.

"Do I need to call someone?" he asked.

"No, I just need to rest."

Detective Harris closed a notepad and stood. "I'd like to take a quick look out back. You go get some rest, Sienna."

"I'll help you up to bed," Jordan said. He rubbed Sienna's back as he stood.

Sienna stood to go to bed and, for the first time, noticed the burgundy book from the study lying on the coffee table. "What's this doing here?" she asked as she picked it up and inspected the title. "*Charlotte's Web*. This was Kira's favorite as a little girl."

"I was thinking about her and looking at the book when the police arrived," Jordan said.

"Kira stopped eating pork at the age of nine because of Wilbur. By age thirteen, she didn't eat any meat at all, because of this book. Once she understood where meat came from, she refused to eat it. She loved animals so much. She had a tender heart," she said, opening the cover.

She turned to the title page, and a fresh, deep purple leaf the color of fruit slipped free and fluttered to the ground. Sienna gasped and skittered back from the leaf as though it was an exotic, poisonous snake preparing to strike. The book fell to the floor and landed open on the first page of the story. Another maple leaf protruded like an enormous insect.

Jordan picked up the book and the leaves. "I'm sorry. I pressed them in there for her." He crumpled the leaves in his fist and tucked them into his pocket.

"What's the matter?" Officer Rodriguez asked. Sienna remained frozen in place, apoplectic at the sight of the leaves.

"These leaves are from trees near our lake house," Jordan said. "We transplanted one to our backyard. It was Kira's favorite because of its unusual color. They're almost blue when the sun shines through them. Like peacock feathers. That's how she described them. The tree came down with the other big maple. I was going to save a couple of leaves."

Officer Rodriguez put her hand on Sienna's forearm but just as quickly pulled it back as though the expression of sympathy was inappropriate in front of the lead detective. "You mentioned the trees at your lake house yesterday. In the hospital. The painting reminded you of them. They do have a very pretty color, Sienna. I can see why they were her favorite."

"They found dried leaves in her mouth. Those leaves," she said, pointing to the leaves concealed in Jordan's pocket. "I had a vision of those leaves smothering my daughter. But they were blue. Like they were electrified."

Jordan put his arm around her waist and begin guiding her toward the stairs. "Let me get you to bed. You haven't had much sleep, and I know you're exhausted. So am I."

"The blue maple smothered Kai in my vision, too. When I meditated, I saw it," she continued. "These maple leaves have five lobes just like fingers on a hand."

"Maple leaves?" asked Detective Harris. "I'm sorry, calm down, Sienna. I'm confused."

"When I meditated, I saw the maples from the lake attack them. The blue leaves closed over his face. This wasn't an accident. Something happened to my son. And to Kira."

Jordan steered her to the stairs.

"Detective Harris, Officer Rodriguez, as you can see, we're having a tough time right now. It's a surreal mix of emotions we're going through. Neither one of us has had much sleep in the last thirty-six hours. And Sienna's pregnant. That's why she was at the hospital. The doctor said there are complications. I don't want her exerting herself. She really just needs bedrest and sleep. Those were the doctor's orders."

"Mr. Clarke, you take your wife to bed so she can rest. We'll wait down here for you."

"I hope you realize all you've done here is stoke a heartbroken woman's delusions. Those delusions are in her mind because of people saying she was negligent with Kira. Now they're doing it again. You're not helping things, detective. It's probably time you two left."

Sienna took the book from Jordan as he helped her to the stairs. She knew from the detective's expression that he thought she was out of her mind.

She glanced at Officer Rodriguez, who had teared up. Their eyes locked.

Jordan ushered her to their room, whispering in her ear. "Seriously? You're going to tell the police you're having visions of maple trees? You need to put this out of your mind. It's not healthy. You're trying to avoid reality. Did something else happen you don't want to face?"

"I'm not avoiding reality. I'm telling you what I saw. I just don't understand it."

"How long do you think you blacked out in the treehouse? They may ask again. You need to be ready to answer that. You don't want to give them ideas and make them start speculating. Unless, do you think, maybe, did you have some sort of mental break? Do you think it's possible you did something to Kai when you blacked out?"

Sienna sat on the edge of the bed, recalling the very moment she began CPR. She couldn't remember if she started with breathing or chest compressions or how many times she tried both. Specifics were missing. Her mind blocked those seconds like a glitch in a recording. Heat flared in her face as she admonished herself for not trying harder. Shaking her head, she kicked her shoes off and lay on the bed, convinced those details would come when she could bear the pain of them.

"I'm not going to let Facebook or you convince me that I hurt my kids."

"That's not what I'm trying to do! I'm asking because you probably just put that idea in those cops' heads, and that might make them start doubting everything you've said."

CHAPTER THIRTY

JORDAN FINISHED CHANGING INTO JEANS and tennis shoes and stood in the closet in front of a wall of Sienna's clothes—row after row of handbags and shoes. He thought he knew the woman who wore those things. Thought he understood everything about his wife but now felt as though he was in a stranger's closet. If she could hide her abortion from him for so many years, what else was she hiding? What had she experienced wearing some of those clothes on her many business trips without him? Was it all business? What else had she done in those clothes and those shoes? Was she capable of doing things he never imagined?

Jordan suppressed the thoughts, flicked off the light, and stepped out of the closet and over to the bedroom window. He twisted the blinds closed, dousing Sienna in a grey haze of shadow as she rested on the bed.

"You sure you don't need to go back to the hospital?"

Sienna shook her head at him.

"Do you need water or anything before I go back downstairs?"

She just shook her head again, like a child who embarrassed her parents in front of guests. He ran a hand along the top of her foot as he stepped past the bed and paused at the door.

"They're going to ask me about what you just said. What am I supposed to tell them? That my wife is crumbling under the guilt she feels?"

Sienna closed her eyes, but Jordan wanted an answer.

"Is that what's happening, Sienna? Do you want me to call Robin?" When she didn't answer, he switched gears.

"I talked to your mom. She's going to be here in a couple of days. We can figure out what we're going to do then. I told her we need her help. She's trying to get someone to stay with your stepdad. I told her what you've been saying about the trees. She's as worried about you as I am."

He immediately regretted blurting the criticism. He didn't want to agitate her further. He needed her to sleep.

Jordan noticed she had dropped *Charlotte's Web* onto her nightstand, and he wanted to retrieve the book and put it back in the study but left it there anyway.

"It should be quiet so you can sleep a little while. I'm going to get rid of them as fast as I can. I'll check on you in an hour or so. If you're asleep, I won't bother you. Please try and rest."

"I will," Sienna said.

Jordan stepped back into the hall and closed the door as though it had the durability of tissue paper and would rip if he used the slightest force. He started back down the hall to the main staircase but stopped and spun around on his heels toward the other end of the house. Instead, he walked to the narrow back staircase across from Sienna's office, the route originally built for servants that led into the kitchen. Using the wall as a handrail to guide himself down, he emerged at the other end and listened. Officer Rodriguez and Detective Harris were speaking in low voices. Edging into the dining room, he tried to make out their conversation.

"You wouldn't think that if you saw her at the hospital yesterday," Officer Rodriguez said. "She was sobbing and crying, like any mother would. I felt terrible even asking her questions about it."

"I've seen a lot of grieving parents before," Detective Harris said. "Not one tear from her today. She's almost stoic. Instead, we get this story about visions of leaves. I think she's scared. Scared she's in trouble. If it was Shane that died huffing paint under these circumstances, she might be looking at negligent homicide charges if the parents pressed it. She gave the boys the paint. Didn't check on them and couldn't see them to keep an eye on what they were doing."

Jordan fought the urge to interrupt the exchange and press the detective to explain what constituted negligent homicide. Instead, he remained quiet and still and listened.

"I think she's all cried out. Believe me, what I witnessed yesterday was an honest, sincere, emotional breakdown. I really don't know how to explain what she's talking about now. Maybe she's gone from an emotional breakdown to a full nervous breakdown. I don't know," Officer Rodriguez said.

"Play devil's advocate with me, will you? She's not crazy; she's not having a nervous breakdown. She's putting on an act with this garbage about visions trying to get our sympathy and to get us to say she has suffered enough. Get us to move on from looking any closer at whether she was negligent. This time or with the daughter. Possibly even get us to move on from looking for evidence of foul play."

"The obvious act would be sobbing and crying. If she were going to put on an act, she would go that route. It could be a defense mechanism. An escape mechanism. When she was her most vulnerable yesterday in the hospital grief room all alone, unable to reach her husband, her son in the morgue, her daughter in the grave, she saw a painting on the wall that resembled a happier place and reminded her of happier memories. The meadow at their lake house. The whole idea got lodged in her mind when she was in a state of shock, and she's clinging to it," Officer Rodriguez said.

Jordan silently agreed, nodding. It was apparent to them too that Sienna was in an extremely frail state of mind.

"That's very possible. But until we have toxicology, I'm not closing the door on any possibility. We have to just keep digging. Keep asking questions. What do you make of Sienna saying her mind went dormant in the treehouse? That she detached? Does that strike you as unusual?" Detective Harris said.

"I don't mean any disrespect, sir, but I just think she meant she had to separate herself from her emotions in order to act and try and save him. That's all."

"Officer Rodriguez, we've never worked this closely together on a case before. I wanted you here because you took her initial statement. Take my advice. Always try every angle of each piece of the puzzle. Twist it and turn it and flip it around to see if it fits into place. When you're convinced the pieces just won't snap together to make a pretty picture, then move on to different pieces. That's all I'm trying to get you to do. Sort the pieces of the puzzle on the table. Turn each piece right side up and look at the whole."

"Her husband is right," Officer Rodriguez said. "She's being tortured by people making all kinds of assumptions. Two child deaths at this house. I heard talk at the station this morning . . . "

"If I had hard evidence this was something other than huffing, I'd call in the FBI, and that reporter would turn this into national news. I'd have Shane in custody. He was the last one with Kai. I'd have her in custody, too. Technically, she was the last one with him. This house, this neighborhood would be on lockdown."

"I don't see anything to suggest it's not huffing. The wind blew the bag away from his face or the witnesses just don't remember everything exactly as it happened. Shane isn't acting. I don't think Sienna is, either."

"This kid may very well be a victim of the tragedy of drug abuse crippling this country," Detective Harris said. "Thousands die every year. I just don't know what to make of his mother. She doesn't think it's an accident. Mind you, no one ever wants to believe their kid could do something like this, but she's outright denying it."

"Devil's advocate, then. I can see she's in pain. I can feel it. Even if she isn't sobbing and putting it all on display. I think the artwork triggered her, and she conflated grief with suspicion, conflated grief with guilt. I can't even begin to imagine the level of misguided guilt any mother must feel when her child dies. She found her son in the treehouse, and she did her best to help him. There's no motive for anything else."

"Rodriguez, I've encountered some pretty shocking reasons that motivated people to do terrible things. But sometimes they aren't shocking at all. They're clichés from movies. Psychopaths can be patient and look for opportunity. And they are narcissistic enough to think they can get away with anything."

"Neither one of us thinks she's a psychopath, sir."

"Most likely, we've got a grieving mother refusing to believe her son would be reckless and frankly do something so stupid. It's easier for her to believe something else must have happened. To say it wasn't an accident. It's a tragic case for sure, but not remarkable. I'll feel better when toxicology results come in. They should show acidosis or high levels of toxins in his blood serum. Then I can chalk it up to a distraught, already unbalanced mother denying the truth about her son's actions. A terrible coincidence, losing two children in a year. I'm interested to see if she keeps this up after getting some sleep. I'm going to talk with her again after I consult with the medical examiner after he has finished his review of Kira's autopsy."

"The medical examiner is going to review Kira's autopsy, too?" Officer Rodriguez asked.

"The same medical examiner performed both. He told me he had an obligation to review Kira's results as well. To document there weren't any concerning similarities."

Sally appeared from the kitchen, her tags rattling, and she joined Jordan in the dining room. He quickly crept from the shadows of the dining room back to the kitchen and opened the refrigerator. After pulling two bottles of water, he lingered in the refrigerator door playing devil's advocate also.

He had waited for Officer Rodriguez to offer some explanation for Sienna's irrational comments other than she was losing her mind. He pondered what reopening Kira's autopsy might do to Sienna's sanity and if he could protest it. But they were only talking about reviewing the results, and he wondered if they would find something different, something new. He returned to the living room.

⋄⋄⋄

"Can I offer either of you some water?" he asked, interrupting their quiet debate.

They each accepted a bottle, and the detective took a gulp. "Thank you. It's hot outside," he said, setting the container on the end table. "So, your wife is pregnant?"

"Yes, a couple months along."

"Congratulations."

"Congratulations," Officer Rodriguez echoed.

Jordan resumed a seat on the sofa. "It's difficult to celebrate one child when we're grieving for another. You can see why she's in such a state. Saying those irrational things. I'm going to suggest she talk with a grief counselor right away. I just wish I could have been with her yesterday, doing something to help her, comfort her at least. Or let her comfort me. Maybe if she had something else to focus on all night, she wouldn't be talking like this now. If I hadn't gotten drunk. Hadn't gotten arrested." He leaned forward with his face in his hands then rubbed his eyes.

"You didn't seem surprised when she said she had visions of leaves and that this wasn't an accident," Detective Harris said.

"She said the same thing to me earlier this morning. Said she went up into the treehouse because our neighbor told her she sensed Kai there after his death. I'm sure that's where this, this stuff about leaves and visions all started. Desperation fed by a well-intentioned neighbor. She's not in her right mind. Hopefully, some rest will help. Besides, if Shane did deliberately hurt Kai, the investigators would have found evidence. Or is it too early in the investigation to say?"

"Child-on-child murder is extremely rare, Mr. Clarke. Ideally, Shane will be better able to tell us what happened when we talk with him again. I'd like to question Sienna again as well after she has gotten some sleep and her nerves are settled down a little. Tomorrow morning, perhaps. I noticed you focused speculation on Shane, not your wife. Do you have any concerns about her to share with us? About her finding Kai in the treehouse?"

"None of us have been ourselves since Kira died. Sienna pretends to be doing better lately, but I think it's an act. An attempt to shield Kai from her depression. She was taking anti-depressants for months. She's emotionally susceptible. Surely you can understand that. She speaks about the tree with these purple and blue leaves as a *mother tree*. That's what she called it. She's talking about herself, really. I think she's trying to deflect some guilt. She was the only person around when Kira died, and she blames herself."

Jordan looked from the detective to the officer, trying to read their reactions, but both seemed practiced at concealing their emotions. He took a breath and continued trying to sound rational and controlled.

"Kira's death was an accident, but at first there were questions about her not having other serious injuries after falling from the treehouse. No broken bones. Only the head injury. But then they figured out the leaves cushioned her fall. She hit her head on a thick root protruding up into the leaves. No one saw Kira fall. Or maybe she jumped. We don't know. But they quickly figured out her death was accidental. The fact that Sienna was under the microscope for Kira's death scarred her. It haunts her. She was home alone with Kai, too, so naturally she is already blaming herself for his accident, and it manifests with these meditation visions. She knows too much about trees. How they protect each other. She moved here from Texas to study forests. She's clinging to something familiar, I think."

Jordan's eyes filled with tears, and his lip quivered. Voices of people gathered out front drew everyone's attention.

"This neighborhood is usually very quiet," Jordan said. "That's a riot, a mob scene compared to the absence of life you'll usually notice. Lots of older people in this neighborhood. Not a lot of kids out playing."

"It's a nice neighborhood. It seems very private. Every house seems private," Officer Rodriguez offered.

"Sienna and I fell in love with this place. All the trees around the property and between the houses. The marsh behind us that extends as far as the eye can see that prevents anyone from building back there. We thought this was the perfect place to raise our family. If we hadn't bought it, we'd still be a family." He sat on the sofa and rubbed his eyes again. Fatigue was taking over. "I really need to try and get some rest. A couple of hours at least, then we can try and focus on the funeral services."

"I'm sorry, but funeral services have to be put on hold until our investigation is complete. A few more days."

"What? No. You heard the irrational things she's been saying. The projecting. Delaying his funeral will only make things worse. She needs to have a funeral. Say goodbye and allow herself to grieve."

"A few days, no more. You can do the planning, just don't set a date." He stood again, as did Officer Rodriguez. "We'll let you rest, Mr. Clarke. I'm sorry there isn't anything we can do about the ruckus in front of your house. It might calm down if you and Sienna come into the police department to answer our follow-up questions, give DNA samples or fingerprints if needed. Better than having us come back unless we need to."

"Agreed. My phone and car are still at the hotel, but I've got Kai's phone, and we have Sienna's, too. What would DNA and fingerprints be for?"

"Forensics will match them up with anything found at the scene during the investigation. To account for everything. We'll be in touch again tomorrow. Thank you for speaking with us," he said, extending his hand.

Jordan shook hands with both cops and escorted them to the door. Officer Rodriguez motioned toward the news van.

"Don't let them get under your skin. Get some rest, Mr. Clarke."

Jordan didn't wait for them to get down from the porch before shutting the door. He listened as the small crowd of neighbors and the news crew reignited their questions. A female voice called out, "Are we safe here? Is that woman dangerous?"

CHAPTER THIRTY-ONE

IT WAS DAYLIGHT WHEN SIENNA awoke, but she needed the dark. She wanted to crane her head to see the time on the bedside clock, but her entire body was weak and sore. Breathing seemed to take energy she didn't have.

She had been dreaming of Kai's funeral. It was an amalgamation of Kira's funeral and every representation of a church she had ever entered.

She tried recalling the dream. She remembered tilting her head toward the vaulted ceiling, wiping away tears spilling down her cheeks, and consciously willing herself to breathe deeply. The numbness that cradled her during her interview with the police continued into the dream but was less than vivid, like a dull current of a weak battery.

In the dream, she felt numb as hundreds of mourners turned their tear-streaked faces in unison to see her as she stepped inside the cathedral staged for a funeral. In the dim light, Kai's silver coffin glistened.

Opening her eyes again, she lifted her head from the pillow. It was three-thirty in the afternoon. She'd been asleep for a couple of hours but didn't feel rested. Letting her head fall back to the pillow, she tried to sleep some more, but her mind wouldn't allow it. She needed to focus on Kai's funeral arrangements. Needed to call her mother back. And Monica was probably expecting a call, too. She had too many things to attend to. Sleep would have to wait.

As she willed herself to get up, focus on what she needed to do, it struck her that in her dream, she was the only member of Kai's family present. She pondered Jordan's accusation that she wasn't facing her own reality. That maybe she hurt the kids and blocked it out. That whatever she did to them had manifested in her meditation.

Then she thought about how her fixation on the leaves must have looked from his perspective. She couldn't blame him for wondering what she was talking about—or hiding. Sienna took a deep breath and exhaled, letting go of her anger toward him.

She opened her eyes again. The burgundy spine of the book with *Charlotte's Web* in gold lettering stared back. Closing her eyes, she recollected reading the book to her precious daughter. The grief counselor, Robin, had said that memories she didn't know she had would come to her. Images of reading *Charlotte's Web* was one of them. She tried to wring joy from the memory.

The password! Maybe she tried the wrong favorite book title as the password. Kira was always reading something and had been focused on a young adult vampire trilogy at the time of her death. But maybe her favorite story from childhood was the password. Climbing from the bed, Sienna slipped on her shoes and crept to the door. The house was quiet. She stepped into the hall and down to Kira's room. Without needing to brace herself, she stepped inside and closed the door behind her.

Sienna lifted the laptop lid and urged the system to boot faster. When the password screen came up, she typed *Charlotte's*

Web, but the computer denied her access. She tried *Wilbur* and *E.B. White,* but to no avail. She tried upper case, lower case, first letter capitalization, but nothing worked. Frustrated, she flipped the pages of the book like shuffling cards, pondering what she was missing.

Then it struck her. She typed *Some Pig* and pressed the enter key. The computer buzzed to life for the first time since her daughter's death. Sienna's heartbeat quickened, and she sucked in a short breath of delight.

She clicked on the Windows home button, and a list of options popped up, including Kira's most recently used apps and file locations. Scanning them, she looked for anything related to her music. Nothing jumped out.

Then she opened her browser and clicked on the history. She read through the list of websites for anything that might hint at where she would find Kira's music, but they were mostly news sites. Optimistic her music had to be on the computer, she went back to the home button and pulled up Kira's recent activity. Other than the web browser, she had last opened her photos folder, so Sienna clicked on it.

The folder contained over three thousand pics. Selfie after selfie. Pictures of Kira's friends. Screenshots from her phone of things she liked on Instagram. Sienna was about to close the folder and continue searching for music but noticed a subfolder with a date instead of a name. The label read *October 20,* two days before Kira died. She clicked on it, and inside were a series of video clips. Intrigued, she played the first one.

It opened with Kira standing on their deck at the lake house, recording herself with her cellphone as she narrated the video. The familiar reds, oranges, and yellows of fall color from the forest of trees around the lake in the background framed her face.

"Hi, guys, I'm going on an adventure," she had said.

Sienna hit the pause button. Staring into Kira's face, a rush of love and gratitude came over her as she relished the fresh image of her beautiful little girl. The school T-shirt she wore was still folded in her dresser. Kira's smile beamed from her lips and through her eyes, as was her way. The morning sun that radiated through her chestnut hair shimmered on the rippling lake behind her with the brilliance of a million gold coins. Sienna put a hand at the base of her throat, and felt her heart beating, and returned a smile to Kira, then restarted the video.

"I'm alone," Kira said, "so I'm going to record it and post it on Instagram when I have Wi-Fi again. I'm going to talk with you along the way, so it feels like my friends are with me. I'm at our lake house. We were here a couple months ago and found a meadow full of beautiful maple trees. They have deep purply-blue leaves. When the sun shines through them, they look indigo, like as in deep blue. Indigo is what they use to dye jeans for those of you who don't know. The leaves are so pretty. I want to see what a big group of them looks like in the fall.

"My dad brought me out here this weekend. We were supposed to take the boat out. My brother was supposed to come, too, but he bailed on us to have a sleepover with his friend's cousins. And now my dad bailed on me. He had to go back to town to show a house and won't be back for a few hours. That's my dad. If he thinks he can make a sale, everything else has to wait!

"I'm supposed to stay in and read. But why should I, right? If he's not going to do what he said, why should I? I'm going out there to photograph the trees. My mom wants to study them. She's on another business trip, but I wish she was here. She'll be excited to see the pictures. So anyway, it's just me. Oh, and Sally." The camera panned down to the yellow Lab. "Say hi, Sally!" The camera returned to Kira. "We're going on a hike in the woods. I'll record another video when I get there and maybe one along the way."

The recording ended with Kira waving to the audience.

Sienna restarted the video and paused it the instant Kira's face came into focus. She kissed her fingertips and pressed them to the screen over Kira's lips. She smiled at her daughter, grateful for the fresh encounter with her and the reminder of how intrepid she was.

She sat for a moment thinking about that weekend before Kira's death. While she was out of town, Jordan planned to take the kids out to the lake, and Kira said she wanted him to guide them on a hike back to the meadow. But when Sienna asked her about it once they were all back home, Kira said she didn't make it out to see the trees. Kira sounded and acted strangely evasive, she remembered. Knowing her daughter's expressions and mannerisms so well, it was apparent to Sienna Kira wasn't giving her the whole story. At the time, she assumed Jordan backed out of the hike when Kai stayed behind. She figured Kira must have had an argument with her dad about the trek, making it a sore subject, so she didn't push her.

Tucking her hair behind her ear, Sienna clicked on the next video. Again, Kira popped onto the screen. She was in the forest, but this time she had her hoodie tied around her waist. It was still early in the day as light shined directly overhead filtered by the maple branches, which had lost most of their leaves that crunched under her feet as she walked. There were occasional clusters of brilliant color refusing to yield to the season.

"Okay, guys, so I thought I knew exactly how to get to the meadow. Turns out, I don't. I've been walking over an hour. I should have reached it by now. There isn't an established trail that leads to it. I've turned, and I'm walking east now. This will eventually take me to a dirt fire road that leads in and out of the state forest behind our property, so you can't ever really get lost here even though it feels like it. So, just a quick reminder. Always be prepared. My mom works in forests, and we hike like all the time. I have water," which Kira held up to the screen. "I made sure to bring some for Sally, too, so don't think I forgot about her." The dog stood by obediently in the background looking in various directions as Kira paused for the recording. "I have my sweatshirt in case it gets cooler. I also have my compass on my phone, and I know the direction that leads me out of here. Sorry, guys, this adventure is going to have to be a two-part series. I'll try to find the meadow again next time. I'm heading back."

Sienna closed the video and counted four more clips and clicked on the next one. Sally appeared on the screen, barking her familiar alert bark. "Guys, I'm a little freaked out," Kira said off screen. She panned the camera around. Ahead in the distance, a group of thirty or forty maples with deep purple leaves with crisp, midnight blue edges shined in the sun like masses of plastic streamer flags decorating the forest. They fluttered on a breeze in the center of the meadow. She had found the meadow. Kira and Sally walked toward the trees through knee-high grasses.

"I don't know how I ended up here. I was walking east. I thought. Maybe my compass isn't working since I don't have a cell signal, but I don't think it needs one. I don't know. But here it is. This is the meadow. Isn't this place amazing?" She continued panning from one side of the meadow to the other using swift and uncontrolled movements of a novice videographer. "These trees are special. My mom studies trees and said this leaf color is pretty rare. Like maple plums. We dug one up and moved it to our house, but seeing this many of them grouped together is amazing. They are prettier than I even remember. They haven't really started changing for fall. This species must be able to take colder weather."

Kira turned the camera back to her face, her eyes red and puffy. Clearly, she'd been crying. "So, I thought I was lost. I've been walking for at least two hours. I went in different directions, trying to find the road, but instead, I found the meadow. Hush, Sally," she said to quiet her barking. "When I got here, I walked all around the meadow until I found this tree." Panning down, she directed the camera to the fallen tree struck by lightning the day they rediscovered the meadow. "We were here when lightning struck this tree, and it caught fire. It was so intense. That was like the scariest day of my life. This is the direction back to our lake house, though. Now I know which way to head back. So, I'm going to take a bunch of pictures, and I'm going to find my dad's old treehouse." She spun the camera back to the trees in a dizzying swoop. "Inside there, my dad built a treehouse when he was a kid about my age. I'll make another recording when I find it."

Sienna rewound the video to where Kira focused on the mother tree in the center. She paused it, letting the deep purple and blue brilliance of the tree fill the screen. Seeing it again didn't terrify her like she would have guessed. It thrilled her. The tree was majestic and glorious. The glossy leaves shined in the sun with the iridescence of countless feathers as though the tree might flutter and lift into the sky.

Sienna recalled Kira saying she hadn't gone back to the meadow that weekend after she asked her about it. She asked if her dad had taken her back to see the maples like she wanted, but Kira had said no. Obviously, she did go back out there, so why would she have lied about it? It occurred to Sienna that was the reason Kira had acted strange when she asked her about the meadow. Because Kira lied straight to her mom's face.

Confused but still marveling at the beauty of the trees, Sienna pressed play. Kira held her cellphone camera on the tree for twenty seconds. As the wind caused the leaves to flutter, they sparkled and glimmered in the sun like gems. All the word's amethysts ever polished and cut and set to adorn a neck or finger or ears, all sapphires ever mined were dangling and twinkling on the tree.

Sienna realized she had been holding her breath the entire time Kira focused the camera on the tree. Staring at it was all-consuming, and it captivated her with its beauty. Sienna smiled. *She's magnificent*, she thought. *She, the mother tree, is a she*. Her lips broke into a smile at the idea that her daughter appreciated the significance and wonder and splendor of the tree as much as she did. Her fear of it vanished.

Closing her eyes, she remembered all the horrible visions of her children that stalked her in the treehouse while meditating. They were the same images. The leaves and saplings were there, but she didn't feel repulsion; she felt something entirely different. The tree no longer frightened or repulsed her.

Sienna realized she had been staring at the wall only after her gaze returned to the computer screen as her reaction to the recalled images morphed. It dawned on her that her mind warned her when she meditated.

She closed the video and right clicked on properties, hoping she could tell what time Kira recorded the video, but she didn't see it and didn't know where else to look.

She clicked on the next video.

"Guys, tell me I'm crazy." Kira had the camera pointed at the sky. A vast pale blue expanse with a single cloud puff like a cotton ball hovered overhead. "This cloud doesn't move. Trust me. It's the only cloud, so it stands out. But watch. It doesn't move. It doesn't drift or anything. Watch. It's like it's frozen." She brought the camera back to her face. "It's true. It's stuck there like this is the top of the world, and the cloud has nowhere to go." She aimed the camera back at the cloud. "I just had to show you that. See, it's still stuck there."

Sienna could hear Kira's voice, but the camera captured the tree in the background. Sienna felt the royal purple and blue maple summoning her. She needed to see it. Touch its leaves.

CHAPTER THIRTY-TWO

SIENNA SLIPPED FROM KIRA'S ROOM and into her bathroom to answer her ringing phone but didn't get to it in time. She missed Yvonne's call and noticed a couple of unread text messages, too.

The first was from her mom. "Call me when you wake up. I love you. I'll get there as fast as I can. I'm working on it."

The second text was from Monica. "Gary and I are heartbroken for you and Jordan. If you need anything, we'll be over there day or night. Don't hesitate. We are praying for you both and for Kai."

Sienna stared at the words in the text bubble, and her heart sank. Monica said she would come by the house. She didn't know if she wanted to see her or anyone. But it hurt that rather than insisting on coming over and consoling her, insisting on holding her friend as she cried, insisting on sharing in her pain hoping to help her endure it, Monica chose to leave it to Sienna to beg for support. It hadn't felt like they were best friends for months. Now it felt like they were acquaintances who occasionally bumped into each other at a seminar or convention. It was the type of message a colleague would send.

She swiped to the next text. It was from Yvonne. "Just checking on you, sweetheart. I know you might not have an appetite, but you have to eat. I've got some food I want to bring by when you're ready. I hope you're sleeping. Text me when you wake up and I'll pop over for two minutes."

She had a second message from Yvonne. "Sweetheart if you're sleeping, I hope you have your phone on silent. I don't want to wake you, but I do want you to know I'm here. I've got some food for you two. I'm a shoulder you can cry on if you need me."

As she was reading, a third message from Yvonne popped up. "I just called but didn't get an answer. I'd like to stop by just for a minute and give you a hug and make sure you're okay. See if there is anything you or Jordan need. I'm your neighbor, and I'm your friend. Let me help if I can. Call me back." Yvonne added thoughts and prayers emojis.

Slipping the phone into her back pocket, Sienna headed downstairs in search of Jordan, despite having no desire to see him. She tried to grapple with his remarks but knew raw emotion would surface when she saw him.

She found Jordan asleep on the sofa and Sally on the floor next to him. Peeking out front before waking Jordan, she saw two news vans outside, but fewer neighbors. *The afternoon heat must have them trapped inside,* she figured. They could be outraged, but only if it was cool enough.

There were remnants of a sandwich on a plate on the coffee table along with a banana peel and orange peel. The thought of eating food right then seemed like a chore she couldn't suffer. Like cleaning house or running errands. But she knew she should eat and couldn't blame him for managing to do it.

Before Sienna had the chance to nudge him, Jordan opened his eyes. His eyes again made her think of blue sapphire. They radiated the light that also brightened his face and gleamed in his hair. She stepped to the end of the sofa.

"It's after three-thirty. This is about the time that Kai came into the office asking for the paint. It's only been one day."

Jordan sat up, and his legs bumped Sally. She stood and waddled toward the back door. "I'll let her out," he said, rising from the sofa, grabbing his plate.

Sienna sat on the sofa where he'd been sleeping. "You get much sleep?" she asked when he returned.

"Some. Enough. I see another van has shown up. I imagine there will be others. That will bring the neighbors back. You don't want to hear what's being said."

"Couldn't be worse than what's online."

A quiet stillness enveloped them. Before it got awkward or he tried to apologize for his earlier remarks, she said, "Did you know Kira went out to the meadow with the maples all alone the last time she was at the lake house?"

"What? No. Why do you say that?"

"I was searching for some of her music on her laptop and found some pictures and videos she took that day."

"Pictures of what?"

"The trees mostly. For her Instagram."

"I thought her phone was broken in her fall."

"She transferred them. She lied to me. I asked her about the hike out there, and she said she didn't go. I knew she was hiding something. I'm not surprised she didn't tell either one of us. She knows she shouldn't have been way out there by herself and knew we'd be pissed. Silly girl."

"Kai wanted to use her laptop a couple of months ago. He said it needed a password. I told him I didn't know it but that I wanted him to leave it alone anyway. It felt too soon to start distributing her things. You knew the password?"

"I guessed it. *Some Pig.*"

Jordan huffed his amusement. "So did you find her music?"

"No, but I'm still looking. It's nice to see the lake through her eyes," she said.

"Earlier, I was thinking we could go out to the lake. Overnight. Maybe two days. Escape from the torture of these idiots outside. Let all this settle down."

"We can't. We have the funeral to attend to. My mom's coming. Other family, too."

"Detective Harris said the medical examiner is going to hold Kai's body for a couple of days. We got Kira back after two days. We don't have to stay to make funeral plans. I'm sure I can get someone from the funeral home to drive out to us if that's what you want. I think we should do the same things we did for Kira."

Sienna didn't comment. She replayed the ornate funeral service from her dream.

"We're more experienced at funeral planning than anyone ever should be," Jordan said. "We can have them drive out, or it can wait two days until they release him. Either way, I don't want reporters or neighbors stressing you out. We have to protect the baby. Maybe they'll leave us alone by the end of the night, or maybe there will be other news crews that camp out. When Detective Harris and Officer Rodriguez left, they had to dodge questions from the neighbors and the reporters. It was chaotic. I don't want you subjected to this," he said, waving toward the spectators out front. "We can't stay here."

Sienna knew he was right; the duress caused by the media and neighbors wasn't good for the pregnancy. She could make an appointment to see her OBGYN tomorrow or the next day. It seemed a good idea to get away from their house that should be bustling with the sounds of her kids. Being there was no different from driving down the main street of so many small towns across America with all their storefronts boarded up. Everything in sight was a reminder of what used to be and a reminder of what would never be again.

"Your mom would probably encourage you to walk the lake, find your peace out there since she can't be here for a few days. I say we go now before more reporters show up and before the crowd returns. I'll drive your car. You can sleep."

The video of the maples in the meadow surged to the forefront of her mind. The alluring color, its grandeur. The tree beckoned her. Their leaves twinkling in the autumn sun in Kira's video called to her. She nodded her agreement. "Okay, but what about your car? Your phone?"

"I guess they can stay there for now. I don't know for sure my phone is even there. I called it earlier, but no one answered. They might tow my car. It's in front of the hotel, not in the guest lot behind it. If I send my assistant or ask someone else, they'll want to know why it's there."

Sienna's phone chimed and vibrated in her pocket, signaling a new text. "They might tow it," she said as she pulled her phone out. "It's Yvonne. She has called and texted a few times. She said she has some food for us. She's worried about me. She found me hanging out of the treehouse. There's no telling what she thinks. Probably that I'm going to hurt myself. Or that I'm going to lose the baby. I can't ignore her. I need to respond." She read the text aloud.

"Can I pop in for literally one minute and check on you? Drop off some food and help with anything you need?"

Sienna looked up. "I appreciate her concern. It was so good of her to stay with me in the hospital this morning. I'm going to tell her we're up and that she can drop off the food."

She typed and sent a quick response and set her phone on the sofa. "Maybe Yvonne would get your car and your phone, so we can go ahead and leave for the lake. She already knows about your arrest and everything that's happened."

The voices from the street reactivated. Sienna craned her

neck to see the commotion outside. "They're probably hounding Yvonne out there. The neighbors saw her with me when the ambulance was here this morning."

Jordan stood to open the door for Yvonne with a chorus of galvanized neighbors trying to get her to answer questions from the street.

"These people are relentless," Yvonne said, hurrying inside toting a large, white rectangular bag in each hand. "I ordered you some Italian. This stuff can sit in the refrigerator for a couple of days and will easily heat up in the microwave. This way, no one has to cook."

Sienna stood and greeted her in the entry as Yvonne passed the bags off to Jordan, who carried them into the kitchen. "You didn't have to do that, but I appreciate that you did."

"Thanks for checking on us. I managed to sleep a little. Jordan did, too," she said as he returned to the living room.

Yvonne stepped over to Jordan and gave him a quick hug.

"The baby's okay, too. I don't have any pain at all right now," Sienna said.

"Your baby will know how much he or she is loved by how much pain you're in over losing Kira and Kai."

"I'm worried my sadness could affect the baby. A mother shouldn't be grieving while she's carrying a child. My mood could influence development. I want to be positive, but my heart is broken."

"You only hurt this much because of love. The baby can feel love above all else. It will be fine," she said, rubbing Sienna's arm. "Okay, I just wanted to give you both a hug and let you know I'm here for you if you need anything. You don't want to step foot outside. Trust me. That reporter is an asshole. All right, I don't want to intrude any further. I'll let you be, but before I go, is there anything you need?"

"We're going to drive out to our lake house for a night or two and get away from the crowd. It's a little over an hour away, so we want to head that way now."

"I think that's a good idea. It's probably quiet and private. The opposite of what you'll find on the street outside."

"The kids loved it out there. We were always happy there. It's calling to me. I think it will be good for me. I feel different there."

Jordan stepped from the living room, joining them in the foyer. "We could use a favor. I was arrested at Library Bar in the Montrose Hotel yesterday. My car is there, and my phone, too, I think. I can use Find My iPhone to be sure. I'm worried my car is going to get towed and my phone might disappear. If we got you an Uber, would you be willing to get my phone and drive my car back to your house? I hate to inconvenience you, but I really don't have the patience to try and explain to anyone else what happened yesterday."

"My friend Robby works at Library Bar. I go there sometimes. Before my divorce, I went there a lot," Yvonne said, issuing a frown. "Too much, probably. Actually, I think he told me about you. Well, I didn't know it was you, but he told me a man was arrested there yesterday."

Jordan ran the back of his fingers over the stubble on his chin and neck. "That was me. God, I hope I didn't offend your friend. I'm so embarrassed."

Yvonne pulled her cellphone from the pocket in the thigh of her leggings only there to hold a phone. "It's almost four. He's probably there by now. Let me call and see if they have your phone."

"It's an iPhone in a Louis Vuitton case," Jordan said.

Sienna and Jordan inspected the food and placed it in the refrigerator while she made the call. Yvonne joined them.

"Your phone is there, and your car is still out front," Yvonne said. "I told him not to let anyone tow it."

"Let us get the Uber for you," Sienna said.

"Please. You two get ready to go. When you get back, your

car will be in my garage, and I'll have your phone. I'll charge it. I'll head over there now," Yvonne said, accepting the keys from Jordan and making her way to the front door.

Sienna followed her and gave her another quick hug in the foyer. "Thanks for your help."

"Text me when you're ready to leave, and I'll back my car out and block the street so the media can't follow you," she said with a wink. "An hour might not seem like a long drive, but when you're emotional, it could feel like an eternity, so drive safe. Be safe."

"I'll pack a few things," Jordan said as Sienna closed the door. "My running shoes. It's been so long I don't remember exactly what I have there. Do you want me to pack a few things for you?"

"I can do it. I want my good robe." Sienna headed up the stairs. Having a task was a welcome distraction.

As she climbed, she decided she might want to stay at the lake until they released Kai. There she and Jordan could have their own space. At home, they would be captive to the patrolling media and neighbors, locked inside together with no escape. She detoured on her way to the closet and stopped in Kira's room. She lifted *Charlotte's Web* and the laptop along with its power cord from the desk. On her way out the door, she placed the book on Kira's pillow and hugged the computer like it was her daughter.

CHAPTER THIRTY-THREE

SALLY'S TAGS JINGLED WHEN SHE stood on the back seat of Sienna's SUV. She spun in a full circle then plopped in the same spot, waking Sienna from her light sleep in the passenger seat next to Jordan. Sienna opened her eyes into the brightness of the setting sun shining on a forest of trees, the rays lighting a path guiding them to the spot where she would find peace. The area was familiar. They were close to the lake house.

"You were sleeping. That's good," Jordan said. "Honestly, I'm surprised you agreed to go to the lake."

"It'll be good to get away for a while." She opened the window a crack to allow for some air to circulate but also to generate a noise buffer.

"You still afraid of the forest trying to hurt the baby?"

"I needed to rest. My mind has been boiling over with emotions."

"Guilt is a powerful thing. Regret. I mean regret is a powerful thing." He turned on the radio and found the local news and talk station.

The broadcaster babbled on until he reached the traffic and weather segment. He predicted strong winds, some gale force. Sienna thought the weather forecast mimicked her fury of emotions. A tornado swirled inside her.

Minutes later, Jordan pulled off the highway at the last grocery store before the road took them deeper into the forest toward their house. "I'm going to stop at the store. Get the bare essentials. We can have Italian for dinner, but we need breakfast food. Stuff for sandwiches. Especially if you're serious about staying a couple days. Is there anything specific you want or need?"

"Get some water. Orange juice. Did you bring dog food?"

"No, I forgot. I'll get some," he said, pulling into a spot several spaces away from the entrance even though the lot was virtually empty. "Okay, I'll be back in ten or fifteen minutes. Text me if you think of anything."

Sienna locked the door and watched him walk inside, thinking he hadn't heard a word she told him earlier. She never said she feared the forest. In fact, she already felt better now that she was near it. Soothed by the anticipation of stepping into it and walking amongst the trees she loved. They would be at the house soon. Well before dark. She could still take a walk.

❧❧❧

Twisting in the seat, she reached for her bag. Unzipping it in her lap, she pulled Kira's laptop free, opened the lid, switched it on, and returned to the folder with pictures and the subfolder of videos. She was anxious to view the three remaining videos but waited to watch them alone and allow herself to succumb to the idea Kira was talking directly to her. The two of them cloistered away, the only two people on earth, sharing an intimate moment. A mother-daughter moment she would never again have another chance to relish.

She opened the next video. It began with Kira. She had the camera pointed at herself.

"I've taken lots of photos today. Make sure to like them on a separate Instagram post. I'm at the treehouse. Well, what's left of it." Kira panned to the derelict structure as Sally barked off screen. "Sally, quiet girl," she said without taking the phone off the treehouse. "Okay, so it's not much to look at, but it's still cool. They built it so long ago, way out here. I think that's cool." She focused on remnants of the treehouse several feet above. A few lateral logs nestled among the branches. Bright afternoon sunshine filtered through the abundant purple leaves fringed in blue that seemed unaffected by fall. As Kira walked with the camera pointed up, light repeatedly flickered directly into the lens. The dog lumbered along, her tags tinkling off screen. "We don't come out to the lake much. I wish we did. My mom's always on work trips, and my dad works all the time, too. Don't parents know that there are some kids who do want to be outdoors, not just on their phones all the time? We could camp out here with these trees in summer."

Kira pointed the camera at her face without turning it slowly enough to avoid making the world around her whirl into a blur. "Can you imagine waking up under a blue sky and branches covered with these pretty leaves?" The tree's limbs seemed to bend under the weight of the leaves.

Off screen, Sally could be heard barking and her tags rattling. "What are you doing, girl?" She directed the camera to the ground. Sally was a few yards away. Kira stepped over slim severed stumps Sienna remembered from the first visit to the meadow.

Kira focused on a spot where the dog was digging. "What is that?" Only a few inches below the surface, the dog uncovered a sliver of what looked like bone. "Oh, Sally, yuck. Leave that. *Eww.* That's nasty." She shewed the dog away from it. The camera caught a glint of sun reflecting off something in the dirt. "There's something here," Kira said, squatting. She held the camera with one hand while rooting in the soil with the other. "It's an old purse or wallet or something." She uncovered frayed fragments of shiny red vinyl like patent leather. "It's a purse." She found the handle and pulled on it, but it snapped free, leaving the purse embedded. Using her hands, she clawed away more dirt until she freed it and lifted what remained of a disintegrating handbag. Its contents spilled when the bottom fell open. A matching red wallet, a hairbrush, keys, and a few cosmetics landed in the shallow hole she dug them out of.

Kira ignored Sally's barking as she fished the wallet from the pile and opened it. In the spot designed for a driver's license, a high school ID from 1997 revealed the purse belonged to Rhona Adams from Minneapolis, Minnesota.

A voice called out from behind her. "What are you doing here?"

Startled, Kira gasped and dropped the phone. It landed face up and continued recording. The lens captured the seemingly frozen, single bulbous cloud hovering above. Sienna stared at it suspended on the computer screen like a puffy cotton ball she could pluck.

"Dad! You scared me!" Kira said.

"Did you follow me?" It was Jordan's voice.

"No, I didn't follow you. I thought you were back in Madison for the day. You said you had a client."

Sally's tags rattled again, accompanied by the sound of digging. "I found a purse and a wallet."

"You shouldn't be here, Kira."

"I wanted to see the trees again. Someone named Rhona Adams lost her purse out here in 1997."

"Kira, you shouldn't be here!" Jordan shouted. Even Sally seemed startled into suspended animation.

"If you hadn't bailed on me, maybe I wouldn't be out here!"

"You know how mad your mother will be if she finds out you hiked out here alone. Especially after that lightning storm. You will disappoint her, Kira. And you will make her disappointed in herself. She thinks she has taught you to respect the forest. Respect the danger. Clearly, she failed. Clearly, you don't respect her, either, or you wouldn't flagrantly disregard everything she has tried to teach you and Kai. I'm really surprised, Kira. I thought you were more mature and more responsible than this. I really did."

"I'm sorry, Dad. I was mad at you for choosing work instead of being out here with me. I wasn't thinking. Please don't tell her. Please."

"Come on. Let's go."

"What about this stuff?"

"Leave it. That's from over twenty years ago. Probably some kids crossed over from the state forest onto our land without realizing it. Probably camped out."

"We can't leave it. We need to get it back to her."

"Give me the wallet." The foliage rustled against his jeans as she stepped closer and flipped the wallet open. "Four dollars and some pictures. A few slips of paper. There's really nothing to return." The plastic cosmetic cases clicked together as he collected the purse. "This stuff is just trash. Now let's go. We need to walk to the fire road."

"Why? Isn't that twice as far as going straight to the house?"

"On foot, yes, but a section of the fire road bends this way. I drove into the forest. My car is parked that way. I didn't know you were out here. You surprised me, too. My appointment got canceled, so I decided to hike out here. I don't ever get to come out here. I thought you wanted to read down by the lake, so I hiked out here on my own. Let's get going."

More jingling of Sally's tags off camera. "What does she keep digging at? Look!" she gasped. "Those are bones! Is that a hand!"

"Sally, get back!" The phone captured the sound of him kicking or pushing dirt and leaves. "There could be rabies on that."

"Dad, that looked like a skeleton."

"Yes, an animal skeleton. Rabbit bones or a fox. We're in the middle of the forest. A rabbit probably made this purse a home at some point. Now let's get going."

The image of the sky swooped as Kira picked up her phone. The lens captured the opposing vantage, the ground, as Kira held her phone, apparently looking at her screen and noticing it was still recording. Sienna got a hint of the grey sweatshirt knotted at Kira's waist and the white tennis shoes laced on her feet just as the recording ended. Sienna looked up from the laptop, searching for Jordan but not seeing him. The store itself had a low-profile roof and sloping eaves to minimize snow accumulation, but they obscured much of the windows and the activity inside. She replayed the video and scanned forward until she reached the point that Kira pointed the camera at Sally digging. When the white bones were in view, she paused it. It was larger than any rabbit bones. It looked like the forearm bones of a small human arm white against the black soil and debris of leaves and moss like the disturbed grave of a forest pixie.

She looked up again to see Jordan at the front of the store. He was smiling and chatting with the young female clerk. He bagged the groceries as she rang them up. Only then did she realize she was shaking. The arm bones scared her. The terror in Kira's scream and in her voice scared her. It scared her that Jordan didn't mention he saw Kira in the meadow. He was returning and had several brown bags in a small cart. Sienna froze. He wheeled the cart closer to the car. Slapping the laptop lid down, she shoved it back into her bag before he saw it. She had two videos left, but they would have to wait.

She unzipped her cosmetics bag and pulled a bottle of Visine eye drops as he lifted the rear hatch. "My eyes are red and puffy from crying. Did you get everything?" she asked, dosing each eye with a few drops of the liquid.

"Yes. I got some wine, too. I don't suppose you can have any, but I hope you don't mind if I do. I need a drink. I'd like to build a fire down by the lake and try and process all this."

Sienna willed the numbness that had become her coping mechanism to flow down her arms into her fingertips. She closed her eyes and felt a tingling down her legs to her toes. As she set the overnight duffel on the floor between her feet, Jordan hopped into the driver's seat.

Within fifteen minutes, as the evening sun settled into dusk, dousing the world in a soft pink hue, they reached the turn from the highway. The road twisted and turned and curved through the forest of their property, eventually changing from pavement to compressed dirt and crushed granite. The farther they drove from the highway, the taller the towering trees jutted into the sky obscured by limbs hanging overhead, creating a leafy green tunnel as the road narrowed. After another ten minutes, as though they were entering a lost and forbidden forest kingdom, they emerged into the clearing surrounding their two-story lake house perched thirty yards from the shore.

Jordan got out first and opened the back door for Sally. "Come on, girl." The yellow Lab jumped out and darted around the lawn they paid to keep trimmed and manicured all season. Then he moved to the back of the vehicle and unloaded.

Sienna opened her door and allowed the forest air, the cool breeze of dusk mixed with the scent of wood and moss and water of the lake, to swirl around her and ensconce her from pain and sorrow, even if just briefly. The lake water lapped at the dock and the rocks that made up the shoreline. A faint breeze had already picked up as the broadcaster said it would. There was a splashing and licking sound as the waves bobbed against the underside of the dock. Even in the dwindling light of the disappearing sun, Sienna could see whitecaps in the rippling lake.

"Might get too windy for a fire," she said as Jordan passed her carrying everything except the dog kennel and her duffel.

"It's just a breeze. I'll make a small one in the fire ring. It's too warm out for a big fire anyway. I'll get this stuff in the refrigerator and then collect some kindling."

Sienna stepped from the vehicle and retrieved her bag. The wafting air didn't drown out the trilling of bugs and frogs. It seemed to amplify and carry them to her ears. They echoed around her in the circular clearing of their yard, reverberating off the walls of trees surrounding her. Fireflies were already out zipping around the yard, unaffected by the breeze. Sienna thought of her kids who would have run around the yard flapping their arms, hair billowing, pretending to fly in the wind, chasing the fireflies.

"I'm heading upstairs for a few minutes," she said, passing Jordan in the entryway as he returned for the kennel.

"Do I need to carry your bag?"

"I've got it. I'll be down in a minute."

"You okay?"

"A little lightheaded, but I'm glad I'm here."

Jordan stood watching her for a minute. "I'm glad, too," he replied and hurried out to the driveway.

Sienna clicked on the light switches at the base of the stairs, and the entire upper floor burst into view. The open loft area overlooking the living room branched into three bedrooms, and she headed up to the master.

In her bedroom, she opened the double-glass doors and stepped out on the balcony overlooking the lake to see Jordan already pulling logs from the stand where he kept a pristine stack of firewood. Since the fire building had him occupied, she unzipped her duffel on the bed and pulled out the laptop and the cord and carried them into the bathroom. Through the little window, she again peered outside. It was getting darker as dusk pulled a grey blanket over the world, but Jordan was still on his kindling hunt.

Sienna plugged in the laptop and, using her thighs as a desk, sat on the toilet lid and opened the computer. The other video was still open. She minimized it and opened the next unseen clip.

CHAPTER THIRTY-FOUR

A VIDEO OF KIRA RECORDING herself in her bedroom played. The white headboard of her bed against soft pink walls set the backdrop.

"Hi, guys. This is video number four of my Insta story. You have to watch the others first, so if you're watching this one and haven't seen my videos of the forest and the meadow, then you need to stop and watch them first, or this won't make any sense."

Wanting to hear if Jordan came inside, Sienna lowered the volume of the laptop but didn't take her eyes off her daughter speaking into the camera with emphatic hand gestures and an earnest, wide-eyed face. "This is a mystery. A real mystery. Me and my dad are going to try and solve it. I can't post any of my videos until tomorrow, which is why I'm going to upload all of them at the same time. Once my dad confirms what I already know, I'm going to post more videos with the progress of solving the mystery.

"Okay. So, a couple days ago, I was at our lake house with my dad. Way deep in the forest, I found the purse of a girl named Rhona Adams. I've researched online and found out she went missing in 1997. We also found some bones. Well, my dog, Sally, did. You can see in video number three. I think it's an arm. What didn't get recorded was the hand I saw. No doubt in my mind. I saw a hand. Five fingers. I screamed like never before. Even on a roller coaster, or in a haunted house, I never screamed so loud. It was so freaky. My dad thinks I'm crazy. He says they are just animal bones, but he agreed to go out there and check again. He's going to go tomorrow. It's Saturday. I think it's Rhona Adams in our meadow. He's going to let me be the one to call the police and report it. We haven't told my mom yet because she wouldn't let us go look. She'd make us call the police. My dad says it will be cruel to get her family's hopes up, and we'd all look like a bunch of idiots if we don't check first and it turns out he's right and I'm wrong.

"But I'm not wrong!" Kira threw her free hand up for emphasis then fiddled with her hair, seeming to notice her appearance on the screen. "We'll be able to go out there with the police. I want to meet her family and help them figure out what happened to her."

Sienna hit the pause button, listening for Jordan, but there wasn't any sound or sign of him. She resumed the video.

"So, I'm sorry for not telling any of my friends about it yet. Don't be mad. My dad made me promise not to tell anyone. Absolutely no one. Not even Margot. Not even Suzie. He thinks if I started a rumor, a bunch of people would trespass on our property. He's probably right. I can see a bunch of kids wanting to be the ones to find the body like in that old movie. And my mom would kill me if I didn't at least let my dad check first before telling people.

"But I can't stop thinking about it. She just disappeared. It's too much of a coincidence. Her purse! And the bones! I know they are bones. He had me convinced it was just a deer leg or something like that. Rabbit bones. I don't know if he saw the hand. He covered it up so fast. If he had seen it, he would believe me. The more I thought about it, the more certain I am that I saw a hand, and I finally convinced him to go look tomorrow. So, I should be able to post these tomorrow, and then I'll record more. I might start a podcast about it. Comment if you think I should. DM me if you want to be on it.

"Okay. Bye for tonight." Kira held up a peace sign with her free hand, and the video ended.

Sienna right-clicked on the video and reviewed the properties confirming Kira recorded the video the night before her death.

Sienna's breathing became shallow as she peered out the small bathroom window. It was noticeably darker, as though the only two colors that existed in the world were grey and black, but she could still define the lake, the dock, even Jordan's unlit fire bundle. All were in silhouette. But Jordan wasn't there.

She paused and listened but didn't hear him. Opening the bathroom door a few inches, she again listened, but the house was silent. She closed the door and returned to the seat and played the last video.

Before starting it, Sienna right-clicked and found the date of the recording under properties. Kira had recorded it the morning of her death. She clicked play.

Kira was again sitting on her bed. Daylight coming in the side window backlit Kira's face and caused a glare on the video. "Okay, so an update. My dad told me this morning that he can't make it out to the forest today. He says it would take him all day and he has to show some properties to one of his biggest clients who wants to look today instead of tomorrow. He says he can go tomorrow, but I'm starting to think it's not important to him. I'm starting to think he might not even go out there, that he'll just tell me he did. I was so excited thinking this was something he and I were doing together. We were working on a mystery together and were going to help Rhona Adams' family. We haven't told anyone yet. Not my mom. Not my brother. It was just between us. I thought we were doing something special and amazing for Rhona together."

Kira started tearing up. She wiped her eyes without interrupting her commentary. "I told him if he doesn't go out there tomorrow, I'm going to ask my mom to take me to check. If it's not important to him, then why should I wait on him, right?"

※※※

Jordan climbed the stairs. His footsteps ricocheted off the white pine paneled walls and ceiling. Sienna paused the video and listened. A moment later, he spoke to her through the door. "You in there?"

"Yes, I'll be out in a minute."

"You feeling okay?"

"I'm fine. Just tired."

"I'm going to start the fire. I'll be outside if you need me."

She waited for him to leave but didn't hear him walk away. Then he spoke to her again. "I understand if you need to rest instead of coming out. I'm not in much of a talking mood. I'm going to just sit by the fire. Sit and remember the kids."

"That sounds nice. You go ahead. I might join you in a bit."

When she heard him walking down the stairs, the wood creaking and groaning with each step, she restarted the video.

"For now, I'm going to keep researching about Rhona Adams. I know she's there. We just don't know what happened to her," Kira said, her eyes watering and her cheeks red. "This is all information for the podcast. So are these recordings. I might have a podcast episode for each video I do so I can really explain in more detail everything that I've researched and talk more about my dad so you can get to know the other person who made this discovery. If the discovery ever happens, that is." She smiled and rolled her eyes. "So, one more day. Tomorrow is the day one way or another."

The video ended with her again giving a peace sign to the viewer as she wiped her eyes.

Sienna stared at the laptop screen without seeing any of the icons. She recalled Kira's behavior the day she died. Remembered how moody she was then and for a couple of days leading up to that Saturday and how her mood improved when they were playing in the leaves. And she even commented about it to Jordan when he called. She realized it must have been her frustration and disappointment.

Sienna glanced at the bottom corner of the screen. The Wi-Fi icon displayed full strength. The laptop had automatically connected to it. Clicking open the browser, she logged into her iCloud account and drive. After creating a new folder, she transferred copies of all of Kira's videos and her pictures. While they loaded, she remembered Kira mentioning the research she had done on missing persons. Sienna minimized the iCloud and opened Kira's web history on the laptop. She'd looked at it the day before, but nothing stood out then. Scanning the rows of webpage links, she saw one news link after another. She clicked on one, then another, and another. Kira had researched news articles about Rhona Adams and other missing persons from surrounding states, some going back decades. It was the research she had done while waiting on Jordan to confirm they were human bones they found. The thought of a dead young woman would have made anyone moody, gloomy, sad.

Any other time probing through Kira's laptop and her web history would have felt like an invasion of her privacy. For that same reason, Sienna hadn't micro-managed the kids' phone usage and instead let the parental control app keep tabs. It struck her, and she admitted to herself that, when Kira was alive, she'd been too busy to ever check their phones or the computer. But right then, delving into her laptop felt like a way to share a secret with her. Share her private, hidden world.

She logged out of her iCloud and set the laptop on the vanity and got up and peeked outside again. It was darker, and the bathroom light turned the window into a mirror reflecting the room and her image and obscuring Jordan out by the lake. She cranked the window open to see if he was out there. The beginnings of a fire flickered in the distance. Jordan was still working with the kindling. His T-shirt flapped against his body in the wind, and his hair fluttered. He reached for lighter fluid, which was something she had never seen him use on a fire, and she assumed it must be because of the wind.

Joining the clear night sky full of stars and a full moon as his audience, a blaze erupted from the fire pit, painting Jordan in a bright orange glow. The wind whipped the flames, but he didn't let them die down. He tossed a few sticks onto the burning kindling and added more fluid, causing another burst of flames to brighten the night.

Watching him work the fire, Sienna thought about their family trek to the meadow. They might have been walking about in a gravesite. She had to know. Needed to see what Jordan didn't want her to see. What he hadn't told her about. It couldn't wait until morning. But he would never let her go out there this late. It would be completely dark soon. She would be careful and protect the baby.

The fire road! Yes, she'd use the fire road to get to the survey markers of their property line. Jordan said the meadow was a few hundred feet from the property line. She could work her way from the fire road along the property line until she found it on her own.

CHAPTER THIRTY-FIVE

WITH JORDAN PREOCCUPIED MAKING HIS fire, Sienna slipped down to the kitchen, grabbed a flashlight, and then crept into the garage. Tucking the flashlight under her arm, and with Jordan on the back side of the property, she opened the garage and wheeled Kai's kid-sized four-wheeler down the drive as the wind buffeted her face and whipped at her shirt.

She eased the small ATV out onto the dirt road. When she was sure she was far away enough that the whoosh of the wind and the rustling of infinite snapping leaves would shield the engine noise, she fired it up. Grateful for a full moon and a sky full of bright stars, she rode to the spot where the main road forked with the narrow fire road to the right. There she clicked on the flashlight and sped along until the flashlight caught the metal stake spray painted florescent orange like an emergency cone on the side of the road.

All around her was dense forest. As far as she could see, countless massive trees towered over her. She scanned left to right. The trees were endless. All swaying in unison under the force of the wind. Then she climbed off the ATV and turned to face the forest.

Tree limbs heavy with leaves caught the rushing air and undulated like snapping sails attached to masts of ancient wooden ships. They resisted the punishing wind trying to capsize the world. Pulling her hair away from her eyes, Sienna walked another few feet and then entered the forest. Raising her feet high, she trudged through dense undergrowth of ferns and saplings that grabbed at her legs. With an arm outstretched to protect her face, she weaved around enormous tree trunks until she emerged at the meadow a few minutes later.

The grouping of midnight maples stood ahead of her in the meadow straining to defy the gusting air.

They dazzled under the moonlight that sparkled on the glossy surface of the deep purple leaves that radiated a blue hue, like underexposed film. Her heart swelled at the sight of them, and her breath caught in her chest. She inhaled deeply and wiped her eyes, watering from the force of the wind hitting her in the face.

As she stepped deeper into the meadow, the wind began to ease into a cool breeze. With each step, the swirling air settled, as did the stand of maples. They became serene and reminded Sienna of a lullaby as though her footsteps could sing the trees to sleep. By the time she reached the nearest maple, the air was still, leaving her ears ringing from the absence of sound. There were no insects chirping. No night birds hooting. No nocturnal animals prowling.

Sienna looked back to the forest. The trees stood immobile like defiant prisoners after a flogging, bracing for a recurrence. She pulled her phone from her back pocket. It was nine. It had been close to eight-thirty when she watched the videos and Jordan started the fire.

She returned the phone to her pocket and headed for the largest tree in the center of the meadow. All its limbs and leaves melded together, turning them into a single canopy as though a master garden architect precisely planted them to create a dream world, a hidden playground. As she neared the center tree, she realized the maples might also serve as a crypt if Kira was right. Undaunted. Without fear. Feeling comfort and peace, and welcomed, like an invited guest, Sienna headed to the blue mother tree.

Her footsteps snapped twigs and crunched leaves as moonlight filtered through the limbs casting black ticker tape of shadows. Ducking under low hanging branches and stepping over years-old fallen trees, she crept toward the mother tree. When she reached the grouping of slender stumps jutting from the ground, she knew she found her. She took out her phone and pointed its flashlight over them. The sap she remembered from her first visit still glistened from the wounds left when Jordan and his brother had severed the trees years earlier. This was the spot in the video where Kira stood recording the treehouse and Sally unburied the bones.

Sienna shined her flashlight up into the branches. There it was. The treehouse hovered above. Not wanting to stand beneath it when it seemed the few remaining logs could slip free at any moment, she moved forward several feet.

Lightheadedness caused her head to spin. Her vision blurred, and tiny stars zipped across her eyes. It was the walking, she figured. Not eating and the lack of sleep had her overtaxed, but she ignored it, willed herself to stay focused, and turned to find the grave.

In Kira's video, Sally dug by the severed stumps nearest to the mother tree. Sienna dropped to her knees and pushed her fingers into the earth, searching for any soft or loose spots in the soil. She crawled around, moving away leaves and twigs and forest decay, but only found compacted, hard dirt underneath until she hit an area that gave way to her hands. A loamy section of soil. She pawed away the earth in the same fashion as the dog. Handful by handful, she clawed away at the ground. Then she felt something solid.

Carefully she traced it with her fingers and cleared away the dirt, sweeping it gently like an archeologist unearthing a rare artifact. The bones of fingers. Joints. She felt them in the dirt. A hand. Sienna brushed away more dirt and freed the bones. A generous moon poured light onto them. A hand and arm. The pointy fingertips didn't frighten her, but her first thought was of the bruises on Kai's face. Fingertip bruises the police had said.

A silver bracelet clung to the bones. Sienna laced her fingers into the hand without revulsion or fear, and lifting the hand, she slipped the bracelet free. Charms dangled from it. Initials. *R* and *A*.

Sienna released the hand back into the soil and placed a few leaves over it to provide it with dignity like closing a lid on a coffin then stood and wiped her hands on her jeans. There was movement behind her. The crunching of leaves and twigs. Something big! Afraid to yell, afraid to run, she stopped and turned toward the source without uttering a sound.

CHAPTER THIRTY-SIX

A FLASHLIGHT BEAM CLICKED ON and shined into Sienna's eyes.

"It's me, Sienna!" Jordan said from several yards away. "I just watched Kira's videos. When I couldn't find you around the house, I drove into the forest on the fire road, figuring you would be here."

She stood defiant, ready to confront him as he approached and moved the light out of her face. "I found the grave, Jordan."

"Good!" he said, stepping closer. "I'm glad you did. It's time you knew."

"What happened to her?" she whispered, afraid of the answer.

"Listen to me. Let me explain."

"Her name was Rhona Adams. She disappeared. She was wearing this." She showed him the tarnished silver bracelet in her palm. "What's she doing out here?"

"Lance killed her when we were teenagers."

Hearing it spoken aloud made her feel sick. Her stomach churned. "Oh my god."

Running her hands through her hair, she stood, looked up to the sky peeking through the canopy, and took a long deep breath.

"You knew what he did? You knew?" she asked, trying to slow her breathing.

"Yes."

"We have to go call the police!" She hurried around him toward the fire road.

He caught up with her. "Slow down. You're going to hurt yourself or the baby."

Sienna stopped and faced him. "Why didn't you call the police?"

He stepped closer to her and held up his arms to block her from continuing and turned off the flashlight. The moonlight illuminated his face. A resurgent breeze swirled his hair and pressed his shirt flat against his chest. The trees in the forest behind him began swaying as the wind resumed.

"I was seventeen. He was nineteen."

As her own hair fluttered around her face, Sienna stepped around him and walked toward the fire road. "We have to report it," she said as a branch caught her hair.

He held up his hands, urging her to listen. "Please stop. Let me tell you everything."

"Oh god! What did you do to Kira?" She scurried between trees with her arms outstretched to protect her face.

Jordan caught up and stepped in front of her. "Kira? What? What are you talking about? This has nothing to do with Kira."

Sienna walked at a diagonal out of the maples and into the meadow as the wind picked up and churned the grasses at their knees. Jordan matched her gait and again blocked her.

"I never hurt anyone. But I made a mistake. I was a scared kid. I didn't tell anyone what Lance did. That's what I did wrong."

He stepped closer as Sienna continued deeper into the meadow. The gusts picked up with each step. He kept pace.

"Lance brought a girl out to the lake house. It was a girl he met in Minneapolis. My mom and dad were trying to get him to go to a technical school there. They said they'd pay for the whole thing. Get him an apartment, so they could get him out of the house. He wasn't working. Wasn't in school. Wasn't doing anything. He was already a bum by then. He would just watch TV all day. They made him go check it out."

Sienna kept glancing at him as she rushed ahead. "I don't understand why you didn't report it."

He ran ahead and again blocked her path.

"Stop, will you please stop and listen? He went there to check out the school and had a one-night stand with this girl he met at a bar. She was a high school girl. Underage. She hung around some of the places the college kids did. She got pregnant. The only reason he even found out about it was because we went back to Minneapolis for a Vikings' game a couple months later. We stayed overnight, and he took me back to that bar. And what do you know? Here comes this girl.

"She didn't even know his name, didn't know his phone number. She said she thought she'd never see him again. She was drinking and seemed high on something. Pregnant and underage, but that apparently didn't matter. She said she was basically homeless and staying with friends after her parents kicked her out when they found out she got pregnant. Said she wanted him to take responsibility. Wanted him to take care of her and the baby. She kept saying he had to help her. It was his baby.

"He didn't have any money! He had nothing! He knew my mom would cut him off and throw him out too for screwing up that badly. All he could think to do was bring her to the lake. He told her how nice it was. Said she could stay until they figured things out. She had nothing and no one, so she agreed.

"She was high on something. She wasn't worried about the baby. A jacket that was too big for her hid the pregnancy, but when she took it off later, there was no doubt. She was a few months along. Lance convinced her it was a good idea to stay at the lake. A safe place to take some time to figure things out. I don't know what he was thinking.

"He might have decided right then to do something to her. I don't know. We got in the car and came out here. She slept most of the way. He got her inside, and she was still under the influence of whatever it was. He got her into bed.

"She woke up the next morning pretty freaked out. Didn't know where she was. She wanted to leave. She started raising hell when he said she should stay so they could figure things out. She made all kinds of threats. Said she would say he raped her if he didn't take her back right then. So, Lance told her he'd take her back. I wasn't going all the way back to Minneapolis. I told him to leave me here. I'd figure some other way back to Madison. A few hours later, Lance comes back. He looked like shit. He was sweaty."

"She disappeared in November. I read it. Kira researched it."

"Yes, there was a foot or two of snow outside. He had mud all over his clothes. His nose and cheeks were as red as tomatoes. He had dried snot on his face. He told me he accidentally hurt her. Said he took her out to the meadow and needed my help. I was freaking out. I thought she was still alive then. Just hurt. He got me out there with him so we could help her. Didn't say a word the entire walk. There she was, lying in the snow.

"He had strangled her to death. She was blue. He didn't want to get in trouble for getting an underage girl pregnant. Didn't want her saying he raped her. The ground was frozen. It's hard to dig a hole without a shovel. He cleared away the snow and made sort of a pit in the leaves and then covered her up with leaves and snow."

Without taking his eyes off Sienna, Jordan clasped his hands together around the flashlight as though praying to it.

"All these years, I've been so ashamed. I didn't hurt her. I didn't even help bury her. But I kept his secret. That fucking loser. I kept his secret. I couldn't tell anyone. He kept saying I had to keep quiet because I was an accomplice. After a while, that became true because I didn't report what I knew right away. I was seventeen, but they would have put me away for life for what Lance did! Not me! He buried her and then went crazy wailing on the treehouse. He tore it apart. That's why it looks like it does. He wanted to erase any sign we were ever out here so he could walk away and forget it. That's why he drinks. That's why he's a nobody. A bum. He's eaten up by guilt for what he did. That's why I don't talk to him, and he doesn't talk to me."

Jordan ran a hand through his hair and cupped the back of his neck. "I'm sorry. I'm sorry I could never tell you something like this. You understand that, don't you? How could I ever tell you my brother killed someone and I kept it a secret for him? I'm so ashamed. I don't even know her full name."

Sienna stepped back several feet. "Kira died the day you were supposed to come out here." As she took more steps back, she was oblivious to the wind gusts tugging at their clothes. "She died the day you were supposed to tell her what you found here."

"I was going to tell her I came out here and confirmed it was just animal bones. She saw a hand, though. She knew better. She kept researching about her online. I thought I might have to tell Lance to move the bones. I know that's the wrong thing to do, but I'd make him get rid of the bones before I'd ever hurt her. You know that. I would never choose him over Kira."

"It was the same day."

"Are you accusing me of doing something to Kira?"

"Kira caught you out here. You didn't know she was out here."

"I was hiking! You hike all the time!"

Her mind swirled. "Kai must have found out. Saw the videos. He confronted you, didn't he? And you hurt him, too," she barked, walking through the whipping grass toward the forest, Jordan matching her stride.

"I was in jail! Sienna! Stop! I was in jail when Kai died, remember? The police came over to our house to get my statement. This is some paranoid delusion. It's insane."

"They weren't accidents!"

"Enough. Stop. I'm going to get you some help, Sienna. You need help." He blocked her path. "Robin told me you were trying to make sense of something that will never make sense.

"Don't treat me the way the world is treating you. It was an awful coincidence. I would never do anything to hurt them. I loved them. I still love them. You know it." He stepped closer, leaving only two feet between then. "Say something."

Sienna had never seen him lay a hand on their kids. He never spanked them. She'd never seen him hurt anyone. She clenched her teeth and swallowed hard, trying to rein in her emotions. Yes, Jordan had been in jail and she was the one home with Kai. And with Kira.

"Let's go call the police." Sienna took the flashlight and led the way back into the forest toward the fire road. The wind whipped the trees and their clothes as they reached the tree line.

They continued on several yards, ducking under branches and stepping over logs and around saplings and tall ferns, before Jordan spoke. "I don't want to go to jail, Sienna."

She stopped and faced him. The grownup version of Kai stared back. Under the night sky that turned the world a velvety midnight blue, Jordan's face was youthful and flawless. "You're not going to jail. We'll get you a really good lawyer. You can testify against Lance. Her family will want the person who killed her to be punished, not you for coming forward.

"Surely, they look at not reporting a crime differently from committing it. It's going to be fine. I understand you were a scared kid. I understand why you didn't tell anyone before. Not wanting to risk your family. But it's time now. It's the right thing to do."

Jordan nodded without saying a word.

She shined the flashlight into the forest. "Come on, let's get back. I want to help this girl after all this time. Same thing Kira wanted."

CHAPTER THIRTY-SEVEN

FIERCE WINDS CUT THROUGH THE trees again on their way to the fire road, ripping leaves from branches. Sienna hurried forward, limbs and twigs catching her hair and scraping her skin, but she didn't slow down.

The air rushed around their ears, preventing them from hearing the creaking of trunks and crashing of limbs or even each other's voices. It was another ten minutes before they emerged from the forest and climbed into the SUV. Jordan spoke to her as they slammed the doors.

"Do you have any pain?"

"I shouldn't be out here doing this, I know. But I had to find her," Sienna said.

They remained silent as Jordan maneuvered the vehicle through the towering tree trunks on the winding dirt road as leaves and debris buffeted the windshield. Minutes later, the lights from the house became Sienna's homing beacon as Jordan drove into the clearing.

"It might not be a good idea to tell the police about Kira's video," Jordan said as he brought the car to a stop. "Honestly, I think we need to sit down and catch our breath, maybe sleep, try and get some real sleep, and in the morning, figure out exactly what to tell the police."

Sienna stepped from the car. "What do you mean? Tell them what you told me."

"I'm thinking about you here. The police in Madison already think you've lost your mind. They're questioning your veracity. Telling them about her video is just going to complicate things. This could really set off alarms."

Sally came running from the deck. Sienna greeted her and climbed the steps of the porch to the back door.

Jordan rested his hand on the doorframe. "Let's wait until after Kai's funeral to call the police. They might put me right in jail. They'll arrest me for sure. Maybe I can get a good lawyer who can work out some sort of plea since I was a minor and I didn't hurt anyone. Maybe I can get probation and not have to go to prison, but I don't want to miss Kai's funeral. I know what I did was wrong, but I didn't hurt anyone. I don't want to miss my son's funeral because of a stupid mistake I made when I was a kid myself. Can you understand that?"

"I can. I don't know what to say. It doesn't feel right not to report it immediately."

"Sienna, it's been two decades. Can you give me one more week?"

"I hope I'm not betraying her by waiting," she said and turned and walked through the mudroom into the kitchen.

Sally and Jordan followed. "I betrayed her. Not you. It was me. You're making it right."

"I'm going to take a bath and go to bed. We can talk in the morning."

"Don't you need to eat? You definitely need to hydrate. Do

you want me to heat up the Italian? That hike has earned us some carbs. We can go into a carb coma and fall asleep."

Without realizing it, Sienna placed her hand on her abdomen. "Yes, okay." She nodded. "I'll try and eat after my bath. Thirty minutes."

She left without waiting for a response. By the time she reached the top of the stairs, Jordan had uncorked the wine with an echoing pop. "Put some lavender or something in your bath," he said. "Something soothing. Let the fragrance take your mind somewhere else. Try and get your mind off things."

Jordan opened the refrigerator door and pulled takeout containers for dinner. Stepping into the bedroom, the lights left on, she noticed Kira's laptop on the bed and intuitively knew Jordan had deleted the videos. She carried it into the bathroom and started the bath. As it filled, she sat on the tub's edge, rebooted the laptop, and confirmed it.

She understood how worried he was about jail but didn't see how he could erase the last images of their daughter. Logging back into her iCloud drive, she verified she still had copies of her own. With the volume off, she played the first one to visit her daughter and see her smiling, excited face. Before she could play another, Jordan knocked on the door.

She closed the lid and set the laptop on the counter. "It's open," she said, turning down the bathwater.

He stepped into the room and extended his hand with a tall glass tumbler of orange juice. "You asked me to buy this for you. I haven't seen you drink anything all day. Drink this down, and I'll leave you alone."

She accepted the glass and took a gulp. "Thanks."

"Finish it. You need to hydrate. There is a sallowness to your eyes. Do you want spaghetti or fettuccine alfredo? Both smell delicious."

Sienna handed him the empty glass. "Alfredo sounds good."

She noticed him glance at the laptop but was grateful he didn't ask her about it. Maybe someday she'd tell him about the copies of Kira's videos. For now, they would remain hers and Kira's mother-daughter secret.

The bathwater steamed up the mirror as she turned off the faucet and stepped into the bedroom. Grabbing her overnight bag from the bed, she carried it back into the bathroom and pulled out her favorite robe and her toiletry case and set them aside. She dug her hand into her jeans pocket and pulled out the corroded bracelet and fingered the charms in her palm. Besides the initials, the bracelet held a book charm, a music charm, and a UM charm, which she let coil up into her hand, and then she tucked them away in the side pocket of her bag. After washing her face in the sink and as she put away her cosmetics, her phone chimed. She pulled it from her back pocket. The screen displayed an alert.

It was a push notification from the parental control app she set up on the kids' phones. She clicked on the alert, which directed her to log in to her account to view an urgent email message regarding the phone associated with Kai's number. An unread email marked "URGENT! Potential Suicidal Ideation Detected!" flashed on her screen.

The email opened with two long paragraphs of legal gibberish, including recommendations from child psychologists about what a parent should do and say when they suspect a child is having suicidal thoughts. She skipped through all of it, trying to find the monitored activity that triggered the alert.

Three quarters down, she found it. The email listed recent web search activity of concern: *Can fingerprints be lifted off a plastic grocery bag?*

Difference between suffocation, asphyxiation and smothering.

Can an autopsy discern between head injury from a fall or blunt object?

Exhuming a body for second autopsy.

Who was Rhona Adams last seen with?

Rate of maternal suicide following death of a child.

Famous suicides in a lake or river.

Virginia Woolf suicide by drowning.

Each search originated on Kai's phone earlier that day, except for the last two. They were within the last couple of hours. Soon after they arrived.

Sienna continued scanning the email. It included a link to an online chat accessed two days earlier. The day before Kai died. *PlayStation-Communities App.* Adrenaline surging and her heart pounding, Sienna clicked the link.

The app took her directly to the chat string. Having seen Kai's PlayStation username displayed on the screen thousands of times, she instantly recognized it—*flylikeaKAIte*. His chat was first on the string.

flylikeaKAIte: "Anyone ever get a message from a dead person?"

Raven: "Whoa! Why?"

Needles: "yeah prince and michael Jackson talk to me all the time"

flylikeaKAIte: "I just got a message from my dead sister."

BeyondRoyale: "sounds like flylikeaKAIte is crazy, probably a school shooter."

Raven: "are you serious?? how???"

flylikeaKAIte: "It came from Anchor"

ChadisMikel: "What's Anchor?"

flylikeaKAIte: "I'm not a school shooter. I'm only 13. It's a podcast app. My sister installed it on the iPad we shared until she died."

flylikeaKAIte: "I never noticed it before. She has tons of apps on it I just use it for movies and games."

2piece: "If you think he's a school shooter call the police."

flylikeaKAIte: "I was playing a game last night in my dad's office while he worked and a notification popped up the kind with a little red dot on the apps icon and a 1 inside of it. I opened the app and a notice said there was only sixty days left of a one-year free trial. My sister died ten months ago in sixty days it will be a year."

Trinity: "is your sister an iPad?"

Jinxd: "I use anchor for my podcast."

flylikeaKAIte: "my sister used the anchor app to start a podcast but she never launched it. It's not live but she had some audio files already loaded on it. I'm pretty sure they were vidoes from her phone but the app just had audio it was really weird to hear her voice."

Raven: "what did she say?!!"

flylikeaKAIte: "She thinks she found a human skeleton from a missing girl out by our lake house and wanted to do a podcast about it."

THEplayer: "This is bullshit"

Mayhem: "has anyone use Speaker for a podcast? Its free. I tried it but I didn't get any subscribers."

Raven: "OMG!!! What are you going to do???"

Velour: "how did you sister die?"

TurboZ: "I'm 12."

Carerra: "so you heard your dead sisters voice on a podcast not in some sort of weird satanic way right"

flylikeaKAIte: "She and my dad were going to try and solve a missing person case but she died before they could. My dad says it was just animal bones not human. I told him I want to go out there and see what she saw so he's going to take me tomorrow or the next day so we can finish her podcast and dedicate it to her. It was my idea to finish her podcast and make it live."

Jinxd: "sounds super creepy!!!! I would listen to that podcast."

flylikeaKAIte: "My dad wants to figure out a way to get my

mom to be part of it. She's sad a lot because of my sister and hasn't been back to the lake house. My dad doesn't want me to tell her yet because it would make her depressed again if we go out there and there's nothing. He wants to make sure first."

Carerra: "report it."

flylikeaKAIte: "I had to promised not to tell anyone not my mom or my friends until we check it out. He said we can make this something we can do as a family like Kira wanted to do with him."

Raven: "so sad!!!!"

Raja: "You should tell your mommy and go to bed."

Eureka: "Is Kira a podcast app?"

flylikeaKAIte: "Kira was her name she hit her head in a fall."

Raven: "OMG for real?!!"

TurboZ: "I wish I had a lake house id go fishing all the time."

flylikeaKAIte: "If we find something out there because of Kira that would make my mom happy again. I hope we find something. I want to tell her but she would be too disappointed if theres nothing out there so I have to wait."

THEplayA: "I wouldn't be out in no woods with a skeleton id call the police."

Raja: "Anyone playing Fortnite today?"

🔥🔥🔥

Sienna scrolled but found no other entries from Kai. Swiping back to the top of the chat string, she reread Kai's entries twice. She returned to the email, searching for guidance on viewing the actual documents accessed by Kai's phone, but her eyes didn't want to cooperate. As she scrolled, her lids kept falling halfway closed until she forced them open wide again, only to fall a second later.

Pausing, she let her mind process it all. Her heartbeat quickened, pumping blood throbbed in her temples when she remembered Kira acting abnormally after her last trip to the lake. Something happened, that was for sure, but back then, she didn't know what. Only now, Sienna knew Kira had found a girl's remains and kept it secret for her dad. And not long after Kira died, she also remembered Jordan got a new phone. It was odd he hadn't mentioned needing one. She logged back into her iCloud, pulled up the devices on their account, and found Jordan's phone. Yes, he activated his new phone the day Kira died.

The blood drained from her face as Sienna imagined Jordan striking Kira with his phone and in that very minute knew Kira's head wound wasn't from a tree root in her fall. Her mind spun, and her mouth went dry as she thought back to that day. He had called minutes before. She told him she was outside alone. But he must have already known that. Must have been watching them. He did the same the day Kai died! Watched!

She remembered Kai saying Jordan suggested he paint the treehouse, but Jordan never mentioned it to her. Then it clicked. The website about huffing she found in Kai's room. Jordan must have printed it and left it laying out for Kai and Shane. He wanted them to know how to huff. He wanted him to die from it. It was him all along.

The familiar red panic hives flared on her neck. Her instincts, her subconscious, tried to help her see they weren't accidents. Jordan was protecting himself because of what he did to Rhona. *Not Lance. Him!* She recalled the first time in the meadow when she noticed the severed stumps and dug into the bark with her penknife. "He didn't want me around them," she mumbled. "He kept trying to pull me away and get me to look at the treehouse." It was the narcissist in him, she realized, that compelled him to take his family out to the meadow in the first place. To mock fate and prove to himself he could get away with anything.

Sienna blinked and held her lids closed several seconds, picturing her children's faces before forcing her eyes open again.

CHAPTER THIRTY-EIGHT

YVONNE SCROLLED ON HER PHONE, Googling article after article about the increased risks and complications inherent in having a baby with fibroid tumors. Reclining by her pool like most summer nights, she tossed the phone onto the chaise lounge and re-crossed her legs, trying to get comfortable again. The dire predictions that tried to convince any reader that a pregnancy with fibroids would most certainly end in heartbreak had her scalp tingling with anxiety sweat. She wanted nothing more than a new baby for Sienna and Jordan.

A cool breeze tugged at her green robe as she took a sip of water from the bottle on the side table. She wanted a glass of wine and a cigarette but wasn't about to have either. Trying to fathom all Sienna faced, her own divorce and recent reliance on alcohol and nicotine seemed trivial. Right then, she decided she was done with both.

Grabbing her phone, she hopped up from the chaise and walked into the kitchen. Her crossbody purse holding her cigarettes was there on the counter where she left it. Opening it up, she pulled the cigarettes and lighter out, crushed them in her fist, and tossed them into the trash. She pulled the bottle of red wine from the refrigerator and poured its contents down the sink.

The cigarettes called her from the trash. A reflex response she knew, but it was real none the less. She shook her head. No, she would not smoke. She marched to the pantry and took the half-empty carton of cigarettes and tossed them into the trash, too. Yvonne crossed her arms and leaned against the sink again. Meditation would help. That's what she needed to do.

Yvonne walked upstairs and changed into fresh leggings, a sports top, a jacket, and tennis shoes then spotted her purse on the island in the closet. She remembered Jordan's phone was inside and that she told him she would charge it. She carried his phone into her bathroom and connected it to her charger then opened the folio cover to turn it off. There on the inside of the cover was a thumb-sized swab of dried blue paint.

Time stood still. Yvonne's neck and cheeks prickled with a thousand needles as her nerves flared. It was the same blue paint she'd seen on Kai's face. The same paint on his body. The same paint the kids took into the treehouse. *How could the paint, that same blue paint, get on Jordan's phone?*

Her mind raced. There had to be an explanation. Jordan's phone had been at the bar since yesterday. The police took the paint and the bag, and the rags, everything the night before. *Had he come home? Did he help the kids with the paint? He couldn't have. He was in jail, wasn't he?*

Goosebumps tingled down her arms and across her back. No, maybe it wasn't fresh. Perhaps it was an old stain. "It must be," she whispered as she looked up at herself in the bathroom mirror. A wide-eyed, mouth agape expression stared back, and it made her feel silly.

"Humph," she scoffed aloud, rolled her eyes, and told herself she was unjustifiably worried. But telling herself it was silly didn't cure the sinking feeling in her stomach. She wondered if she should call the police. At least report the unexpected presence of blue paint on Jordan's phone. Questioned if she had an obligation to call. No, she couldn't. Doing that would destroy him and Sienna in the public eye. Whatever the reasonable explanation, the media and the public would crucify them. She couldn't contact the police over nothing. That's what it was. *Nothing.*

She pulled her phone from her bag, saw it was almost nine-thirty, and dialed her friend Robby at work. "Hey, sweetheart, you really busy?"

"No, I only have one table. The bar has been dead tonight. What's up?"

"Well, I'm curious. Was there anything unusual about my neighbor yesterday?"

"You mean other than getting trashed, being loud and cursing people out, and assaulting another customer? Nah. Nothing unusual."

Yvonne chuckled. "No, I mean before that. Can you tell me what happened when he got there? Anything stand out?"

"Ooh, are we playing Nancy Drew? Why? What's going on?"

"Stop, no, I'm just curious."

"Well, I noticed him right away, of course. Who wouldn't? He's gorgeous. But also, because he took a booth, and before I could get to him, he hopped up to the bar and ordered directly from the bartender. I thought that was rude. Customers like that are always a handful. And I was right. He tossed his drink back, hit the bathroom, and then ordered another the second he saw me."

"What time was that?"

"Right after I started my shift. Around four. Speaking of someone seeing me and demanding a damn drink, my table is looking at me. We're closing in thirty minutes, so they're getting a check instead. I've got to go. Bye, babe."

"Call me back!" she said.

Trying to convince herself she was being silly, she set her phone down and crossed her arms but couldn't resist opening the phone cover and again scrutinizing the blue paint. There was no question. It was the same paint. Her concern for Sienna resurged.

Yvonne decided to meditate and send Sienna good thoughts. Leaving her phone and wine and cigarettes behind, she stepped back out to the pool, thinking that Jordan's anger with the lawn crew for refusing to finish destroying the tree and treehouse seemed odd now, too. Maybe he was trying to destroy evidence. No. She was letting negativity seep in. Surely, he was the genuine loving husband and father he seemed.

Yvonne shook her head, thinking that her own husband was never the man people thought he was. A successful, powerful lawyer, yes. He doted on her when she was on his arm at parties, yes. He loved the idea of her but didn't love her. Only she knew that for sure.

Taking a seat on the edge of the pool, the colorful LED pool lights turning the backyard into an amusement park's midway, she crossed her legs and began her breathing. Within minutes, she reached her practiced state of tranquility and tried to imagine holding Sienna in a tight hug. But Jordan kept popping into her mind. Him standing over Sienna with blue paint dripping from his hands like a fiend. A ghastly ghoul with paint dripping like blood. Concentrating harder, she shoved him aside and pictured Sienna at her lake house. Pictured her walking the forest and finding strength among the maples as the sun shined on her and reflected off the shiny purple maple leaves with blue edges. Stepping over to her through the grassy meadow, she saw herself pull Sienna into her arms and hug her tight, doing her best to comfort her friend. Sending her positive energy, positive thoughts, she whispered to her. "You're strong, my friend. Be strong for your baby. I'm sending you all my strength to redouble yours."

CHAPTER THIRTY-NINE

JORDAN LEFT SIENNA TO TAKE her bath. At the base of the stairs, he opened his overnight bag he sat by the front door, pulled out a small bundle wrapped in plastic, and jogged with it out to the firepit. Sally was asleep on the porch but jumped up on alert when his footsteps stomped on the wooden decking as he passed her, and she followed him down to the lake.

As he expected, the fire smoldered as a pile of glowing ash. It had almost died out after he abandoned it to drive into the forest and trek into the meadow to find Sienna. He shook his head, still astonished that she remembered the route back to the meadow. Glancing up to the bathroom window, he looked for any movement or shadow to indicate Sienna was out of the bath, but the house and lighted window was still and silent.

Sloshing the lighter fluid in the bottle, he confirmed it was still nearly full. Despite the wind, he kneeled, unspooled the dry cleaner garment bag, and lifted out his dress shoes. The wind caught the bag and tried to rip it from his fingers like a magician pulling a tablecloth from under a place setting of china. He managed to wad it into a ball and shove it into his pocket. He placed the shoes in the firepit soles up. The moonlight illuminated the dried blue paint on the heel. Opening the lighter fluid bottle, he held it close to the shoes to keep the wind from blowing the flammable liquid out of the pit and squeezed a thick stream, saturating the loafers. The acrid fumes drifted away on the breeze.

Before striking the lighter, he turned the shoes over and emptied half the bottle of the lighter fluid into them, where it pooled and reflected the moon overhead. Again, he glanced up at the bathroom window. Still no movement. With the plastic bottle in one hand, he held out his arm holding the lighter in the other and clicked the igniter. A small orange flame protruded and flickered like the tongue of a demon tasting its prey on the night air. Jordan gave it the meal it desired.

The lighter fluid burst into flames two feet tall, and he yanked his arm back. He lurched backward a few feet and watched for a moment. The flames reflected in his eyes as the fire consumed the shoes. Wind stoked the fire, giving it oxygen, helping it to burn hot. Before the flames died down, he tossed several large twigs and kindling into the pit then moved upwind and again sprayed the fluid, turning the bottle into a mini flamethrower.

After another few minutes tending the fire, adding kindling and more lighter fluid, and checking the bathroom window for movement, the shoes ceased to exist. Tossing in a few small logs, Jordan splashed the rest of the flammable liquid into the fire for good measure to destroy the only thing that linked him to the treehouse that he couldn't otherwise explain. He ran it through his mind again. *My sweat DNA? The rags from my T-shirts. My fingerprints? The treehouse, my son, his paint.* No, there wasn't anything other than the shoes. That was his only slip-up, and now they might as well never have existed at all.

Setting the empty bottle near the wood stack, he used his

poker to stoke the burning logs and root into the base of the fire, exposing ruby red embers. He tossed in more tinder, and the fire coughed glowing orange embers into the air. The wind dispersed them over the lake as he jogged back to the house.

Sally returned through the mudroom with him, and he listened for Sienna. It had been fifteen minutes or more. There was no sign of her. At the sink, he poured dish soap over both hands and, with a little water, generated a thick lather up past his elbows trying to rid his body of the smoke and petroleum odors. After toweling, he pulled the orange juice from the refrigerator and poured another generous glass. He shoved his hand into his pocket and pulled out the six remaining Valium pills, and using the base of his wineglass, he crushed them between paper towels into a fine white dust then mixed half of them into the juice and the other half into Sienna's alfredo. Taking a sip of the juice and spoon of sauce, he tasted for any hint of the pills but couldn't discern one. After chomping on a breadstick and washing it down with another glass of wine, he headed upstairs.

With the glass in hand, he listened at the bathroom door but didn't hear a sound. Thinking she might have slipped under the water, he swung the door open wide without knocking to find Sienna sitting on the edge of the tub.

CHAPTER FORTY

STARTLED BY JORDAN BARGING INTO the bathroom, Sienna quickly stood from the tub, but her legs were unstable, and she grabbed onto the edge of the counter for support.

"What the hell?" She tucked her phone into her back pocket.

Jordan stepped into the room, holding a glass of orange juice. "I'm sorry. I was just coming to check on you, but I didn't hear anything and got scared for a second."

Sienna rubbed her bleary eyes and ran a hand through her hair. "I got distracted looking for Kira's music on her computer and haven't even gotten in the bath yet. I was about to call my mom really quickly to say we're here and doing okay and then just go to bed. I'm too tired to even take a bath."

He extended his arm, proffering the juice. "Well, here, have some more juice then. You need the calories and sugar."

"No, I don't want it."

He lightly waved the glass in front of her. "Drink."

"No, too much acid. I drank that last glass on a completely

empty stomach, and now it's upset." On her feet, dizziness taunted. Dizziness she suddenly feared came from something in the juice he gave her. She wanted out, but he stood in the doorway.

"Well, come down and have a bite, then."

Feeling trapped and vulnerable, and hoping it would get him to back up, she nodded. "Okay. I'll eat a little."

Jordan backed into the bedroom, and Sienna walked past him, but he followed closely behind down the stairs. Clinging to the banister, she ambled as vertigo and a spinning head threatened to rob her of balance.

In the kitchen, she rounded the island, looking for the car keys, but they weren't visible. Instead, he had place settings for their meal ready in front of the barstools.

Stepping to the microwave, Jordan reached in to retrieve the food. "I had a couple bites of the fettuccine. It's so good, but I wanted to wait for you to eat."

With his back to her, Sienna opened a drawer and quietly withdrew the longest butcher knife they had. She held it low against her leg and turned to slip into the living room. "Um, all that juice. I need to pee again."

When Jordan shut the microwave, its door reflected the room and Sienna's movements behind him. His head snapped toward her, his eyes wide.

"What are you doing with that knife?"

Feeling her senses dull with every passing minute, Sienna gripped the eight-inch blade using both hands, elbows tucked at her sides, and pointed it at him.

"You killed Kira and Kai because they found out about Rhona Adams. You killed her— not Lance. You buried her in the maples. He knows what you did to her. That's why he hates you."

"Oh my god, this again. You are insane. You've completely lost your fucking mind." He set the food on the bar and stepped to block the doorway.

"Kai heard Kira's podcast on the iPad two days ago. The day before he died," she said, pointing the knife ready to strike, not taking her eyes off him.

His jaw clenched, and the muscles bulged in his cheeks. "You're wrong. I was going to have Lance take care of the girl's remains and then show Kai some animal bones. That would've been the end of the whole thing. I didn't kill him."

"Kira had evidence of her on the video! I saw it myself. Kira saw a hand. She would have exposed you even if you moved the body. I'm sure you destroyed the purse. You could even move the body, but she knew her name. So did Kai. Kira saw her remains. People who knew her can identify you," she said, reaching for her phone in her back pocket.

Before she could grab it, Jordan took a quick step closer and raised his hands in protest. "Wait! Don't! There's something else I have to tell you."

Sienna quickly gripped the knife with both hands again, trying to keep him at bay. She shuffled back as he advanced. "Stay there! Don't fucking move! You can tell the police!" Stars sparkled before her eyes, and she blinked them away.

Jordan stopped and held his hands up. "Okay. I'll stay here, but listen to me. I didn't kill Kira or Kai, but Lance might have. I told him the kids found out."

Her vision blurred. "I know you used Kai's phone to Google about fingerprints, autopsies, about Rhona, about suicide." She slurred the words as she clumsily pulled the phone from her pocket, nearly dropping it.

Jordan took Kai's phone from his pocket and waved it at her, taking a step forward. "Yes, I looked up those things. I wanted to know if the police could find Lance's fingerprints on the bag." He took several quick steps closer but stayed just out of reach of the knife.

Sienna tightened her grip on the knife in one hand, her

phone in the other, but her head was spinning faster, and her legs threatened to buckle. She tried swiping the phone open but didn't have the dexterity to enter her passcode. "I'm not joking. Step back, or I'll sink this into your chest."

He didn't budge. Sienna stepped toward him and swung the knife in the air, aiming for his torso. "Get back!" she shouted but didn't know if she was close or not. Her depth perception zoomed in and out.

Jordan backed up a few steps. "Please, hear me out. What you're doing is absolutely insane. Please. Lance has nothing to lose. He'll kill all of us to protect himself."

Sienna again tried to open her phone but staggered to the side and hit the island with her hip. Jordan moved closer around the island.

"If you call the police, I can't protect you from him."

Sienna swung the knife and backed away from him, struggling to keep her eyes open. Her eyelids fell halfway before she forced them open wide, only for them to flutter again. "Stay back," she said in a low, faltering voice.

Jordan advanced, and she tried to step back but didn't have the coordination.

As if in slow motion, she leaned into the island. "You drugged me," she said.

Her phone rang. Before she could react, Jordan lunged forward and knocked the knife from her hand. Sienna tried to answer the phone, but Jordan was faster, held her arm, and slipped the phone free.

"It's Yvonne. Jesus, this woman." But he didn't answer.

"You did kill them," Sienna slurred.

Helpless and with her head bobbing, she watched Jordan open the web browser on her phone and type an entry. An image of Virginia Woolf pulled up on the screen.

Using his shirt, he wiped off the phone and then turned it off.

"Give me your hand," he said, lifting Sienna's hand and putting the phone in her palm then manually closed her fingers around it.

She tried to grip the phone, but her fingers felt phantom, as though they couldn't affect matter in this dimension.

He took the phone back from her. The realization he meant to make it seem she researched Virginia Woolf's suicide by drowning struck her with another blow. It was all a plan. A plan to make her seem crazy. Seem suicidal. A guilty conscience that made her kill herself.

Wobbly on her feet, Sienna could barely focus, and it took every ounce of her strength to force her eyelids open.

"You're a monster. You killed my babies," she slurred as her legs buckled, and she collapsed.

Jordan caught her before she hit the floor and swept her up in his arms.

Looking up at him through fuzzy vision, seeing him stare down into her face, his eyes glistened a bright sapphire blue, as if electrified like the glistening blue leaves in her meditation. She realized too late what her mind tried to tell her, but what her heart didn't want her to know. The maples were the blue of Jordan's eyes. The warning she felt from the tree was actually a subconscious warning.

"It was you." Struggling to formulate her words, she mumbled mostly to herself as her eyelids fluttered. She felt him carrying her through the mudroom and into the garage. He set her down on the concrete floor. Straining to open her eyes, she saw him with his back to her rummaging through their wall of camping supplies. *My phone!* She slowly moved her hand to her back pocket, but it wasn't there. Through sheer will, with her eyes blurring in and out of focus, she rolled onto her side and managed to push herself up onto her knees.

As Jordan shoved backpacks and canteens and campfire pans around on the shelf, Sienna grabbed a nearby croquet mallet from its stand and used it as a cane to help her to her feet. With her head lolling and knees trembling, she raised the mallet. Letting gravity pull her weight back to the ground, she fell toward him, swinging the mallet against the side of his head. The crack to his skull sent him to the floor on his side as she tumbled facing him. Motionless and with his eyes closed, the two lay prone only a foot away from each other as though they were settling into bed to sleep for the night. Her eyes fell shut as she lost consciousness.

CHAPTER FORTY-ONE

SIENNA WAS DREAMING OF JORDAN. Him standing over her with blue paint dripping from his hands like a fiend. A ghastly ghoul with paint dripping like blood. Then he vanished. She was walking in the meadow and found strength as the sun shined on her and reflected off the shiny purple maple leaves with blue edges. Her father was there. Not the sickly man he was at the end of his life, but the healthy and robust version of him. Her father walked through the grasses and pulled her into his arms, hugging her tight. She felt safe and comforted. He whispered to her. "You're strong. Be strong for your baby. I'm sending you all my strength to redouble yours. I love you, baby girl."

A gust of cool night air whipped in her face. Weak and groggy, she woke with a start and tried to sit up but fell back when sobering pain wracked her abdomen that forced her eyes open wide.

Through blurry vision, stars danced in her eyes. It took her a moment to discern the moon and night sky shining above the tree line in the distance. She didn't know how long she'd been unconscious. Something blocked her peripheral vision, and she squinted, trying to make it out. When she tried to lift a hand to clear away the obstruction, she found her arms restricted at her sides. Panic rose in her chest, but all she could do was wiggle, trying to free her hands. She heard a whimpering, muffled by the obstruction. She froze and listened.

"I'm so sorry. I'm so sorry," Jordan cried, his voice a low whine. "God, please forgive me."

Sienna couldn't see him. She turned her head, trying to see, and realized she was inside a sleeping bag zipped up tight around her face leaving only her eyes, nose, and mouth exposed. Her mind registered movement. A bobbing and swaying motion of her entire body. *Water!* She was in their fishing boat. Instead of using the motor, Jordan paddled them on the lake. The water sloshed each time he dipped the oars.

"What are you doing?" she mumbled, her head still foggy from the Valium.

"You're awake."

She still couldn't see him. She struggled to get free, but she had no room to move and realized she was inside Kira's red junior sleeping bag. Kicking her legs with no result, she tried to turn onto her side. Terror surged through her body.

"Why couldn't you just believe me?" He sniffled then sighed.

Sienna's eyes watered from the wind on her face. She squinted away the tears and inhaled deeply. Then she felt more movement as Jordan climbed over the seat and set a foot near her torso.

"This is just about far enough, I think. I'll have to swim back."

She sensed Jordan wasn't talking to her, as though she was already dead. Trying to focus, she could see only the night sky and trees writhing in the wind. The image of Virginia Woolf on her screen flashed in her mind. Instantly, she knew he meant to make it seem she killed herself the same way by taking sedatives and weighing herself down in a river. The sleeping bag was too tight. It restricted her arms, but she wrestled and twisted with the little strength she had, trying to get a hand free.

"I never wanted this. I never wanted any of this to happen. Rhona wouldn't listen to me either. She got hysterical. Said that I raped her. It wasn't rape. I'm so sorry. I'm so sorry."

Without the use of her hands, all she could do was flip onto her side and, for the first time, saw Jordan's face. He stood only feet from her in the middle of the flat-bottom boat. Dozens of fireflies zipped around the shore like a meteor shower.

"Don't. Don't make this uglier than it is."

Sienna watched Jordan pull the oars into the boat and maneuver them underneath the seat. With him distracted, she wiggled an arm up toward the zipper. Before she had it, Jordan put her in a bearhug and lifted her up. She struggled in his grip. Panic flared, and she whipped her head back and forth but couldn't stop him. He got her up onto the seat next to him.

"I'm sorry. Please forgive me," Jordan said, his voice breaking.

Sienna felt him place an arm against her back and slip the other beneath her thighs. She could feel his breath on her cheeks as he leaned over to pick her up. His face was inches from hers. As he lifted, she jutted her neck forward and latched onto his nose with her teeth.

Jordan screamed as she held him by the tip of his nose as he flailed his arms. His wailing echoed off the lake and the trees. Wiggling her arm in the bag up to her face, Sienna found the zipper and yanked it down, setting her arms free. At the same time, she clenched her jaw harder, releasing all of her hate and anger through her mandible, biting half his nose off.

Jordan fell onto the side of the boat and somersaulted over the edge as she fell onto her back. The sobering pain gave her strength, and the cool wind ripped through her hair, stirring her fight or flight instinct as she spit his skin and cartilage out of her mouth.

Jordan bobbed back to the surface and latched onto the boat's edge. Blood poured from his face, and his panicked screaming ricocheted across the forest, sending panic prickling up her back. She blinked, and her vision snapped as clear and crisp as peering through focused binoculars.

As though moving underwater, Sienna yanked the zipper to her feet as Jordan howled and tried to pull himself into the boat. She threw the sleeping bag on him, and he fell back into the water. Before he could latch back onto the side, she slid to the back and clicked the motor's ignition switch. It roared to life, and she turned the gas to full throttle, racing toward shore.

Jordan held onto the boat with one hand and jerked the boat's edge toward the waterline. Sienna let go of the throttle and reached for an oar as frigid water rushed over the side and sprayed her face and body. The boat coasted toward shore as Jordan again pulled the edge down into the water.

As she raised the oar to swing it down on him, Jordan capsized the boat, sending her into the lake on her back. The chilly water poured into her nose and sent a surge of energy through her limbs. She dove deep, and the water canceled out Jordan's horrific screeching. Kicking with both legs, she stayed under as long as she could while swimming toward the shore. When she resurfaced, Jordan's high-pitched squealing had turned to a deep-throated groan as he climbed back into the boat.

Diving under, Sienna pulled at the water with both arms toward the lakeshore. Jordan had the motor churning, but she was almost on land. She dove under again and swam with wide, outstretched arms. When her lungs were about to burst, she bobbed up above the surface just enough to breathe as the motorboat roared closer.

Her hands brushed against the stalks of lily pads and then reeds. She surfaced and stood near the shore with water breaking against the rocks. Fireflies buzzed around her as she sloshed through the water up to her hips. The dock was two hundred feet away, and the lake house was nothing more than a candlelight in the distance. The motorboat's engine gunned behind her. She looked back over her shoulder. Jordan was motoring to the left of her. As she climbed on the rocks out of the lake, struggling to keep her balance and not slip, the engine revved. He saw her.

"Sienna!" Jordan shouted.

She scurried from the water as he raced closer to shore, the engine roaring at full throttle. Water dripped from her hair and into her eyes. Afraid she couldn't make it to the house, she launched into the forest, trees swaying under the force of the winds. Unimaginable pain gripped her abdomen, but she kept running and reached the tree line, where she ducked into the cover of thousands of trees with branches heaving and leaves fluttering in the gusting air.

The boat's engine slowed to a chug and then cut out, its metal bottom scraping against rocks.

"I see you, Sienna!" Jordan said, his voice echoing.

Grateful for the moonlight and the stars, she bobbed around trees and under branches, trying to put distance between her and Jordan as twigs and leaves slapped into her face. Her waterlogged shoes squished with every step. A fallen log blocked her path, but she was running with too much momentum to stop. She jumped over it and landed hard, bending at the knees to break the fall, and she got a glimpse of her shoes. Her blood mixed with the water and streaked them a grisly, oily black. Terror surged over her as she ran. When she ducked under low branches, she noticed the blood had darkened her jeans down her legs, too.

"You can't get away!"

He wasn't far behind. Panting, Sienna could barely catch her breath as the wind slapped saplings into her face and forest floor debris grabbed at her ankles, but she continued deeper, looking for somewhere to hide.

Terrified a tree would topple on her at any moment, Sienna

repeatedly glanced up. Century-old tree trunks that touched the sky heaved side to side and swayed in a circular motion. Raising her knees high as she charged forward, and with her hands outstretched to protect her eyes and face from saplings and tree branches, she ignored the pain in her abdomen that warned her to stop. Warned her something was wrong.

Ahead, she recognized two large oaks growing close together, creating an enormous wooden *V*. It was a landmark she knew from hiking the property, but it meant the meadow and the fire road beyond it were still a thirty-minute hike away. Twenty minutes if she ran it, but she didn't think she had the strength.

Ducking behind the oaks, she leaned against the trunks for support and inhaled deeply as she clenched her abdomen and listened for Jordan. The wind was drying her hair and her shirt, but her jeans stayed wet with fresh blood. She could feel it trickle down her legs and pool in her shoes.

Peering around the tree, she looked for him. The wind rustled in her ears and obliterated the sound of him trailing her. A pale moonglow lit the forest floor. Rays of moonlight that beamed over the trees flickered from the orchestra of trees conducted into a frenzy by the wind. But she didn't see Jordan.

Sienna darted away from the shelter of the trunks to race deeper into the woods when Jordan stepped into her path, ready to catch her with outstretched arms. Blood covered the lower half of his face and covered his shirt like a monster after devouring the throat of a victim. A pulpy black hole where his nose belonged oozed glistening blood. Sienna stopped, slid on the fallen leaves, and fell onto her backside.

CHAPTER FORTY-TWO

SIENNA TWISTED AWAY FROM HIM, jumped up, and ran. As she ducked around trees, pain jabbed with every step. But Jordan stayed close on her heels, crashing through the branches after her.

"I'm sorry it has to be like this," he said, only a few yards behind.

Ducking under a low branch, she swiped a bat-sized log from the ground and raced forward.

"I'm sorry, I can't let you get away!"

The pain in her lower abdomen was unbearable. She pushed forward as thicker steams of blood spilled into her shoes. A different lightheadedness began to take hold. Tilting her head up, she sucked in deep breaths just as Jordan jumped in front of her.

He stood before her with the wind whipping his hair.

"Stop running. With every step you take, you're killing another child," he said. "If you keep running, you only have yourself to blame for the death of the baby."

Sienna gripped a log by her feet and raised it with both hands ready to swing. "Stay away from me."

"You've probably already lost it. Your lower body is covered in blood. I can see it even in this light. And your face is pale as a ghost."

He lunged at her.

Sienna swung the log, and Jordan pulled back out of reach, but with all her strength and momentum, she spun in a circle and brought the log around again, crashing it into his shoulder, knocking him to the ground.

She fell at the same time, the pain in her abdomen pulling her off her feet, slamming her to the forest floor. As she lay on her back, the trees swayed in unison as the branches covered in leaves whipped like flailing arms and hands.

Jordan jumped on top of her, pinning her hands in the ground over her head. "You're woozy from blood loss. I'm surprised you made it this far. Just let it happen. Close your eyes. I'll stay here with you. I love you, Sienna."

Sienna strained to stay focused. Her mouth was dry, and she felt cold. "Murderer," she said, the words creaking from her throat. His blood dripped onto her neck.

"We both are, Sienna. You killed our first child. You aborted it. You said you did what you had to do. Don't you see? I did what I had to do, too. I had to."

"Only a monster would kill his own kids. You're a psychopath," she spat at him. His destroyed face hovered above her, but she refused to avert her eyes and give him the satisfaction of intimidating her. She glowered at him even as her strength faded.

Jordan gurgled globs of blood that fell onto her as he spoke.

"It's not my fault. Kira made me do it. It was her fault. She was going inside to tell you. If she had just let it go, this wouldn't have happened. I was in the marsh, watching all of you playing in the leaves that day. I called you when you sent Kai inside and left her outside alone. You didn't mention the meadow or Rhona to me, so I knew she hadn't said anything yet. I went up to her. She was mad at me, so I lied and told her I went to the lake house that morning and that it was just animal bones. She didn't believe me and tried to storm away, saying she was going to tell you she found Rhona Adams. I couldn't let her do that. I had no choice."

The trees rocked in the wind over his shoulders like sentinels. Kai's words flashed in her mind. He said the trees surrounding the mother tree were like *"the Queen's Guard in London with their colors flying, there to protect her in the center."* As leaves siphoned from branches swirled, and her hair whipped to join with his hair dancing on his head, Sienna asked the trees all around, asked the mother tree, asked Kira, and Kai, asked God, and the universe to help her. To save her from this man.

Jordan leaned his weight, pressing her wrists into the soil as he spewed his guilt.

Sienna tried to pull her arms free, but the pain in her abdomen sapped her strength. "You're grotesque."

She stopped struggling and relaxed her arms and felt him ease his grip.

"Kira is the one who put those recordings on the iPad. If she hadn't done that, Kai never would have known. She wouldn't let it go. She just kept digging and digging. Once Kai found out, he was just like Kira. Wouldn't let it go. He wanted to finish what she started. I watched Kai from the marsh, and when I saw that chubby little punk Shane running away bawling hysterically, I knew they tried huffing. I found Kai up there choking and turning blue, and I knew what I had to do. I didn't have a choice. I don't have a choice now. You wouldn't believe me."

Fueled by anger, Sienna gritted her teeth and flung her head forward, headbutting Jordan in his wound.

Jordan shrieked and fell onto his side, cupping what remained of his nose as fresh blood poured through his fingers.

As Jordan rocked in a fetal position and howled, Sienna tried to stand, but her body wouldn't cooperate. She got onto her hands and knees, but her legs couldn't raise her off the ground. Slowly, a couple of feet at a time, she crawled away from him, buffeted by the wind in her face. Each time her palm found purchase, she clawed at the soil and dragged herself forward and pushed off with her knees.

Jordan's crying faded, but he continued rocking side-to-side, holding his face.

Twigs and debris poked into Sienna's hands, but she didn't stop. A gale surged into the forest and blasted into her face and pulled at her hair, but she crawled on.

Ahead, she recognized the rotting, fallen tree leaning against a smaller one, the same tree Jordan had them all duck under when he guided them on their first visit to the meadow. Sienna closed her eyes and pictured the mother tree not far away now. Knowing she was close, and the fire road was just beyond, gave her strength. She sat up and managed to get to her feet and stagger to the propped-up tree.

Jordan was getting up, too. First onto one knee, then the other.

Sienna leaned into the tree. Using her body weight, she tried to shove it free and topple it onto Jordan, but it didn't budge. With the last of her strength, she heaved the tree. Shooting pain pulled her to her knees, but the tree remained petrified in place.

Jordan was on his feet.

Dropping onto her hands and knees, she crawled away from him, blood trailing behind. Her arms and legs became heavier, leaden, and she struggled to slide them along the ground. The wind tore around her, and she collapsed onto her stomach, unable to go on.

Jordan staggered toward her, his face blackened with blood that spilled between his fingers and ran down his shirt. Grisly and deranged, he stepped over ferns and stomped saplings without taking his eyes off her.

Sienna pushed herself upright on her knees, ready to face him, to fight him. Jordan stepped closer, his head lowered, his eyes focused on her.

He crept closer. A squall of wind erupted through the forest, pulling at limbs and tree trunks as though a doorway into space had opened. The downed tree resting on its neighbor gave way. He walked into its path, never breaking eye contact with Sienna. With a crash, the ancient tree toppled onto his lower back. Jordan screamed as the tree slammed him into the ground, crushing him and obliterating his legs and spine.

Jordan's screams reverberated through the trees. Forcing her eyes open, Sienna glimpsed him coughing and gurgling blood as the gusts settled and debris in the air swirled like pennant flags in a parade.

Jordan's contorted body and limbs lay in tortured angles. His eyelids closed as he died. She blocked him out. Tried to sift the sounds of the forest, the rustling leaves, the blowing wind, from his final moans.

With the last of her energy, she got back onto her hands and knees and dragged herself toward the meadow and the maples and the fire road beyond. Taking deep breaths, she crawled as the wind fell to wafting air that kissed her cheeks. Without the rush of air in her ears, she could hear Jordan whimpering behind her. She could also smell her own blood, but she crawled forward.

The windstorm died, and the forest settled. Then she heard it. A tone. Then another. A piano. Jordan's death groan gave way to a high register piano note followed by a soft, musical chord.

As she hauled herself forward, the melody flooded back to her, and with it came a static electricity in the air that sent shivers down her spine, reviving her with hope. *Kira's music!* Gentle at first, a twinkle of high notes, delicate and softly played, then the chords using middle *C*. Sienna let the melody envelope her and give her the strength to crawl to the fire road beyond the meadow.

The swell of Kira's soaring music, keys tinkling, filled the night around her. Sienna let it wrap her up and protect her. It sparked her determination and forced her to pull herself onto her feet. She focused on her daughter's melody, a pure harmony, a twinkling of sound that turned the forest into a grand concert hall as though Kira sat before her on the piano. She let Kira's music replace the pain of scrapes and cuts to her hands and knees, the pain in her abdomen, and the agony of knowing her husband killed her children.

The chords rang across the sky, a crescendo that lifted her like shoulders she could drape her arms across and let them carry her the rest of the way. She felt so light as if drifting on the chorus, as light as air, no pain. Oblivious to Jordan's final breath as she left him behind in the forest and stepped out into the meadow, she staggered on to the maples. She sat beneath the largest tree in the middle only feet from the severed stumps that served as Rhona Adams' grave marker.

She lay under the trees. Nestled into the earth, wispy ferns grazing her cheek, the breeze ruffling the leaves overhead as moonlight flickered, her breathing slowed and became shallow. Staring into the night sky, her arms out at her sides, she focused on Kira's music and let it lull her to sleep.

CHAPTER FORTY-THREE

BEHIND HER EYES, SIENNA SAW a black grand piano
positioned on an elevated stage framed by a floor-to-ceiling drape
of velvety royal blue. The stage itself was a gleaming polished
hardwood. In the foreground, an orchestra pit warmed up.
The woodwinds melded with the brass and string instruments,
heightening the anticipation of hundreds of people seated in the
great hall. Sienna leaned forward over the railing of the prestigious
first opera box seat. She looked around at the people in the plush
red velvet seats below and across to those occupying the other
gilded boxes suspended over the crowd. Everyone dressed in
black tie and gowns, the room was there to witness a classical
performance featuring Kira Clarke.

Sienna leaned back into her seat, and Kai placed his hand
over hers and squeezed. It was much bigger than hers. A young
man's hand. She looked into his grey-blue eyes twinkling in the
low light from the crystal chandeliers, and he smiled at her.

She leaned her head into his shoulder. He was much taller than her. This twenty-year-old Kai with his tuxedo and slick groomed hair. With his other hand, Kai held the hand of his boyfriend, also there to celebrate Kira's performance. Sienna caught the young man's eye, and they both smiled at each other. He was good for Kai. Her sensitive Kai, who she knew from a young age would grow up to be a man who would fall in love with another man just as special as he was. And he'd found him. That made her happy.

The lights dimmed and raised, signaling the concert was about to start. Rather than fall silent, for a moment, the voices of the audience raised with delight as people clamored for their seats.

Slowly the lights fell to a low steady amber glow, and hushed voices dropped silent. The stage fell to black, then a single spotlight ignited over the piano. Its lacquered surface shimmered, as did a twenty-two-year-old Kira in her midnight blue sequin gown sitting on the bench before the piano keys. Her eyes quickly darted over the crowd then up to the box where Sienna gestured a small wave.

Kira blinked, and a little smile tugged at the corners of her mouth, signaling she saw her mother and her brother up there in awe. Then Kira returned her attention to the piano. Only the piano, and then positioned her hands over the keys like a magician, a sorceress, a goddess, ready to perform her magic.

The conductor, only visible to those in box seats, raised his arms and spoke to his orchestra, but Sienna couldn't hear what he said as though he was talking deep inside of a cave. A moment later, with vigor and with finesse, wand in hand, he signaled the start of the music. At once, the performance commenced.

The concerto featuring Kira on piano solo erupted through the theater. Kira's practiced performance, her radiance mesmerized all those in attendance, and when her fingers frantically released the final chords from the keys, the room leaped to its feet and roared, signaling the arrival of her dominance in the world of classical piano. She had all she ever wanted. To perform beautiful music that people loved.

After she finished her second encore and the curtain fell, an usher entered the box and helped Sienna, Kai, and his guest down the stairs to a backstage room where Kira and other musicians greeted their family and friends.

Sienna entered the room, holding Kai's hand, and together they strode to Kira, whose beaming smile captured the scene. All eyes were on her, but she only saw her mother and her brother. The three embraced in a hug.

Sienna squeezed them as tightly as she ever had. Squeezed them as tight as she had after the lightning storm in the meadow when she thought she might lose them. Squeezed them and kissed them both. And they clung to her. Through their arms, she could feel love radiating. Could feel their hearts beating in time with hers. In that moment, she wanted nothing more than to be with her children forever. To stay with them and never let them go. To succumb to the pain, to the bleeding, the shallow breathing, and to the stalling heartbeat that signaled in moments, she would be with them again. Wherever they were.

As if reading her thoughts, Kai turned and whispered in her ear, "Our sister can't wait to meet you."

CHAPTER FORTY-FOUR

"I CAN'T BELIEVE I LET you talk me into this," Robby said without taking his eyes off the road as Yvonne slowly drove them deeper into the forest with the top down on her roadster.

"You wouldn't be in bed for hours anyway," Yvonne said, glancing from the dark dirt road ahead and the navigation screen on the console. "You said it yourself. We're both night owls. Okay, the navigation doesn't have guidance for the last couple of miles. This is too remote. I'm not sure if this is right."

Hardwood trees created a tunnel as the road split and narrowed. The tires kicked up rocks that showered the underside of the car.

"How do you know it's the right address?"

"I used the county central appraisal district website. Sienna told me their lake house was about an hour away from Madison, so I looked at the counties within that radius and one by one searched for their names. I found their house next to mine right away. It took me about fifteen minutes to find this address. This was the only other one."

"Yeah, well, you've gotten us lost. This doesn't even seem like a road. You go too much farther, and we'll forget how to get out of here."

The headlights shined ahead of the little sports car but couldn't penetrate into the wall of trees on each side of the road. After another mile of crawling deeper into the forest encountering no other paths or structures, Yvonne stopped to turn the car around. Before she could, a dog barked in the distance, an alert bark Yvonne recognized. She turned to Robby.

"That's Sally. The Clarke's Lab."

"What? No. How would you know?"

"We're close." Yvonne stepped out of the car and stared into the forest. "We have to go this way."

"You're insane. We drove out here to see if their lights were on. To make sure she was okay and give the man his phone, not traipse through the forest in the dark."

"She might be in danger, Robby."

"What the fuck are you talking about?"

"Their son died huffing blue paint. I saw it on his face. I found that same paint on Jordan's phone. I have a feeling something's wrong. I've called and called and texted, but there's no response."

"Why the hell didn't you tell me? What are we doing here? We should call the police."

The dog continued barking. Two quick barks, then a break. Then two sharp barks and a break. Over and over.

"Sienna!" Yvonne called out, and the dog's barking intensified. "Sally! Come here, girl!"

"Get back in the car, Yvonne. That might not be the dog you think it is. That could be a wolf or a coyote."

"I know that bark."

"I'm serious. Get in the car."

Yvonne sat back down, and Sally bolted into the road ahead of them.

"That is Sally!" Yvonne got back out of the car and greeted the dog with a ruffle of her neck. "Come on." Yvonne turned on her cellphone flashlight and stepped into the woods.

Robby turned on his phone light, too. "This is nuts!"

"SIENNA!" Yvonne said as she trudged through the forest, her cellphone lighting the way.

"You have no idea where you're going," Robby said, but Yvonne continued rushing forward.

A few minutes in, they stepped into the meadow, leaving the dense forest behind. In the center, a grouping of Crimson King maple trees with veiny branches tangled and intertwined, creating a web in the sky filled with feathery leaves that appeared black under the moonlight. She stepped toward them, and Robby followed.

Lifting their legs high to step through tall grasses, they neared the grove, and Sally charged ahead. "SIENNA!" Yvonne shouted, racing after the dog.

Then she found her. Lying beneath a large tree in the center of the grove, Sienna, blood-covered and immobile, sent a surge of horror through Yvonne. "Oh my god! Sienna!" she said, racing to her.

Yvonne fell to her knees at Sienna's side. Her cellphone light revealed the broad pool of blood that darkened her clothing and painted her hands. Staring into Sienna's pale face, she shook her by the arms, trying to revive her. "Sienna!"

"Oh god! Is she alive?" Robby asked.

Sienna's eyes fluttered but never opened.

Yvonne squeezed her hand and looked to Robby. "We have to get her out of here." She felt Sienna's hand relax and go limp in hers.

Robbie tried to dial 9-1-1, but he didn't have a signal. Neither did Yvonne. He kneeled next to Sienna and hefted her up with an arm under her neck and one under her thighs. Yvonne used her cellphone flashlight to lead them back to the fire road.

"Sienna, can you hear me?" Yvonne asked. Unsure if Sienna had already left this world to join her children in the next one, she listened for Sienna's spirit.

EIGHTEEN MONTHS LATER

YVONNE WAS BUSY WITH THE final arrangements. She made a pass around the sunny room, adjusting the flowers as more guests arrived.

Sienna locked eyes with her mom, and they both smiled. For a few seconds, everyone else became invisible to her. She didn't hear the voices of children laughing or people chatting. The colorful party streamers in shades of pink and yellow that decorated Yvonne's pool house studio were as invisible to her as the clouds of pink and white balloons that hovered in clusters around the room. She didn't smell the sweet vanilla ice cream or the chocolate cake. She focused all her senses on her mother holding her daughter on her first birthday. Her baby girl with her grey-blue eyes and Jordan's chestnut hair. The same hair color as her sister Kira and her brother Kai.

It wasn't until Robin lit the candles on the white birthday cake and the group of her friends began singing "Happy Birthday" that she allowed herself to see the rest of the room, filled with people who loved her and who loved her daughter, there to celebrate as she turned one year old.

With Olivia content in her grandma's arms, Sienna stepped to Yvonne handing out cake with the late summer sun shining on her through the windows and French doors. The rays brightened Yvonne's green eyes and red hair.

"Thank you for putting this party together for her. You went to too much trouble," Sienna said, taking a glass of champagne from the bar.

"I'm her godmother. Of course I'm always going to spoil the hell out of her. It's my job," Yvonne said, smiling and touching Sienna on the upper arm. "Really, Robin and Monica did most of the work. We all just want you to know we're here for you. No matter what. We are family."

Robin finished cutting the cake and setting plates for everyone to take as a few young children in party hats claimed their piece. "Yes, this little baby girl has lots of aunties who love her."

Officer Rodriguez handed a piece of cake to Sienna. "Lots of aunties who will always protect her."

Sienna accepted the cake and squeezed the officer's hand. "Thank you, Lisa. I'm lucky to have all of you, and so is Olivia."

Monica swallowed a gulp of champagne and refilled her glass from the bottle chilling in an ice bucket. "And lots of cousins. Cousins who can babysit. In a few years, these kids of mine can be the babysitters when we go out for cocktails."

The group was laughing as Dr. Singh stepped into the studio carrying a wrapped gift. "I'm sorry I'm late. Happy birthday, Olivia," she said, placing the shiny box on the bar and bending to greet the baby.

"Hi, Marta! Thanks for coming!" Sienna said with a cheery smile.

"Can I hold her?"

Sienna's mom handed off the baby and then mingled outside

with Monica monitoring her kids running around the backyard and pool, leaving Sienna with Yvonne, Robin, Marta, and Lisa.

"She's such a pretty little girl," Marta said. "And how's Mom doing?"

Sienna crossed her arms, hugging herself, and looked around at her friends, making eye contact with each of them.

"Having everyone's support has saved me. Yvonne was there for me from the moment I found Kai. The rest of you were in the grief room with me when I broke down and ever since. Working with Robin all this time has helped me understand why I fixated on the painting that looked like the maples in our meadow. What did you call it? You said it wasn't a mental break down. It was the start of a mental repair."

"Yes, your mind found a way to focus your pain and grief to keep you from collapsing under the weight of it and helped you slowly put together the pieces of what you already knew. Your subconscious suspicions about Jordan."

Yvonne shook her head. "The mind is capable of some remarkable things to protect us. Self-preservation is an instinct."

"That's what motivated Jordan," Sienna said. "Self-preservation. Selfish instincts. That's all he had. He died in that forest. Robin has helped me learn I have to leave him there. I'll never be able to think about him without anger taking hold of me, so I leave him there dead in the forest. I'm glad Rhona's family has some closure now. For some reason, they don't hate me. You'd think they would. My husband killed their daughter. They are kind people. I'm glad they'll never be ruined by knowing Jordan."

Marta turned to Lisa. "It's your work, your investigation, that has given that family some of the missing pieces. And Sienna, too."

"Yes, tell them what you were saying before the party started," Sienna said while nodding.

Lisa smiled and looked outside at the kids playing then shook Olivia's foot inside its little white bootie. "We're here to celebrate.

I didn't mean to bring up negativity."

"You didn't," Sienna said. "No, the answers you've gotten have helped keep me going."

Lisa turned back to Marta. "I was giving Sienna's mom an update on our findings."

"The last time I saw you, you had worked with the phone company and triangulated Jordan's cell phone," Marta said.

"Yes, he pinged back at the house around the time of Kai's death and Kira's, too. Forensics confirmed Kira's head wound was more likely from the edge of a cellphone than the bulging tree roots as originally concluded and as Jordan referenced in our interview. CCTV cameras also picked up his vehicle in the area at those times," Lisa said. She turned back to Sienna. "Are you sure you want to talk about this today?"

Marta spoke first. "Forgive me. I just meant to commend Lisa for her diligent work."

"Trust me. It's fine," Sienna said. "Not knowing has been torture. The answers you've gotten me and the Adamses mean the world."

"The Adamses were proactive from the start," Lisa said. "They helped track down those two friends of Rhona who confirmed it was Jordan she met at the bar. When we showed them pictures of him from back then, and others in a lineup, they both identified Jordan as the person they last saw Rhona with. Not Lance— Jordan. Lance has been fully cooperative. His lie detector test and Rhona's two friends support his statement. He knew what Jordan did but was afraid of what Jordan might do if he reported it."

Robin and Yvonne were shaking their heads, listening to the details.

With Monica and Sienna's mom outside monitoring the children, Lisa continued. "What I was telling Sienna's mom earlier is that we obtained a statement from the cellmate who woke Jordan while he was talking in his sleep. You know I watched hours of surveillance video and spotted the moment Jordan crossed his foot over his leg while in jail. The camera caught the sole of his shoe. There was paint on the heel, which Jordan saw. His expression showed surprise, and he quickly put his foot to the floor, and he later burned those shoes. On video later that night, I saw a cellmate kick Jordan's feet off the bench. Moments before Jordan had been sleeping, but his lips were moving. He was talking in his sleep. His cellmate remembered what Jordan said. 'Sienna will kill herself.' Apparently, he had his plan all along."

Sienna had already heard it all. She stayed in frequent contact with Lisa. It never shocked her that Jordan planned to kill her to protect himself and keep the secret in the meadow.

She remembered when she finally forced herself to return to the meadow not long after Olivia was born. Rhona's remains were relocated, but she wanted to visit the plaque she had installed under the mother tree. It was in November when she visited. The same month Rhona died. The enormous tree was dormant then. Gone were all the deep purple leaves fringed with a pretty midnight blue. It occurred to her then, staring at the bare branches, the leaves withered under a foot of snow, that Jordan treated his family the way a maple treated its leaves. As deciduous. As something he could simply let go when he no longer needed it, just like a maple tree in winter.

Olivia started to fuss, so Sienna took her back from Marta.

"It's still hard for me to keep from blaming myself. For not putting it together and protecting Kira and Kai. The counseling helps. So does the meditation."

"I'm trying to convince Sienna to lead some meditation classes at the studio," Yvonne said.

"I just might. I get to visit my kids when I meditate. When I was meditating this morning, I remembered a forgotten memory. It was from the day Sally came to live with us. Jordan had the kids at the lake. It was a few weeks before Christmas, and they'd been begging for a dog for months. I decided to surprise them. I flew back into town from a seminar and stopped at the pound before driving out there. Sally was a couple of years old. She slept on a towel next to me on the drive. When we pulled up at the house, I sat out front and had a talk with Sally that I didn't remember until I meditated. I held Sally's face up to mine. She cocked her head and stared at me with puppy eyes, and I told her she was about to meet two of the best kids in the world. That she was going to love them as much as I did. I asked her to please take care of us and protect our family."

Sienna shifted Olivia to her other arm and smiled down at her as she talked.

"I forgot all about my little pact with Sally. I took her inside, and the kids fell to pieces. They were so young. Six and five. Sally was in heaven, licking faces and rolling around on the floor with them. When I was in deep meditation, I remembered that day. It was a vivid memory. Like I was reliving it. Every aspect of it. I pictured the curve of Kira and Kai's ears, and the shape of their chins, just like Olivia's. I remembered Kai's cowlick at his temple, and Kira's long wavy chestnut brown hair she liked in a ponytail. I remembered the clothes they had on and the winter boots. I remembered the evergreen scent of our Christmas tree and the low evening light coming in through the windows that turned the world blue.

"As we meditated, I imagined myself with Olivia in my arms, and I got to introduce her to them. Kai ran his hand across the little hairs on her head, and Kira kissed her on the cheek. It felt real. I remembered every detail about them. I remembered the smell of their hair and the sound of their voices. I remembered Kira's facial expressions and Kai's mannerisms as they talked. I could see and remember their fingerprints. They put their arms around me, and I remembered exactly what it felt like to hug my babies."